Deadly
Curiosities
Book 2
Vendetta

First published 2016 by Solaris
an imprint of Rebellion Publishing Ltd,
Riverside House, Osney Mead,
Oxford, OX2 0ES, UK

www.solarisbooks.com

ISBN: 978 1 78108 403 8
Copyright © Gail Z. Martin 2016

10 9 8 7 6 5 4 3 2 1

A CIP catalogue record for this book is available
from the British Library.

Designed & typeset by Rebellion Publishing

Printed in the US

Deadly
Curiosities
Book 2
Vendetta
GAIL Z. MARTIN

SOLARIS

For my wonderful husband Larry
and my children, Kyrie, Chandler, and Cody,
and all of the extended family who rallied
to help with the events that inspired this story.
Much love and gratitude to you!

Chapter One

"WATCH OUT, CASSIDY!" Teag's warning was a heartbeat too late. The dark wraith screeched in fury and his clawed hand raked across my shoulder, opening four bloody cuts. I ducked out of reach and flung up my left hand with its protective bracelet. The ghostly figure of a large, angry dog appeared by my side, teeth bared, snarling at the wraith.

The ghost dog sprang at the wraith, striking it square on, driving it back so I could get out of the way. It wasn't the first time a soul-sucking creature of death showed up in the break room of my store, but it also wasn't something I had planned on when I opened the velvet jewelry box.

"Cover me!" I shouted to Teag, trying to figure out how fast I could get to a weapon that I could use against the billowing, monstrous shape.

"Go!" Teag said to me. He turned to the wraith with a wicked grin and snatched down a fishing net made of clothesline rope from a hook on the wall. "See how you like this!" he yelled, throwing the net over the wraith.

Normal rope would have gone right through the wraith's dark form. Wraiths are like that – solid when they want to be, insubstantial when you want to hit them. But the magic woven into the net meant it stuck, catching the wraith in a web of power. It wouldn't hold forever, but it could buy us precious seconds, and that delay might be the difference between life and death.

If I'd expected a fight to the death, I would have made sure my weapons were closer. I had to dive for the door to my office and grab my athame from atop my desk. The athame focused my magic, and I opened myself to the powerful memories and emotions that I connected with it, drawing strength. The wraith surged forward, straining at the energy of the rope net that glowed like silver. The ghost dog harried the wraith, snapping at its heels, keeping it occupied.

I swung back into the room and leveled the athame at the wraith, channeling my magic. A cone of blinding white light surged from the athame, and when the cold power struck the wraith, it shrieked and twisted, forced back toward the wall. It looked as if the white light was burning through the wraith, like fire on paper, and with one last ear-piercing scream, the deadly apparition vanished.

The ghost dog looked back at me, wagged its tail, and winked out. I slumped back against the wall, feeling suddenly drained. Magic takes energy, and I was still pretty new at learning to channel mine for big stuff, like fighting off monsters. Then again, with the amount of practice we'd been getting lately, I figured I'd be up to speed in no time.

"Nice net," I said, managing a grin.

Teag returned a tired smile. "Good shooting." His expression grew serious. "You're bleeding."

I sighed and sat down in one of the chairs at the small table, eying the overturned jewelry box mistrustfully. For now, at least, the box seemed harmless. "I didn't move fast enough," I said.

"You weren't expecting an attack," Teag replied.

"I'm beginning to think I should always expect an attack, and be pleasantly surprised when an antique is just an antique, instead of a demon portal to the realms of the dead." The wraith's claws must have taken a swipe at my energy as well as my shoulder, and I hoped that didn't include shreds of my soul as well.

Teag retrieved the souped-up first aid kit we keep in one of the cupboards. Unfortunately, we need it a lot. It's not your average office supply store kit. It's got surgical needles and sutures, sterile bandages, prescription painkillers and antibiotics, plus healing herbs and potions supplied by our friendly neighborhood Voodoo mambo and root workers.

Then again, Trifles and Folly wasn't your average antique store, and Teag and I had a few extra abilities they don't teach in business school.

I'm Cassidy Kincaide, the current owner of Trifles and Folly, an antique and curio store in beautiful, historic, haunted Charleston, South Carolina. The store has been in my family almost since Charleston was founded, close to three hundred and fifty years ago, and we have a big secret to go with that success. We do much more than sell interesting, expensive, old stuff. Our real job is getting dangerous magical items off the market and out of the wrong hands. When we succeed, nobody notices. When we fail, lots of people die.

I inherited Trifles and Folly from my Uncle Evan. Teag is my assistant store manager, best friend and occasional bodyguard, and Sorren is my silent partner – a nearly six-hundred-year-old vampire who is part of a secret collaboration of mortals and immortals called the Alliance, dedicated to getting rid of items with dark magic before they can hurt anyone. The antiques that don't have any magical juice, Trifles and Folly resells. Those that are just unsettling but not dangerous, we neutralize so that they won't cause a problem. Items that are magically malicious or so tainted with bad emotions that they will hurt people, we lock up or destroy.

I shrugged out of the shoulder of my shirt and winced as Teag cleaned the deep scratches. "Do you think it'll come back?" Teag asked as he daubed carefully at the damage the wraith had done.

I sighed. "No way to tell until we know more about what it was and why it came in the first place. And that means taking a look at what's in that jewelry box."

Magic runs in my family, and the person chosen to run Trifles and Folly needs all the magic he or she can summon, because we keep Charleston – and the world – safe from things that go bump in the night. My magic is psychometry, the ability to read the history of an object by touching it. Not every object, thank goodness, just those that have been touched by strong emotion or powerful energy. Heartfelt emotion is one of the strongest sources of power. That's why a tattered old dog collar is my protective bracelet – summoning the ghost of my golden retriever, Bo – and my grandmother's mixing spoon is my athame, used handle-side out. Both items have a strong emotional connection for me, and in both cases, the protection of the beings associated with the items resonates enough to fend off some seriously nasty creatures.

The salve Teag smoothed on my cuts included plantain, comfrey, and rose to prevent infection and slow the bleeding. The herbs had been mixed by Mrs. Teller, a powerful root worker, so they carried a supernatural level of healing and protection. Teag covered the scratches with gauze and then pulled out a small woven patch of cloth imbued with his magic, which he taped down over the gauze to keep it in place. Teag is a Weaver, someone who can send energy and intent into woven and knotted fabric. He's also able to weave together strands of information that would elude a regular person, making him an awesome researcher and an amazing hacker.

"Is that one of the patches you made?" I asked, slipping my shoulder back into my shirt.

Teag grinned. "Yeah, you'll have to let me know how that works. The patches are a bit of an experiment right now."

I paused for a moment, focusing on my wounded shoulder. "There's a tingle of magic from the salve and from the patch," I said, paying close attention to what I was feeling. "The cuts don't hurt as much as they did before, and where you bandaged it feels warm... like sunlight on a summer day."

Teag nodded. "That means that the poultice and the patch I wove are speeding the healing and driving out infection." Supernatural predators often had bad stuff on their claws, either poison or a taint that could be as deadly as the cuts themselves.

I went over to the fridge and poured us both glasses of iced tea, made the Charleston way, so sweet the fillings in your teeth stand up and wave. I needed a moment before I took on handling that antique jewelry box, and I figured that Teag wouldn't mind a break either in case something else tried to kill us. Fortunately, the shop was closed, so we didn't have to worry about the safety of customers or our part-time assistant, Maggie.

We drank the iced tea in silence, stealing glances toward the little velvet box on the table. Both of us knew we had to deal with it, and given what we had just survived, neither of us were looking forward to the prospect.

I finished my sweet tea, and couldn't postpone the inevitable. "Okay," I said. "Let's see what was so special about this little jewelry box."

"You feel up to it?" Teag asked.

I gave him a look that didn't need words. "As ready as I'm going to be. And you're supposed to be having dinner with Anthony tonight. That gives us about an hour and a half for me to read the mojo on the jewelry box, get knocked flat on my ass, and come back to my senses without making you late for your date." I was being intentionally flippant, but the reality was much more dangerous, and we both knew it.

"Do you think we should wait for Sorren?" Teag asked.

I thought about it for a moment, then shook my head. "Kinda late now, don't ya think?" I asked with a wry half-smile. "Besides, he's in Boston, taking care of whatever-it-was that made him up and leave on a moment's notice. I think I'll be okay. Let's get it over with." I moved my chair closer to the box on the table.

The velvet was worn and faded. It was too big for a ring box, and I wondered if it had originally held a pair of earrings, or maybe a dainty bracelet. The wraith had shown up a few seconds after I opened the box, but as I thought back over what had happened, I realized that the wraith hadn't come *from* the box. That was important, because it meant the wraith hadn't been trapped inside. But why had it shown up at all?

Hard experience taught me to look before I touched. I was also learning to see what I could learn without making contact with an item. Practice was sharpening my ability to use the magic I was born with but had only recently begun trying to control. I held out my hand, palm down, over the faded blue velvet and closed my eyes, concentrating.

The sense of overwhelming loss made me sway in my chair. Second-hand grief welled up in my throat, as tears stung my eyes. Beneath those darker emotions, I felt the remnants of something joyful, sullied now by whatever had been taken away. Dimly, as if in a faded photograph, I saw an image of a couple in their twenties, hand in hand. Then, as I watched, the young man's image faded away to nothing, leaving the woman all alone.

Magical seeing – things like psychometry, clairvoyance, and being a psychic – requires a lot of reading between the lines. I wish it were as clear-cut as it seems on television, where ghosts speak in complete sentences and visions are in high-definition with the volume turned up. In real life, images are distorted, murky, and incomplete. Spirits move their mouths, but often no sound emerges. The little snip of stone tape memory we see leaves a lot of room for interpretation. And that's the problem. When we don't have full information, we have to guess. Sometimes, we're right and the problem gets solved. Other times, we guess wrong, and someone gets dead.

Then I realized what was causing the extra buzz that my magic had picked up from the velvet-flocked box; this item came with its very own ghost.

In general, my psychic gift of reading the history of objects doesn't give me any special power to see ghosts. Oh, I've seen more than a few ghosts – then again, I live in Charleston, which is one of the most haunted cities in North America. I think it's written somewhere that every house built before 1950 has to be haunted, and every native-born Charlestonian has a yearly quota of ghostly sightings. Given the nature of what we do at Trifles and Folly, seeing ghosts comes with the territory. Some of the spirits have been helpful. Others have been lost, not even sure that they are really dead. And some of those ghosts have been downright pissed off and dangerous.

In this case, the ghost was terrified out of its ever-lovin' mind.

As I reached toward the box again, my fingers hovering over the velvet, the ghost welled up at me in a rush, so fast that I rocked onto the back legs of the chair, and might have gone over backward if Teag hadn't been standing behind me. Most of the time, ghosts hang back, but this one got right in my face, so to speak, screaming soundlessly, eyes wide with fear.

"Are you okay?" Teag was worried. I gestured to him that I was fine. So far, this ghost wasn't trying to hurt me. It just really wanted to get my attention. Maybe I had been the first living person it had ever had a chance to contact. Or maybe the wraith that had come after Teag and me wasn't really looking for us at all. Perhaps it had a different kind of prey in mind.

That left me stuck between two bad options. I really didn't want to make the level of connection that would happen if I touched or held the jewelry box. It was already clear that the box had a history of tragedy, and if I made contact, I would feel that sad background as forcefully as if I had lived it myself. On the other hand, whoever's spirit was still connected to the jewelry box was in torment, and might suffer forever if I didn't do something about it.

I reached out and picked up the box.

The first image I saw was of pearl earrings; dainty round balls with a lustrous glow, classy and always in style. Judging from the box, and the name of a local jewelry store I knew had gone out of business before 1900, I figured that the gift had been given back in the Victorian period. Then I looked into the box, and I knew for certain. Inside was a dark round circle, braided from brown, human hair.

Gotta love the Victorians; they knew how to make mourning a life-long, high-art spectacle. By modern standards, the old customs seem mawkish, even macabre. But in a time when most families buried as many of their children as they saw live to adulthood, when few people lived past their forties and a lot of folks died young from cholera, smallpox, and other terrors we've since vanquished, and when the Civil War killed half a million young husbands, lovers, fathers, sons, and brothers, our great-great grandparents had a lot to mourn.

They mourned in style, with whole wardrobes of black crepe clothing, elaborate social rituals and an entire etiquette for grief. On the other hand, these were real people and their loss was just as real as it is for modern folks. They tried to hang on to the memory of their departed beloveds. Sometimes, they took pictures of the corpse, dressed up in its Sunday best, perhaps the only picture of the person they would ever have. And other times, they clipped a lock or two of hair and plaited it into jewelry, something to remember the person by, or something they could keep with them all the time. These were *memento mori* in the full, original meaning of the word, 'to remember death'.

The beautiful, ghastly wreath of hair was a piece of Victorian death jewelry.

The vision was sudden and overwhelming.

I was cold, so cold. One moment I had been sweating on a battlefield in Virginia, and the next... the next there was nothing. They say you never hear the bullet that gets you. How could you, when all around you the sound of hundreds of rifles crashes like thunder? I remembered a loud noise, a sharp, sudden pain and then falling into darkness.

And waking up. Only, not really. When I emerged from the darkness, my body didn't come with me. Women sobbed. Men pretended that they weren't crying. My little sister fainted and had to be carried from the room. I wanted to tell them I was still there, wanted to tell them how much I loved them, but 'I' wasn't 'me' anymore. I was up here, and the rest of me was down there, not moving, gray with death.

I thought I had been frightened on the battlefield. That fear paled in comparison to how terrified I was now. I thought that the Almighty would have gathered me to his bosom by now, if I were worthy. I'd heard tell all my life about bright lights and a land of milk and honey. Since I was still here, maybe that bright light wasn't going to come for me. I didn't have words for how afraid I was of what that meant for my immortal soul, so I just stayed where I was, looking for Amelia, my beloved. She always knew how to make sense of things.

Then I saw her. Oh dear Lord, had grief for me done that to her? My pretty Amelia, so young and happy, looked gaunt and frail, hollow-eyed. Her father walked her to the casket, as if she could barely stand. She nearly collapsed, sagging almost to her knees, before he collected her and helped her stand next to me to say good-bye.

I wanted to touch her, to tell her I was near, but I couldn't. And then she leaned over and kissed my forehead, and carefully snipped some of my hair where it was the longest. Hot tears fell on my cold skin, but somehow, I felt them. No one faulted her for weeping. We were going to marry in the spring.

I couldn't go back and I couldn't go on, so I followed my Amelia home. And since the Almighty didn't seem to want me, I did the best I could, watching over my girl. I had nowhere else to be. She plaited my hair into a memorial wreath, and she wore it on a chain around her neck. And if, when she touched it, she thought she imagined my presence, I was closer than she knew.

Abruptly, I was Cassidy again. I saw time flow by like an old movie. The scene changed, years passed. Amelia died, still grieving her lost love. The hair wreath went into the velvet box that had once held a gift that gave great joy. The young man's ghost remained, too afraid to move on. And then, the shadows came.

This time, I didn't enter the ghost's thoughts as fully as before, except to feel terror in every cell and sinew of my body. After a hundred years of quiet darkness, not exactly heaven but far removed from hell, something appeared in the everlasting night. It was not the Father Almighty.

Like watching a movie with the sound turned off, something I could see but not influence, I saw the wraith stalk the young man's ghost. Tad. His name had been Tad. Thaddeus, maybe, but no one called him that. Just Tad. Lonely, afraid, desperate for company, he had gotten too close the first time, only to lose part of what little he had left to the wraith's hunger. After that, there was terror. Hiding. Fear of being found, of having the last little bit of self destroyed after all these long years. The darkness was so vast. Suddenly, the everlasting night that had seemed to be the enemy became an ally, a place to play a deadly game of hide-and-seek. And finally, the young man's spirit got the answer it had been seeking. There are some things worse than death. Being consumed is one of them.

When I came back to myself, I was screaming. Teag held me by the shoulders, shaking me gently, calling my name. We've done this a lot, unfortunately.

"Come back, Cassidy!" His eyes were worried. I guessed that I'd been pretty far gone. I've never gone so deep into a vision that I haven't been able to find my way back, but there's always a first time. And if there was a first time, it was likely to be the last time.

I nodded groggily, like a drunk sobering up on coffee. The terror and loss of the young man from the vision stayed with me, frightening and sad. "I'm okay," I managed. Teag's look told me that he sincerely doubted that.

Instead of arguing, he pushed another glass of sweet tea into my hand, and waited while I gulped it down. The icy cold liquid shocked me back to myself, and the sugar rushed through my veins like elixir. Only then did I realize I was shaking and sobbing, grieving for two lovers who had been dead for more than a hundred and fifty years.

I dragged the back of my hand over my eyes and took a deep breath to steady myself. Teag waited patiently. "I saw the story behind the memorial jewelry," I said, carefully laying the velvet box aside. "Young lovers. Civil War." Unfortunately, that story was a common refrain with the pieces we often saw at Trifles and Folly, although rarely had the past made such an impact. "I'd expect a piece like that to have a lot of mojo," I added, trying to get my voice to stop quailing. "But there's a ghost attached to it, and the thing we fought off tried to destroy him."

Teag frowned, alarmed. "That monster attacks ghosts?"

I nodded. "Yeah. It took a bite out of him. And I have the feeling that whatever that thing was, it went away, but it's not really gone."

"Then we've got a big problem," Teag said. "Because Charleston is a spookfest, and that monster is going to have an all-you-can-eat buffet if we don't do something about it."

Chapter Two

THE NEXT MORNING, I woke up feeling more refreshed than usual, something I attributed to the magic in the salve and bandage. The cuts on my shoulder were healing well, and they hurt a lot less than I would have expected. I fed my little Maltese dog, Baxter, grabbed some peanut butter toast for breakfast, and headed to the store. It was a warm fall day, typical for Charleston, and my strawberry-blonde hair was staying in place for once. One look at my hair and my pale skin, and there's no doubting my Scots-Irish blood.

I was surprised when my phone rang on the way in to the store. It was Kell Winston, and he sounded worried.

"Could you meet me at Honeysuckle Café?" Kell asked. "I need to talk to you."

Kell was an acquaintance; a college friend of Anthony's and someone Teag and I had worked with on occasion. The sudden, urgent request caught me by surprise.

"Sure," I replied. "In fact, I'm heading that way right now to grab coffee. Want to meet me there?"

"Done. See you in about fifteen minutes." Kell ended the call, and I stared at my phone for a moment, trying to figure out what was going on and wondering if it could have anything to do with the ghost-eater we had run into the day before.

Honeysuckle Café is my favorite place to grab a latte. It's a local coffee house on King Street, and thrives because of – and in spite of – being one-of-a-kind instead of a national chain. Inside, the café feels like a comfy living room with overstuffed chairs, piles of books, and vases of fresh flowers. People linger to actually have a conversation.

Although I was in a pretty good mood when I left the house, as I got closer to the coffee shop, the worse I felt about Tad's ghost, like I had failed him. *I let him down. He's in danger, and I can't help him. Some big bad monster hunter I am. Total effing failure.* I caught my mood spiraling, and pulled myself out my thoughts. It took me a few minutes of giving myself a silent pep talk to shake off the awful feeling of guilt that had overwhelmed me. In fact, I was so deep in thought that I didn't hear Rick ask me a question when I got to the head of the line.

"Big or little?" Rick, the barista, asked.

"Big – but I'm going with the chai latte special today," I replied. The coffee bar at Honeysuckle Café is Rick's stage, and he's one of the reasons the place is so popular with King Street merchants and tourists. A sign on the wall over the espresso machine reads 'Rick's Place' and with his long face and bedroom eyes, Rick is a dead-ringer for Bogart. He plays up the resemblance with a wardrobe of vintage clothing and snappy fedoras.

"Hi Cassidy!" Trina, the café owner, waved from over by the register. I thanked Rick for my latte and headed over to pay for it. The café has good food and great coffee, but the real reason I love going is because Rick and Trina hear all the news in Charleston, and are happy to pass it on.

"What's new?" I asked as Trina rang up my order.

"You ought to ask Drea," Trina replied, handing me my change. "They've had some excitement with the ghost tours." I raised an eyebrow, encouraging her to go on.

"Valerie told me that she had to cut last night's tour short because the ghosts were frightening the tourists and throwing rocks," Trina nodded. Drea Andrews owned Andrews Carriage Rides, and Valerie was one of her most popular tour guides. I'd known both of them for a long time.

I frowned. "And she's sure it wasn't just teenagers playing a dangerous prank?"

"She's sure." Drea had come up behind me in line, back for a coffee to-go. "I was going to stop over at Trifles and Folly to tell you about it." While we waited for her coffee, Drea continued the story. "Valerie's been doing the ghost tour for years, and nothing fazes her. She swears that the regular ghosts know her and leave the guests alone."

"But not last night?"

Drea paid for her coffee. "Nope. Valerie said that there were cold spots all over town. She heard knocking on fences, saw shadows that shouldn't have been there, had an orb flash right in front of the group – and got pelted with pebbles even though no one was in sight."

"Wow," I replied. "I guess the customers got their money's worth." The ghost tours were Drea's most sought-after excursions.

Drea didn't look pleased. "There could have been injuries. Thank goodness no one was hurt."

We said good-bye and I went to grab some extra napkins before I found a seat to wait for Kell. I didn't even look up when someone came to the cream and sugar station until the newcomer spoke to me.

"Have you ever had the triple-pumpkin latte?" the man asked. "I took a chance and got it, and now I'm hoping I'll like it."

I glanced up at the best looking man I had seen in a long time, including on TV and in the movies. He had dark hair and blue eyes, and although his jacket-over-jeans combo was casual, I recognized the brand names of the clothes and knew they didn't come cheap.

"It's very good," I replied offhandedly. I was still thinking about what Drea had said, and it had me worried.

"I figured that you'd know," he said, and nodded toward my cup. Out of the corner of my eye, I saw that the rest of the women and some of the men had noticed the stranger. I glanced outside through the picture window, wondering where the production truck was and racking my brain for which show he might be on.

"Yeah," I said. "This is my favorite place to get a latte."

I expected him to grab some packets of sweetener and a stir stick and be on his way, so when he gave me a high-wattage smile and turned like he meant to chat, I was surprised. *Isn't your producer waiting for you? Since when do they send the on-air talent for coffee?*

"I take it you're not a tourist?" he said. Behind us, I could hear a muted buzz of conversation as the folks in the coffee shop tried to place the newcomer.

Cute though he was, something put me on guard. I hoped it wasn't just being out of practice. It's been about a year since my last 'romance'. "Nope. I live here. Most of my life. Charleston is a nice place."

On one hand, I hesitated to ask a question because I wasn't really in the mood to flirt. And on the other, I've been raised to be polite – unless I'm kicking demon ass. "New in town?" I asked, letting politeness win out, for now.

His smile reached his eyes, which were Caribbean-sea blue and crinkled a little around the edges. Maybe that's what put my guard up. Not only was he my type, he was a little too much my type to be true. I'm cynical. So sue me.

"Everyone says how beautiful Charleston is," he said. "So I came to find out for myself. And it is," he added with a little extra emphasis to let me know he wasn't talking about the city. *Was that actually a pick-up line?*

I reached for the sweetener packs at the same instant as Mr. Tall-Dark-and-Perfect, and my hand brushed his. Magic tingled so hot it burned, and I stifled a yelp. I saw a flash of something in his eyes that went deeper than surprise. He hid it well, but I thought I saw a glint of anger.

"I got us a table in the back." Kell Winston came up just then, tall and lean with light brown hair, blue eyes, and dark summer tan – looking like he should be on a yacht somewhere rather than in a coffee shop. He stepped in between Coffee Guy and me, sparing me from having to say something. "I'm glad you could meet me," Kell added. Whether Kell was oblivious to the good-looking stranger or was ignoring him intentionally I wasn't sure.

"Enjoy your visit," I said to the newcomer as I gathered my things, trying to be neighborly without giving him any ideas. Something about the guy was sending my gut warnings into overdrive, and I've learned to trust my intuition.

"See you around," he said, grabbing his cup of coffee. There was nothing unusual about the way he said it, but I wondered whether it was a promise or a threat.

"Sorry to interrupt," Kell said. "I know you've got to open the shop. So I really appreciate you meeting me here on such short notice." We found a table away from everyone else, and I took a sip of my latte, waiting for him to go on.

"I don't know who else to tell about this." Kell said. "But I know you've dealt some with ghosts, and frankly, I have no idea what to make of things."

I sipped my chai, letting Kell take his time telling his story. Kell runs the Southern Paranormal Observation and Outreach Klub, better known as SPOOK, a local group of high-tech ghost hunters. Unlike some of the ghost shows on television, Kell and his group aren't sensationalists. They do their research, and seem dedicated to understanding the true nature of ghosts and spirits from 'beyond'.

Of course, Kell had no idea about what we really do at Trifles and Folly, although he's pretty sure I have some type of psychic gift. Especially after the last time Teag and I went out with his group. We were attacked in an old crypt by a deranged vampire's ghost, and barely managed to fight it off. That kind of thing makes an impression, and so I wasn't surprised that Kell had called me when his team ran into something they couldn't explain.

"What happened?" I asked.

Kell looked genuinely worried. "In the last couple of weeks, there's been a real uptick in supernatural activity all around Charleston," Kell replied. "We've tried to figure out what's causing it. Moon phases. Tides. The alignment of the planets. The season of the year. The wobble in the Earth's rotation. You name it, I've looked into it. I can't figure it out."

"What makes you think the ghosts are riled up?" I asked. My chai latte was hot and seasoned with pumpkin and nutmeg. It was the perfect drink for a fall day, but given the topic, the tea did little to soothe my nerves.

"I know most people think we're just thrill-chasers," Kell said. "But most of us, especially our core group, really want to know what causes paranormal activity and what's on the other side."

Most of what I'd seen on the other side wasn't friendly. Personally, I wasn't in a hurry to cross over and see more of it. Much as Kell thought he wanted answers, I was pretty sure that he didn't want to know the truth.

"So we don't just observe a site one time," Kell went on. "We do our best to visit the sites a couple of times a year and take new readings. That way, we know if sites get more or less haunted, and whether the phenomena changes if there's a new owner, for example, or a renovation."

"And you found changes."

Kell nodded. "Not just in one site, but in all the ones we've re-surveyed in the last month," he said. "Big changes. But what has me worried is, the ghosts are not only more active, but they've gotten aggressive."

"How so?"

Kell ran a hand through his hair. "Geez, you're going to think I'm nuts."

I smiled, although inside I felt a growing worry. "No, I promise. I definitely won't think you're nuts."

Kell looked at me a little sheepishly. "All right then. Most of the paranormal activity we've documented is pretty passive. Readings on the EMF monitor. Voices or footsteps where there aren't any people. Hazy images. Objects that have been moved – usually a very short distance."

"And now?"

"Now, it's like every ghost in Charleston suddenly took poltergeist lessons," Kell said. "Instead of a light touch on someone's shoulder, it's a shove. Instead of a chair rocking gently, the chair suddenly tips over. We didn't just get fog on a window last night, it actually iced up." He shook his head. "It's the first time in all the years that I've been ghost hunting that I'm actually getting scared."

"Has anyone gotten hurt?"

"No. At least, not yet," Kell replied. "And none of us have gotten the feeling that the ghosts are trying to attack us. If anything, they seem... frightened."

"What could scare a ghost?" I asked, although I had a pretty good idea.

"That's what I've been wondering. So I've been doing some research. I've been going through everything I can get my hands on, and there are a few situations that I've found like this, all from long ago. But I don't know if I can believe what the researchers at the time said was the cause."

"How weird could it be?" I asked, crossing my fingers under the table that Kell hadn't stumbled onto the truth.

Kell looked like he was prepared for me to laugh at him. "I only found three mentions. And all three times – different countries, different time periods, different ghost hunters – the researchers blamed witches with the power to destroy restless spirits." He gave a weak smile. "Crazy, huh?"

It might not be, but I couldn't tell him that. For one thing, Kell didn't know about the Alliance, and I wasn't going to let him in on the secret. The fewer who knew, the better. He had a medium and a clairvoyant on his team, but none of them had the level of power that could stop a curse or fight a wizard of real power, and I didn't want them to get hurt playing out of their league.

"Do you really think anyone has the power to hurt the dead?"

Kell sighed. "Before all this happened, I would have said no. Now, I don't know. Something has riled up the ghosts. It's got to the point where Melissa won't go out with us anymore because she says she can't stand to hear the ghosts screaming in her head." He frowned. "The last time we went out, Melissa literally got sick from the impressions she received. She said that something was destroying the spirits. Isn't that awful? But Melissa isn't the kind to make something like that up."

"How did you think I might be able to help?"

Kell set the empty cup back on the table and hesitated as if he were searching for just what to say. "I don't know. Just hearing me out helps. I didn't know if you'd come upon any old books, or charms, or sacred objects that we might be able to use to protect the spirits." He looked at me earnestly. "They're dead, Cassidy. Most of them had some kind of tragedy that kept them stuck here. They've suffered enough, first in life, and then by not getting to go on to wherever it is we're supposed to go when we die. They weren't bothering anyone. And now, thinking that someone – or something – is hurting them, it makes me angry." Kell gave a self-deprecating chuckle. "Listen to me. I make it sound like they're a bunch of stray cats."

My mind was leaping ahead. "Actually, that's not a bad idea," I replied.

Kell looked confused. "Stray cats?"

I shook my head. "No. Charms. Protections." Something else occurred to me. "Did you find any ghosts that didn't fit the pattern? Any that hadn't been damaged?"

Kell nodded. "A few. They were still riled up but Melissa didn't get the same sense of panic."

"Did those ghosts have anything in common?"

"Yeah. They were inside old churches. Consecrated ground."

In other words, inside very powerful, heavily reinforced wardings. "You know, I think I may have a couple of ideas that might help with this," I said. "I know some people who have a lot more experience with the supernatural than I do," I added, fudging just a little. "How about if I go talk to them, and let you know what they say? Maybe I can get you some charms and amulets and you can take them to where the ghosts were causing a problem."

Kell reached out and took my hand. "Cassidy, if you can do that, I'll be your raving fan forever," he swore. "Thank you. Just having you believe me matters. And if you can come up with something that helps – that would be amazing."

I smiled. "Give me a day or two to track people down. I'll call you as soon as I know anything."

"And I will happily buy you dinner for your effort," he said. "Promise."

My cheeks flushed and I drew back my hand, but not before giving his a friendly squeeze. "Thanks. That sounds fun. But first let's see if I can actually come up with something."

Kell and I parted company at the corner with a promise to have lunch together soon. I was deep in thought as I walked back to Trifles and Folly. I wondered if the wraith Teag and I had encountered was bothering other ghosts, not just Tad's spirit. I got my answer when I walked into the store and saw Alicia Peters talking with Teag.

Alicia gave me a friendly wave. "Hi Alicia!" I said. Alicia is a powerful spirit medium, someone Sorren and I had worked with on occasion. I had thought about calling her to see what she made of the hair necklace. The fact that she showed up on her own told me something big was going on.

"Hi Cassidy," Alicia replied. "I thought I had better stop by and see what's up, since the ghosts are climbing the walls, so to speak." Alicia's strong Lowcountry accent gave her a smooth drawl. Her dark, shoulder-length hair was tied back in a ponytail, and she had a twinset on over a dressy pair of jeans.

"I've got the front of the store," Teag said, volunteering to handle customers since this was Maggie's day off. "Why don't you and Alicia go in the back?"

I led the way, and offered to make Alicia a cup of tea from our pot, but she shook her head, looking preoccupied. "No thanks. I'm jittery enough."

"You don't usually stop in unless there's trouble," I said. "What's up?"

Alicia knows about my magic, and she also knows about Sorren and the Alliance. "Last night, something panicked a lot of ghosts in Charleston," she said. "You and I have seen some mighty strange things that haven't sent the ghosts into a flurry. This did."

"I heard something like that from Drea over with the ghost tours."

Alicia nodded. "I'm not surprised. Valerie has some ability as a medium; that's why her tourists always get the best glimpses of the ghosts."

I gave Alicia a quick recap of what had happened with the *memento mori*. She listened intently, looking more worried as I went on. "Do you still have the jewelry box?" she asked.

I wasn't about to handle it again, but I led her into the office, where the box sat on the corner of my desk, waiting for Sorren to come get it. "That's it," I said, pointing to the box. "Can you pick up anything about Tad?"

Alicia walked close to the velvet box and bent down to look at it carefully. I brought my desk chair around to the other side and she sat down then I closed the door, in case things got loud. "I can sense the spirit that is tied to the hair necklace," Alicia said.

"Tad," I replied. "I saw his memories, but I couldn't actually communicate with him."

Alicia nodded. "I'd like to go into trance and talk to him. I'll channel him and you can ask the questions."

"Do you need anything?" When I had worked with Alicia before, it was always part of something big, so I wasn't sure what a 'casual' reading entailed.

Alicia smiled but shook her head. "No, thank you. I'll be fine. Give me a few minutes to get grounded, and then we'll see what Tad can tell us about what's going on." I watched Alicia take several deep, slow breaths and saw her entire body relax. She closed her eyes, and leaned against the back of the tall chair.

"Tad?" she called quietly. "I know you're scared. I'm here to help, but I need to know what's going on. If you're there, Tad, come talk to me."

I waited, and realized I was holding my breath. Alicia was silent, but beneath her closed eyelids, I could see her eyes flickering back and forth as if she were dreaming. She shifted in the chair, and just like that, I knew that Tad was with us. Something about her posture seemed less like her and more masculine.

"Tad?" I asked hesitantly.

"I saw you," a voice replied. The voice came from Alicia's mouth, but it was deeper, and the accent was different. "You fought off the bad thing."

He meant the wraith. "Yes," I replied. "Do you know where you are?"

The ghost was quiet for a moment. "I'm a long way from home," he replied. "And I can't make any sense out of most of what I see. Folks move around so fast, do strange things. I wish I could sleep. But I don't dare."

I could hear the confusion and weariness in his voice, and my heart went out to him. "Because of the bad thing?" I asked gently.

"It eats you if you sleep."

"Has it always been around?" I asked. I hoped not. More than one hundred and fifty years was a long time to run from something in the dark.

"No," Tad's spirit answered. "It came... not long ago..." Alicia's face mirrored the ghost's confusion. I doubted Tad could be more specific. Ghosts don't pay attention to the passage of time the way living people do.

"Did something happen to bring the bad thing? Did it wake up?" I struggled to ask questions the ghost might be able to answer.

Tad was quiet for a minute. "The dark has been quiet for a very long time," he said, and I could hear the loneliness in his voice. "I rested. I didn't try to bother

anyone. If I can't go on from here, the quiet will do."
He paused again, longer this time. "Then 'it' showed
up. I didn't know what was happening until it hurt me.
I didn't know anything could hurt me anymore." He
sounded afraid. "It came out of the dark, and it took
a bite out of me before I knew what was happening.
I... ran. I didn't know how to fight it." Shame tinged
his words, and I remembered that Tad was a soldier.
Running away had to be hard.

"There wasn't anything else that happened before the
bad thing came?" I pressed. "Anything at all?"

"I heard a voice, far away. Someone I didn't know. I
couldn't make out what he was saying. It woke me up,
or the bad thing would have gotten me in my sleep. And
then, I saw a line in the darkness that looked like fire. It
came and went real fast. After that, the bad thing was
there in the dark with me."

Sounds like someone is messing with magic, I thought.
*Who summoned the wraith? And how did they open
a door for it?* Important questions, but I knew Tad
couldn't answer them.

"Have you seen the bad thing since last night?" I
asked.

"No. But it might come back. Then what?"

"I don't know yet," I admitted. "But my friends and I
are going to do our best to send it away."

"Thank you," Tad said. "I'd like to go back to sleep."

Alicia was rousing from her trance. She shivered, and
I knew she was back again when she opened her eyes.

"Did you hear any of that?" I asked. Sometimes,
mediums don't remember anything after a session.

"Yes," Alicia replied. "And I don't like the sound of
it. But it squares with what Valerie saw on her ghost

tour. A predator that eats ghosts. That's bad – and Charleston has a lot of ghostly prey."

I went to the kitchen and came back with a cold glass of sweet tea. There's not much that can't be made better with a glass of cold tea. Alicia drank it gratefully, and after a few moments, the color came back to her face.

"If you heard what Tad said, did you get anything from his thoughts that I might not have picked up?" I asked, leaning against my desk, well away from the problematic jewelry box.

Alicia frowned, thinking back over the ghostly encounter. "Tad didn't really have the words to tell you what he saw when the wraith appeared," she replied. "Magic certainly isn't in his vocabulary. What I got out of the memories I saw was that someone called the wraith forth from... somewhere. So we've got two problems – the wraith, and whoever summoned it."

I had been thinking the same thing, but hearing Alicia put my fears into words sent a shiver down my spine. "Yeah," I said. "That's what I got out of it, too. And that means we've got a heap of trouble."

"Are you going to call the woman who brought in the jewelry box?" Teag asked after Alicia left and I had given him a recap of what we had discovered. Before Teag came to Trifles and Folly, he had been working on his doctorate in history at the university. He still looks like a grad student, mid-twenties, good-looking, tall and slender with a mop of dark, skater-boy hair and a wicked sense of humor. Now, he pushed a lock of hair out of his eyes and gave me a look that was deadly serious.

"I'm not sure she can tell us more than she did when she sold it to us," I said, leaning against the counter. "That jewelry box has been in the family for over a hundred years without bothering anyone, and just recently, she starts getting bad dreams and blames the box. Pretty odd if you ask me."

Teag nodded. "I agree, especially that she'd single out the jewelry box. I wonder why – and what she saw in her dreams."

I remembered the woman who had brought in the velvet jewelry box. She looked tired and guilty. That's not as surprising as it sounds. A lot of people feel pressured to keep everything they inherit. Sometimes, they've hated that item since childhood. Maybe the piece doesn't work with their lifestyle or they just don't have room for it. That's when the guilt hits, and they sneak into Trifles and Folly like we're their fence for stolen goods.

For our customers, we're a mix of antique appraiser, treasure hunt, and confessional. People bring us grandma's unwanted silver flatware and want to know what it's worth. Buyers love finding one-of-a-kind items, and collectors hope they'll stumble on an overlooked Picasso sketch worth a million dollars. But before those items go into the glass cases out front, we talk to the people who own the pieces, and that's usually when we know whether we're in for trouble.

"Let me give it a try," I said. "I'll see if I can steer the conversation back to her dream." It was a long shot. The woman who had sold us the piece looked very uncomfortable even admitting that bad dreams had anything to do with her decision to part with the heirloom. Now that the box was no longer her problem, I was betting she'd revise her memories to conveniently forget all about the bad dreams. It's amazing what people can ignore when the truth makes them too uncomfortable.

I went into the office and dialed the number Teag gave me. A woman answered on the third ring.

"Mrs. Hendricks? This is Cassidy Kincaide from Trifles and Folly, the store where you sold that marvelous Victorian heirloom. I have a couple of questions for you, if you don't mind. Our customers love to have information about the pieces they purchase, and there's a lady who wants to know more." Technically, that was true, although I was the 'lady'.

"You won't give out my contact information, will you?" Mrs. Hendricks asked suspiciously. But when I assured her that we would keep her name confidential, she opened up, to my surprise.

"That necklace has been in my family for a long time," Mrs. Hendricks said. She sounded like she might be in her sixties, with an accent that told me she had lived in or near Charleston all her life. "Thaddeus Anderson was engaged to marry my great, great-aunt Amelia. He died in the Battle of Rivers Bridge. He was just twenty-two years old."

"Your family must have been very proud of him."

"We are," she replied in a mellifluous cadence I could have listened to all day. "Of course, he died before great-aunt Amelia married him, so there were no children. She never married. But Amelia lived into her nineties, and she kept a photograph of Thaddeus with her at all times. She was buried with that photograph."

I frowned. "But not with the necklace?" That seemed strange, especially given Amelia's life-long devotion, and the fact that a hair necklace wasn't likely to be something anyone else would want.

Mrs. Hendricks chuckled. "Well now, you'd think so, wouldn't you? And the stories vary as to why. One story says that the box with the necklace had been misplaced when Amelia went into the nursing home, and it wasn't found until after she died. Another story says that they tried to bury her with it, but something kept thumping on the inside of the casket lid until the mortician removed that necklace. And the third story says that one of my great-uncles, a rather greedy man, thought the necklace might be valuable and refused to let them bury her with it. Take your pick."

I was betting on story number two, although I didn't tell her that. "How long ago did your great-aunt Amelia die?"

"She died in nineteen forty," Mrs. Hendricks said.

"So the necklace has been in the family all these years since Amelia's death. What led you to sell it now?"

Mrs. Hendricks was quiet for a moment, and I was afraid she was going to refuse to answer. "Some of great-aunt Amelia's things came down to me through my mother," she said. "Dishes and such. My parents have moved to Florida, and when they cleaned out their house, my mother gave me what she wanted me to have. That included a box of Amelia's things, and in the box was the necklace. That was about a month ago."

I waited, hoping she would go on. "I knew about the hair necklace because it's a family story. But of course, something like that is very personal to the one who made it. Not like regular jewelry. No one else would ever wear it." She paused again. "Frankly, it gave me the creeps," she admitted with an embarrassed chuckle.

"Were there ever any ghost stories connected to the necklace?" I asked. "I'm sure someone is bound to ask."

Mrs. Hendricks hesitated a little longer before she spoke. "When I found the necklace in that box, I didn't like the way it made me feel," she said. "It seemed unlucky. I try to create positive energy in my home. So I thought I would let someone else appreciate it, since my own children have no interest in that sort of thing."

I had the feeling Mrs. Hendricks had said all she planned to say about the subject. "Thank you very much," I said. "You've been generous with your time."

"I hope it finds a good home," she said, and paused. "But I do hope no one tries to wear it. It's just... strange."

I thanked her again and hung up. The necklace was indeed 'strange', but not in the way Mrs. Hendricks thought. Or perhaps, some latent magic warned her that the memento was not benign. That left Teag and me with a problem item to deal with, and no idea what to do about it.

And I had a nagging suspicion that whatever had come after Tad's ghost would be back.

Chapter Three

WE CLOSED THE store right at five, and even if Sorren was back in town, it wasn't dark enough for him to be out and about yet, so Teag invited me to join him and Anthony at Jocko's Pizzeria, our favorite place to grab a couple of slices and a cold beer.

Jocko's is run by Giacomo Rossi, 'Jack' to his friends. Jack gave us a wave and a hearty "hello" from behind the counter. Just walking into Jocko's makes me feel good. It always smells of fresh herbs, ripe tomatoes, warm cheese, and freshly-baked crusts.

"You want the usual?" Jack called. Teag shot him a thumbs-up and we went to our favorite booth in the back. Teag and I ate at Jocko's at least once a week.

One of the things that makes Charleston such a foodie town is the fact that a large number of our restaurants aren't chains. They're one-of-a-kind places you can only visit here in the Holy City. We love good food almost as much as we love history and sweet tea, which is saying a lot.

The best restaurants have a history of their own that makes them special. In this case, Jocko's had a mural on the wall that told the Rossi family history, and picked up with the turning point in Jack's life that brought him to Charleston. Jack had been a stock trader in the North Tower of the World Trade Center in New York back on September 11, 2001, and when he survived the attack, he decided that life was too short to spend behind a desk. So he quit his job, moved his family to Charleston and opened up Jocko's using some of his mother's recipes. The rest, as they say, is history.

We had just ordered drinks when Anthony joined us. Anthony Benton was the blond-haired, blue-eyed epitome of a Battery Row favorite son, and a partner in the family law firm. He and Teag were a long-time couple, and although Anthony didn't know everything about our work with the Alliance, he knew enough to worry about both of us.

"Did I miss much?" he asked, slipping into the booth beside Teag and giving him a quick peck on the cheek. The waiter brought pale ale for Teag, a red wine for me, and a Chardonnay for Anthony.

"We've got a rampaging evil spirit that's attacking ghosts," Teag replied matter-of-factly. Anthony looked from Teag to me and back again.

"Seriously?"

I nodded drolly. "Yeah. All in a day's work. How about you?"

Anthony took a sip of his wine. "Honestly, I'd trade you. This big case is running me ragged. And it's tough getting anything done at City Hall right now, since the police are going crazy trying to track down two disappearances in as many days." Anthony is a lawyer, and that means he talks to a lot of people in law enforcement. While he's bound by confidentiality, in some situations, when he can, he passes along information that might help with what we do.

"Disappearances?" I keep an eye on the headlines and I'm pretty well connected to the grapevine. Teag's Google-fu is strong, so between the two of us, we usually know what's going on in town, and then some. This was new.

Anthony looked around, assured himself no one was close enough to overhear, and dropped his voice. "Yeah. They've kept it out of the news, but given the weird stuff you two deal with, I figured I should mention it. Two people walked down perfectly normal staircases and never reached the bottom."

That was interesting. "Do the people have anything in common?" I asked.

Anthony hesitated. "Age, gender, location – all different. Other people walked up and down those stairs without a problem, before and after the disappearances."

"When you say 'disappeared' –" Teag began.

Anthony met his gaze. "I mean up and vanished. Witnesses said they saw the victims start down the stairs and then just disappear before they reached the bottom."

It had taken Anthony a while to warm up to the idea that Teag and I dealt with real magic. Teag believes that the 'intuition' Anthony uses so successfully in the courtroom is his own magic skill, but so far, he hasn't convinced Anthony of that. But the times that Anthony has gone along to help out, he's seen enough to accept the fact that the spooky stuff is real. He's also seen Teag and me get pretty beat up fighting off supernatural nasties, and he's helped us fend off a few surly spooks himself. I can't blame him for worrying.

"What kind of explanation are the cops coming up with?" I asked.

Anthony's mouth was a grim line. "Nothing to do with ghosts, I can assure you. Mostly, they think the witnesses are mistaken. Or that the victims are either playing a prank or don't want to be found."

The server brought out our pizza, and we fell silent as we ate. My mind kept pinging back and forth between two things that didn't seem to have a logical connection: Tad's ghostly stalker, and the disappearances. I've learned the hard way that there aren't a lot of coincidences when you're dealing with supernatural predators. Unfortunately, sometimes you only see the connections in hindsight, when it's too little, too late.

"Heading home?" Teag asked Anthony when we finally finished our feeding frenzy. Teag and Anthony had moved in together a few months ago, a big step forward for them. Even so, with the crazy hours they both kept, it was still a challenge to get a lot of quality time.

Anthony shook his head. "Not for a while. I have some more files to go over before a case tomorrow. I shouldn't be terribly late, but that's why I figured I'd meet you for dinner rather than have you wait up."

I could tell Teag was glad not to be the only one working late. Sorren was supposed to be headed back from Boston, and I suspected trouble was afoot. It might be a long night.

SORREN WAS WAITING for us when we got back to Trifles and Folly. I flicked on the light in the back room, and jumped to find him sitting quietly at the table in the dark.

44

"Geez! Can't you turn on a light or something?" I covered my surprise with some good-natured annoyance. Then again, Sorren didn't need light. His vampire senses were sharper than mortals' abilities, and he was stronger and faster, too. I knew he'd used his key to get into the store, but he didn't need one. Long ago, when he was mortal, he had been the best jewel thief in Belgium.

"I assumed you'd be expecting me," Sorren replied, a slight smile letting me know he enjoyed the banter. Sorren looks like he's in his twenties, the age he was when he was turned back in the 1400s. His hair is an unremarkable shade of blond, his blue-gray eyes are the color of the sea before a storm, and his features are pleasant without being memorable, something that was helpful back in his thieving days. Right now, he was wearing a t-shirt and trendy jeans with sneakers. Since his skin wasn't unnaturally pale, I figured he had fed recently. Sorren was very good at passing for mortal. But Teag and I had seen what he could do in a fight. Anyone who took him for just another twenty-something was making a fatal mistake.

"We just went out for a bite," I said.

"So did I." Sorren's voice was droll, but his eyes held a hint of mischief. *Ha, ha. Vampire jokes. Did you hear the one about...*

"The jewelry box I called you about is on my desk," I said. Sorren walked over, picked up the velvet case and brought it back to the table, turning his attention to its funereal jewelry. The piece that caused me such a jolt had no effect on Sorren. He says that's because he doesn't *have* magic; the Dark Gift *is* magic. Handling objects with bad juju doesn't knock him flat on his ass. "Did your trip go as planned?" I asked.

Sorren looked preoccupied. "As well as could be expected," he replied. "There was an attack on my Boston operation. Two of my people are in the hospital. The damage to the store was contained, but it required my attention."

He looked down at the velvet box in his hands, and I got the feeling he had said all he planned to say about Boston. "The Victorians had a lot to mourn," Sorren said quietly as he looked at the hair necklace. "The War killed so many, and then there were the epidemics," he added. From his tone, I wondered if he was thinking aloud rather than speaking to Teag and me. I knew Charleston's history pretty well, and the last half of the 1800s was rough by any standards. War, Yellow Fever, earthquake, violent storms, fire... I'm sure the hardy souls who survived must have believed the world was coming to an end.

"I was going to give Father Anne a call to see if we could set Tad's spirit free," I said. "Maybe even help him cross over."

Sorren nodded. "Good idea. I'm sure she'll be up for it. She's done that kind of thing before."

"What about the *thing* that tried to eat him?" I asked. "That isn't something we hear about every day. Maybe it's also causing problems for the ghost tours and Kell's people – scaring the ghosts and making them more aggressive."

He frowned. "I don't have a good answer. There are plenty of unfriendly creatures that can move back and forth across the boundary between life and death. I'm going to have to ask around." He gave a lopsided grin. "Sounds like something the Briggs Society might know."

When I want to find something out, I go on the internet. Teag digs into the Web's dark, ensorcelled recesses. Sorren navigates the complicated politics of Charleston's immortal and magical community, as well as his contacts around the world. The Briggs Society was one of those communities, a place I'd heard Sorren talk about but never visited myself, an organization dedicated to explorers of all kinds.

"Do you think we're in danger?"

"I'm not sure," he replied. "For now, assume the worst. Don't take any chances. I'll have Lucinda strengthen the wardings around the shop and around your houses. You can always relax once we find out there's nothing to worry about."

It was a nice thought. But finding 'nothing to worry about' seemed about as unlikely as snow in a Charleston summer.

THE NEXT MORNING, I got in early to make a phone call. Tad's ghost was still bound to that old hair necklace, still vulnerable to whatever had taken a bite out of him. After a hundred and fifty years, I figured he deserved better than hanging around a jewelry box.

If there was someone who would know about getting spirits unstuck, it would be Father Anne, Assistant Rector of St. Hildegard's Episcopal Church. She was also a member of the St. Expeditus Society, a group of renegade Anglican priests who helped put down supernatural threats. I'd worked with her before, and I thought Tad's problem sounded like it was right up her alley.

Unfortunately, I got her voice mail, so I left her a rather vague but urgent message, and chafed at the delay. As I ended the call, I heard someone rapping at the door to the shop, and found Maggie peering in through the window. "It's going to be a good day, I can just feel it!" Maggie greeted me when she came in the door.

She's our part-time helper, and a real god-send. Maggie retired from her teaching job and decided that yoga, travel, and her grandchildren just weren't enough to keep her busy, so she works a couple of days a week at Trifles and Folly, and helps out when we need extra coverage. She's sixty and sassy, as she likes to put it, with short silver hair and lively blue eyes. Her fashion sense is pure Woodstock, but her business sense is all Wall Street. Teag and I love having her around.

"Hi, Maggie!" I said, as I headed to finish the work I had started earlier, re-arranging the front window display. Drea had clued me in to a big tea industry conference in town, so I figured featuring our stock of antique silver tea services would be a good idea. Charleston has one of the only tea plantations in North America, just down the road, and as Trina and Rick can attest, Charlestonians love their tea as much as they adore their coffee.

"Oh, pretty!" Maggie said, and went back outside to size up the display from the customers' perspective. She came back in smiling brightly.

"I think the big set needs to be moved a little to the right," she suggested. "It looks off-center. My heavens, those pieces are gorgeous!" She lifted a silver creamer from the set I was just about to put in the display.

"They *are* beautiful," I agreed. One of the occupational hazards of running a shop like Trifles and Folly is that sometimes you want to take the pretty shiny things home with you. I had already snagged a small tea set for myself – paid for at wholesale price – and I had my eye on a coffee set as well.

"Glad I don't have to polish them before every holiday dinner," Maggie said, as she went over to tuck her purse into a cubby in the office. She emerged a few moments later with her own hot cup of tea in a big yellow mug that had a giant smiley-face. That was Maggie's style – retro wonderful.

"Well, back in the day, folks had servants to do the polishing," I replied, maneuvering the other set into place. Here at Trifles and Folly, we didn't have the luxury of servants, so Teag, Maggie, and I all knew first-hand the joys of silver polishing.

"Oh, my mom had a set when I was a kid," Maggie added, grabbing the duster and making the rounds of the shelves. Her broomstick skirt twirled and swished with every movement. "I felt like a princess every time she used it for her card club when the meeting was at our house. She'd make those little tea sandwiches without the crust, and some special cookies, and my sisters and I got the leftovers." Maggie chuckled.

"When I went to that antiques conference in London, I did high tea at a swanky hotel, the Grosvenor House," I said, adding a bouquet of silk flowers in a silver vase and some pretty vintage napkins to the window scene. "I felt like I'd been dropped into the lap of luxury."

I straightened and dusted off my hands, then went outside and gave my tableau a critical eye. Arranging the front window was one of my favorite things to do at the store, and I was well aware of the fact that by setting up a new window display, I was deliberately not thinking about soul-eating spirit-bullies and strange disappearances. Until we had a better idea of what was going on, there wasn't anything Teag and I could do, and I was resolved to not let it bother me.

Maggie was just finishing the dusting. Trifles and Folly has been in the same location since the store's founding. We're right on King Street, in the heart of downtown. The store has a big front window in a black, wooden facade with the name of the store painted in big, gold letters overhead. On either side of the shop are two huge, ornate antique lamp sconces that look opulent and very 1800s.

Inside, Trifles and Folly looks well-worn. Our treasures are displayed on open wooden shelves, in glass jewelry cases, and in a big, glass cabinet. Paintings and old portraits hang on the walls, along with an antique rug or two. Behind the scenes, my Uncle Evan brought the store into the modern world with computers, but out front Teag and I try to keep an old-world feel to the place.

"Isn't today your day for the nursing home visits?" Maggie asked as she took the trays of jewelry out of the safe I had opened and began to arrange them inside the glass cases.

"Yep. And I swear, Baxter knew it from the moment he woke up this morning."

"That dog is a real go-getter," Maggie laughed. "Mark my words, he'll be on the cover of a magazine someday, and then there'll be no living with him!"

Baxter may look like a six-pound cotton ball, but he's got sixty pounds of attitude. He's all waggles and licks for people he likes, but I've seen him tear off like a maniac after someone he thinks is dangerous, and his high-pitched bark could make your ears bleed.

"He absolutely loves being a therapy dog," I said, and stopped by the register to take a drink of my coffee while it was still warm. "And you should see the residents' faces when we bring in animals. Even the ones who don't talk light up and pay attention to the dogs and cats."

Baxter and I had only recently begun working with Animals for Alzheimer's, a local program where therapy animals came into nursing homes to help residents reconnect with the world. The program had been so popular that patients outside the Alzheimer's ward began insisting we bring the animals over for them to see as well. I always got teary-eyed when I saw the sheer joy on the residents' faces as they petted Baxter's silky white hair. He seemed to like it too, and he was always on his best behavior.

"I think Bax honestly enjoyed the therapy dog training," I said, finishing my coffee in a gulp. "Maltese have always been companion dogs. I wish I could bring him to the store with me. But since I can't, this helps make up for him being at home."

Dogs are sensitive to the supernatural. I had tried to bring Baxter with me on several occasions, but every time, he'd find the Spookies and decide it was his job to guard them and growl at them all day. Then again, it was the same reason I hadn't been able to stay in the apartment on the second floor that we now used as storage. Even though I wasn't handling the objects, just being close to them all the time had really set my nerves on edge.

Maggie chuckled. "You really ought to try him out in doggie daycare again."

I sighed. "I know. But the last time, he kept stealing the big dogs' toys."

"Baxter likes to be king of the hill," Maggie replied. "But he's such a love. And he really does like the other dogs."

"Yeah, I'll have to try again. I just feel like the parent of 'that' child, the one that throws blocks or something." I flipped the sign on the door to 'open'.

The morning was slow. Customers didn't wander in until closer to lunch. I could tell from the way Teag acted that he was mulling over what Anthony had said about the stairway disappearances. Just then, my phone buzzed in my pocket and I pulled it out to see a call from Father Anne.

"Cassidy! Wonderful to hear from you!" Father Anne is definitely not what most people think of when they picture an Episcopalian priest. She's in her thirties with a short, edgy haircut and a custom-designed tattoo of the three patron saints of the St. Expeditus Society on her arm. I've seen her wear a clerical collar with a black t-shirt, and she's partial to Doc Martens boots when we've got some ghost-whuppin' to do.

"Great to hear from you, too," I replied. "You got my message?"

"Suitably cryptic," she replied with a chuckle. "You gonna tell me what's really going on?"

"In a nutshell: Civil War ghost trapped in a piece of Victorian death jewelry being menaced by bullies from beyond. I wanted to see if you can help send him on his way."

"Ooh, that sounds like fun," Father Anne replied. "I've been tied up in vestry meetings, and I'm so ready for a change that I'd say yes if you wanted to do a girl's night out two-for-one root canal."

Yikes. "Hopefully, it won't be exciting at all. Can I count you in?"

Father Anne laughed. "Absolutely. Tomorrow? Then we can go set this poor ghost on his way."

"It's on the calendar." We got the place and time straightened out, and I put the phone back in my pocket. "Looks like we can at least get Thaddeus squared away," I said. "And with luck, whatever came after him, won't come after us." Yeah, right.

Chapter Four

BY NOON, I had already decided to do some digging for information on my own. "Why don't I pick up lunch and bring it back?" I suggested. "How about take-out from Forbidden City?" We all liked Chinese food, and offering to go grab lunches from our favorite place guaranteed no one would mind me stepping out for a while, even if we did get busy.

Teag raised an eyebrow. "You're going to go see Mrs. Teller, aren't you?"

I grinned. "Busted. Of course. Who else might know something useful about restless ghosts?"

"Just don't let the food get cold," he added with a grin. "How about you see Mrs. Teller on the way over, then bring lunch back while it's still hot?"

"Geez," I said with an exaggerated eye roll. "You mess up one time and no one lets you forget it."

Teag and Maggie gave me their orders. "And don't forget the egg roll!" Maggie added with a grin.

"Got it!" I replied, heading for the door. "I won't be long."

I stepped out of Trifles and Folly's air conditioning

into the warmth of fall in Charleston. The sun was bright, the sky was clear and my mood began to lift despite the sweat that was beading my forehead.

The thought of restless ghosts and ghost-eating monsters had kept me awake last night. I'm still fairly new to running Trifles and Folly and working with the Alliance, so I haven't gotten used to knowing about all kinds of terrifying supernatural threats that normal people are lucky enough not to believe even exist. I accept the responsibility that comes with my magic and inheriting the shop, but sometimes, I really think that fate picked the wrong person when it aimed its fickle finger at me.

The attack on Sorren's Boston operation also bothered me. I knew he had other stores like Trifles and Folly all over the world, helping the Alliance keep people safe from dangerous magic and haunted objects. Beyond warning us to be careful, Sorren had said little. I could tell he was worried and guessed that he blamed himself for what had happened. Teag and I had done some digging online. According to the news, a gas leak had caused an explosion in the old store. The building was badly damaged, and the store's two managers were in the hospital.

The Boston fire department hadn't considered it suspicious. On the other hand, the fire department didn't know about the Alliance, or the many supernatural enemies Sorren had made over the centuries. I tried to convince myself that bad things can happen without involving hell spawn. Gas leaks happen. But we didn't believe the report, and I didn't think Sorren did, either.

The weather coaxed me out of my worries. Fall is one of my favorite times of year in Charleston. The days, while still quite warm, were cooler than at the peak of the summer. While the gardens weren't quite the riot of blooms they had been a few months earlier, pansies and mums had traded places with petunias and verbena. Evenings were pleasant, warm enough to be on the porch.

Valerie passed in one of Andrews Carriage Rides' horse-drawn wagons. She had a full load of tourists, and she waved as she went by. I waved back. Lucky for us, tourism here doesn't end with Labor Day. There are plenty of people who want to enjoy Charleston's beautiful scenery and wonderful food when the climate is a little more moderate. I was beginning to hope that Maggie's prediction of this being a good day might actually be on target.

I swung by Honeysuckle Café to pick up a pumpkin-spice latte on my way. Rick and Trina both greeted me with a hearty hello.

"Anything new?" I asked as I waited for Rick to fix the latte.

"You just missed a bunch of cops," Rick replied, as the steam whistled into the cup of milk. "Some guy disappeared over at the Old Jail, or so his girlfriend says. Claims he headed down a flight of stairs and never got to the bottom." He handed me the latte. "Weird, huh?"

I felt a chill run down my spine. Unlike the other disappearances Anthony had told us about, this one hadn't been hushed up. "Yeah, kinda creepy," I replied. "Figures it would happen at the Jail, doesn't it?"

"I steer clear of that place," Rick said. "Big with tourists. Never could understand why. That place, it's bad news."

I nodded in agreement, but I suspected my reasons were a little more concrete than Rick's for avoiding a place that was a top tourist attraction. Charleston's Old

Jail had been the site of harsh judgment and human misery for a very long time, and deaths and suffering can permanently stain a building's energy. That's why so many locations that hit the 'most haunted' list tend to be abandoned hospitals, madhouses, battlefields, and penitentiaries. I'd also heard some of Sorren's stories about the Old Jail, back when it still held prisoners and used its gallows. Just thinking about it made me touch the agate necklace around my throat for protection.

"Let me know if they find the guy," I said as I paid for the coffee and headed out the door. But deep inside, I know that no matter how hard the police searched, they weren't going to turn up anything.

My bad mood flooded back. *You're supposed to be protecting people in Charleston against the supernatural. Some job you're doing. This is all your fault.* I felt so overwhelmed with guilt that tears started and I blinked them back furiously.

Wait a minute! I argued with myself. *No one said I was supposed to know everything. We're working on it. We'll figure it out.* I managed to push the wave of guilt back so that it didn't stop me in my tracks, but the awful feeling lingered that I had let everyone down. *Maybe I need to go to the doctor. This isn't like me.* I'm a pretty realistic person, and I've seen stuff working for the Alliance that would send most cops running for the hills, but I work at staying relatively optimistic. I have my faults, but pessimism isn't usually one of them. *Probably working too much. Overtired. I'll take a nice, ghost-free vacation once we deal with the disappearances.*

As I left the café, I spotted the guy who had chatted me up about the latte sitting at a table by the window in a restaurant across the street. He saw me, waved and smiled, but made no move to call me over or get up. That was fine with me. I gave a half-hearted smile and wave, then walked briskly down the block.

What bothered me about him? I still wasn't sure. Maybe it was the too good-looking part. Something about Coffee Guy seemed fake, although I couldn't put my finger on why. My gut feeling told me that Coffee Guy wasn't what he seemed.

And then there was the zap of magic when I brushed his hand. That didn't happen often. Usually, only when I touched someone else who had magic. So that meant the stranger had some kind of power of his own, and from the look in his eyes when I got jolted, he didn't like that my magic outed him. Curiouser and curiouser. And now there he was again, popping up along my path. *Coincidence? Maybe. Stalker? Too soon to tell. Friend or foe? Not sure, but until proven otherwise, he goes in the 'foe' category.*

I cut through the Charleston City Market on my way to Forbidden City. The Market is the heart of historic Charleston, and buildings take up the main section of Market Square.

Charlestonians have been buying produce, spices, and baked goods at the City Market for hundreds of years. Nowadays, shoppers can find fresh fruits and vegetables, locally-made jams, jellies, and pastries, artisan-roasted coffee, Charleston-raised tea, and a wide selection of craft and art objects sold by the people who made them.

Walking through the City Market is my favorite way to lift my mood and clear my head. I shop there a lot, so many of the merchants know me. The smell of the coffee, pastries, and spices makes me happy, and I love to see so many beautiful things on display. I waved hello to friends as I walked by, although I didn't stop to chat like I usually do.

Near the main outside doors, sat an elderly woman and her daughter weaving beautiful, complex baskets from sweetgrass. Completed baskets lay on a large cloth on the ground near their feet. Charleston sweetgrass baskets are a local art, passed down from generation to generation, and they sell for hundreds – sometimes thousands – of dollars. Baskets like these are in the Smithsonian and other museums, a handcraft with roots tracing back to the Gullah people and the region's freed and escaped slaves. And in my opinion, no one made more beautiful sweetgrass baskets than Mrs. Teller and her daughter, Niella.

"I wondered when you'd come 'round here, Cassidy," Mrs. Teller said, not looking up from the complicated pattern her agile fingers wove. She had been making baskets all her life, and she made it look easy, but the strips of grass were tough and sharp, and novices ended up with bloody fingers.

"It was a nice day for a walk," I said.

Niella nodded. "Sure is. Lots of tourists walking around. Let's hope they feel like taking a little bit of Charleston home with them."

"You heard about the men that disappeared?" Mrs. Teller asked, looking up at me with piercing, black eyes. Close-cropped gray hair was a stark contrast against her dark skin. I wasn't sure how old she was. But I knew her skill as a powerful root worker was a force to be reckoned with.

"Yes. But I'm not sure what to make of it," I replied.

Mrs. Teller cocked her head at me as if she were

certain that I wasn't telling the whole truth. "Oh child. I think you do. Bad things are happening all over town. People been coming to me for days for charms and blessings. I give them what I can," she said with a sigh, "but what's comin' is bigger than I can put a root on, you know what I mean?"

"Mama –" Niella said, a warning for her mother not to speak of things too loudly, or maybe not to call the evil by name. Niella and Mrs. Teller know about my magic, and about Sorren. Teag takes Weaving lessons from Mrs. Teller to learn more about controlling his power, something he's also pretty new at doing. Still, Niella's right to be careful. Most people in Charleston don't believe in magic, or in the kinds of supernatural threats we do our best to protect them from. We try to keep it that way.

"What do you know about the disappearances?" I asked quietly.

Mrs. Teller went back to her weaving. "I know I've been called out to bless a dozen staircases in the last two days," she replied. "And I know there are people who are mighty scared."

"We're trying to figure out what's going on," I said.

Mrs. Teller nodded sagely. "Figured as much. Blessing those stairs might help keep the dark away, and I can send some folks away with *gris-gris* bags and jack balls, but this nonsense is gonna have to stop."

"Mama's trying to tell you that if you need us, we'll be there to help," Niella said, with a sidelong glance at her mother.

Mrs. Teller glared back. "I don't need you to speak my mind for me," she snapped. "But she's right. I knew one of those men who disappeared."

"You did? Was there anything unusual about him?"

Mrs. Teller shook her head. "He didn't have 'abilities', if that's what you mean. Nobody special. Just a friend. He'd been in a bit of trouble, but he was just getting everything straightened out and now –" She sighed. "If Niella and I can help, you just give a holler, you hear?"

I smiled. "I do hear you," I replied. "And if we need your 'abilities', I'll let you know."

Mrs. Teller nodded. "Good enough," she said, fingers still flying on her weaving. "Now best you get on. And you tell Teag for me that it's been too long since he's been 'round for a lesson."

"I'll be sure to let him know," I said, giving a wave and heading off. The day was bright, but my thoughts were dark as I headed to Forbidden City to pick up lunch.

Teag was busy with a customer when I got back to the store. I carried the bags of food into the break room, and Maggie followed me. "A strange man came looking for someone named Sorren," she said, a worried expression on her face. "I told him I didn't know anyone by that name. Teag was in the back, so he wasn't there to shoo this fellow away. Looked like a rough sort."

"Did he say anything else?" I asked, glancing at the door.

"He said he'd be back. That there was a reckoning to be had. And that this Sorren fellow had better be prepared to finish what he started."

"What did he look like?" I asked. I didn't know whether to take what the stranger said as a pronouncement of fact, or a threat. And until I knew whose side he was on, I intended to be very careful.

"Big guy, about as tall as my husband, maybe six foot six or so," Maggie replied. "He had a leather jacket on, funny with the heat to wear that, don't you think? And it was pretty beat up, plenty of scratches. He looked like he'd been in a few fights himself. Had a scar that wound around one eye and down his cheek, and he was missing part of an ear. His hands were all scarred up, too, and he had several big silver rings that looked like they'd hurt if you got hit with them."

Yikes. "Thanks, Maggie," I said. "We'll keep an eye out for him. If you see him again, make sure you yell for Teag or me." I managed a smile. "Now why don't you sit down and eat, and I'll cover for you and Teag."

I went up front to handle any customers while Teag and Maggie ate, then came back to finish my lunch after they were done. *Mrs. Teller was right. There's a storm brewing. And unless we figure something out, fast, we're going to be smack dab in the middle of it.*

THAT EVENING, BAXTER and I had some old people to cheer up. I closed up shop at Trifles and Folly, warning Teag and Maggie to be extra careful. The stranger who had been looking for Sorren didn't come back, and I didn't spot Coffee Guy anywhere near the store. I headed home to get changed and have a bite to eat. My little blue Mini Cooper slid into a parking space near the curb and I checked all around me before I got out, but there were no lurking strangers or ominous shadows.

I live in what Charlestonians call a 'single house'. The house is turned with the narrow side toward the street, so the main door in from the sidewalk enters the broad front porch, not the house itself. What most folks call a 'front' door actually looks into a small walled private garden. The house had been in my family for a long time, and when I moved back to Charleston after I inherited the store, my parents were just about to move to Charlotte, so they sold me the house at a discount, and we all got a good deal.

Baxter was already yipping and squeaking when I turned the key in the lock. I paid close attention as I touched the doorknob, using my magic to sense whether anyone else had tried to open the door since I left, but it was undisturbed. Thanks to Sorren, our friend Lucinda the Voudon mambo had placed wards around my house and Teag's place, to keep bad things at bay. I wondered whether Sorren's people in Boston had similar wards, and whether our protections would be any good against whatever was eating ghosts. I shivered, even though the night was warm.

"All right, all right," I said as Baxter jumped and danced on his hind legs. I set down my purse and scooped Bax into my arms, getting my nose licked in the process. My senses were on high alert as I took Baxter around the block, even though it was still light outside and plenty of people were making their way home from work or out for a stroll. Once we got home, Baxter ate his kibble enthusiastically while I heated up a slice of leftover pizza and changed into jeans and a t-shirt.

"Ready, Bax?" I asked, and he pirouetted on his hind legs. "Save the fancy tricks for the old ladies," I said, tussling his fur as I put his harness on him. "They like it when you show off."

Baxter enjoys riding in the car, and I have a carrier seat for him so he can ride safely and still see out the window. We didn't have far to go. Palmetto Meadows is one of Charleston's most popular 'active living' communities, and from the outside, it looked like a big turn-of-the-century seaside inn. On the inside, some parts of the building looked like a fancy condominium with apartments for the most mobile residents, other sections resembled a hotel with single rooms and a big dining hall, and a third wing had more of a hospital feel.

We headed up the walkway, past the manicured front lawn. Halfway along the sidewalk, I felt a familiar frisson of energy. Baxter sensed it too and looked up at me. *Who raised wards around an old folks' home?* I wondered. Because that was exactly what the energy felt like. Very, very odd.

Everyone waved to Baxter and me as we checked in at the front desk and headed for the third wing. When Baxter and I had gone through therapy dog classes, he had done exceptionally well with Alzheimer's patients, so that was where we spent most of our time.

"Hey Cassidy! Hey Baxter!" Judy, one of the nurses, greeted us and buzzed us into the secure unit. "What's up? This isn't your usual night." She winked at me. "Although I had a feeling you might be coming." I'd talked enough with Judy to know she had some magic of her own, including a bit of foresight.

I nodded. "Had an appointment last night, so I checked with the front office to make sure we could come tonight," I replied. "We'll be back on schedule next week."

Judy laughed. "I don't think anyone here would mind if Baxter came every day," she said. "He's a popular fellow."

I swear Baxter strutted as we headed for the social room, as if he knew he was a furry little celebrity. The residents' faces lit up when they saw him. Mrs. Macallen always saved pretzels to give Baxter, and she would slip them to him when she thought no one was looking. Mrs. Talheimer kept a bit of apple or a bite of broccoli for him. Baxter made out like a bandit, and I figured that as long as he didn't get sick, it was fine for him to get a few treats since he made everyone so happy.

"It's good to see you, Baxter." Mrs. Peterson's voice was shaky, but she had no trouble leaning over in her wheelchair to scratch Baxter behind the ears as he put his paws on her legs. He weighs all of six pounds, so he's not going to knock anyone over, and he seems to know which of the residents like to have him jump up and which don't.

We made a slow circle around the social room, making sure everyone who wanted to pet Baxter got their turn. Big glass windows opened onto a nice patio and walled garden, a safe place for the residents to get fresh air without any danger of wandering away. Baxter and I had gotten about halfway around the room when I spotted a couple sitting on a bench out on the patio. I recognized the woman from our weekly visits. Mrs. Butler was ninety-four, and she was talking animatedly with her visitor. I stopped dead in my tracks. Sorren was sitting in the moonlight next to her, holding her hand.

For a moment, I couldn't stop staring. Sorren was chatting with Mrs. Butler and looking more natural, more relaxed, more *alive*, than I had ever seen him. It was obvious from their body language that they knew each other very well. The tilt of the woman's head, the way she reached out a veined hand to touch his arm, they weren't the touch of a grandmother to a great-grandson. They were the flirtation of a young woman to her beau.

Suddenly, I felt as if I were intruding, and I turned my back to the window, in part so I would stop staring, and also because I didn't want Sorren to sense me there. He was so happy, an adjective I can't usually use to describe him. Six hundred years, give or take a few decades, weighs on a person. He's seen a lot of history first-hand, much of it tragic, and lost a lot of people who were friends and colleagues. Sorren is an old soul in the body of a grad student. And while I knew it was none of my business, I couldn't help but be filled with questions.

"He's such a good boy." Mr. Thompson's thready voice cut through my reverie. He was a stoop-shouldered man in a striped bathrobe, t-shirt, and sweatpants, with corduroy slippers trodden down on the heels. A wooden cane was tucked into the seat of the wheelchair next to him. Long ago, he must have been built like a linebacker. Now, he was all bones and angles, with skin that no longer fit. Behind his thumbprint-marred reading glasses, Mr. Thompson's blue eyes were watery, but I saw a flash of something in them as he petted Baxter, something that might have been a memory of the person he used to be.

"What? Oh. Baxter. Yes, he is a very good boy," I replied, pulling out of my thoughts. "He's taken quite a shine to you."

Mr. Thompson laughed, something between a chuckle and a wheeze. "Well, I always had dogs, you know," he said. "All my life, until I came here. I wouldn't let them bring me here, you know, until Tilly died. Little rat terrier, lived to be fifteen years old. *Fifteen*. You know, in dog years, that's one hundred and five." He smiled. "Believe it or not, that made her even older than I am!"

I reached down to ruffle Baxter's ears, and Mr. Thompson's hand brushed mine. I felt a sharp tingle like an electric shock, and drew back. From the surprise in his expression, he felt it too. "Sorry. Static electricity," I murmured. But I didn't believe it. I know magic when I feel it, and that was what had zapped me, I was certain of it.

From the pocket of his bathrobe, Mr. Thompson withdrew a battered old pocket watch. The crystal was cracked, and the hands were in the wrong position for the hour. I bet it hadn't worked in a long time. "I need to go to my room," he said abruptly. "Got to get ready." He peered at me over his reading glasses, and his tone had a sudden urgency. "Watch yourself," he warned, dropping his voice. "They're coming. The Judge comes at midnight." He gave me a look that seemed to stare through me to my bones, as if I ought to understand what he couldn't quite put into words. For a moment, I saw stark terror that seemed utterly rational, not a product of dementia.

"Be careful," Mr. Thompson admonished once more. Then he nodded to Baxter and me and wheeled himself across the room and toward the hallway with more vigor than I would have imagined he possessed.

When I looked up, the old woman in the walled garden was alone. Sorren was gone.

Baxter and I finished our rounds, and stopped by the nurses' station. Bax had fans there, too, and the ladies usually brought a doggy biscuit or two for him. At this rate, he'd be a porker unless we started taking longer walks. "Mr. Thompson certainly likes dogs," I said, ruffling Baxter's fur as he chewed his treat.

Judy chuckled. "Did he tell you about Tilly?" I nodded. "She passed away thirty years ago, according to his son." She shook her head. "That's the thing with Alzheimer's. These folks get unstuck in time."

Unstuck in time. I thought again about the woman in the courtyard. "You know, Mrs. Butler didn't get a chance to see Baxter tonight," I said. "She was out in the courtyard with a visitor."

"Oh, that must have been her great-grandson, Mr. Sorrensson," Judy said. "It's not your usual evening to visit, so you wouldn't have met him. Comes every week, or nearly so. Pays all her bills, sees she's taken care of right. Nice young man. Must run some kind of software company to be so young and have that kind of money."

"I just didn't want her to be disappointed for missing Baxter."

"That's the thing about our residents. She won't know which day it is, and she won't remember, so she won't be disappointed." Judy chuckled. "Although it's funny. We remind her in the morning when her great-grandson is coming to visit, and she insists on getting her hair done and having one of the nurses help her do her makeup and put on her best dress." She sighed. "Then again, most of our folks here are lucky to get any personal visitors, so I guess it is a big occasion when someone takes the time to come around."

"They looked like they were having a good conversation," I said, remembering what I had glimpsed. Baxter was working on his second biscuit, so he was in no hurry.

"I'm glad Mr. Sorrensson comes to see her," Judy says. "Most of the time, Mrs. Butler won't say much, and she's very confused. But when he stops in, she lights up and chatters." Judy shook her head. "Amazing what effect a visitor can have, isn't it?"

Especially when that visitor was immortal. *Does glamouring her make her remember the old times?* I wondered. I could imagine the headline now: *Vampires cure Alzheimer's*.

"Does Mr. Thompson like detective movies?" I asked. "I can bring some, if he does."

Judy looked at me, puzzled. "Not that I know of, why?"

I laughed it off. "Oh, just something he said. It was very *Maltese Falcon*."

She nodded. "Is he talking about the Judge again?" A cold chill went up my spine. "He does that. All day long, he's a pretty happy fellow. But he gets edgy come nightfall – some of our folks here do – and that's when the superstitions take hold."

"Superstitions?"

Judy gave a shrug that said oddities came with the territory. "Old people with dementia can be a lot like kids, you know? They have their routines, their rituals, their lucky rabbit's foot. Calms them down, helps them sleep. Some of our folks want a cup of hot milk before bedtime. Others want to have someone read aloud, or they want to tell us a story, like they're the ones putting a child to bed. If we possibly can, we do what they want. We try to make them happy."

"What about Mr. Thompson?"

"Oh, as quirks go, it's nothing much. But housekeeping has fits. He keeps taking the salt shakers from the dining room, and we find them dumped out on the big circular rug under his bed." She gave me a 'what-can-you-do' smile. "Go figure."

I was rattled by what I learned about Mr. Thompson. That sweet old man was looking more and more like an addled adept, and I was ready to bet a cup of coffee and a dozen doughnuts that his salt circle meant that on some level, he knew something bad was heading our way.

We said good-bye and headed out to the car. Baxter's low growl alerted me to trouble. I stopped at the place on the sidewalk just inside where I had felt the shimmer of invisible wards. The flat expanse of parking lot sprawled ahead of me, lit by tall security lights that bathed the lot in an amber glow. Except for one spot that was pitch black. Not just dark, lightless. There's a difference. Shadows around the edges of a well-lit place aren't opaque; usually, they're a deep gray. This spot was completely dark, the kind of dark that isn't natural.

Baxter growled again, baring his teeth this time. Baxter has the heart of a warrior, and small as he is, he's got the same dog-sharp senses of hearing and smell as any German Shepherd. I'd only heard him make this sound when he and I had been under attack from nasty spirits.

Something evil was out there. It was between me and my car, and I was going to bet that it was faster than I was.

I let the old dog collar slip down under my sleeve to jangle around my wrist, and my ghost dog, Bo, appeared beside me. I wasn't worried about any of the residents seeing a ghost. Sadly, anything they claimed to see would likely be discounted. That's one of the dangers with dementia: the monsters you see might be real, and no one will believe you.

Bo's growl was a deep rumble. I reached into my tote bag and pulled out my wooden spoon athame. I decided that keeping the spoon and the dog collar with me was a pretty good idea. But I still hadn't moved. I had no idea whether or not the cold light force I could muster up with my athame would have any effect on the shadow. And I had no guarantee that making the shadow back off long enough to get into my car would keep it from attacking me once I was on the road.

Decisions, decisions. I could call Sorren or Teag, but that might just put them in danger without knowing what we were up against. Then again, I couldn't stay here all night.

Just as I was reaching for my cell phone, I saw something silver streak across the lot, like a metallic baseball. The metal ball landed right in front of the dark shadow, and when it hit the asphalt, it burst into a blindingly bright light and a sharp pulse of high-pitched sound that made Baxter howl and gave me an instant headache.

The dark shadow writhed and winked out of existence.

"You can come out now, Cassidy. It's gone." The voice was familiar, but not someone I expected to see here, or now. Chuck Pettis walked out of the darkness on the edge of the parking lot.

I'd met Chuck a while ago when we were fending off some other bad nasties. He's in his mid-fifties, with short-cropped, graying hair and a too-thin frame. Don't let the gray hair fool you. He's smart and tough, and he's fought enough supernatural bad guys to be sneaky, too.

"How did you know there was going to be something in the parking lot?" I asked, giving the area one more sweep before I crossed the wardings.

"Because I come here a couple of nights a week to play cards with an old neighbor of mine, and I got bad vibes the last few times I came over," Chuck replied. "So I started carrying." He didn't necessarily mean a gun, although knowing Chuck, he probably had at least one of those close at hand. I knew he meant weapons like I had just seen, things that could take out a supernatural foe. He'd had plenty of practice, back when he worked with a Black Ops military unit – the kind of Black Ops that bagged paranormal threats, not run-of-the-mill terrorists.

"Why would something like that want into an Alzheimer's unit?" I asked. Chuck fell in step next to me, giving Baxter and me an escort to my blue Mini Cooper.

"If I had to guess, it's because of Old Man Thompson," Chuck replied. He was just a few feet away from me, close enough that I could hear him ticking. Chuck has an obsession about timepieces, and he never goes out without wearing a vest covered with working wristwatches. Teag and I call him 'Clockman'.

"Why him?" I asked. Chuck stood guard as I got into the car.

"Because back in the day, my Ops unit had that sweet old man on a watch list," Chuck replied. "Once upon a time, he was the most powerful sorcerer in Charleston." He bent down and looked through the window. "Trouble's coming. I can feel it. Be careful, Cassidy. Call me if you need me." And with that, Chuck straightened, slapped his hand on the car roof in farewell, and watched until I was out of sight.

Chapter Five

"WHAT DO YOU think it's worth?" The stranger who stood on the other side of the counter tapped his toe, anxious to be anywhere but here. That much was pretty clear. He was as jumpy as a junkie overdue for a fix, and for all I knew, he might be one. I didn't think so, though. I was pretty sure that the problem lay right in front of me, nestled in a silk-lined box.

"That depends," I replied. "Do you know what it is?"

The man shook his head. He was short and muscular like a boxer, with the flinty-eyed squint of a hustler. "No idea. Weirds me out, that's why I want to get rid of it. Had no idea what we were getting when I bought that batch of unclaimed luggage, and now I'm beginning to think it was a bad idea."

I straightened up, careful not to touch the box. In it lay a skull covered with intricate beadwork in the *veve* of Baron Samedi, one of the Voudon Loas associated with death. I had seen my friends Lucinda and Caliel at work, and, once or twice, I'd glimpsed the Baron's spirit. Whether my would-be customer knew it or not, the Loas were not to be trifled with.

"It's a Voudon relic – you probably call it Voodoo," I said. "There's more of a market for something like this down in New Orleans, which means fewer potential buyers here, and that affects the price." I named a dollar figure that I thought was low. The stranger jumped at it.

"It's yours," he said. "Cash?"

I nodded. "We can do that. But I will need to record your name, address, and a phone number, just in case there are questions."

Hustler Dude looked nervous. "Why would there be questions?"

I shrugged. "It could happen. Especially if that turns out to be a real skull."

Hustler Dude blanched as if he hadn't considered that possibility. "Oh man," he said, taking a step back. "Do you think it could be?"

I shrugged again, although my spidey sense was tingling. I was betting that it was not only real, but it had been used by someone with power and know-how in some honest-to-gods Voudon rituals. And as with the hair necklace, I had the definite impression that a trapped ghost was connected to the beaded skull, and that ghost was scared witless. Hustler Dude didn't need to know any of that. "No idea. But it didn't come from Joe's Juju Junk Shoppe."

"Where's that?" he asked, wide-eyed.

I resisted the urge to face-palm or roll my eyes. "I made it up," I said. Across the store, I could see Teag hiding a snicker. "What I meant was, I think it's the real deal. Do you want to sell it?" I repeated my price.

I could see him torn between the greedy hope that he could find someone to pay more, and the strong desire to get rid of the damned thing. And I was willing to bet that there had been some hard-to-explain circumstance that spooked Hustler Dude. "Okay," he said. "Sold."

The grinning, bejewelled skull lay nestled in the satin lining of its box, and the similarity to a coffin had not escaped me. I sent Hustler Dude over to Teag to get his money, but I already knew who I needed to talk to about the relic – Lucinda.

As soon as Hustler Dude was out of the door, Teag looked at me and shook his head. "Sometimes, Cassidy, I really wonder about your sanity."

"Touch that silk and tell me that isn't an active relic," I challenged.

"I didn't question whether or not it was active," he said archly. "I questioned your sanity."

"Yeah, well. That's been in short supply lately." The dark shadow at the nursing home spooked me more than I wanted to let on, especially after the attack in Boston. I was grateful for Chuck's help, and I had a suspicion that Lucinda might have been the one to set the wards. Now with the skull, I had an excuse to go see her right away.

"Think you two can handle the shop for a while?" I asked. "I want to see what Lucinda makes of this." I pulled out a plastic bag. "And can you please put the skull in this? I don't want to touch it." Teag gave me an exaggerated, long-suffering look as he put on a pair of gloves, picked up the skull and put it in the sack and then slid it into my tote bag.

"Go. Get rid of it before it causes problems." He shook his head. "That thing is so tacky, it looks like it belongs in a New Orleans airport gift shop."

"Maybe that's where it came from," I replied. Teag's glare told me that he doubted that was the case.

"Let me know if you hear from Sorren," I said. Odds were slim, since it was daylight. Apparently, a vampire of Sorren's age could be awake during daylight hours as long as he stayed somewhere dark, but that wakefulness came at a cost, and so Sorren usually slept. If he contacted us now, I would know we were really in trouble.

"Yeah. Yeah. Get out of here," Teag said, making a shooing motion with his hands. "We'll be fine."

I hoped he was right as I gathered up my tote bag. But as I headed out into the bright Charleston sunshine, I had a pretty good idea of where to find Lucinda, and I hoped she would know what I had just gotten myself into.

It didn't take long to walk down to the Lowcountry Museum of Charleston. I make a yearly donation to the museum, so I got an email every time they have a new exhibit. That meant I knew all about the 'Voodoo and You' special exhibition curated by Dr. Lucinda Walker, College of Charleston Humanities Department. And I was counting on Lucinda to be at the museum, overseeing the installation of her exhibition, so I could figure out just how much trouble we were in.

As much as I love history, I avoid museums. My magic reads the history of objects that have been imprinted with strong emotion or magic. That pretty much covers the pieces in museums. It's caused me some unpleasant experiences, especially the time I took a wrong turn and ended up in a 'Plagues and Pestilence' exhibition.

"Hello, Cassidy! To what do we owe the pleasure of your visit?" Alistair McKinnon, Curator of the Lowcountry Museum, spotted me and came my way with a wave.

"Hi, Alistair," I replied. "Have you seen Lucinda Walker?"

He raised an eyebrow. "You skip attending an exhibition on imported porcelain dishes and show up early for a Voodoo exhibition?" Alistair knows about my magic, but not about Sorren and the Alliance. Or perhaps I should say he doesn't 'remember' that he knows Sorren. He's been a big help when I'm trying to research something in Charleston's past, and I've helped him out when the museum happens across dangerously haunted acquisitions.

"I promise not to touch anything," I said with a wry grin. "You won't have to scrape me off the floor again."

Alistair chuckled. "No harm done, but that encounter couldn't have been pleasant for you." No kidding. In addition to the horrific vision I experienced, there was the utter humiliation of having caused a scene in public.

"Goes with the territory," I replied. Boy, and how. We chatted for a few more minutes, then Alistair directed me into the wing of the second floor where traveling exhibitions were showcased, and I promised to meet up with him for lunch soon. Alistair went back to his office, and I climbed the steps to the next floor, trying to get a feel for the museum's vibes without knocking myself into a full-blown vision.

What's on display at the museum varies by the season and the themed exhibits. Like any similar institution, the Lowcountry Museum has a much larger collection than is ever out for viewing at any given time. I'd been down to the storage area in the basement once, and that was enough for me. It didn't go well.

Sometimes when I had tried to attend an event at the museum, I knew from the sensation I got just walking through the door that it would be better to turn around and go home. Today, the museum felt pretty neutral. I picked up on something strong and negative – but not dangerous – down on the first floor, and another hotspot at the far end of the second floor, and resolved not to go anywhere near those areas. On one hand, I was pleased to have gained enough ability with my magic to sense some problems without having to be right on top of a troubling item. On the other hand, anything I could sense from that far away was probably a doozie.

Ahead and on the right, I saw where the new temporary exhibition was being installed. 'Voodoo and You: Loas and the Lowcountry' the banner read. From inside the room, I could hear boxes and glass cases being moved around, and the sound of Lucinda's voice. I poked my head into the room. Lucinda is a tall, slim woman with skin the color of espresso and shoulder-length hair done up into a mane of hundreds of tightly-woven braids. Today she was dressed in a business-casual tan pantsuit with a richly-hued animal print silk scarf and tastefully-sized gold hoop earrings. I could see that Lucinda was in her element, directing the museum staff on where to place the artifacts.

"Dr. Walker!" I called from the doorway, and Lucinda turned to greet me with a big smile.

"Cassidy! Come on in. How do you like the chaos? This'll be a fine exhibition when we're through," she added, "but it's wild as a hurricane in here right now!"

Lucinda's energy is infectious. Whether she's giving an academic presentation or helping Sorren, Teag, and me fight off rampaging supernatural threats, Lucinda has a zest for living that is as powerful as a gale-force wind. "What brings you over here in the middle of the day?"

I grimaced. "We made an acquisition at the store that seems like it's more in line with your area of expertise,"

I replied. Lucinda sobered, understanding the potential for problems.

"Okay," she said, drawing out the word. She strode over to where her helpers were arranging some display cabinets to give them instructions, then walked back toward me.

"They'll be busy with that for a little while," she said, and motioned for me to follow her into a small side room that was currently empty except for a large table. "Now, what did you bring me?"

I put my tote bag onto the table and gingerly drew out the bag that held the beaded skull. Lucinda frowned, then walked counter-clockwise around the table, raising a quick, defensive warding around us. When she came back, she reached into the bag and lifted out the silk-lined box with cautious reverence. "Oh, oh, oh. What do we have here?" she said when she opened the box and stared down at the skull.

I told her about the unclaimed baggage sale and the man who had brought the skull in to Trifles and Folly. She listened as she carefully took the skull out of its box and turned it around in her hands to see the full decoration.

"You didn't touch it, did you?" Lucinda's dark eyes met my gaze.

"Are you kidding?"

"Good. Because it's got some bad juju stuck to it, like stink on a skunk." She lifted a small round magnifying lens that was on a chain around her neck and bent to get a better look at the beading.

"That's the Baron's *veve*, isn't it?" I asked.

Lucinda nodded. "Yes it is. But not everyone who calls on the Baron has good intentions. Some of them don't know what they're messing with. They think he's some kind of supernatural frat boy, and they find out fast he does not like to be disrespected." Baron Samedi, one of the Voudon Ghedes, helps to conduct souls to the afterlife. Tradition holds that the Baron's spirit likes cigars, rum, and dirty jokes. I always figured that his excesses had something to do with standing on the threshold between life and death, since the Baron is also the Loa of resurrection. If someone summoned the Baron without the proper deference, the situation could go bad very quickly.

Lucinda is a scary-powerful mambo, and together, she and Sorren and Teag and I have done battle with some supernatural creatures that definitely deserve the name 'monster'. So I wasn't surprised when she bowed her head, chanting softly as she cradled the beaded skull in her hands. I saw a shiver run through her body and knew that one of the Loas had heard her call.

"Not one of mine." The voice came from Lucinda's mouth, but it was a man's voice, smooth in a riverboat gambler sort of way. Something about the way Lucinda stood, the expression on her face, told me that she was not herself, and I held my breath. Being face-to-face with Baron Samedi had not been on my to-do list for the day.

"I will take this soul," the voice said. "It has been wronged. Best you watch the shadows. Bad things are a'comin'." I could feel magic in the air, thick as roux. It felt different, and not just because of how strong it was. Magic done by mortals, even powerful mortals, feels one way. Magic done by supernatural creatures is different, in a way that words aren't designed to express. The power that flickered in the air for an instant was not of this world. I shivered, and tried not to attract its notice.

With that, another tremor ran through Lucinda's form, and when she raised her head, she was merely human once again.

"What was so special about that skull that it got a visit from… him?" I hesitated to say the Baron's name. When dealing with insanely powerful otherworldly spirits, it's best not to invoke them unless you're prepared for a visit.

Lucinda placed the beaded skull back in its box. "Someone had misused their magic to make this abomination," she replied, and from the anger in her tone, I knew she wasn't critiquing the artwork. "It's a human skull, and a human soul was trapped inside. The beadwork was done in a way that secured the spells. And if that wasn't bad enough, something was draining that captive soul."

"That's the second time in as many days we've run into something feeding on souls."

Lucinda fixed me with a worried look. "Child, that is not good. Does Sorren know?"

I nodded. "And he isn't sure what's behind it. Which worries me."

"Is it all right with you if I keep the skull?"

"Yeah. We bought it for you, to keep it from going astray," I replied.

"Good call. Even now, I wouldn't want someone with bad intent to get a hold of it," she said, and glanced over her shoulder toward where the workers sounded as if they were finishing their assignment. "Look, I need to get the exhibition up and running, so I've got to go, but if you need me, call me," she added. And with that, Lucinda headed back to the other room, picking up where she had left off.

I headed back to Trifles and Folly, glad to be free of the beaded skull. My tote felt lighter without it, and I felt a psychic burden lift as well. Then I remembered that we still had not freed Tad's spirit from the hair necklace, and I hoped that Father Anne would be able to send him on his way. Although Tad seemed resigned to being adrift in the world of the living, I had no desire to see him become a casualty in what was looking like it would be a nasty fight. And while Tad was already dead, I had seen enough to know that there were fates much worse than lack of a pulse.

I was deep in thought, and stumbled over the Ghost Bike. The mangled bike had been painted white as a memorial to a fallen cyclist and chained to a light post close to the scene of the accident. The newspaper had dubbed such memorials 'Ghost Bikes', and they had been popping up all over town in the last several months. They reminded me of the roadside shrines grieving families put up by the side of the highway to commemorate the site of a fatal wreck. And just like with the homemade shrines, I felt a jolt of otherworldly energy as my leg brushed the bike's painted tire.

"Yikes!" I yelped, less because I had nearly fallen than because I was unprepared for the vision that came with the physical contact.

A bump beneath the front wheel, the blare of a car horn, too close and coming up too fast. Frantically struggling to regain control, then falling and impact... and then, something evil in the darkness, hungry and relentless. In the next instant, I saw the darkness overwhelm the cyclist's hapless ghost, consuming his flickering light until nothing remained.

"Hey lady, are you all right?" A man in the coveralls of a local lawn service peered at me with concern. I realized I was steadying myself against the lamp post, trying to catch my breath.

"I'm fine," I said sheepishly. "I stumbled and almost fell – must have caught my toe on something."

"You might want to sit down. You're pale as a ghost."

Not quite, I thought. "Thanks. I just needed to catch my breath." The man went on his way, and I took another moment to steady myself. I glanced back at the Ghost Bike, and saw a small laminated card with the name of the dead cyclist and the date of the fatal accident, along with a short description of what had happened. And while I knew that the bikes that were painted and used for the memorials weren't always the actual bikes from the accidents, I wondered if the people creating the shrines realized that at least in some cases, spirits that did not move on attached themselves to the bikes.

When I got back to the shop, I found a sign on the door that said 'Back in fifteen minutes' and the door itself was locked. Worried, I unlocked the door and stepped inside, locking it behind me.

"Teag? Maggie? What's up?"

"We're back here, Cassidy," Teag replied, and I could hear the worry in his voice. I headed for the back, and found Maggie seated in one of the chairs at our break room table looking much the worse for wear. She had a bloody gash on one side of her head, and blood marked her face and shirt. Maggie held a plastic bag full of ice against a rapidly-growing bruise that looked likely to become a goose egg. She also had her left leg propped up on a chair with a swelling ankle and more ice.

"What happened?" I asked.

"I went next door to take the newest batch of fountain pens over to Craig Murdoch," she said. Teag and I knew Craig fairly well. He was the owner of Deckle Edge Bookstore, my favorite place in Charleston to look for out-of-print copies of special books. We gave Craig first dibs when we got in boxes of old books from an auction or estate sale, and he had a standing order for whatever beautiful vintage Parker and Waterman pens we acquired.

"Did you fall?" I couldn't imagine what could have happened to Maggie between here and the next store. "Please don't tell me that someone mugged you!"

Maggie started to shake her head, then swallowed hard at the discomfort and reconsidered. "Craig loved the pens. But everything was higgledy-piggeldy in the shop because he was bringing out his seasonal books. He and that new assistant of his were also putting up some fall decorations, and I volunteered to help bring a load of garlands and plastic pumpkins up from the basement."

Uh-oh. "And then what?" I asked, although I was afraid I could guess.

"Craig sent Jonathan ahead and asked him to show me where the pumpkins were stored. You know what their basement stairs look like – the shop is very similar to Trifles and Folly. Ten steps down at the most, into a big room with a few support beams."

Except that ours also had a locked safe-room where a vampire could spend the day in an emergency. That was a feature only Teag, Sorren, and I knew about.

"Jonathan was three steps ahead of me," Maggie continued. "The lights were on. Craig was right behind me. But then – and you're not going to believe me –

Jonathan started to disappear. He kept on walking, but I couldn't see his legs. And before I could say anything, he was gone completely. And I was falling – it felt as if someone had pushed me square in the chest."

"Just gone?"

Maggie met my gaze. "I know it sounds crazy. Craig saw – or rather, didn't see – the same thing. One instant, Jonathan was in front of me, and the next he was gone."

"You searched the cellar?" I couldn't imagine how someone could have pulled off such a prank, but it was worth exhausting the mundane explanations before assuming a supernatural attack.

"Craig did. I was nearly knocked cold," Maggie replied. "Whatever took Jonathan pushed me so hard I fell. There are a few moments I don't completely remember, except that something really scary and strange was happening and I didn't dare fall forward."

"I'm glad you didn't," I said with heartfelt relief. I had met Craig's new assistant, and Maggie's account made my skin prickle with fear for his safety. "What then?"

"Craig helped me back up the steps, and then he went back to the basement. I wouldn't have gone back down those steps for a million dollars, but this time, Craig went down just fine. Said the basement was just how it always was. But there was no trace of Jonathan."

"Wow," I replied, exchanging a meaningful glance with Teag.

"Craig tried calling and texting Jonathan's cell phone, but he didn't get an answer." She paused. "Funny thing – we thought we heard the phone ring a couple of times, then nothing. But there was no one around, and we didn't find the phone."

"What's Craig going to do?" Teag asked.

"He was beside himself. You can imagine. But how can you call the police about it? Can you imagine what they'd say if he tried to tell them someone disappeared on his way down the basement stairs?"

A few weeks ago, her skepticism would have been dead on. Now, I was betting Craig would be surprised to find out the police might take his report more seriously than he imagined.

"Was there any reason Jonathan might have had to run away?" I asked. Not all employees are trustworthy. I wondered if Craig might find the till short a few hundred – or thousand – dollars, or some items missing from stock.

"Jonathan hadn't mentioned any personal problems, and Craig said there weren't any issues with his performance, but he told me he would double check to make sure nothing was gone." Maggie sighed. "I really liked Jonathan. He was good with customers, and he was just getting his life back together."

A warning prickled down my spine. "What do you mean?"

Maggie's face grew pink. "I shouldn't have said anything. But I guess it will come out, if Jonathan really is missing. He hadn't been in Charleston long. Moved here from Upstate, near Columbia, after he'd had a bit of trouble. Got accused of vehicular manslaughter because a drunk wandered out in front of his car, but he was acquitted. Poor fellow."

"Why don't you take the rest of the afternoon off?" I suggested. "Teag can drive you home."

Teag looked at me. "Are you sure you'll be all right while I'm gone?"

I nodded. "Sure thing. But I promise you – I won't go near the basement."

Teag hesitated. "Check your voice mail. Sorren left a message that he had to go out of town unexpectedly – said we were to be careful."

I wondered if that meant more problems in Boston. With the wards Lucinda had set around the shop, I was pretty sure we would be safe in the store, but I wasn't about to push my luck. I was worried about Maggie. I was worried about Sorren. And right now, there wasn't a damn thing I could do about any of it. So I poured myself a cup of coffee and flipped the sign in the window, figuring that chatting with some tourists with money to spend might take my mind off things.

It wasn't long before a big man in a leather jacket and more scars than a cage fighter walked into Trifles and Folly. He just didn't seem to be the type to be shopping for antiques.

"I'm looking for Sorren," the man said abruptly. His voice was rough, and I bet he liked his whiskey straight.

"Excuse me?"

This guy was easily over six feet tall, with broad shoulders and muscles that didn't come from the gym. He had scars on his hands from fights and a scar on his neck that looked like someone had tried and failed to slit his throat. A particularly ugly scar marred his face.

"I believed the hippie when she said she didn't know, but I don't believe you," he replied. His voice wasn't implying a threat – so far – but his light blue eyes had a killer's coldness to them.

"You need to leave." If the best defense is a good offense, I intended to start offending. Charleston prides itself on manners, but it also has a reputation for starting fights (big ones, like the Civil War) and finishing what gets started. And right now, he'd gotten my back up.

"Tell Sorren that Daniel's in town. Tell him I'm watching the Watcher."

"Daniel who?"

His smile revealed a mouthful of teeth that looked like they had been rearranged a few times, and not by a dentist. "Daniel Hunter. He'll remember me." His smile froze into something more like a grimace. "Sorry about your uncle. He should have gotten out of the game sooner. I hope you know what you're doing, taking over for him."

That did it. "Get out," I said. "Get the hell out, and stay out." I felt a tingle as the dog collar on my left wrist jangled, and then a low, angry growl filled the air. The big man looked surprised, then annoyed when he saw the glowing shape of a large dog with its spectral teeth bared, but he backed up mighty quickly when that ghost-dog took a step toward him, head lowered, ready to leap.

"I said, get the hell out of my shop."

Daniel Hunter gave me a baleful look, glanced back at the angry dog, and headed for the door. "Just tell Sorren. He'd better watch out. And you'd best watch out, too." With that, he walked out of the door, but I noticed that he never turned his back on Bo's ghost. When the door slammed shut, the ghost dog looked over at me, wagged his tail, and vanished.

I sat down on the stool behind the counter and took a long, shaky breath. Sure, I had faced down some pretty nasty supernatural threats with Sorren and Teag. I trained in martial arts with Teag, and while he was good enough to have won several championships in both Filipino and Brazilian styles of combat, I could hold my own. That didn't mean I relished a fight, not with a bad nasty from beyond, or from a big bruiser who seemed to think he could push me around.

I replayed what Daniel had said. His delivery had been flat, and his manner was menacing. But had he meant it as a threat, or a warning? And was 'Hunter' really his last name, or his job? No way to tell. I pulled out my phone and texted Sorren, giving him a quick recap. He definitely needed to bring me up to speed on this whole situation – and Teag, too. I don't mind putting my life on the line to keep Charleston, and the world, safe. But I do need to understand what I'm fighting. So the next time I saw Sorren, he was going to get a tart piece of my mind.

Chapter Six

FOR ONCE, I was happy that we didn't get any more customers that afternoon at Trifles and Folly. By the time Teag got back from settling Maggie safely at her house, it was time to close up.

"I'm meeting Anthony for dinner," Teag said with a smile. "He's working on that big case, so we have to grab time together when we can. Otherwise, we don't cross paths even though we're in the same house." I wished them well. My last boyfriend had kept a similarly crazy schedule as an emergency room doctor, and coupled with my odd hours with the Alliance, which I couldn't talk about, things didn't go smoothly. Maybe someday.

"Anyhow," Teag continued, "Text me if Sorren shows up. I want to know more about what's going on. And in the meantime, I'm going to see what I can find on the Darke Web." Teag's Weaver magic works for more than textiles. He's fantastic at weaving data strands together; his magic can hack into just about any system and never leave a trace. He's also good at navigating the darker corners of the internet. Criminals and low-lifes haunt the Dark Web, pages regular people aren't meant to find. But the supernatural community has the Darke Web, spelled and protected with ensorcelled encryption to keep out prying eyes. Teag takes it as a challenge to break through, and I've never known him to fail.

"Go for it," I replied. "Just be careful." On the mundane internet, you might get a computer virus. On the Darke Web, a daemon really is demonic, and it might just follow you home.

Teag grinned, and gave me a mock bow. "As you wish," he said. Then he headed out, and I locked the door behind him.

When I got home, Baxter danced in circles, and when I picked him up to snuggle him, he licked my nose several times, then wiggled to be put down. I knew what he wanted. It was time for a walk.

Charleston is a walking city. It's the kind of place where neighbors nod to each other when they pass or say "nice evening" even if they don't actually know each other. No matter what the season, taking a walk along the old brick garden walls, the beautiful wrought-iron gates and the big old live oak trees brightens my mood.

Often, I'll take Baxter down to White Point Gardens on the Battery if I want to get a nice harbor breeze. But tonight, that didn't sound like such a good idea. White Point Gardens is a beautiful spot now, with a great view of Charleston Harbor. But long ago, that park was where the gallows stood to hang pirates, making it a place where many a soul has been trapped. I had no desire to go looking for more restless ghosts.

Baxter didn't care where we went as long as he got to enjoy the fresh air. We were heading home when I heard the clip-clop of hooves and looked up to see Valerie leading one of her carriage tours. I waved, expecting her to wave back and keep moving. To my surprise, she paused beside me.

"Hi, Cassidy," she said, and all the passengers, thinking this was part of the tour, echoed her greeting. I grinned and waved again.

"I'm trying out a new route tomorrow evening, and I was hoping you'd go through it with me. You know so much about Charleston's history, I'd love to have you help me break it in."

Valerie is pretty much an expert on Charleston's history herself, so I knew that part was total bunk. But I did remember what Drea had told me, about Valerie being worried about something she saw on a ghost tour, and I figured she really wanted me to ride supernatural shotgun. And despite the potential danger, it sounded like fun.

"Count me in," I said. "Just give me a call and let me know when."

After Valerie and her carriage had moved on, Baxter and I continued on our way. Up ahead, I saw another Ghost Bike with its memorial photo and plaque. I was going to go around it when I noticed a man on the other side of the street who seemed to be more interested in Bax and me than he was in just taking a walk on a nice night. I stayed on the sidewalk, and picked up my pace.

If someone gets hurt on the ghost hunts, it's because you weren't on top of things, I found myself thinking. I had been in a pretty good mood before, but now my thoughts circled the drain. *You're supposed to be protecting Charleston, and you're failing. People are going to die, and it's all going to be your fault.* I felt such a sudden flood of guilt that I teared up and stumbled. I put my hand out to catch myself, and steadied myself on the white painted frame of the Ghost Bike.

That's when Baxter lowered his head and began to growl. All of a sudden, the Ghost Bike shuddered so violently that it felt like it was going to break away from the fasteners that held it to the light pole. The wheels spun like they were caught in a hurricane, and the chain securing the bike whipped back and forth. Baxter was barking his 'stranger danger' bark, doing his best impersonation of a Doberman. All of that seemed far away. Steadying myself against the Ghost Bike plunged me into darkness.

A beautiful day, sun on my shoulders, wind against my face. Then a car swerved too close. By the time I heard the crunch of gravel, it was too late. I felt myself flying through the air, landing on the road, almost unconscious but still aware enough to see the grill of the car and the undercarriage coming right for me... pain... then darkness.

I wasn't alone in the dark. There was something in the shadows, some new dark terror. It stalked me, after so long alone. Predator. Before I knew it, the Darkness had its claws or its teeth into me, ripping, tearing. Tried to pull free, tried to push it away...

My left hand found the agate spindle whorl in my jeans pocket and closed around it. That old Norse magic anchor sent a jolt of power through me. I felt magic radiate from me, separating me from the spirit of the dead bicyclist. In another heartbeat, within wherever-it-was the ghost and its stalker existed, my magic formed a wall of flame in between the bike's ghost rider and the supernatural predator. The predator drew back with an ear-splitting screech and the ghostly rider retreated, injured but still himself.

The blast of magic broke me out of the vision of the Ghost Bike spirit, just in time to see that the man who had been watching us was now striding closer. Something about the way he moved made me think he wasn't coming to help.

I didn't want to summon Bo's ghost. I didn't want whatever had taken a bite out of the Ghost Rider – and Tad – to get its spectral claws into Bo. And I didn't know who or what the guy headed my way was, but he looked like trouble. My wooden athame slid down from my sleeve into my hand. Steadying myself against the light pole, I focused my power into my athame, and let loose with an icy white blast of power that caught the stranger in the chest and knocked him back across the street, against a fence and flat on his ass.

Baxter was still barking his head off, and I hoped that someone would get annoyed and come out to see what was going on. I didn't plan to wait around. While my would-be stalker was climbing to his feet, I grabbed Baxter and ran.

The street was strangely deserted. Normally, I'd have passed a half dozen people by this time. I wondered if there was something about the weird guy which drove the other pedestrians away. I wondered, but I didn't slow down. I was afraid to look over my shoulder to see if he was getting closer. It wasn't until Baxter and I burst through the wardings inside my piazza doorway that I stopped running. I collapsed onto the porch, heaving for breath, while Baxter tried to cheer me up by licking my nose.

For a little while, Bax and I sat on the piazza – that's what Charlestonians call the side porches on single houses. My phone buzzed and I saw the text from Sorren, *Be there as soon as it's dark*. Then Baxter and I went inside and I got dinner for both of us. Shortly after sunset, Baxter began to bark when a knock came at the door.

"Glad you could make it," I said, opening the door. I'd given Sorren permission to enter long ago. He swore permission was a technicality that could be gotten around, and as a former jewel thief, I figured he would know.

"Such a good dog," Sorren said in a calm, smooth voice as he knelt down and scratched behind Baxter's ears. And just like that, Baxter stopped barking and sat down with a goofy expression. I sighed. Sorren's ability to glamour the pup came in handy, but it always seemed like cheating.

"If you hadn't already figured it out, something dangerous is brewing," Sorren said.

Thank you, Captain Obvious. I didn't say anything, but I did give him a look. "Come on in."

Sorren had fed recently, which brought normal color to his skin. He doesn't talk about how he feeds, and I don't ask, but he did tell me once that he no longer needed or wanted to kill in order to eat, and that he was blood-sworn never to cause harm to me or my family. I assumed that included Baxter, and Teag by extension.

"You left me a rather cryptic message," he said, settling onto the couch.

"A guy came looking for you. He was a real jerk."

Sorren looked as if he would have let out a long sigh, if he had needed to breathe. "Daniel."

"Yeah. Where do you dig these folks up?" I asked.

Sorren chuckled. "In this case, no digging was required. Daniel is indeed a Hunter. And if there is a Hunter in Charleston, then we're right to be concerned. They don't waste their time on rumors."

"What's a Watcher?" I asked.

Sorren frowned. "Where did you hear that term?"

"Daniel Hunter said to tell you there was a Watcher in town."

Sorren's frown deepened, and he looked lost in thought. "That is worrisome," he said, in a tone that made me guess his comment was a gross understatement. "Watchers are supernatural creatures that judge – and eat – beings they believe to be flawed. That's bad enough, but someone – a powerful wizard – has to bring the Watchers through from the Other Side."

"But wait," I said, doing my best imitation of a television commercial voice-over, "there's more." I filled him in on what had happened to Maggie over at Craig's store. He listened intently as I told him about the missing assistant, and about what I had learned from Mrs. Teller and Lucinda. I finished up by telling him about the incident with the Ghost Bike and the weird guy.

"Did you feel odd before the incident happened?" Sorren asked.

"Odd how?"

Sorren shrugged. "Did you have any unnatural emotions that seemed to just come out of nowhere?"

I thought of the strange, crippling guilt that I had felt right before I stumbled into the Ghost Bike, and how it had happened before with Coffee Guy. "Yeah," I replied. "If suddenly feeling like the worst person in the world and a total failure counts."

Sorren nodded. "It counts. That's exactly what I meant. And I'm afraid it means Daniel Hunter is correct. Watchers feed on guilt and judgment. When they're around, people feel overwhelmed by negative emotions, and it's worse if you're paranormally sensitive."

"What about the wraiths? The thing that attacked Tad's ghost and the shadow that took a bite out of the ghost rider?"

"If Daniel is right about Watchers, if what you saw was really a Watcher, then the wraiths were Reapers, supernatural creatures that prey on ghosts. I'm inclined to believe that's the case, but there are other monsters that can do similar things, and if we want to fight them, we have to be sure." He leaned back and closed his eyes. "Have you heard it said that animals can sense a storm coming?"

"Baxter certainly can," I said. "Bo could, too."

"All of this activity, it's a storm warning. The ghosts feel it. Anyone with a hint – or more than a hint – of power feels it. And the only problem is, we don't know yet whether it's a hurricane, a tornado or a volcanic eruption, so to speak. Until we have a better idea of what's coming for us, we don't know who's behind it or how to fight it." He paused. "But I'm certain of one thing. Someone with a lot of magic power is gunning for me. This isn't random. It's personal."

I sat with that sobering observation for a moment without saying anything. "Other than Daniel Hunter showing up and the attack in Boston, what makes you think someone's after you?"

Sorren looked more worried than I had ever seen him. "The Boston store was the second Alliance outpost I opened when America was still a colony. I thought it was protected. Obviously, I was wrong." I could hear recrimination heavy in his voice. "Like with Trifles and Folly, that store has been in my partner's family for centuries. Your counterpart is still in the hospital. Teag's counterpart died from his injuries earlier today."

I swallowed hard, and saw in Sorren's face how much the failure to protect his people had hurt him.

"There have been scattered attacks at other locations. Antwerp. Vancouver. Some at the offices that hide other parts of the Alliance's business. And something very personal." He met my gaze. Looking into a vampire's eyes will glamour most people, but I'm immune. "Three houses that I once owned have all burned down, just in the last month. Too many to be a coincidence."

When I had given Sorren my recap, I left out meeting up with old Mr. Thompson at the nursing home, and the part about Chuck Pettis using some of his military-issue anti-supernatural equipment. That would require admitting that I had been at Palmetto Meadows when Sorren was there, and I didn't want to let on, at least, not yet. I hadn't meant to pry when I saw him with Mrs. Butler. And although I was dying of curiosity, if their relationship was as I suspected, it was decidedly none of my business. The nursing home was warded, so at least we didn't have to worry about that.

"I know that look, Cassidy," Sorren said. "Is there something else?"

I sighed and shook my head. "Just a lot going on. Even things like the Ghost Bikes that don't usually pull me into a vision seem turbo-charged with energy. Now maybe I know why."

"And those kinds of things are going to keep happening until we stop the storm," Sorren replied.

"Do you know who's behind this?"

He shook his head. "I've existed for almost six hundred years, Cassidy, and five hundred of those I've worked with the Alliance. I've made a lot of enemies in that time. Believe me, the Alliance is on the case, using their resources to figure out who and why. Right now we've got theories, but nothing solid. Too many possibilities, not enough facts to narrow things down. I've got calls in, but longer-lived people in the supernatural community have a very different sense of time. Urgency isn't really part of their world."

He paused. "I can only stay here in Charleston briefly. I need to help in Boston, and there are things I have to track down that might make a difference. I'm going to look into what – who – could bring a Watcher here and why, and see if there's another explanation. But I wanted to warn you and Teag. There may be more attacks – especially if I'm right about this being a vendetta." He got up to leave. "Until I get back, keep your eyes open and watch out for anything unusual. I'll return as soon as I can."

It wasn't until he was gone that I realized I hadn't mentioned the guy in the café.

You know, most people – female and male – would feel pretty lucky to have a guy that looks like that trying to start a conversation, I told myself. *You look at him and decide he's some kind of scary stalker. Maybe you're just paranoid.*

Maybe I was, but for good cause. And even though I still couldn't figure out why, Coffee Guy made the hair on the back of my neck stand up. Personally, I don't find that attractive in a man. I wasn't giving him the benefit of the doubt, not when so many weird things were going on.

My phone buzzed again, and I startled. It was Kell.

"What's up?" I asked.

"I told you about some of the weird stuff we've been seeing," Kell said. "Then I thought, maybe I should show you. So... our group is going out to take a look at a haunted house that's giving the real estate agent fits.

We've been there before and it was active, but apparently not like this. Do you and Teag want to come?"

"When?"

Kell chuckled. "Wow. I should use the haunted house bit to get company more often," he joked. "Day after tomorrow? We generally go after it's dark enough that the ghosts will move but the neighbors won't call the cops."

"Works for me. And I'll let Teag know right away."

"Great." He paused. "I really appreciate you taking this seriously. I think there's something going on, but it's not anything I can explain."

"Let's see what we can find out," I said, trying to sound more chipper than I felt. I was afraid there was more at work than jumpy ghosts. "See you then."

"DON'T FORGET, I have an appointment at noon with Father Anne," I said to Teag the next morning. Today was the day she and I were going to free poor Tad's spirit from the hair wreath necklace.

He nodded. "I'll stay with Maggie, in case we do get those busloads of Canadian tourists you were expecting," he added with a grin.

Maggie had to keep her swollen ankle elevated, and she looked like she had been in a car wreck, but she insisted on coming in at least for part of the day, and had a doctor's note to back her up. We were busier than usual, so the morning passed quickly. I sold a vintage tea set to a woman who was delighted to find one just like her grandmother's. A brass lantern, an old seafarer's telescope, and more vintage jewelry found new homes, which made for a profitable morning.

"Are you sure you're okay meeting Father Anne without extra back-up?" Teag asked in a low voice when he followed me into the break room. I knew what he meant. Father Anne and I were both pretty good at watching out for ourselves, but with someone attacking Sorren's interests, it never hurt to take extra precautions.

"That's one reason I suggested she and I meet at noon," I replied. "It's a good time for working light magic, but not as good for dark magic." Everyone thinks of midnight as the witching hour. They forget that noon has also traditionally been believed to be just as friendly for supernatural workings. Both midnight and noon are 'liminal times', when the veil between our realm and the next thins and magic becomes easier to work. Most creatures and people who are up to no good don't like doing their dirty deeds in daylight. Add to that the fact that a number of supernatural creatures are allergic to direct sunlight, and I figured we would be safe.

"Be careful," Teag admonished.

"Don't worry," I replied, grabbing my purse. But I knew he would.

I revved up my little blue Mini Cooper and headed out for Magnolia Cemetery. Magnolia Cemetery is a jewel. It was built on land that had once been a rice plantation, back in the 1850s. Old graves, lots of famous dead people, and beautiful huge live oaks make it a top attraction for visiting historians, tourists, and walkers.

The cemetery is just outside of town. I wanted to arrive early so that Father Anne could work her blessing exactly at noon. The supernatural can be surprisingly punctual.

A lot of Charleston's cemeteries are all located on the same stretch of road, on or near Huguenin Avenue. Magnolia Cemetery is the biggest. The whole street is like a suburb of the dead. On the way out of town, I passed a couple more of the Ghost Bikes, forlornly chained to the fences and posts near where tragedies had occurred.

Thinking about the Ghost Bikes got me to notice a white cross marker near the corner of Huguenin Avenue and Brigade Street. There's an overgrown corner that's thick with brush. Poking out of the high weeds was a homemade cross with a small, sad wreath of faded silk flowers looped over the top. The name on the shrine was too faded to read. Drive along highways in a lot of the South and you'll see similar memorials, placed by family where a loved one met a tragic end. I've always wondered whether the spirits hang around those memorials or whether they move on. Just in case, I always say a blessing for the departed when I pass by.

Father Anne was waiting for me at the front gates of Magnolia Cemetery wearing a black shirt with a clerical collar over jeans and Doc Martens. She grinned and waved when she saw me.

"Hi Cassidy," she said as I pulled up and parked by the side of the cemetery roadway. "Beautiful day for a walk, isn't it?"

We left our cars near the main gate and strolled into the peaceful grounds. I had forgotten how beautiful it was there. In the bright sunlight, with the fall flowers, I could almost push my thoughts away from all the weird things that had happened, and the danger that surrounded Sorren. Almost.

The jewelry box with the hair wreath was in a canvas tote bag. Father Anne and I walked down one of the paths toward the part of the cemetery where we would try to lay Tad's soul to rest. I glanced around to see if there were people nearby.

Crazy as it seems, cemeteries can be busy places. Joggers and walkers like the car-free side roads, and the landscaping is gorgeous. On nice days, you might even see someone on one of the benches, reading a book. Most of the time in Charleston, you'll spot tourists following a map of the graves of famous people, and here in the South, families still come to plant flowers or decorate a relative's plot.

Today was quiet. The wind rustled through the live oaks, making the Spanish moss flutter. Teag had already searched for Tad's grave. We hadn't found one for him, but there were a lot of Civil War dead buried in Magnolia Cemetery, many of whom were unidentified. Father Anne and I walked to the section with soldiers' graves, and then Father Anne stepped off the asphalt path into an empty section of yard. "This all right?"

I nodded, and handed her the canvas bag. Father Anne opened the velvet-flocked case and looked at the memorial wreath for a moment in silence. I guessed she was honoring the grief Tad's fiancée felt when she made and wore the wreath, and the loss that separated the two lovers.

"Ready?" she asked. Father Anne and I had a lengthy discussion the night before on exactly what type of service might be appropriate. Apparently, there's nothing in the *Book of Common Prayer* for releasing a trapped spirit from an old piece of jewelry. Exorcism didn't seem quite right, because Tad's ghost wasn't a demon. On the other hand, there wasn't a body to bury. In the end, Father Anne decided to write her own comments, based rather loosely on the 1662 ritual for burial at sea.

"Ready."

I'm used to seeing Father Anne in the wee hours of the morning when we're covered with blood from kicking demon ass. I've never made it to Saint Hildegard's Church when she was giving the homily. So I had to admit I was a little surprised to see the change come over her bearing as she prepared to say the burial ritual. Father Anne stood a little taller, and her manner was somber and circumspect. There was just something different about her as she moved into her priestly role.

In the distance, I heard church bells begin to chime the noon hour.

Given what we do at Trifles and Folly, I see a lot of rituals. Voodoo, Hoodoo, Wiccan, Native American, Christian, and probably all the others as well – there are certain things that we humans need from our sacred space. Words matter, and so do actions. There's a reason why holy men and women, priests and priestesses, and practitioners, say certain things in a certain way in a certain place at a certain time. Rituals prepare the worker to face the unknown, and they open a thin spot between our reality and somewhere else with a degree of safety. In other words, how you do it matters.

We were on consecrated ground, within the cemetery walls. Father Anne was a consecrated person, ordained in the traditions of her faith. She had an iron cross on a chain around her neck, a protective symbol. And now, as she spoke words that resonated with more than four hundred years of sacred repetition, I could feel power rising around us.

"Almighty God, with whom do live the spirits of them that depart hence in the Lord..."

I don't think it was my imagination that the air trembled above the box Father Anne held in her outstretched hand. As Father Anne said the words of the burial rite, the shimmer grew a little more visible.

Father Anne didn't try to say the whole burial service. That wasn't why we were here. Tad's mortal remains were long gone. We came to lay his spirit to rest, and from the subtle iridescence that floated just above the velvet box, I had the feeling that Tad was finally going to be able to move on.

"...be with us all evermore. Amen." Father Anne finished the prayer, and the faint shimmering glow rippled once and then winked out. She looked at me and held out the box. "Do you want to see if he's really gone?"

I nodded and took a deep breath, then reached out to take the box. I felt a tingle of old power, and dimly, I could sense images from the vision I had seen before. But Tad's lonely ghost had departed. I slipped the box into my pocket. "He's gone."

Father Anne smiled. "Well, that's my good deed for the day, I suppose. Tad was long overdue to make it home." At first, we didn't say much as we headed back to our cars. Then I had a question that I couldn't get out of my mind.

"If you can lay a ghost to rest, how come Charleston has so many restless spirits?"

Father Anne shrugged. "Monkey's fist."

"Come again?"

"Didn't you ever hear the story about how people trap monkeys by putting a banana in a bottle? When the monkey reaches in, his hand fits. But when he makes a fist and grabs the banana, his hand is too big to come out. Unless he lets go of the banana, he's stuck."

Since I hadn't seen any ghosts holding bottled bananas, I was confused.

She chuckled. "Some of the ghosts are stone tape recordings – memories, not really spirits. A few, like Tad, got lost on the way to that bright light at the end of the tunnel. And probably a few more are actually trapped by something nefarious, like a cursed object. But it's my bet that the majority of ghosts are here because there's something they don't want to let go of – like the monkey's banana."

Father Anne shrugged. "They might be holding on to memories, or love, or vengeance, or maybe they just want to be heard. But if that's the case, then they can get free on their own when they're ready, by letting go and walking away."

Put that way, it sounded like the spirits of the dearly departed needed a supernatural shrink more than an exorcist. "Yeah," I replied. "But do the ghosts know that?"

"Probably," she said as we came into view of our cars. "How many times have you struggled with something, only to realize that you actually knew what to do all along?" She gave a sad smile. "They might be dead, but they're only human."

We had parked our cars not far inside the entrance gate, near where the large central pond divides one side of the cemetery from another. Father Anne gave me a hug and said good-bye.

"Call me if you need something," she said. "There's been some strange stuff going on lately. If there's a way I can help, count me in."

I thanked her profusely, then waved as she drove off. That's when I heard something stirring in the pond.

I turned sharply. Nothing moved along the banks of the pond, but I saw a ripple in its dark waters. A sign warned visitors not to feed the alligators. It's the

Coastal South. If there's water, there's gonna be 'gators. I watched for a moment, and could have sworn I saw something long and black move beneath the water, but it was there and gone too quickly to be sure.

I decided that now was a good time to leave, so I got into the car and headed out, watching all around me. There didn't seem to be anything unusual, so I made the turn onto Huguenin Avenue and headed back to town.

The afternoon's work had done a real number on my mood. Even though we had released Tad's spirit, I had been struggling with a feeling of guilt that had been growing on me since I arrived at the cemetery. *People are going to die, and it's all my fault. I'm just not cut out for this. My magic isn't strong enough. If I'd have been any good at this, Jonathan wouldn't have disappeared. All my fault –*

Whoa. This is not like me. I was starting to wonder if I needed to see a therapist. I took a deep breath, and then another. The awful guilt receded, but I knew it was at the edge of my mind, waiting for an opening to rush back in and smother me. *What's wrong with me? Is the pressure finally getting to me?*

Even after I pushed away the terrible guilt, I couldn't shake the feeling that something was wrong. Taking the velvet box with the hair wreath out of my pocket didn't ease my mind. Huguenin is a lonely road. Low brick walls lined the sides of the road, with cemeteries on either side. Although it was broad daylight, I felt a chill go down my back.

I blinked, and saw a man coming down the street toward me. He was walking down the middle of the road, and his posture raised a primal fear in me. Tall and raw-boned, the stranger held his hands away from his sides like a marshal in an Old West movie about to go into a gunfight. He wore jeans and a dark t-shirt with a collared shirt open over top. Something about the way he moved was all wrong. That's when I realized I recognized him. Mr. Super-Handsome himself. Coffee Guy. And I did not think he had shown up here just to chat about a latte.

Unfortunately, there was nowhere to go and no one was in sight, except for Coffee Guy, who seemed to have appeared out of nowhere. He was a little too perfect to be trusted. Maybe a little too perfect to be human.

Options? Not many. If this guy was faster than a human, he could probably be on me before I could get anywhere to call for help. There wasn't a whole lot out here besides the cemeteries. Turning around wouldn't work, since the road that intersected behind me was currently closed for water main repairs. No one had expected a traffic jam at the cemetery, or the need to outrun a renegade underwear model.

I kept the car moving, picking up speed to be a little more threatening. Coffee Guy kept walking right down the center of the street, and there was no mistaking the fact that his attention was completely on me. He looked like trouble, and not in an attractive kind of way.

He stared at me, head down but gaze lifted. It made me think of the way a wolf moves right before the kill. People talk about a smoldering gaze like something sexy, but I was pretty sure that the look in this guy's eyes was more hellfire than attraction.

I gunned the gas a little, revving the engine and moving faster. Still, the stranger kept walking straight for me. I could run him down, but that could raise awkward questions if he turned out to be a real underwear model.

Or, I could speed up and play a game of chicken, betting that he would jump out of my way. I didn't think he looked sane enough to count on that. Option number three was to get to the cross-street before he did, and hope he didn't have any tricks up his sleeve.

Coffee Guy just beat me to the cross-street when a car shot from the side street and hit him at full speed, tossing his body up in the air. For a horrible moment, I saw a young man fly limply from a terrible collision. And then, I saw something even more horrible. Coffee Guy twisted in mid-air like a gymnast from an impact that should have killed him. He landed in a crouch, and the illusion wavered.

My, what big teeth you have.

The magazine cover model was gone, and in his place was one butt-ugly monster. Big and muscular, with arms and legs too long to be human, the monster resembled a bloody skinned carcass. He was big enough that the dent in the car that hit him could have been from a deer or a moose. His head was oversized for the body, with a lantern jaw and sharp teeth, cat-slitted eyes that glowed red, and his infernal gaze was locked right on me.

I couldn't see a driver in the car that had hit the creature, and I was hoping they had the good sense to get the hell out of there. The monster rushed toward me, and I had a choice to make. Ram him again with a car that was much smaller and lighter than the sedan that hadn't put a scratch on him, or stand and fight. I didn't much care for either one, so I came up with Plan C. I decided to do both.

I have another weapon that's like my athame but it shoots fire, an old walking stick that belonged to Sorren's maker, Alard. I'd left it in the car, just in case.

Now, I grabbed the walking stick in my left hand so I could level it out the driver's side window like a lance, bracing my elbow against the window frame. I gripped the steering wheel with my right hand. Then I called up my will, reached out my touch magic to the resonance and memories in the walking stick, and floored the gas.

A stream of fire shot from the walking stick, striking the monster squarely in the chest. My Mini Cooper peeled rubber as I pushed its acceleration to the limits, swerving past the creature to get clear. I was pretty sure I was going to make it, before the monster leaped toward me, landing on the hood of my car. Its body was blackened and charred with strips of burned flesh hanging down in tatters, and its toothy maw pressed up against the windshield, terrifyingly close.

He was too close to blast again with my walking stick, and I sure as hell couldn't drive into town this way. Gravel and loose bits of asphalt crunched under my tires, and I had an idea that was either going to set me free or get me dead.

Before I could second-guess myself, I picked up speed, then pulled the handbrake and hit the gas. The Mini Cooper started to doughnut, spinning in a circle so hard my seat belt seized up. I had a death grip on the steering wheel. The engine whined and the car went into its second loop, careening into the turn. The monster lost its grip and fell off the hood, leaving a trail of claw marks across the metal. Suddenly free of the extra weight, the Mini Cooper skidded off the road and into the brush, knocking over the white roadside shrine.

My ears were ringing from the impact of the sudden stop, and I was pretty sure my neck would be sore tomorrow, but the airbag didn't inflate and I wasn't dead. Stunned, it took me a moment to struggle with my seatbelt. Blood was running down my face from a cut over my left eye. I reached for the walking stick and my spoon-athame, prepared to fight that thing once more.

Shots rang out. I didn't need to see the gun to know it was big, and the noise was deafening. My head was spinning. The car door refused to budge and I had to kick it open. When I crawled out, I stopped cold at what I saw.

Daniel Hunter stood in the middle of the street in a wide-legged shooting stance, plugging the monster with bullet after bullet. The creature staggered, but it did not stop. At this rate, if Daniel didn't have any other tricks up his sleeve, we were both going to die.

Something crunched under my foot. I looked down, and saw part of the broken white memorial cross. The air around me shimmered, and I could make out the faint images of two young men in their late teens. They were watching me as if they could see me, but I couldn't hear what they were trying to say. My hands shook as I raised the walking stick, determined to go down fighting, although I wasn't sure I had enough juice in me to send another blast.

The ghosts moved closer, and I was aware of the broken memorial under my foot. Even through the sole of my shoe, I could sense the deep emotions of the person who had placed the marker. Wrenching grief, dark loneliness, and deep, true love.

Terrified, bleeding and out of good ideas, I plunged my magic down into that broken marker and pulled hard.

An orange jet of fire streamed from the walking stick and hit the monster in its head and shoulders. The creature shrieked and writhed. Filled with the borrowed energy of the shrine, I kept him bathed in flame too bright to watch. Smoke and the smell of burned and rotten meat filled the air. Daniel produced a shotgun from somewhere, and aimed for the thing's knees.

The monster tottered for a few seconds before collapsing onto the roadway. It jerked once, then went still. The monster's head was a charred skull, and most of its upper body had been burned away or shot to pieces. Daniel sauntered up to the body and pumped one more round into it for good measure. As I watched in stunned silence, the corpse vanished.

The ghosts of the two young men turned to me with sad smiles and disappeared as well.

Daniel bent down and picked up something from the asphalt, and I realized he was gathering spent shells. I collapsed against the side of my wrecked car. Now that the crisis was over, I felt drained and light-headed. And I didn't even want to think about the Mini Cooper.

After a few minutes, Daniel loped over. "You all right?" he asked, giving me a once-over from head to toe. He frowned as he saw the blood on my face, and stepped closer. I wasn't in the mood to fight about it as he checked my scalp.

"Looks worse than it is," he said. "You can move everything?" I nodded. "Seeing double?" I shook my head gingerly. "Headache?" My nod was imperceptible. "Neck hurts?" I had the feeling from his questions that Daniel had been in enough fights and wrecks to have some experience with the subject.

In the distance, sirens wailed. "Look, I've got to get out of here," he said. I moved to argue, but he shook his head. "No buts. You've got a reason to be here. I don't. Tell them a deer jumped out of the woods. If they ask you about the charred mark on the road, play dumb. Tell them you didn't see it. Don't worry – that thing isn't coming back soon."

Maybe not, but it's likely to have friends.

Daniel sprinted away and drove off. I dug my cell phone out of my purse and called Teag. He nearly had a conniption when I told him what happened.

"No, don't come out here," I said. "I'll have them take me to St. Francis. But I'll need a ride home from there. And someone's going to have to tow the car." Despite the headache and the sore neck, I was with it enough to bemoan my poor mangled Mini Cooper. I was sure it had given its all for me.

Teag reluctantly agreed to meet me at the hospital. I shifted in my seat, and saw the broken bits of the memorial by my foot. A pang of guilt shot through me for ruining the shrine.

I bent down and picked up the pieces. Someone had gone to a lot of effort to create the memorial for two young men who died before their time. I had already felt the initial images from the memorial when the ghosts appeared, so handling the wooden pieces now didn't send me into a swoon. Still, the longing and loss was clear, as was the love that went into the homemade marker. I resolved to replace it. That's when I looked up and saw the ghosts of the two young men standing by my car, waiting with me until help arrived.

The police sirens were so loud that I thought my head would explode. A police car, an ambulance and a fire truck roared down the road and stopped when they saw my car.

"What happened?" the officer asked, taking in my disheveled condition and the ruined car.

"Deer," I said. "Came out of nowhere. Wrecked my car," I said ruefully.

The rest of the questions were a blur, and since I felt woozy, I mostly concentrated on not passing out. I must have looked pretty bad, because the cop never even tried to ask me about the scorch mark on the pavement.

Two very nice EMTs loaded me onto a gurney. "A precaution," one said as I tried to object.

"My car –" I protested.

One of the EMTs, a big man who looked more like a linebacker than an emergency medical technician shook his head. "Honey," he said, "that car's not going anywhere. They're gonna have to haul it out."

I blinked back tears. Then I got mad. It didn't matter that the monster who wrecked my Mini Cooper had been run over, shot, and incinerated. Someone had sent him, and he, she or it was going to answer to me before this was over.

I don't remember much about the time at the hospital. I was poked and prodded and asked the same questions over and over again. They made me take a Breathalyzer test and took blood to make sure I wasn't on something. Huh. If I'd have told them what really happened, they'd have been sure I was using.

Finally, when they had cleaned me up and run all their tests, they let Teag come in to see me. He paused in the doorway and shook his head. "Oh Cassidy," he said with a little moan. "I am so sorry I didn't go with you."

I dismissed his comment with a gesture. "Someone had to mind the store. Maggie couldn't do it alone," I said. "And it's not as bad as it looks. Scalp wounds bleed a lot. I'm going to have a nasty bruise from the seatbelt, but other than some sore muscles, I'm good to go."

"I found out where they towed the Mini Cooper," he said. "No estimate yet, but I made sure they had your contact information."

"Thanks," I replied. I wanted to tell him what really happened, but there were too many people around. From the look he gave me, I was pretty sure that he had figured out it wasn't as simple as I had made it sound.

Another hour passed before they let me leave. The emergency room doctor gave me a bottle of pain pills and instructions on what to watch out for. The worst part was having to leave in a wheelchair, but Teag didn't mind pushing me out.

"Anthony insisted I take his car so you'd be more comfortable," Teag said. His old Volvo was reliable and safe, but Anthony referred to it as a beater. To be honest, I didn't mind, although the Lexus was more like sitting on a leather couch in a comfortable, mobile living room.

"Tell him thanks for me," I mumbled. Despite the pills, every movement hurt.

I swore a lot as Teag helped me into the car. He waited until we were out of the parking lot before he stole a sideways glance at me. "Okay. Spill."

I gave him a very abbreviated recap of what Father Anne and I did at the cemetery, about the monster's appearance, and Daniel Hunter's unexpected arrival.

"I don't know whether to be annoyed because he was following you, or happy that he saved you," Teag replied.

"Yeah, I'm with you," I agreed. "But on the whole, I'm glad he showed up."

"You didn't see him tailing you?"

"No. I checked on the way out." I paused, because it hurt to talk too much. "Maybe he didn't follow me.

If he's a supernatural hit man with woo-woo powers, maybe he was tracking the monster."

Teag shrugged. "Possible. I wish we knew more about him. I'm still not sure I trust him."

Neither did I. On the other hand, Daniel didn't like monsters, and that was a point in his favor.

It was dark by the time I got home. I was surprised to see that the lights were on in my house. I turned to Teag, but before I could ask, he chuckled.

"When Maggie heard me on the phone with you, she insisted on staying the night with you," Teag said. "She's already taken Baxter out and given him his dinner."

"What a pair we'll make," I said ruefully. "She's on crutches, and I look like I hit the side of a building."

"You got lucky," Teag replied, and all the humor had gone out of his voice. "You might not have been able to fight off the monster on your own if Daniel hadn't shown up. That move with the car was suicidal – and brilliant. But it put you right where another driver didn't get to walk away from a wreck."

I told him about the ghosts of the two young men, and the bits of the broken memorial I had saved to reconstruct. The power the ghosts had shared with me when I made my last stand against the monster played a big role in my survival. I wasn't sure how I could thank them, but I was resolved to try.

"Oh, and I left a message for Sorren." Teag tried to sound off-handed about it, but I glared at him. "Hey," he said defensively. "It's not like it was an average traffic accident and after the attack in Boston and the other stuff you told me about, he'd want to know. Something big, brutal, and supernatural is going out of its way to stalk you. That's not the kind of thing we can keep from Sorren."

I wanted to argue, but I didn't have the energy. So, I glared at him.

He grinned patiently. "Sucks when I'm right."

Baxter greeted me with bounces and yips, and I coveted Sorren's ability to glamour him. Glad as I was to be loved, right now those high-pitched barks felt like ice picks in my brain. I scooped Baxter up and he tried to lick me, then he stopped cold at the strange antiseptic smells and gave me a curious look. I cuddled him close as Maggie bustled up.

"Oh my goodness," she said shaking her head. "You are a hot mess."

"Bed," I managed. After the ride with Teag, I was talked out, and totally exhausted.

"Good heavens, go right ahead," Maggie said, overflowing with maternal concern. I noticed that she was dressed in a pair of classic men's-style linen PJs with a terrycloth robe over the top. "I wasn't sure how you'd feel about taking the stairs, so I made a bed for you on the couch. Teag got your roll-away out of the guest room, and set it up for me in the dining room. That way, if you need anything I can hear you."

I hugged Baxter, looked at Maggie with her crutches and then looked back to Teag and felt overwhelmed at my good fortune. "You are both the absolute best," I said, trying not to tear up because I knew it would make my headache worse.

"Get some sleep," Teag said. "Don't worry about the store tomorrow, either of you. I can handle it myself."

"Thank you both so much," I said, suddenly too weary to stay awake. I noticed that someone had set out my pajamas on the couch, and I headed into the bathroom to change while Teag and Maggie conspired near the front door. On one hand, it tweaked my pride to need help. On the other, I was exhausted and in pain, and couldn't do for myself. I decided to leave off thinking about it until tomorrow. Teag was gone by the time I came out of the bathroom.

"Do you want a cup of hot chocolate? Or tea?" Maggie asked. "Bourbon, maybe?" I remembered that she had children and grandchildren. Mothering seemed to come naturally to her. I managed a wan smile.

"No thanks. Just bed."

"You go ahead and get comfortable," Maggie said, bustling around despite her crutches. "I'll make sure all the doors are locked and turn out the lights."

I was too tired to argue. Every muscle and joint hurt as I eased myself onto the couch and lifted Baxter up to nestle in to the bend of my knees. I was home. I was safe. I was among friends.

Just in case, I made sure that my athame and the walking stick were within reach.

Chapter Seven

I INSISTED ON going in to the store around noon the next day, and Maggie refused to let me come by myself, so we drove together in the rental car Teag had arranged. Fortunately, things were quiet, and both of us could spend the afternoon seated behind the counter. That was good, since we were still recuperating.

"If you feel up to it, Anthony wanted me to invite you over for dinner tomorrow night," Teag said after we closed up at the end of the day and Maggie had gone. "Nothing fancy," he added. "He's planning to pick up take-out, but he said he's found out a couple of things and he wanted to tell you about them. Oh, and I did talk to Sorren. He was really worried about you but he knew Maggie was at your house, so he grilled me on the details and gave me strict orders for both of us to take full precautions. He said we're not to go anywhere without our 'tools'. He's really upset, Cassidy. I've never heard him so distracted. But on the Boston situation, he did say the other guy is going to pull through and that he'd connect with us as soon as he possibly could."

I felt chills down my spine. Sorren was our rock and to think of him being rattled was more than a little disconcerting – but then he'd just lost a friend and seen others he'd known for years get hurt. That's when I remembered my promise to Kell.

"What are you doing tonight?" I asked. "Valerie wants me to go on one of her ghost tours to see the kind of weird stuff that's going on, and then Kell wants us to go through a haunted house where he found some more weird stuff." I sighed. "And I also told Kell that I'd see if I could find some kind of charms to protect the ghosts that are causing his people so much trouble."

"If the disturbances they're seeing are tied into what happened to Tad's ghost and the Ghost Bikers, maybe Kell's ghosts have a reason to be agitated," Teag said. "How about this? I'm overdue to go see Mrs. Teller. I'll ask her for some Hoodoo charms to help Kell's ghosts, and then I'll plan on going with you on the ghost tour and to the haunted house." He managed a grin. "After what happened at the cemetery, I vote for strength in numbers."

"Works for me. I just need to swing by the house to take Baxter for a walk and make sure he gets his dinner." Until we knew what we were fighting, I was not taking Baxter beyond my own little walled garden.

"When are we supposed to meet up with Valerie?" Teag asked.

"Six. At the carriage stable. So we should be done in plenty of time to meet up with Kell and his SPOOK folks at the old house."

"I'll see you there," Teag said. "Sounds like fun."

After the shop closed, I went home and grabbed leftovers for dinner while Baxter ate. After what happened the last time we took a walk, tonight we played in my garden to burn off some of Bax's energy. He loves to chase a Frisbee, and so I threw and he chased until his tongue was hanging out. It was good exercise for both of us. Back in college, I had actually won a few Frisbee golf tournaments. Nice to see that my aim was still good.

We came back inside, and I selected a few items from the drawer where I keep most of my magical protections. Not all supernatural threats react to the same charms or defenses. Just in the time I'd taken over Trifles and Folly, we'd faced enough ghouls, demons, and otherworldly bad guys for me to have amassed a growing collection of tools to help keep them at bay and keep me relatively safe.

I gulped a couple of ibuprofen tablets and made sure to take some of the odd 'tea' Niella had dropped off earlier in the day for me and Maggie. I don't know what Mrs. Teller put into her mixture, but I credited it with making both of us feel much more recovered from our injuries.

I wasn't going to take any chances tonight, walking around with Valerie. From what she had already seen, the ghosts weren't in a good mood, as the incidents with the Ghost Bikers confirmed. Kell's experiences made it even more likely that frightened ghosts could cause trouble. And then there was Daniel Hunter, the wild card. Despite his help at the cemetery, the guy seemed like trouble and I didn't put it past him to shadow me. Not to mention wraiths and homicidal underwear models.

I pulled several defensive amulets out of the drawer and put them in my oversized purse, then picked up the antique walking stick Sorren had given me. It had belonged to his maker, Alard, and my touch magic activated Alard's memories and the residue of his power. And of course, I had my spoon-athame and Bo's collar.

After dinner, I took Baxter out again and sat on the steps while he explored the garden, giving myself a chance to decompress and just enjoy the beautiful day. Which meant that I was doubly annoyed when I spotted a figure near my gate and Baxter began to growl.

Daniel Hunter was lurking outside my house. "I need to talk to you," he said over top of my gate.

I backed away from him, and Baxter started to go ballistic. "You need to see me at my store during business hours," I said. "Thanks for your help yesterday. I did deliver your message to Sorren. But don't stalk me at my house."

"Maybe I was just in the neighborhood." His smirk let me know he was baiting me.

"You want to talk to Sorren, talk to Sorren," I replied, wondering whether the wardings on my house would keep Daniel at bay.

"I can't find him. That's why I need you to help me connect."

"Did it ever occur to you that Sorren will let you find him when he's damn good and ready?" I snapped. "I'm not his appointment-keeper. I already told you: I delivered your message. You want more? Give me a business card. Or a cell phone number. I'll make sure he gets it."

Daniel tried to open my gate. There was a shimmer of light and a spark of electricity as the wards flared, then a deep, warning growl and Bo's ghost stood between the gate and me. Most people aren't afraid of Golden Retrievers. But any time a big dog bares its teeth, raises its hackles and advances with its head down, it's time to pay attention, especially when in life that dog could put ninety pounds of muscle behind a flying leap.

"Just back away slowly," I said, enjoying the startled look on Daniel's face. "My house is warded. I'm tired of playing games. You show up and drop cryptic warnings about Watchers but you're not giving me information I can give to Sorren that will actually do any good. So, give me your phone number if you really want to help out." To my surprise, he rattled off a number, and then repeated it so I could store it in my cell phone.

I glared at him mistrustfully. "All right. Thanks. But I'm still not okay with you just showing up here. I'm going in my house now, and when I come back out, you'd better be gone."

Daniel gave me an appraising look. "I hope you've got more tricks up your sleeve," he said. "Because Watchers are bad news and Reapers are nothing to fool with."

"Are you going to keep lurking around the shadows?" I raised my chin defiantly.

Daniel's glare gave me the impression he wasn't used to being challenged. "Tell Sorren 'Alliance protocols'. He'll know what that means." Then he turned and walked down the street, and disappeared around a corner.

Bo's ghost raised his head, gave me the wide doggy smile I remembered, wagged his tail and vanished. Baxter stopped going absolutely nuts once Daniel walked away. Bo and Baxter seemed to have an understanding. I leaned on the front porch and tried to stop shaking.

"Come on, Bax," I said. "We've got things to do."

I changed clothes and gathered my things to go out. Baxter gave me his best little blinky-eyed guilt-producing stare as I got ready. "I won't be long," I promised. "Then you can sit on the couch with me and we'll watch a movie. With popcorn." Baxter likes popcorn, and I knew from the wag of his tail that he was fine with that plan.

Teag and I met up with Valerie at the downtown barn where the carriage horses stay during the day. Andrews Carriage Rides has its barn near the Charleston City Market. Tourists love to come in and see the horses, and getting to walk through the stables is one of my favorite things, too. Drea's family has always been exceptionally careful about how the horses are treated. She says that she dotes on the horses the way I spoil Baxter.

Valerie was waiting for us. Teag had brought Anthony along, and they both waved. "Hey, it's a rare chance to combine work and a romantic nighttime walk past haunted houses," Teag joked. I noticed he had his messenger bag with him, likely full of some of his magical tools. He also carried his long staff, and I saw him note my walking stick. Anthony was wearing a scarf Teag had woven, and I was willing to bet that it had protective magic bound into its threads and into the weaving itself.

"Please don't think I'm a cheap date," Anthony deadpanned. Valerie and I laughed. Anthony rocked *GQ* style, while Teag was more on the *Rolling Stone* or rumpled grad student side of fashion. Somehow, they looked right together.

"Thanks for coming," Valerie said. I was surprised that she seemed a little nervous. Valerie is a history geek and a big Charleston supporter, so writing and researching the tours she gives is a dream job for her. She's usually incredibly happy when she's leading tours, and getting to work with the horses is the icing on the cake.

Tonight, Valerie seemed subdued. Due to noise restrictions, horse-drawn carriages can't go through certain parts of the city after business hours, so most evening tours are done on foot. That made for an up-close experience that tourists usually enjoyed, but if the ghosts decided to be dangerous, being on foot could cause some real problems.

"Would you rather drive the route in a car?" I asked.

Valerie shook her head. "That's the thing – I'm going to have to do the route on foot all the other times, so if there's something out there that shouldn't be, I need to know now, and not when I've got a group full of tourists."

I knew Valerie wouldn't even consider giving up the ghost tours. They were some of the company's most popular attractions, and people came to Charleston just to go for a spooky tour specifically with her. Besides, there was no way I could explain why taking a break might be a good idea, at least until we fought off some psycho ghost-eating monsters and a supernatural predator who could look like an underwear model. Yeah. I can just imagine that conversation. Not.

Then again, even if we did somehow persuade Valerie not to do her tours, the other companies in town would still be doing theirs, and the risk would be just as real. So we might as well see what we were in for.

The sun had set, and Charleston glowed with gaslights on some of the historic streets as well as twinkle lights set into trees here and there. The area around the Charleston City Market was busy, but as we turned off onto smaller streets, we left the crowds behind. I walked behind Valerie, with Anthony behind me and Teag bringing up the rear.

I took a deep breath. Even in the fall, it seems like Charleston always smells of flowers. We headed down a narrow cobblestone street. Brick garden walls rose on either side of us, overhung with crepe myrtles and live oaks, gated with wrought iron. Somewhere nearby, water bubbled in a fountain. This was the kind of experience that drew thousands of people to Charleston and created fond memories and plenty of tourist spending.

But even as I drank in the historic atmosphere, I could sense that something was not quite right. I glanced back at Teag and he gave me a nod. He was feeling it, too. I noticed him slip a hand into his pocket and pull out a woven ball on a tether of braided twine. It was a jack ball, a Hoodoo protective charm. Teag nonchalantly began to swing it clockwise, and I felt the space around us calm with the talisman's cleansing power.

"We're coming up on the first location where things started to get weird," Valerie said. Up ahead I saw a brick building that dated from the early 1700s. It had been many things over the years, most of them salacious. Brothels, taverns, gambling houses, and speakeasies had all made the two-story brick building their home. Some people might wonder why certain locations seem to attract dark pursuits, but I believe that at least some of the time it has to do with the natural energy of a site, the currents of power that flow through it and around it, the history and blood that have soaked into its foundations.

The building's latest incarnation was as The Wallace Inn. It was a bar that attracted tourists who believed a night on the town wasn't complete if you could remember it the next day. The Wallace Inn always seemed to be in trouble for something: its liquor license, the health inspector, bar fights, and occasionally, a missing person or two. I got a bad feeling just walking past the Inn.

Now, that warning prickle was much stronger. There was no way I wanted my back to the place, not when its energy was juiced up. Teag and I practically walked backwards for half a block just to keep an eye on the Inn as we walked by.

I heard a crack, and saw a small rock bounce away from the wooden fence behind me. More stones flew. Some missed us, while others pelted Teag and Anthony as they ran down the sidewalk away from the Inn. No one else was around.

"Did you see that?" Teag asked.

"Yeah. Classic poltergeist move," I replied. "But I've never heard about The Wallace Inn having any dangerous ghosts."

Teag shook his head. "There's a story about a lovelorn girl who hanged herself in one of the upstairs rooms, and a petty thief who haunts the old stables because he supposedly got knifed there two hundred years ago, but those are standard tavern lore."

I didn't like the rock-throwing ghosts. Not only could one of Valerie's guests get hurt, but when the supernatural begins to take physical action in the mortal world, things are likely to go bad quickly. Doing more than showing up and being seen takes power, and whatever was hanging around The Wallace Inn was both powerful and aggressive.

Valerie already had us into the next block, and thankfully the angry ghosts from the Inn did not follow. "Well, that was new," Anthony said. "I've been by here a million times and never had anything throw rocks at me."

"The next tour spot is the Hallen House," Valerie said. "Let me know what you pick up."

I knew the stories about the Hallen House, how the owner had been a rum smuggler and a pirate, then turned respectable when he gave up his ship and swore off the sea. Rumor said the house was haunted by members of his dead crew who had followed him home, or by ghosts from the islands trapped in cursed trinkets the captain brought back from his voyages. Nowadays, Hallen House was home to an accounting firm. The building was said to have a ghost or two, but so did every old house in Charleston.

I reached up and touched the agate necklace I wore. Agate is a stone of protection, as is the onyx in my bracelet and the black tourmaline in my ring. Just feeling the gemstone under my fingertips calmed me and stilled my jittery magic.

No rocks flew as we strolled past Hallen House. But despite the street lights and the glowing porch lights, the house seemed darker than it should be. Something moved in the shadows. I reached for my athame. Its magic is powerful, and not quite as destructive as the cane.

"You see it?" Teag murmured.

"Yeah," I replied.

"I feel like we're in one of those movies where the monster pops out of the shadows," Anthony muttered.

As we passed in front of Hallen House, the gate to the walled garden suddenly slammed shut. Shutters began to rumble against the fasteners holding them open. Too-dark shadows gathered around the sides of the building.

"Look!" Anthony said, eyes wide, pointing toward one of the upstairs windows. We could see a corpse-white face against the darkness, staring down at us. The apparition couldn't have gotten any clearer if she had lifted the sash and stuck her head out into the night.

Valerie gasped as she turned to look. After another few seconds, the ghost vanished.

"That wouldn't be hard to fake," Anthony said, although from the uncertainty in his voice, I think he was trying to convince himself.

"No," Teag replied thoughtfully. "But why would they? It's an accounting firm. I could see where a bar might benefit from being haunted, but accountants aren't supposed to be interesting. I wouldn't think their clients would like the notoriety."

"Now you see what the problem is," Valerie said. "Visitors want to get a thrill, not get scared out of their sneakers."

I suspected that Teag and I were taking this all better than the average tourist because we had faced down much worse. Anthony might be spooked, but he was used to keeping a poker face in the courtroom. Tourists looking for a mild shiver wouldn't consider this fun. *Are the ghosts amped up because they're afraid of the Reapers? Is that why they've suddenly gotten aggressive, because they're scared of being eaten by wraiths?*

I knew most of the ghost stories that Valerie told, but she was such a good storyteller I didn't mind hearing them again. Charleston had more than its share of pirates, rogues, gamblers, tragic love affairs, and scandals, so tales of dirty deeds and tawdry goings-on made for thrilling fare. *It's all fun and games until someone ends up as a ghost...*

Valerie took us past St. Philip's Church and its beautiful cemetery. Behind crumbling brick walls, tombstones stretched off into the darkness. These were old graves, some dating back to the early 1700s. The cemetery had long been said to be haunted, and it seemed right out of Hollywood's idea for a horror movie: stones that were sometimes crooked or barely legible, lonely corners shadowed by huge trees, and a Southern Gothic moonlight and magnolias vibe that was the real thing. But tonight, none of those ghosts showed up, not even an orb. "Consecrated ground," I murmured to Teag.

"I was thinking the same thing," he replied.

When we reached the Old Slave Mart, it was a different story. Charleston is a beautiful city with a bloody past. Tens of thousands of enslaved Africans and people from the Caribbean were auctioned like cattle at the Old Slave Mart. Anyone with a hint of a psychic gift finds the building very uncomfortable because of its stone tape images and the impression so much grief and misery left in every inch of its construction. Although the building has been converted to a museum and gallery, I couldn't bring myself to visit after the first time, which went badly, to say the least.

Moans rose from the darkened building. As we passed in front of the big stone façade, I heard screams and wails. Something invisible and angry shook the huge iron gates at the building's arched main entrance. Dark, human-shaped shadows slipped along the walls. Inside the darkened building, momentary bursts of light were visible, as if camera flashes were going off. Impossible, since the building had been closed up for hours.

"Definitely more than your guests bargain for," Anthony observed, looking rattled by the ghostly noises.

"One more stop," Valerie said. We walked in silence for several blocks, thinking about what we had seen. So far, the ghosts had been unusually active. Yes, Charleston is one of the most haunted cities in the

United States, but that doesn't mean that every night looks like something out of a horror movie. Charleston is a city of subtlety, manners, and decorum (at least in public), and our ghosts are subtle, too. Usually, they're not out to scare anyone. They're just trapped in an infinite memory loop, or trying to get a message across a gap in time they can't bridge. Some of their stories are tragic, others are horrific, but fortunately most of them aren't dangerous.

Now, the ghosts were restless, and I don't think they were practicing for Halloween. There was an edge of desperation about the hauntings we had seen, and it squared with what Tad's ghost had told us about the wraiths and what I had witnessed with the ghostly bike riders. That made me even more curious about these Reapers and whether they and the Watcher had anything to do with Sorren's other problems.

Valerie turned down Queen Street. The Old Jail was a tourist favorite, especially for evening ghost tours. It once held Charleston's most notorious criminals, including Lavinia Fisher, a female serial killer who ran an inn. I usually steered clear of the Old Jail. The psychic echoes of the long-ago executions were unpleasantly strong even if I took pains not to touch anything, and the malice of the long-ago inmates left an indelible impression.

Someone vanished on the steps here just a few days ago, I thought. *Did the Reapers have a hand in it?*

Traffic was quiet tonight. I wondered if people without psychic ability could still sense that something was wrong and avoided places where the ghosts were active. We drew alongside the Old Jail, and right away, I could feel a wave of cold air completely out of place in this season. It was like stepping into a meat locker.

A foul smell hung in the air, and the hair on the back of my neck stood up.

Have a message for the devil? I'll be seeing him soon.

"Did you hear that?" I asked.

"Not clearly," Anthony replied. Teag nodded, and so did Valerie. We all recognized the words. It was the statement Lavinia Fisher made moments before her hanging a century ago.

I eyed the open area around the Old Jail. Once, it had been a potter's field, the place criminals and vagrants were buried when no one else wanted them. Now, I could feel the gaze of all those spirits watching us. Ghost hunters like Kell have often talked about how angry some ghosts seem, jealous of the living. Tonight, I was certain that if those ghosts could have hitched a ride with us, to somewhere safe and warm, they would have done so in a heartbeat.

The sudden sound of a metal cup against iron bars made me jump. I looked to the jail's gates, but there was no one in sight. We had barely moved forward when I heard a snap, a thud and a creak that sounded suspiciously like a weighted rope swinging back and forth against wood, though no one had been hanged here in over one hundred years.

"Look!" Anthony said. Several blue-white orbs glowed dimly as they bobbed and wove through the darkness of the lawn beside the jail.

Coming for us.

All four of us heard the voice that time, and I could see from their expressions that Valerie and Anthony had had enough.

"Let's go," I said, a little more sharply than I intended. We vamoosed, right back to the main street and the safety of bright street lights. Even so, I kept a white-knuckled grip on my athame, and I saw that Teag held his staff as if ready for trouble.

"You've seen what I mean, right?" Valerie asked as she headed us back to the stables.

"Have you heard anything from the guides at other companies?" Teag asked.

"Everyone's scared. Some of the guides are saying it's pranksters, but I don't think they really believe it."

"How are the other guides handling it?" I asked.

"What can they do?" Valerie replied. "We've tried to let people know when they book that the tours are 'intense'. Some people think it's all a big joke. Others leave the tour and want their money back. It's been getting steadily worse over the last two weeks. You should see the comments we've gotten online."

Valerie stuck to main routes on our way back, and while I spotted a few shifty shadows and we passed through some odd cold spots, we saw nothing like the ghostly activity from the main sites. "I cancelled tonight's tours so I could show you around," she said as we came back to the stables.

"Do you have any ideas of how to make it safer for my customers?" she asked. We followed her into the barn, where the horses looked up in curiosity, then went back to their hay.

"Other than the rock throwing, none of the ghosts actually did anything that might cause harm," I mused. "Could you avoid the Inn, until things calm down?" If this kept up, Mrs. Teller was going to be a rich woman making charms to soothe the ghosts. Worse, if all the spirits were restless because of the Reapers, Charleston's ghosts could be in real danger, and so far I had no idea of how to stop them from getting eaten.

"I can," she said, giving a round of fresh water and carrots to the horses. "But what if the ghosts get bolder? What if they do more than just rattle the gates and windows?"

"We've had some weird things happen at the shop lately too," I said. "Have you tried putting a root on whatever is making the ghosts bonkers?" Here in the Lowcountry, wise people take the idea of having a Hoodoo woman like Mrs. Teller 'put a root on' someone very seriously. "I bet she's got some charms you can use when you take your tours around that might help, until we can figure out why the ghosts are acting up."

Valerie nodded. "I know Mrs. Teller. I'll go down tomorrow morning and see what she can do. At least it might make things calm down until someone can get to the bottom of the problem." The look she gave me said I was on her short list of people who might do that.

"I'd be grateful for anything you can figure out on how to stop the disturbances," Valerie said. "I'm afraid this is going to ruin the ghost tour business – or worse, someone will get hurt."

Despite Valerie's protests, we insisted on sticking around until she had finished checking on the horses. Her car was parked near Teag's and Anthony's, in a side lot one block up. The parking lot usually seemed well lit, but tonight, the security lights gave a dim glow, and the shadows around the lot's edges were darker than I remembered.

Valerie got in her car, but when she turned the key, nothing happened. "Darn," she muttered. "I've been having problems with the battery. I guess it finally gave out."

I hoped it was that simple. "Why don't I drop Valerie off at her house?" Anthony volunteered. I held my breath when Anthony tried his key, but to my relief, the engine roared to life. Valerie accepted Anthony's offer gratefully, and we watched them head out of the lot.

That's when the shadows engulfed Teag's car. "I really don't like the look of that," I said. I held the athame in my right hand, walking stick in my left, and jangled the dog collar. Bo's ghost appeared at my side. Immediately, he began to growl.

"Neither do I." Teag held his staff defensively. It's almost as tall as he is, made of ash, solid enough to give bad guys a solid thumping. Even without magic, Teag can whup ass with a fighting stave. But he's enhanced the stave with carved runes and woven charms imbued with power, making it even more dangerous to bad things that go bump in the night.

"Let's move toward the car and see if the shadows draw back," I said. "Maybe it's a warning, not a throw-down."

We moved slowly, me facing forward and Teag behind me, facing away. The air grew colder, and there was a sense of foreboding that made me want to run away. I kept going, one foot in front of the other, until we were nearly to the car.

As I reached for the door, the shadows surged forward. For a moment, they nearly blotted out the overhead light. I closed my hand tight around the handle of my grandmother's wooden spoon and tapped into the warm, safe memories. A cone of cold, blindingly bright white light flared from the athame, forcing back the darkness.

Teag began to murmur under his breath. He reached down to several macramé knots that hung from his belt loops, and loosened one of them, sending a surge of stored magical power through his staff. He swung the staff in a semi-circle behind us, and the darkness crept back, just beyond the reach of his staff.

My teeth were chattering. Light frost glittered on the windshield. Murmured voices were all around us, so many that I couldn't make them out clearly, only a word here and there.

Help us... save us... beg for mercy... hunting us... destroyed... feed on us... mercy...

The speakers might have been long dead, but there was no mistaking the cold terror in their voices. Something had frightened the dead out of their wits, scared them badly enough to beg the living for help, to use what precious energy they hoarded to make themselves seen and heard to us.

"We're trying to help," I said, addressing the darkness. I'm not a psychic. For all I knew, talking out loud without being a medium was like yelling at your cell phone without a signal.

"Who's doing this? Who is trying to hurt you?" The spirits remained silent, but I took it as a good sign that they had not surged toward us. "Is it the Reapers? We're trying to stop the things hunting you. Please, help us do our job."

Teag and I exchanged a glance. If it came to a fight, he and I had the skills and the weapons to do some damage. I hoped it wouldn't get that far. "Do you think they heard me?"

Just then, the darkness rolled back like the tide, away from the rental car and back toward the edges of the lot. "Thank you," I said. "We will find an answer."

Hurry...

Chapter Eight

KELL HAD INVITED Teag and me to come out with his group and see the havoc the ghosts were causing, so here we were at the place everyone called the 'murder house'.

The big white house on the outskirts of the city was stunning in its day. Teag and I had called up everything we could online. It didn't take us long to find details. The Blake house was built in 1936, and the white-columned mansion was large and impressive. A brick and wrought iron fence faced the street, opening onto a long curved driveway. Even now, after years of neglect and vandalism, I could imagine what the old place must have looked like in its heyday.

"Given the nickname," Teag said, "I guess restless ghosts aren't surprising."

Kell grinned. "Nobody's surprised that the Blake house has ghosts. We're surprised how much the ghosts have changed."

I had the floor plan to the house in a pocket of my jacket. The Blake house had been on and off the market for a long time, so details were easy to find. Once I read the house's history, it didn't surprise me that the house hadn't sold. Some stains don't wash clean.

"I'm surprised the place is still standing," I commented. The front door and the large French doors on the first floor were boarded up. Upstairs, some of the windows were broken and the rest were filthy. Knee-high weeds and overgrown bushes nearly hid the house from the road.

"Must have been amazing when it was built," Kell said, looking up at the big home.

"I heard it had its own movie room, back in the 1930s." Pete was a short, wiry ginger with the look of a welter-weight wrestler.

"I heard it had air conditioning, even way back then," Calista added. She was rocking a goth librarian vibe, even dressed to explore.

Tarleton, as the Blakes called their new home, was once a showpiece. Magnolias flanked the wide front porch, an old live oak graced the front yard and there was a swimming pool in the back. The mansion was meant to impress.

"They bombed with the name," Kell sniffed. "The only worse thing they could have called it would have been 'Sherman's Acres'."

I couldn't resist chuckling. Kell was right. Charleston has a long memory, and doesn't forgive easily. Banastre Tarleton was a British general who laid siege to Charleston during the Revolutionary War and tried to burn Middleburg Plantation, a local historic treasure. That made him about as popular as Civil War General William Tecumseh Sherman, who burned his way through the South on his march to the sea. Folks are still a mite touchy about all that, even now.

"You ready to go in?" Drew, a tall skinny young man with black hair tied back in a ponytail looked around, bobbing up and down on his toes with nervous energy. "I don't like standing around out here."

"For all the bucks the Blakes sunk into this place, they didn't live here long," Teag observed.

We had found out a lot about Manfred and Bethanne Blake, and the information ranged from sad to sordid. The Blakes made their money selling automobiles and managed to hang onto it despite the Great Depression. They were new in Charleston and eager to earn a place in the local social register. That's easier said than done.

Charleston's old money families have been around since Blackbeard sailed the seas. They know each other, marry each other and see each other for golf and benefit dances. It's clubby and close-knit, so breaking in to that crowd, even with a wad of cash, takes patience and finesse. The Blakes were short on those two traits. They didn't even know that the natural habitat of Charleston blue-bloods is South of Broad Street. The Blakes were screwed before they ever set foot in their new dream house.

"Before we go in," I said, rummaging in my messenger bag, "I have something for each of you." I pulled out four agate necklaces and four smooth pieces of onyx, one for each of them. "And once we're done, I have those charms to help calm down the ghosts that I promised we'd get for you," I said to Kell. Teag patted his messenger bag.

"Take these," I said, distributing the onyx and agate pieces to the team. Kell and Pete put their necklaces on immediately and tucked the loose piece of onyx into their pockets. Calista looked at the stones skeptically. Drew shoved his in his pocket without a second glance.

"What are they?" Calista asked, examining the stones in the moonlight.

"Agate and onyx are good for protective energy," I said, and lifted my right hand to the necklace at my throat, while fluttering the fingers of my left hand to show my bracelet. Teag held up his hand to show a silver and onyx ring as well.

"Just for good measure, I had the pieces blessed by a Voudon mambo – and an Episcopalian priest," I added. "They aren't a bullet-proof vest, but they should have enough juice to make most ghosts want to give you some space."Drew's expression let me know he didn't believe a word I said. Calista looked like she was debating the idea, then slipped the stone into her pocket and put on the necklace.

"You read about the murder?" Kell asked as we walked toward Tarleton. Long ago, when lights blazed through its windows and the grounds were manicured, it must have been a beautiful place. Now, the ruined home was silent and brooding.

"Yeah," Teag replied. Houses have personalities. Some houses have a personality disorder, especially when the house is the site of a tragedy or horrific crime. Tarleton was one of them.

"It didn't happen right away, did it?" I asked. "The Blakes owned the house for fifteen years, but they traveled a lot. Then he retired and they decided to get to know the neighbors."

Kell nodded. "Fancy society dinner, lots of local big-wigs invited, caterers brought in from Columbia, even some famous movie stars were supposed to show up," Teag continued. "Then everything went wrong in a big way."

That was an understatement. The technical term is clusterfuck.

"The swing band from Atlanta that they booked didn't show up. Claimed they got a telegram cancelling the gig," Teag said.

"And then the movie stars backed out at the last minute," I added. "The caterers came, so there was a mountain of expensive food, a full bar for a crowd of people, plus flowers and waiters. But two hours before the big event, the Blakes got one phone call after another from the guests expressing their regrets at not being able to attend."

"In other words, after it was too late to get out of paying for all that food," Teag said.

"Which is where the stories start to differ," I jumped in. "Most accounts suggest that one of the Blakes' guests was catty enough to sabotage the party by cancelling the entertainment and getting the other guests to accept and then back out."

"Other people blamed it on a streak of bad luck. Maybe even a curse," Teag added.

"And it went downhill from there," I said. "It looks like Manfred Blake's mistress picked that night to confront him, probably intending to make a scene at his fancy party. Instead, both of the Blakes were stinking drunk and mean as skunks, having a roaring fight over who was to blame. Bethanne shot the mistress, and then Manfred shot Bethanne and later, when he sobered up, put a bullet in his own head."

"The house sat empty while the whole sordid story played out in the courts," Kell said. "Relatives didn't want the place, and neither did anyone else. It changed hands twice since the Blakes, both times to out-of-towners. Nobody stayed long."

"The last buyer got the place at a fire sale price hoping the land might be worth something," Teag said. "I don't think the current owner ever meant to live in it."

Kell nodded. "It's been vacant for at least ten years, to the point where the cops threatened the owners if they didn't keep the vandals and the vagrants out."

"Do we actually have permission to be here, or is this on the downlow?" I asked.

Kell grinned. "Actually, I'm friends with the real estate agent who got saddled with this place. He had some weird experiences out here, and asked us to look into it. So I've got the key to the back door and a note in my pocket giving us permission in case the cops come by."

From the look of the place, the cops didn't go out of their way to come around. The grand pillars were marred with graffiti, and the weeds around the front porch were littered with trash. I was glad I had worn hiking boots.

The back yard was worse. Old papers and plastic bags were strewn all over, along with the rusted remains of lawn furniture, and the burned remains of a broken picnic table. Two empty garage bays stood like eye sockets. Vandals had stripped the outside light fixtures. It was a shame to see a grand old house like this.

We all came armed with really big flashlights, and everyone had cans of pepper spray. Teag brought his staff, and I had the dog collar on my left wrist, my athame up my right sleeve where it could be in my hand with the flick of my wrist, and the agate Viking spindle whorl in my pocket. It amplified my power, and if Kell was right about the spirits being juiced up, then I wanted an edge of my own. I left Alard's walking stick at home, because I didn't think burning down the house would help.

"What's that smell?" My nose wrinkled as the breeze brought a whiff of something dead.

Kell grimaced. "That's the swimming pool, or what's left of it," he replied. "You can imagine – or maybe it's better if you can't. It's full of rain water and debris, so it blooms with algae all summer and there's no telling what kind of trash is in there. Perfect place to hide a body or two, if you ask me."

Unfortunately, Kell probably wasn't the only person who had ever thought of that. I had no desire to go closer.

"Where are the hot spots?" Teag asked. He was wearing his *agimat* and hamsa amulets, and the hand-made vest into which he and Mrs. Teller had woven magical protections. I was sure he had a few other surprises hidden away, just in case.

"Don't worry. You can't miss them," Kell said with a nervous chuckle. He led us inside. No one spoke as we walked into the kitchen. What was left of the décor screamed 1980s. The appliances had been torn out and so had some of the custom-made cabinets. Dirt and mildew covered the tile floor. Kell played his light across the walls. It was a commercial kitchen designed for people with servants.

"According to the stories, the mistress, Karla Waters, came in through the kitchen," Kell said. We followed him from the kitchen into the dining room. Even without furniture, I could imagine a grand banquet set with candles and crystal for guests who never came. Paint peeled from the walls, and the ceiling was discolored.

"She found the Blakes in the dining room, drunk and having a food fight," Kell continued. "Bethanne Blake went after Karla with her nails and a dinner fork. But Karla had a gun."

"So why didn't Karla just shoot Bethanne?" I asked. Drew, Pete, and Calista had moved away from us, wandering the room with their ghost hunting equipment in hand. Drew had an EMF reader, looking for electromagnetic frequency spikes. Pete wore a pair of smartglasses that could capture video, and another small camera attached to his hat. Calista set out microphones and a tablet computer to run all her devices.

"No one knows," Kell replied. "But the theory is that Karla came to speak her mind, and she wanted them both to hear her out. Don't forget – she expected to show up when everyone would be on good behavior in front of the rich neighbors. I don't think Karla ever expected two surly drunks."

"So there was a struggle," I filled in. Kell nodded. "And the gun went off when it was pointed at Karla. End of mistress."

"Yep," Kell confirmed. He led us out of the dining room into a dilapidated grand foyer. Overhead, a huge crystal chandelier hung amid layers of cobwebs.

"Problem was, Manfred Blake was fond of Karla, in fact, fonder than he was of Bethanne," Kell said. "When the police got here, it looked like a war zone. Ming vases shattered. Bullet holes in the walls. Apparently the Blakes threw everything they could pick up and heave at each other, with some shooting in between."

"And when the dust settled, Bethanne was dead, too, with a hole in her chest," Teag supplied.

"Uh huh. So Manfred Blake goes and finishes off a bottle of his best whiskey and eats more of the party food and falls asleep in a drunken stupor," Kell said. "And when he remembered what had happened, he went out to the garage, put his gun in his mouth and pulled the trigger. That was the end of the Blakes' assault on Charleston society."

My footsteps echoed as I walked slowly around the perimeter of the foyer. It didn't take much psychic wattage to know bad energy had never left Tarleton. I wondered if the people who had purchased the house had actually visited it, or just taken a broker's word for its condition. Anyone with the paranormal sensitivity of a turnip could have felt the resonance. Anger. Jealousy. Betrayal. Shame.

"Out of curiosity," I asked, "did anyone ever find out who cancelled the entertainment?"

Kell shook his head. "No. But if you get some of the old guard talking – and liquored up with good Glenfiddich – the name Lillian Heath comes up."

The Heath family was Charleston royalty. They were the equivalent of the Mayflower settlers for the Holy City, and they had done well for themselves. Sorren had hinted on more than one occasion it was because the women in the family were witches who had an edge when it came to financial investment. Because of their blue blood, wealth, and social position, the Heaths would be formidable enemies. Even now, a word from the current Heath brothers could make or break business ventures, and their wives were equally influential. Lillian Heath would have been the Heath brothers' grandmother.

"What do you know about the other owners?" I asked as we climbed the broad, curving staircase. The carpet was mildewed and rotting. Grime covered the carved teak balustrade.

"The first couple talked about making it a bed and breakfast," Kell said as he led us up the stairs. "But there were problems from the start."

We all gathered at the top of the stairs overlooking the foyer. For just a second, I could see the foyer as it had been in Tarleton's heyday. When I blinked, the vision was gone, but it was far too detailed and real to have just been my imagination. I removed my hand from the railing and promised myself I wasn't going to touch anything else. Hell, this place was so haunted I was picking up the resonance through the soles of my shoes.

"What kind of problems?" Teag asked. The upstairs hallway stretched into darkness to my left, with closed doors all the way down. A shorter hallway ended in a few steps up and a closed door.

"Lights that went on and off on their own," Kell replied. "Cold spots. Foggy windows. Drafts even when doors were shut. Strange noises."

"Did these people not watch any horror movies?" I asked. "Those aren't construction issues. Those are exorcist issues."

Kell shrugged. "Not everyone believes," he replied. "So the first new owners sank a lot of money into trying to fix the place. Then the wife had a nervous breakdown and ended up in a psychiatric hospital because she was hearing voices."

"And the husband?" Teag asked.

"A series of business failures ruined him financially. A year later, he shot himself."

"Score two for the house," I muttered.

Kell led us down the long hallway. "What's in the other direction?" Teag asked.

"Those stairs go to the attic," Kell replied. "The house has a full attic and full basement, plus a detached garage. It's cavernous."

"And your group has been everywhere?" I asked.

Kell gave a bark of a laugh. "No. We never get that far."

I looked down the dark hallway. "What's down here?" I asked.

"Bedrooms," Kell replied. "All but one of them are 'hot', supernaturally." He stopped at the first room and opened the door. The furniture was gone, but draperies still hung forlornly from rods above the filthy windows. It was easy to tell where pictures once hung because of the rectangular spots on the wallpaper.

"We think this was the master bedroom," Kell said.

An overwhelming sadness came over me, along with a seething rage that I knew was not my own. Instinctively, I backed up toward the doorway. "I can't imagine trying to spend the night in there," I murmured.

"We've spotted a woman's ghost by the windows," Kell reported. "This is also one of the rooms that the new owners had problems heating."

It was cold as a freezer. "Let's keep going," I urged, running my hands up and down my arms. I clasped one hand around the agate necklace, and the coldness receded.

"This next room might have been a guest room," Kell continued as we moved down the hallway. Faint moonlight straggled into the corridor from the windows. "We haven't seen as much supernatural activity in it."

"How soon did the house sell after the first owners lived here?" Teag asked. I noticed that he touched the *agimat* charm that hung around his neck.

"The house sat vacant but maintained for about ten years," Kell replied. "A caretaker visited occasionally to check on things. Apparently, they needed a new caretaker just about every year. No one wanted to stick around."

"I'm getting some weird jumps in the EMF readings," Drew said, turning in a slow one-eighty from just inside the doorway. None of Kell's team ventured far from the group upstairs.

"I'm getting some weird flashes in the photo stream," Pete said. His wearable technology gave him a slightly unfocused expression as he looked at and not through his lenses. "The camera snaps shots every twenty seconds, and I see them on my glasses. It's picking up sparkly things in the air that we're not seeing live."

"Picking up some activity downstairs," Calista said, flicking through displays on her tablet. "Movement, sounds. Temperature fluctuation."

"This is just the pre-game warm-up," Kell said.

We left the door to the second room open as well. Room three was on the opposite side of the hall, and the faded pastel colors and stencils of toys and animals made it clear that the room was decorated for a child. I frowned. "I thought you said the Blakes didn't have children."

"They didn't. Neither did the Tanners, the first new owners," Kell replied. "But the Robertsons did. They bought the place from a real estate speculator who lost his shirt when a plan to build a mall fell through. The Robertsons bought the house about five years after the property went into foreclosure."

I couldn't imagine anyone thinking that Tarleton would be a healthy place to raise a family. "The Robertsons had two young daughters," Kell said. Calista, Drew, and Pete moved into the room just far enough to monitor. "This was back in the mid-nineties. Things went okay for a while."

"Maybe the house took a while to wake up," Teag said.

I had the feeling that all around us, the house was indeed waking up. I didn't need Calista's recording equipment to hear faint scuffling sounds downstairs. Over our heads, boards creaked as if someone was walking in the attic.

"The girls started telling tales about invisible friends, a 'bad lady' in the dining room who chased them, and a man with no head in the garage."

"Uh oh."

"Mrs. Robertson began having migraine headaches. Mr. Robertson was traveling a lot. Both girls had night terrors," Kell said. "The family dog wouldn't enter certain rooms, and it would wake up and begin barking at nothing."

Nothing you could see.

"There were a lot of weird goings-on," Kell added. "It got so bad, Mrs. Robertson called in a medium and had a séance."

"We're having some weird goings-on ourselves," Calista said. "The equipment is picking up vocalizations too low for us to hear. Listen." She tapped her tablet, and we heard a deep voice that sounded distorted.

Leave us.

"Play that again," Kell ordered.

Leave us.

"Sounds like someone doesn't like company," Teag commented.

"The first time we came here, more than a year ago, we picked up some orbs and a little EMF agitation," Calista said.

"When we came back last month, we got a bit of a woman's voice, saw some strange shadows, got hit by pebbles and rocks and had a bunch of other poltergeisty stuff," Pete added, splitting his attention between us and what he was watching on his glasses.

"The readings are way more extreme this time," Drew chimed in. "Pegging the red zone. I've never seen anything like this."

"What happened when the Robertsons held their séance? I asked.

"They got more than they bargained for," Kell replied. "The medium went into her trance and began to speak in a man's voice, threatening them. The Robertsons moved out shortly afterwards, and a developer bought the land and just let the house go to rot."

Out in the hallway, I heard the squeak of footsteps on the floorboards, but no one was in the hallway. From downstairs, the faint sounds of a piano and voices were unmistakable.

"Yeah, you heard that," Drew confirmed, noticing my expression. He checked his equipment. "I picked up some audio."

"Let's take a look at the last two rooms," Kell said. "Just in case we decide to make a fast getaway." Above our heads, I heard a scraping sound, as if someone were shoving a heavy piece of furniture or dragging a trunk.

"How do we know there isn't someone up there?" Teag asked. "Maybe squatters moved in."

Calista adjusted the sensors on her equipment, and held up a metal wand connected to her tablet. "I'm picking up six heartbeats and six separate thermo readings in here," she said. "If there's anyone upstairs, they're cold and they don't have a beating heart."

Teag and I exchanged a glance. I wasn't going to say so, but that didn't rule out vampires and other supernatural creatures.

The fourth room looked like it might have been an office. Paint peeled from the walls and cockroaches skittered past. On the hardwood floor, someone had made a large circle with charcoal and salt, like the kind used to do powerful magic. It had been smudged open. I could still feel the remnants of magic, dark and stained.

"No ghosts," Calista said, looking at her tablet. Pete shook his head. "Nobody home."

"What about the circle?" I asked. "Was it here the last time you visited?"

Kell frowned. "No, or at least, we didn't notice it. Vandals must have gotten in again."

I let him think that, but the residual power I felt wasn't from a bunch of kids with a Ouija board. Someone with real power had been here. I wanted to know why.

"The fifth room has always been the wildcard," Kell said as we moved to the last room in the hallway.

The door slowly swung open as we approached. Inside, dingy curtains hung over the windows. Something skittered beneath the fabric. The sense that someone was present in the room was overwhelming, and all my instincts were screaming for me to run.

I stepped far enough into the room to note that its window overlooked the pool. In the moonlight, the pool was a dark rectangle surrounded by a sagging chainlink fence. Then I saw something that looked like a long, dark tentacle snake from the fetid water and lurch up onto the cracked pavement.

"Y'all, we need to get out of here," I said, backing toward the doorway.

From the darkest corner of the room, a figure began to slide toward us, a shadow with no one to cast it. It had the shape of a woman, with a long, flowing gown, and it was moving fast toward the door. Hundreds of cockroaches swarmed toward us like a living brown tide.

"Run!" Kell yelled.

Slam. Slam-slam-slam. The doors we had left open slammed shut as we ran past. Over our heads something in the attic stamped its feet. Sounds filled the empty house. I heard a child's laughter and a woman sobbing, then the muted echo of a gunshot.

Cockroaches covered every surface, wiggling out of the walls along the baseboard, dropping down from holes in the ceiling, emerging from beneath the wallpaper and crunching beneath our feet as we ran. We brushed them out of our hair and off our clothing, but no matter how many we trod underfoot or slapped away from us, the swarm closed in behind us.

When we had entered, the old house smelled of mold and decay, mildew and dust. Now, the stench of rotting meat was unmistakable, strong enough to make my gorge rise. I kept myself from throwing up because that would require stopping and something might catch up with me. From the look on the faces of my companions, everyone was struggling not to retch.

As we headed for the steps, the door to the attic swung open, revealing a lightless abyss. I heard footsteps coming down the attic stairs, and I did not want to see what was heading to meet us.

"Faster!" Teag shouted. Calista and Drew were in the lead, heading down the grand staircase. Pete was close behind them. Kell was in front of me, and Teag behind me. As Calista reached the midpoint on the stairway, the huge crystal chandelier crashed to the floor, sending shards of glass flying.

Roaches made a living waterfall down the moldering carpet of the stairway. Pete tripped on the last step and went sprawling. The roaches swarmed over him as he screamed and beat them away. Teag and Kell dragged Pete to his feet, swatting the bugs off him.

"My equipment!" Calista yelled, veering toward the dining room.

"Hurry!" Kell urged.

Teag and I maneuvered ourselves to stand at the bottom of the steps while Pete and Drew helped Calista grab the monitoring equipment and Kell held the door open. Shadows were sliding down the walls of the upstairs landing and from around the corner where the attic stairway loomed. "Get them out of here!" Teag yelled to Kell. "We'll buy you some time. Get the van running and wait for us."

"Go!" Teag said, giving Pete a push toward the door.

Calista and the others were already running. I let the athame fall into my hand and focused on its resonance, gathering my will. A cone of cold, white light blasted from the wooden handle, smashing the roaches on the bottom half of the stairway and driving back the shadows with its glare.

Teag and I backed up quickly, never turning our backs on the shadows that were already regrouping and slithering down the walls to the bottom of the steps.

"Run!" Teag yelled as he lobbed one of Chuck's EMF grenades in an underhand toss toward the steps. Together, we dove out of the house and clamored down the front steps. A momentary burst of sound and light flared out of the windows of the first floor, then the ruined house was dark once more.

Teag and I piled into the van before Kell slammed the side door closed. "What the hell was that?" Kell's voice was shaking.

"Tell you later!" I said, remembering the thing that had been hauling itself out of the pool. "Go! Go! Go!"

Drew was driving, and the van laid rubber getting out of the driveway. I had no idea whether any of the neighbors had spotted the light show and called the cops, but if they did, I didn't want to be around to answer questions. Calista was examining her equipment and swearing under her breath.

"Something nearly blew out all my monitors," she said.

Pete managed a brave half-smile. "Thanks for pulling me out back there. I thought I was a goner." His smart-glasses were askew.

"Next time, I'm bringing a big can of Raid," Drew said. "Calling those bugs 'palmetto bugs' doesn't change a thing. I *hate* roaches."

Kell was still looking at Teag and me as if we had grown two heads. "What did you do back there?" I could hear fear in his voice, and beneath it, curiosity.

Teag shrugged. "I used something I've been tinkering around with," he lied. "Sends an EMF pulse and scrambles ghosts' frequencies."

"It would have been nice to have a warning," Calista said, sounding a bit tetchy. "I'm hoping I didn't lose my equipment."

"It got us out of there," I snapped. "Did you really want a closer look at whatever was chasing us?" Calista and the others shook their heads and I realized that they looked more frightened than annoyed.

Kell let out a long breath. "Thanks a lot," he said "Better to lose some equipment than have anyone get hurt."

"I'm guessing the last time wasn't quite that extreme?" I asked.

"Not even close," Pete replied. "We got freaky readings and heard sounds."

"No roaches," Drew agreed, and shivered.

"It's very possible that EMF pulse wiped our recordings," Calista said with a sidelong glare at Teag. "So we may not have any data to show for all our bother." Kell gave her a dirty look, and she shut up.

"You saw what happened in there," Kell said, and I could see that he was badly shaken. "It's not just our imagination, or stories we're making up."

I nodded. "Yeah. We saw. And I don't have a good explanation for you."

Kell met my gaze. "Cassidy, this is Charleston. Ghosts galore. What happens if the rest of them turn dangerous?"

I didn't know what to say. He was absolutely right about the danger. And that meant that Teag and Sorren and I needed to figure out answers before more people got hurt.

Chapter Nine

"EVERY TIME THERE'S a lull, I go out and look up more about Tarleton House," Teag said. The store was busy, but tourists seem to come in bunches with times in-between when the store was empty. Maggie was off, so that left Teag and me to rehash what we had seen the night before.

"And?" I asked.

Teag shrugged. "Kell's recap gels with what I found, even on the Darke Web," he said. "Nothing supernatural about the owners, no dark magic at work." He made a face. "If you make bad enough choices, you can get screwed over just fine without the need for dark magic."

True enough, I thought. I hadn't slept well, even with Baxter cuddled next to me and the lights on. Last night had been like being in a horror movie. Only when you're watching a movie and it gets too intense, you can go out for popcorn, or just shut your eyes. Those aren't options when the big bad wolf is real.

"I did find something else," Teag said. "I was poking around the records on Jonathan, the guy who disappeared next door. Maggie was right – he had been acquitted of some serious charges. When I looked up the other people who've vanished on stairways, it turns out every single one of them was charged with a serious crime and then acquitted."

I frowned. "That's weird."

Teag nodded. "Yeah, it is. So I dug a little deeper. In each case, it turns out that the person who disappeared really did do something wrong, but circumstances factored into the verdict. So for example, Jonathan really did hit and kill a man with his car, but he was acquitted because the pedestrian was drunk and the jury determined that he couldn't have avoided hitting the man."

I could feel a headache coming on, and I rubbed my temples. I was glad that, at least for a few moments, all the tourists had left the store. "Interesting – but I've got no idea how that could possibly have anything to do with the disappearances."

"Neither do I," Teag admitted. "But I thought it was worth mentioning."

"I've tried to reach Daniel Hunter, but he's not answering his cell phone," I said. "Since Sorren isn't here, I want some answers about Watchers and Reapers." I sighed. "Guess Daniel just plans to come and go on his own schedule. That's not helpful." I had left several messages, with no reply. *If we can't count on him and don't know when he'll bother to drop by, he's not much use to us.*

"Don't forget dinner at our place tonight – it's Anthony's treat." Teag chuckled.

"You had me at hello," I said, trying to sound light-hearted. It took a real effort to shake off what had happened on the ghost tour and at Tarleton House.

Really bad things were happening and I was worried that I hadn't heard from Sorren.

The bell on the shop door rang, and we both looked up, expecting a customer. To my surprise, Father Anne walked in, with a large leather-bound book under one arm. "Hey there," she greeted us, and glanced around to see if there were any customers. "Are you busy? Can I talk to you?"

"Sure," I said. "If someone comes in, you and I can go in the back."

"I heard about your accident at the cemetery," she said. "Are you all right?"

I shrugged. "It could have been a lot worse. I'm a little banged up, but nothing that won't heal. Insurance will cover the car, although I'm not sure 'monster damage' is on my policy." Hard to believe that was just a couple of days ago.

"What have you got there?" Teag asked, coming around to stand next to me.

Father Anne set a large ledger-sized book on the counter. It had an old, worn leather binding, and even without getting close to it, I could feel a tingle of power. "I'm glad you called me. I got in touch with some of my people at the St. Expeditus Society. Thought you might want to see this."

She flipped open the book. Two full-page colored prints of paintings stared out at us. The paintings were old, and I did not recognize the name of the artist. But there was no mistaking the subject.

On the left-hand page, I saw a trio of young men who looked like they belonged in an ad for every high-priced sin you could imagine in your fevered dreams. They were handsome, but not anyone's version of the boy next door. Their faces had the chiseled features of a Bernini sculpture, but the thin lips were cruel and haughty, the eyes arrogant and cold.

On the right-hand page, a dozen handsome men stalked forward out of the shadows, but on second glance, they were in the process of transforming into something hideous. One had leathery arms that ended in wicked claws. Another had the cloven hooves and furred legs of a goat. The head and chest on one had changed into a monstrous creature with a gaping maw and slitted eyes.

"Is this what attacked you?" Father Anne asked.

"Yeah. At least he sure looked like he'd belong with them." I wrapped my arms around myself. "So what are they?"

"Nephilim, supernatural creatures born when something from the Other Side seduces a human," Father Anne replied.

"Yeah," I replied, thinking of Coffee Guy's rapid change from handsome heartthrob to ugly monster. "And I bet they hold the illusion just long enough to get what they want." I didn't want to think about how flirty Coffee Guy had been and where that might have ended up.

"Let's just say it doesn't go well for the women they seduce," Father Anne said with an expression that told me I didn't want to ask for details.

"I don't get how these Nephilim guys can just show up. Aren't they Lucifer-fell-from-heaven type angels?" Teag asked, bending forward for a closer look.

Father Anne gave a tired smile. "Actually, that's more legend than fact," she said.

"How do Nephilim decide where and when to appear?" Teag asked.

"It depends," Father Anne said, closing the book. I wondered what else it contained, but I wasn't sure I wanted to know. "Sometimes, they're attracted to where a disaster is about to happen. Imagine vultures with foreknowledge of when there's going to be fresh road kill."

I could live without that image.

"Sometimes, they're drawn by a person with a particular gift – like the monk who painted the original paintings reprinted in this book, or like poor, doomed Gerard Astor, a painter who could see them," she added. "Or a powerful nephilmancer can a summon them to do his bidding. Fortunately, that's a once-in-a-blue-moon kind of thing."

"How long ago was the last blue moon?" Teag asked wryly.

Father Anne gave a wan smile. "It's been about one hundred and fifty years since the last time a nephilmancer showed up on this half of North America. I gather it was quite a battle. Most people remember it as the Great Yellow Fever Epidemic of 1854. Sorren played a big role in defeating that nephilmancer."

"Sorren destroyed him?" I asked.

"That's what the record says. A guy named Sariel. Not that such things are actually recorded anywhere, of course," she said with an exaggerated upward roll of her eyes.

"Of course not." Teag echoed sarcastically.

"So what is a Nephilim doing back in Charleston?" I mused, staring at the big leather book as if it might bite. "And why was he shadowing me?"

Father Anne met my gaze. "That's a very good question."

"What do you know about Watchers and Reapers?" I asked. Father Anne looked a little startled. "Daniel

Hunter mentioned them and so did Sorren. Now I can't get a hold of either Daniel or Sorren, and we just had a run-in with some really bad juju. I feel like I'm in the dark on everything."

Father Anne nodded. "Okay. A nephilmancer – like Sariel – is a sorcerer who can summon Nephilim from the Other Side. He can also call up other supernatural nasties, like Watchers, who punish wrongdoers, and Reapers, who feed on ghosts. It sounds like we've got a nephilmancer on the loose."

"How do we fight them?" Teag asked.

"That's the hard part," Father Anne said. "Because usually, a nephilmancer is after some kind of prize. It's a lot of magic to throw around, so there's got to be something in it for him – or her. Beings like Nephilim and Watchers aren't easily bound, and a nephilmancer brings them through to do something in particular, not just on a whim. We need to figure out the prize, and then we'll have a better idea of how to fight back."

A shiver went down my spine. *Sorren is certain the attacks are personal. Revenge is a very compelling prize for someone with a big grudge. And if the goal is a vendetta against Sorren, then if the sorcerer isn't Sariel, maybe it's someone picking up where he left off, someone who has a dog in this hunt.*

Father Anne left after she made sure I had her personal cell phone number on speed-dial. "Call me if you need me – and I mean that!" she warned as she left the shop. I had no doubt that we were going to need her help, and probably sooner rather than later.

* * *

DINNER WITH ANTHONY was a little later than we had expected.

By the time Teag and I finally arrived, Anthony had already picked up everyone's favorites from Forbidden City and had the table prepped. I had been over to Anthony's house before he and Teag formally moved in together, but I hadn't seen how they had blended their furnishings. The mix was just like the two of them: really different, but it somehow worked.

Teag used to have a studio apartment in a remodeled old house that had a lot of charm but no ghosts. It was full of books, one-of-a-kind art purchased from street sales of artists no one had heard of yet, a loom that took up one corner of the space, and his martial arts equipment.

Anthony's single-house wasn't on Battery Row, but it was South of Broad. The homes there are historic, well-kept and expensive. If I had any question as to whether Anthony was doing well in the family law firm, the house and its furnishings removed all doubt. Like Anthony, nothing was fussy or ostentatious. Instead, the quality was understated, in a way folks tend to do things if they've had money for a while and don't have to show it off or prove anything. Together, their place had an IKEA meets Hepplewhite vibe that worked, in a quirky sort of way.

"I was beginning to worry." Anthony lit a pillar candle in the middle of the table and poured us each a glass of wine. I caught a glimpse of the bottle, and it wasn't a brand with a twist-off top. In the kitchen, a small flat-screen TV was still on, but muted, turned to a local news channel. One glance told me the broadcast was depressingly full of the week's big stories: a serial killer loose in New England, a couple of gruesome murders with unlikely killers, and a workplace shooting. I resolved to block out the bad news and enjoy the evening.

We were starved, so for a few minutes, we dug into the food, passing the entrees family-style and filling our plates.

"So I'd say that we're all in agreement that Valerie's concern about juiced up ghosts wasn't just her imagination," Anthony said finally, when we had nearly finished eating.

I shook my head. "No. It's not."

"Do you know what's causing it?"

"Maybe," Teag replied.

"Something human?"

I sighed. "Not anymore."

Anthony looked as if he were debating what to ask next. Teag and I don't want to cause him any problems with the law firm, so there are some things we don't tell him about, like breaking and entering for a good cause, and he doesn't usually ask too many questions.

"Is the situation that has the ghosts riled up dangerous to you?" Anthony asked finally.

Teag hesitated for a moment, then nodded. "Probably. But we've got back-up, and some tricks of our own."

"Can you stop whatever's doing this?"

"We plan to," I answered. "One way or another."

Anthony thought about that for a moment, then nodded his head. "All right. The less I know, the more plausible my deniability. So let me tell you what I heard today."

He leaned back in his chair and took a sip of his wine. "There's been another missing person. Utility worker went down a flight of steps to the mechanical room beneath an office building, never arrived. One of the other workers said he'd used those stairs earlier without a problem."

"What are people saying?" Teag asked.

"Publicly, they're attributing them to people walking off the job. There's no blood, no evidence of a struggle, and no witnesses. Privately, people are a little weirded out about the whole thing."

I could totally understand that reaction, which seemed pretty rational to me.

"There've also been a number of 'malicious pranks' played around town," Anthony continued. "Previously locked doors standing open. Shutters pulled loose. Garbage cans turned over. That kind of thing. The cops are looking for teenagers." He took another sip of his wine. "But after what we saw with Valerie, I'm inclined to think there might be a connection to your restless ghosts."

"Are the pranks happening anywhere in particular?" I asked.

Anthony nodded. "Mostly around older homes and some of the lesser-known historic buildings. Normally, that kind of thing wouldn't have caught my attention," Anthony said. "Now, after what we saw, I'm wondering if it isn't riled up spirits trying to make themselves heard." Even speculating such a thing was a big step for Anthony, proof that his love for Teag had made him willing to consider the unthinkable. "Of course, I don't dare say that to anyone but you two, and I don't want to be quoted."

"Of course not," I said. Teag made a motion of zipping his lips, and Anthony grinned.

"Anyhow, I thought you ought to know. Oh, and there was something else," he added. "You know those Ghost Bikes? People are reporting all kinds of strange things happening with those."

"Like what?" Teag asked, leaning forward and sipping his wine.

"Wheels spinning when there's no wind. Bikes jostle up and down and rattle the chain with no one around."

No one but the ghosts, trying to get someone's attention, I thought. *Or desperate ghosts trying to get away from Reapers.*

"Do you know if the same is true for the roadside shrines?" I asked, toying with my glass. "The crosses people put up on the side of the highway?" I was thinking about the shrine over by the cemetery, and the ghosts of the two young men who had helped me against Coffee Guy. I hated to think that those spirits might also be running from Reapers. *Damn. We've got to fix this.*

Anthony frowned. "You know, I hadn't connected it. But I overheard a couple of the state cops in line at Honeysuckle Café, and they were talking about how people have been calling in accidents, and when the police show up, there's nothing but a memorial marker. When the people described what they had seen, the details were accurate – for fatal accidents that happened months or years ago."

"I don't even want to know what the morticians in town are running into," Teag commented, and poured himself a second glass of wine.

"Or the gravediggers," I added. Not all of Charleston's cemeteries were consecrated. Public memorial parks might not have the same protections as old churchyards.

Just then, a familiar image flashed on the silent TV screen, and I glanced up. "Oh my God, turn it up!" I said, pointing. Anthony grabbed the remote.

A photo of Palmetto Meadows nursing home filled the screen, with a banner beneath it that read 'Local Nursing Home Reacts to Bomb Threat'.

"...none of the residents were harmed, but police say several patients did require monitoring for stress," the male anchor said.

"Makes you wonder what kind of people are out there, who would think it was funny to phone in a bomb threat to a nursing home," the female anchor replied, shaking her head.

"In other news, a suspicious package in downtown Charleston turns out to be a real bomb," the man continued. A photo of a stretch of King Street flashed up on the screen, filled with ambulances and police – right in front of Trifles and Folly.

"An anonymous call tonight to Charleston police about a suspicious package was too little, too late when a box left on the sidewalk in front of a local business turned out to be a homemade bomb," the man said. "The bomb exploded at eight o'clock in front of an antique shop that's been in the same location for over three hundred years, but for reasons the bomb squad does not yet understand, the blast was deflected backward, away from the curio store. A car on the street and a business on the other side of King Street suffered minor damage. No one was hurt. Authorities are looking for information as to who might have placed the bomb and why that location was selected."

The news anchor looked into the camera. "If you have any knowledge about this crime, we need your help." The phone number for anonymous tips came up on the screen. "And remember: if you see something, say something."

My hand was shaking as I set down my wine glass. Teag reached over and put a hand on my arm. "It's okay, Cassidy. No one was hurt. The store is all right. Everyone's okay."

I blinked back tears, and at the same time, felt a swell of anger fill me. "This time," I said savagely. "But what about next time? The attack in Boston, the retirement center, the cemetery... none of us are safe!"

Anthony looked at us worriedly. "This is where I put on my lawyer hat and remind you that withholding information from a criminal investigation is a crime."

Teag met his gaze. "Even if the perp is somehow connected to ghost-eating supernatural monsters?"

"And a powerful sorcerer who can call up fallen angels?" I added.

Anthony knocked back the rest of his wine in a gulp that didn't do the vintage justice. "Is there any way you might be able to rephrase that if your testimony was required?"

"No." Teag and I spoke in unison.

Anthony sighed. "Assuming that I actually heard you say something just now – which I didn't – and understood what you said – which I didn't – theoretically, would that situation have anything to do with what we might or might not have seen happen on the ghost tour?"

"Yeah," Teag replied, finishing off his glass. "This is the part we weren't going to mention to keep you from worrying."

Anthony said something pointed which was not the kind of phrase they teach at law school. "And you two are involved because, why? You're antique dealers, not paranormal vigilantes...?"

His voice trailed off as he realized what he had just said. Teag and I looked back at him, neither confirming nor denying.

"Oh, no. Please tell me that I didn't just –" A series of emotions crossed Anthony's face. I could tell he was putting the pieces together, especially when the last expression was one of horror.

"Those explosions out at the Navy Yard a while back... how badly you were hurt, you said..."

Teag reached across the table and took Anthony's hand. "Do you remember when you were working on that case about the whistleblower who outed the crooked financial firm? Remember the death threats you got – at the office, and here, where I heard them on the machine and almost had a heart attack?"

"I remember," Anthony said in a choked voice.

"I asked if you would consider dropping the case," Teag said quietly. "And you told me that it was part of your job to take risks. That someone had to take the unpopular cases, the ones that resulted in rulings that could change things for the better. And that you had to do it, because not everyone could."

"I meant me, dammit!" Anthony said with a glare, his voice rising to a shout. "Not you!"

Teag gave a sad smile. "I've found a calling of my own," he said with gentle determination. "Something much bigger than I ever expected to be part of. Something that makes a difference, even though if we do it right, no one will ever know. We aren't alone. We have colleagues – powerful ones. But we're saving lives, Anthony. Because of what we do, lots of people get to live."

"You go up against those things?" Anthony said, not bothering to hide the fear in his voice. "Angry ghosts? Bad magic?" He shook his head. "Isn't there someone else?"

Teag met his gaze. "I have to do it, Tony. Because not everyone can."

Anthony wrapped his arms around Teag and hugged him fiercely. And then, unexpectedly, he reached out and grabbed my hand as well. "Now you listen to me," he said urgently. "I don't like this. I don't understand it. And frankly, it scares the shit out of me. But I love you," he said, looking toward Teag, "and you're one of my best friends," he said, meeting my gaze. "And I am not – *not* – okay with losing either of you. So just don't let that happen. Okay?"

Teag managed a teary smile and hugged Anthony tightly. "Okay," he said, although all three of us knew the promise wasn't really within our full ability to keep.

"Okay," I replied. And I really hoped it would be.

I LEFT SHORTLY after that. Teag and Anthony had things to discuss, and I was a third wheel. I drove the rental car I'd gotten from the insurance company home on the main streets, steering clear of any landmarks with particularly dark histories, and was pleased to find a spot on the curb right in front of the door onto my piazza. Pleased, but not completely surprised. I had asked Lucinda to put a distraction warding on the parking place, something that doesn't so much keep other people from taking the spot as it keeps them from noticing it's even there.

I looked all around before I unlocked my door, worried that I'd find either restless ghosts or Daniel Hunter. I wasn't sure which was worse, but I didn't want to see either. My head ached, and it wasn't from the wine. There was too much going on too fast in too many places, and I didn't have enough of a grip on what we were doing to fix it. I grabbed my purse, shook out the dog collar so that I'd have Bo's ghost as an escort, and kept my walking stick in hand. Forget about blasting something with cold power. Anything that got between me and that gate tonight was going to fry.

Good thing that Sorren was already inside, sitting on my couch, petting my dog.

"Don't," he said as I came through the door and froze. Bo's ghost wagged and winked out. Sorren's tone wasn't compulsion. He had promised he wouldn't use compulsion on me, unless it was truly a life-or-death situation. Because of my family's long bond with Sorren, neither glamouring nor compulsion would work right on me anyhow. But there was a tone of command in Sorren's voice that made me stop in my tracks long enough to think before I reacted.

That was good, since neither my vampire boss nor my dog – or my couch – are flame-proof.

"You're back sooner than I expected. I thought the clean-up in Boston would take longer."

"I need your help."

Sorren didn't look good; he was paler than usual and his eyes looked haunted. There were a lot of things I wanted to ask Sorren, and a lot of things I thought he might say, but that wasn't one of them. "How?" I asked.

"Have you seen the news tonight?" There was a sadness in his voice I hadn't heard before.

I nodded, put down my purse and came closer. Sorren was slumped on the couch, petting Baxter absently. If I hadn't known what he was, I would have pegged him for a grad student who had just failed out. My god, he looked awful.

"Trifles and Folly is okay," I said. "I've already had two phone calls from the police on the way home. No damage." I paused. "You want me to go to Palmetto Meadows, don't you?"

He looked up sharply. "You know?"

I nodded. "Sorry. I didn't mean to pry. I was there a couple of nights ago, when I took Baxter for our therapy dog evening. I saw you in the garden with Mrs. Butler." I paused. "And I also met old Mr. Thompson – the warlock."

Sorren gave a melancholy chuckle. "You never cease to amaze me, Cassidy."

"Do you need me to go over there now and make sure she's all right?" I asked. Going out again was the last thing I wanted to do, but I knew what it was like to be worried about a loved one.

Sorren shook his head. "No, but thank you. I appreciate the offer. When I heard, I went myself, got close enough to make sure there was no real danger. But I didn't dare go in. Too many questions."

I nodded. Sorren had assumed many names over the years, and had been careful to disappear and reinvent himself at regular enough intervals so that no one wondered about his extremely long lifespan and exceptionally youthful appearance. Still, falsifying identification and creating fictitious back stories was harder these days, even for the Witness Protection Program. Fingerprints didn't change, and retina scans didn't lie. The nursing home would not have run a background check on 'Mr. Sorrensson', but the FBI might.

"I can go over first thing in the morning," I offered, and glanced at my watch. "Odds are, the residents are in bed by now anyhow, and there are probably police on watch. I can say that I was worried about the friends Baxter and I have made, and wanted to see if there was anything I could do."

"Thank you, Cassidy," Sorren said raggedly. "There are many things the Dark Gift enables me to do, but often, it's the simplest things it denies me."

Like going abroad in daylight, I thought. Or spending a mortal lifetime with a woman he cared about.

"No problem," I assured him. Belatedly, Baxter seemed to notice that I had arrived home. Sorren carefully put him on the floor, and Baxter waggled his way over, utterly unconcerned about the obvious breach of etiquette. I picked him up and hugged him, then took him back and set him on Sorren's lap. Sorren looked up at me quizzically.

"You look like you need him at the moment more than I do," I replied. I went out to the kitchen. I only had one glass of wine with dinner, but this was definitely shaping up to be a two-glass day.

I brought the wine back in with me and settled into an armchair facing Sorren. Baxter was on his lap with a goofy grin. For a moment, it was awkwardly silent.

"I met her in 1940," Sorren said finally. "She was twenty. I was... older than that," he said with a sad smile. "She loved horses and mint juleps – and me. Even though she figured out quickly enough just what I was," he added, and if he had needed to breathe, he might have sighed. "She had a touch of her mother's Sight."

"I could tell that you two were close," I said, not entirely sure what to say. Technically, Sorren was my boss, or at least, my patron. Then again, in my last job, I had sat with my boss on more than one occasion while she drank herself numb and talked about her divorce. Chalk it up to being a good listener. But more than anything, Sorren was a friend. He'd had my back in a lot of fights. I wanted to hear him out.

"Helen was the last mortal I permitted myself to become romantically involved with," he said quietly.

"Ever. It's just not fair, to either of us... and sometimes it's so hard." He smiled. "But damn, she was a very special woman. Smart. Funny. An amazing dancer. Not afraid of anything. So open to curiosity. Do you have any idea how rare that was back then?"

Or even now, I thought, remembering Anthony's struggle to reconcile himself to what his own senses testified.

He didn't really expect an answer, so I didn't give one. Helen Butler was over ninety years old. There were a lot of things people didn't talk about back then, including vampires. She must have been exceptional to handle that.

"I'm guessing that eventually she found someone else." Since she was 'Mrs.' Butler instead of 'Miss', that was pretty obvious.

Sorren nodded. "We were together for several years. But eventually, it had to end. She wanted a real home, and children. Neither of which I could provide. She did not want to be turned. I looked in on her from a distance, now and again to make sure she was well. The years go so quickly for mortals, and so slowly for us. Her husband died a decade ago. She outlived her children. And then the Alzheimer's set in..."

"And you found a way to reconnect," I supplied. "To make sure she was taken care of."

He looked away. "I can't cure Alzheimer's. But for most people, it makes the past more real than the present. I can glamour her, just a bit, and nudge those memories to the fore. And as far as she's concerned, for a little while, it's seventy years ago, and nothing has changed."

Damn. I couldn't think of anything to say to that, so for a few moments, we were quiet. Finally, Sorren sat up and shook himself out of his mood. "Thank you," he said again. "But there are other things that also need attention."

"Yeah, and I've got some news on that," I replied, filling him in on what I knew of the bombing, what Teag and I had experienced with Valerie, as well as Anthony's news. I added the unexpected visit from Daniel Hunter, plus what we had seen at Tarleton House and Father Anne's Nephilim information.

"Hunter is an asset, but he's also a wild card," Sorren replied, scratching Baxter behind the ears. "I've worked with him once or twice. He's more of a hit man or a bounty hunter than anything else, which means that his real allegiance is to himself."

"Lovely."

Sorren shrugged. "In an all-out fight, he's handy to have around. He's not a member of the Alliance. More of a resource we call in when we need to. So no, I don't entirely trust him. But I think we're going to need some hired guns for this fight, and he's one of the best."

His expression darkened when I told him about Coffee Guy and the attack at Magnolia Cemetery and the paintings in Father Anne's book. He made me repeat some of the details of the attack, and describe exactly what I remembered of the monster.

"You are absolutely certain that the man you saw at Honeysuckle Café became the monster that attacked you outside the cemetery?" Sorren asked.

"Not a doubt in my mind," I said. "I had a bad feeling about the guy, even though he was handsome enough to be on a romance novel cover. He just seemed… too perfect. More like a painting than a person. And when I brushed his hand, I knew he had some kind of magic, and I got the clear impression he didn't want me to know that."

"This isn't good," Sorren said, standing and beginning to pace. "First something taking a bite out of ghosts to feed on their energy. Daniel called it a 'Reaper'. That's certainly one of the kinds of things that are able to do that. There are others. Does Daniel know for sure it was a Reaper, or did he just jump to that conclusion?"

"No idea," I replied. "We don't really have very helpful conversations," I added drily. "But Father Anne told me about Sariel. Do you think he could have survived and come back for revenge?"

Sorren muttered a curse in Dutch under his breath. "That would be extraordinary. We were so sure... Then the staircase disappearances," Sorren mused. "I've been thinking they're unrelated. Maybe so – or maybe not. There are too many distractions!" He looked at me in exasperation.

"But what if the distractions are part of the same problem?" I asked. "The attack in Boston, and at the other sites. The bomb tonight at Trifles and Folly. A Nephilim coming after me. What if this is all tied together with the attacks on your other properties? You said you thought this was personal. What if it *is* Sariel, returned somehow?"

"Now Daniel shows up talking about Alliance protocols – and Watchers," he said. I noticed that he ignored my last question.

"Translation, please."

"Alliance protocols are a series of responses to an escalating supernatural threat. There are precautions to be taken – physically and magically – and protections to be raised. Sort of the magical equivalent of red alert."

"Lovely," I replied.

"Back to the Nephilim. There aren't a lot of beings that can successfully pass themselves off as human, even for a few minutes. The one you met was able to run a solid, stable illusion that fooled a shop full of people and could hold that form to eat and drink. He also chose an extremely attractive form."

"And Coffee Guy was out in broad daylight."

"So he's not a vampire," Sorren said with a grimace. "Shapeshifters generally change from one species to another, not from monsters into cover models. Some demons can do it, too." He shook his head. "I think you're right about it being a Nephilim. But how did it get here and why did it come? They don't just wander around without a purpose."

"I know you think you destroyed Sariel," I said, refusing to let him evade the question. "But is it possible that he survived somehow and came back for revenge? Because that would make this all make a lot more sense."

Sorren ran a hand back through his hair. "God. That was something I hadn't even considered before you mentioned it. That complicates things."

"But is it *possible*? Could it possibly be Sariel?"

Sorren looked pole-axed. "I don't know. I hadn't thought about it." He looked at me. "The next time Daniel shows up, get him to commit to a meeting. Then text me. I want to know why he suddenly decided to come here."

"Not thrilled about it, but I'll get it set up," I said with an expression of distaste. "Oh, I also ran into Clockman over at Palmetto Meadows." I told him about the altercation in the parking lot. "He has a neighbor there. And he seems to be keeping an eye on old Mr. Thompson."

Sorren smiled. "Ah, Chuck Pettis. Another good resource. I asked him to watch Thompson because back in the day, Thompson was a pretty powerful wizard and Chuck already knew all about him. I want to assume that Thompson is out of the game, but wizards can live a long time, and he may not be as frail as he wants people to think."

I guess that hit men and wizards and bad-ass fighters get old, if they're lucky to live long enough, but it's difficult to imagine. Maybe there was more kick left in old Mr. Thompson than Chuck or I imagined. The question was, would he be a friend or a foe?

"There's also a nurse over there, Judy, who has at least a bit of magic," I added. "She's always been very nice to me and she fusses over Baxter, but I was surprised when I found out she had at least enough power to zap me when we brushed hands."

Sorren nodded. "She doesn't know about the Alliance, but she's one of the good guys," he said. "Part of a local coven, fairly talented with white magic." He shrugged. "You can understand that she doesn't broadcast that, given the circumstances."

I understood. Charleston was fine with its ghosts, but old ways of thinking died hard, and some folks in the community had unfriendly feelings toward anything that had to do with magic or witchcraft. Fortunately, those views were fading, but they weren't gone yet and they could certainly cause complications for someone in Judy's position.

"Her secret is safe with me," I said. "Did you have something to do with her being hired?"

Sorren smiled. "Always good to have a person on the inside," he replied. "Someone to watch over Helen – and keep an eye on Edwin Thompson."

"Could she protect them, if it came down to that?"

"Nurses without magic have done amazing things to protect their patients when the chips are down. I suspect her magic would trigger naturally in a dangerous situation, but I have no idea what that would mean, or what experience she has using her talent. Judy's not a bodyguard, just a friend with a little something extra."

"What next?"

Sorren put Baxter down on the floor gently, and stood. "I have some information I need to track down, and I'm still trying to get the Boston office back in order. I also need to talk to Archibald Donnelly over at the Briggs Society, and he's damnably hard to find. We need to talk to Daniel Hunter. There've been more threats against my Alliance sites and my personal safe houses, and now with the bomb at Trifles and Folly and the danger to the nursing home, I'm more certain than ever this is someone's vendetta against me. Someone who's willing to hurt my people to get to me. And if it's really Sariel, if he wasn't destroyed…" His voice trailed off. "So don't take chances," he said after a moment. I'll be back as soon as possible." He leveled a look at me. "Stay safe."

I picked Baxter up and walked Sorren to the door. But as the gate clicked shut behind him, I wondered how exactly I was supposed to avoid taking chances, and what 'safe' really meant under the circumstances.

Chapter Ten

IT'S NEVER A good day when the police are waiting outside your door in the morning.

"Cassidy Kincaide?" the dark-suited woman asked, coming up beside me just as I was unlocking the door to Trifles and Folly. "Detective Monroe, Charleston Police. I'd like to talk with you about the bomb someone left outside your shop last night."

I opened the door and stepped aside so she could enter. Detective Monroe's head turned one way and the other as she took in our merchandise. We had a pretty nice assortment on display at the moment: French mantel clocks, silver tea sets and place settings, vintage china, porcelain figurines, and more. The low jewelers' cases were empty since we put rings and small items in the safe overnight, but it didn't take much imagination to figure out what kinds of pieces we offered.

"Nice place," she said offhandedly. Her lack of interest told me old stuff wasn't her thing. I pegged Detective Monroe for early thirties. She had short dark hair and a no-nonsense attitude that was either career cop or ex-military. And while her voice tried for friendly, her eyes were coldly recording everything.

"You didn't bother to come down to the shop last night," she said as if she were just making conversation.

"I didn't need to," I replied, putting my purse in my office as the detective followed me around. I figured she was going to get a good look at the place one way or the other, and at least if I kept going on about my business I might be ready if customers walked in.

"Why not? Weren't you worried? Someone tried to blow the place up."

I met her gaze. "I saw the report on the news, and the police called me at home. The situation was already taken care of, as far as the bomb went. And if there's a whacko bomber running around Charleston, I couldn't see what the point would be of going down to my store in the dead of night and making a target of myself."

"Do you think you were the target?" Her voice was flat, but she was quick on the uptake. I didn't want her poking around.

"We don't know if the bomb was intended for our store, or if the placement was just an unfortunate coincidence," I said, though I had my own opinions on the matter. "If someone wants to set off a bomb downtown for whatever reason, it's going to be in front of *someone's* business. Right now, we don't know enough to leap to conclusions. We sell antiques. Not what most people consider to be a dangerous profession." That wasn't exactly the truth, but she wouldn't believe me if I told her, so I didn't.

"Your store's been around for a very long time," Monroe said, taking a slow tour of the shelves in the front. She didn't pick anything up to examine, but

I could see her making mental note of the details. "That's unusual."

"Not so much here in Charleston," I replied as I began to move trays of rings and bracelets and watches from the safe into the cases. "People love their history. And there are plenty of good antiques."

"Uh huh." She didn't look like the type who had much use for antiques. "So do you have any enemies, Ms. Kincaide?"

Yeah, but all of them are dead or undead, I thought. Not exactly something I could say out loud. "No one I can think of," I replied.

"Just odd for a random bomb to show up in front of a store and there to be absolutely no connection to the owners," she mused. Her casual manner didn't fool me a bit. Detective Monroe was a pit bull in a suit, and I wanted her gone and paying attention to someone else as quickly as possible.

"I'll be grateful when the police find whoever was responsible," I said, arranging the trays of jewelry carefully. My comment sounded good, but I knew the police weren't going to get to the bottom of this case. Not when supernatural bad guys were involved.

"Have you seen anyone lurking around the store?" she asked. "Anyone who didn't belong?"

Only Daniel Hunter, but he wasn't a problem for the police. "No. We get all types in here, but no one suspicious lately."

"I heard that you sometimes buy pieces from guys who bid on unclaimed baggage and abandoned storage units," Monroe said, taking way too long to make her way around our displays. "Sometimes, those types of people don't come by their merchandise in quite the way they say they do. Have you seen anything odd come through recently from those sources?"

I knew what she was hinting at. Sometimes, people who claimed to job odd lots tended to get a little iffy about ownership, meaning they were fencing stolen goods. In other cases, people who legitimately bid on luggage or storage units discovered later that the things they purchased were hot.

"We've been in business for over three hundred years, Detective," I said, trying to keep my voice neutral. "And that's never been a problem. Certainly it's never caused anyone to try to blow up the store – if the store was really the bomber's target. Are you even investigating the idea that the bomber could have had a different agenda – like mass panic?" I paused. "Did you have any other questions?" I added. "Because I don't think I have anything else to offer."

Monroe looked at me appraisingly. "Wasn't your part-time helper hurt when the guy next door disappeared?"

She damn well knew about Maggie. I was getting tired of playing games. "Yes, Maggie got hurt. Have your officers made any progress in finding the guy who went missing?"

Monroe might have heard the impatience in my voice. I saw a flicker of annoyance in her eyes. "No, we haven't. Seems like your employee got pretty lucky."

I put the last tray in the glass case and straightened up. "Detective Monroe," I said. "I'm a little confused. Last night, someone tried to set off a bomb in front of my store. Whether or not they were aiming for us in particular, that could have destroyed my business. A few days ago, my employee was hurt, as you note, in a yet-unsolved attack. It would seem to me that we're the ones needing the protection, but so far, this conversation has had an unfriendly tone to it, and I'd like to know why."

Monroe stood up sharply. I could see she didn't like to be challenged, but she was in my shop wasting my time, and since my people had been victimized, I'd had it with the insinuations.

"I've heard talk about you and your shop," Monroe replied, and there was a chill in her voice. "People say that strange stuff happens here. There's something a little hinky about this place. I've heard rumors that you specialize in haunted objects, that you think you're some kind of ghost whisperer."

I laughed out loud. "I'm not a medium, Detective. And I am most definitely not a ghost whisperer." Hell no. When I get desperate enough to talk at ghosts, I usually shout.

Monroe shrugged. "Whatever. I don't like charlatans who fill people's heads full of nonsense to inflate their prices."

I reined in my temper, knowing she was probably trying to get a rise out of me. "Detective, I'm betting that you looked into my store's history, and our rating with the business bureaus. If you have something specific to get off your chest, then let's hear it. But I don't appreciate your innuendo and if there's nothing more to discuss, I need to open my shop for the day."

Monroe didn't say anything for a moment. I was betting it was something she learned in cop school, a way to rattle your opponent's nerves. She had no idea that it took a lot more than that to rattle me, after what we dealt with on a regular basis.

"I've found that seemingly 'random' bombings and attacks usually aren't," she replied. "There's usually a tie of some sort, somewhere. And I'm wondering what it is."

"Well, you'll have to let me know when you find out."

"Oh, I will." A little smile touched her lips. "Don't worry about that." Detective Monroe turned and left just as Teag opened the door to come in. She paused, gave him an appraising glance tinged with disapproval, and walked out.

Teag closed the door behind her and waited until she was out of sight. "Who was that?" he asked. I could tell from his tone the Detective hadn't made a good first impression.

"Someone I've decided I don't like," I replied. I made a pot of coffee and heated up water for tea while I told him about my run-in with Monroe.

"If she's got a stick up her ass about anything haunted, she's not going to do too well in Charleston," Teag said, stirring extra sugar into his tea. "I'm guessing she's not from here."

"She didn't say, and I couldn't tell from her voice. Maybe she's just a show-me type." I sighed. "With everything that's been going on, it would have been nice to have a little sympathy."

Teag grimaced. "I live with a lawyer, remember? Cops only give sympathy when they're trying to get a confession out of you. She's got a point about attacks usually having some kind of link, even if it's only in the mind of the attacker. And her instincts are dead on. There is a link, just not something we could tell her about."

"I know. But the whole thing just has me worried, and now Sorren's gone off to chase down 'resources', whatever that means." I recounted the conversation with Sorren the night before.

"Speaking of which, I need to go over to the nursing home, and I'd rather do it in daylight. Can you cover for me?"

Teag nodded. "Sure. And expect to see Maggie later today, even if she is on crutches. I think she's bored recuperating."

I grinned. "That's good. I wouldn't have blamed her if she'd have lit out like a rocket after what she saw."

Teag raised an eyebrow. "I think Maggie's made of sterner stuff than that."

It took me an hour to calm down after Detective Monroe's visit. I tried to tell myself that she was just doing her job, and that it was probably some kind of standard police protocol to insult the victim in order to make sure he or she hadn't staged the incident, but I was still annoyed as hell. There wasn't a whole lot mundane authorities could do in this situation, but if Monroe's attitude didn't change, we weren't likely to get any help, period.

Maggie came in around lunch. I hated to see her on crutches, but she got around like a pro. "I've learned something about myself," she said, and hobbled over to the chair Teag had pulled behind the main counter. "I do not convalesce well." She looked at me intently. "Did you know that there is absolutely nothing worth watching on daytime television?"

Teag and I fussed over her, letting her know how glad we were that she was feeling better. Teag brought her a cup of coffee, and I made sure she had a stool to prop up her sore ankle. She had brought two ice pack wraps, one to use now and one to have in the break room freezer. Once Maggie was set up, Teag gave me a nod and I slipped out to fulfill my promise to Sorren by visiting Palmetto Meadows.

First, I swung by the house to pick up Baxter. He met me at the door hopping around like a crazed fluff-bunny, since he is always up for a car trip. Even though it was broad daylight, I was cautious. I parked as close as I could to the door to the Alzheimer's unit, and scanned the parking lot before I got out of the car. My athame was up the sleeve of my sweater, and Bo's collar was around my other wrist. To my relief, no strange shadows or restless ghosts menaced me as I headed into the nursing home.

"Hi Cassidy! Hi Baxter!" Judy was at the nurses' station when I arrived.

I grinned. "Hey there. I just wanted to stop by and make sure everyone was okay. I saw the news yesterday. Thought people might like a little Baxter time to relax."

"That would be fantastic," Judy replied. She sobered. "Can you believe someone would do something like that? Fortunately, nothing actually happened. But still."

Baxter tugged on his leash to come around the side of the nurses' station, and Judy bent down to pet him and ruffle his ears. "Yep. I think a dose of Baxter is just what the doctor ordered today," she said, smiling at him fondly. "Go on into the activity room. It looked like most of our folks were up and about the last time I checked."

We got a pretty energetic ovation when the residents spotted us, although I knew they were really clapping for Baxter. And despite my ulterior motives of checking up on Mrs. Butler and Mr. Thompson, it made me really happy to see all those faces light up. Baxter toddled into the room like a superstar, knowing he was the center of attention. I could feel the tension in the room ease as we made our rounds.

"Is it that time already?" Mrs. Talheimer reached down to pet Baxter. "Oh, my. I don't have my pretzels with me!"

"That's all right," I replied. "We're not here on our regular day. And the vet says Baxter put on a few ounces. It won't hurt him to miss a few treats."

Mrs. Talheimer gave me a conspiratorial smile. "A couple of pretzels won't make a difference," she said. "And it does make him wag, doesn't it?"

Baxter looked up at me, the poster-dog for innocence, as if he didn't know treats were part of the routine. We moved on. Even though Mrs. Peterson was playing cards with Miss Henderson, they waved us closer so they could fuss over him. I glanced at their cards. I'm not sure whether they were playing any game in particular or both even playing the same game, but they were having a good time. Judy had told me that sometimes they remembered the rules, and sometimes they didn't. Usually, it takes us about an hour to circle the room, but today took longer. It was worth it to watch the residents relax as they petted Baxter and let him nuzzle against their hands.

The great thing about bringing a therapy dog onto an Alzheimer's unit is that even if people have forgotten who they are, lost the memories of their own children, and misplaced their personal history, they remember that they like dogs. And dogs don't care if you remember their names or not, as long as you love them.

"Ho there, Tilly!" I heard Mr. Thompson's voice behind me.

Baxter waggled and headed his direction. Wheelchairs are a danger to little dogs like Maltese, so I lifted him up so Mr. Thompson could pet him. "Good girl, Tilly," he said.

"He likes you," I said as Baxter let the man stroke his fur with his large, gnarled hand.

"Humph," Mr. Thompson replied.

This time, I made sure my hand touched his. Again, I felt the electric charge, and he looked up at me, "You have power," he hissed.

I took a chance. "So do you," I replied quietly.

His eyes widened. "Don't say that! They'll hear you!"

"Who?"

He glanced around and leaned in. "The Judge. He was here, you know. But he didn't get us."

"Is that why you use the salt? For a warding?"

Suspicion glinted in his eyes. "How did you know about that?"

"Like you said – I have some magic, too."

"Then you'd better be careful," Mr. Thompson said, meeting my gaze with a clear-eyed look. "Because they'll come looking for you, too." And with that, he maneuvered his chair around me and headed down the hallway.

What if he's not as befuddled as he wanted to seem? I wondered. It wouldn't be difficult for someone clever to fake dementia. Get to a certain age, and even some medical people see what they expect to see. I wondered if Thompson had been wily enough to hide in plain sight, somewhere that might prompt his enemies to write him off as no longer important. And once again, as I watched him wheel away, I wondered whether old Mr. Thompson was friend or foe.

"Who said you could bring a dog in here?"

I looked up as a dark-haired young nurse I had never seen before made a bee-line over to us. "Baxter's a certified therapy dog," I said, taken-aback. I pointed to the little vest Bax wears that lets people know he's a working dog. "We come here at least once a week."

She scowled at me. "Nobody told me about it."

"It's all right, Becky," Nurse Judy must have seen the confrontation from her desk. "Cassidy and Baxter have cleared all their paperwork." Judy was smiling, but it was strained. I wondered if she had run into other problems with Becky. That was likely, given Becky's attitude.

"If he bites anyone, I'm going on record that I objected," Becky said sullenly.

"That won't be necessary," Judy replied. Her smile had slipped into a tight-lipped look that meant business. I felt a subtle shift in the energy around her, a reminder that Judy had some magic of her own. I didn't pick up any sense of power from Becky, but there was a darkness to her I didn't like. It surprised me the nursing home would hire someone who seemed like such a grouch.

Judy sighed as Becky walked away. "I'm sorry about that," she said. "She's new, and I think she's letting some personal issues affect her work." She raised an eyebrow. "Boyfriend problems."

I nodded sympathetically. "Well, maybe she'll cheer up," I said.

Judy rolled her eyes. "Maybe. Anyhow, she won't bother you and Baxter anymore. I'll make sure of it."

I thanked Judy, and then looked around for Mrs. Butler. She hadn't been in the activities room. I thought she might be napping in her room when I spotted her out in the walled garden. I watched her through the window for a moment. She moved haltingly with the use of a walker. Even though she was closing in on being a century old, it was easy to see the high cheekbones and regular features that must have been striking in her youth.

I led Baxter out into the garden. It was a beautiful place, circled by a high brick wall so residents couldn't wander away. The garden enclosure also provided a lovely view for two of the big floor-to-ceiling windows in the activity room. Mrs. Butler turned at the sound. There was a momentary expression of expectation on her face, followed by confusion, and then resignation. "Hi Mrs. Butler!" I said cheerily. "I brought Baxter for an extra visit this week, and I wanted to make sure you got a chance to see him. You had company the last time we came."

Mrs. Butler sat down shakily on the bench where I had seen her talking with Sorren. "Did I?" she asked, looking at me intently as she tried to place where she had seen me before. "Oh well. What a cute dog. What do you call him?"

"Baxter. He's very friendly, if you want to pet him." My heart broke a little. We go through this every week. She loves petting Baxter, but she just can't remember his name. I sighed. *On the bright side, that makes his visit a new discovery each time.*

"Have you met my young man?" she asked, and looked around as if for someone who had just stepped away. "He was just here."

"I don't believe I've seen him. Does he visit often?"

"Often?" she said, frowning. "Oh, I don't know. But he promised to take me dancing. Only, I can't find my good shoes. Do you know where they went?"

I shook my head. "No. But someone will help you look for them," I replied. I nodded toward Baxter, who was out-doing himself on cuteness. "I think Baxter really likes you."

"Baxter? No, his name isn't Baxter. It's…" She frowned as memory eluded her. "Something else. I'll think of it." She looked down at Baxter. "This little fellow's cute. What do you call him?"

I was used to conversations like this with the residents at Palmetto Meadows. Like an old vinyl record with a scratch in it, words or whole phrases looped over and over again. The same few questions could be asked and answered a dozen times in ten minutes, and only one of us knew about the repetition. It had never bothered me before. Maybe that was because I didn't know any of these folks before the dementia set in, so I didn't expect them to be someone they weren't anymore. I couldn't imagine what it must be like for Sorren.

In almost six hundred years, how many friends has he buried?

I was just in my mid-twenties, and I knew the pain of losing a few people to car accidents and suicide, boating mishaps and unexpected illness. *Multiply that by hundreds, thousands. Maybe more, in a dangerous business like the Alliance.* I didn't want to think it through, so I pushed the thoughts from my mind and forced a smile to my face.

"I've got to get back to my store," I said. "But I'll bring Baxter another day."

"I need to run my errands," Mrs. Butler replied. "If I don't get groceries, there won't be dinner tonight." I wondered which decade of her life her memory had skipped tracks to land on. It made me think of all the time travel movies I'd watched, where people hop from one era to another in the blink of an eye. On TV, it looks exciting and adventurous. Here at the Meadows, there was a glitch in the switch, so that you never knew where your personal time-addling machine was taking you, how long you'd stay, or where you'd go next. And for most of the residents, that time machine went mostly to the past, with brief, sporadic stops in the here and now.

I'd learned after my first couple of visits that it was better to just disappear than to say good-bye, so Baxter and I sidled to the door by the nurses' station and motioned for Judy to buzz us through. Memory Support units have alarmed doors and restricted access so residents don't go wandering. But now, knowing that Mr. Thompson – and possibly other residents – had magic that might put them at risk, I felt better knowing they had another layer of security protecting them.

Something made me glance back as Baxter and I started toward the car. Mr. Thompson sat framed in one of the big glass windows. He was watching us, and his gaze was lucid and sharp. Across his lap was a wooden cane. Mr. Thompson saw me, and nodded. A shiver went down my spine. I knew what my magic could do with a spoon and a walking stick. I wondered whether anyone at Palmetto Meadows realized that Mr. Thompson could likely do a lot more than walk with that cane of his. I just hoped that, if I ever found out exactly what he could do, we were on the same side.

I took Baxter home and gave him a treat, then headed back to the shop. The afternoon was busy with a busload of tourists from Canada. Even though we were into what passes for cooler Fall weather, every person who came in remarked on how warm it was. The tour seemed to have a lot of retired schoolteachers, and they loved our estate jewelry.

"Nine rings, seven pairs of earrings, four bracelets, two old watches, and a necklace!" I tallied up triumphantly when we finally closed for the day. "I think that's the best jewelry day we've had in a long time."

"That should pay the rent," Teag said with a grin. He knew as well as I did that my family had owned the building for centuries, and that because of our work for the Alliance, Sorren would underwrite the shop, even if it didn't pay its own way. Since we spent so much of our time being 'supernatural vigilantes', Sorren paid us very well for the risks we took. But I was happiest when Trifles and Folly actually turned a profit, because aside from all our ghost-busting and demon ass-kicking, I really did love all the marvelous old treasures that came into the store – at least, the ones that didn't try to kill us.

"Well, you can add one more ring and a bracelet to the tally," Maggie said, pulling out her wallet. "One of the reasons I was keen on coming in today – aside from seeing the two of you and getting back to my job, of course – was that I wanted to buy that onyx ring and matching necklace that came in last week."

I knew just the set she was talking about, an art deco onyx and silver combination that looked just as stylish now as it would have done years ago. Since Maggie had commented before on liking it, I had made sure to handle it, assuring myself there were no hidden surprises. The onyx and silver had protective qualities and whoever had owned the pieces before must have been pretty happy, because the impressions I received were positive and energetic.

Teag rang Maggie up. With her employee discount, she got a good deal, and it was worth it to see the smile on her face as she tried the pieces on. "I feel so pretty in these I could just twirl!" Maggie declared, then sighed as she glanced down at her crutches. "But not today," she added ruefully.

"Save the twirling for when you're all patched up," I said.

Maggie gathered her things, then preened at her reflection in the window for a moment as she left the store. I flipped the sign to closed and let out a long breath.

"Wow. What a week."

"No kidding," Teag said. "Oh, and there was one other transaction today while you were out, but I didn't want to bring it up while Maggie was here."

"Sell something?"

"No, but we bought something," he said walking over to the counter. "A sweet pair of dueling pistols."

"Please tell me that the owner wasn't suddenly having bad dreams."

"Not that he mentioned," Teag answered. He pulled out a box from below the counter and opened the top. Inside was a pair of expertly-crafted pistols that would have been beautiful if it weren't for the fact they were made to kill. Charleston had a big problem with dueling back in the 1800s, and a lot of young men died. These pistols looked like they had seen plenty of use.

"What made him sell the pistols?" I asked.

"Said he needed the money because his son's going to college."

I frowned. "How did you set a price? Normally, we'd have the gun appraiser take a look at them."

Teag shrugged. "He told me what he wanted for them, and at that amount, we'd make a profit even if they turn out to be reproductions."

I'm always in favor of an honest bargain, but something about the man's story didn't add up. If the buyer were anybody but Teag, I'd be concerned that the pistols might have been stolen, but Teag was good at running a check for something like that. Then I let my right hand hover over the box, and drew back right away.

"They're Spookies, all right," I said, using our term for an item that was magically dangerous. Even that brief contact gave me a single, searing image of a man in a long dark coat fighting for his life, flares of sickly green light that could only have been magic, and an awful sense of finality that told me the original owner of the guns had not survived the battle.

"Let's put them back in the office," I said, rattled a little from what I had seen. "Were you able to get any provenance on the pistols?" I asked, as Teag closed up the box and carried it to the back.

"A little," he replied. "He said they belonged to a man named Josiah Winfield, back in the 1850s. I got the feeling from what he said that Winfield was kinda like a private investigator, hired to look into problems. Anyhow, the seller claimed that a lot of tall tales got told about Winfield, like stories about him fighting off warlocks and vampires." Teag raised an eyebrow.

"That's why you bought them," I said. "Winfield was probably working for the Alliance. Want to bet he knew my ancestors?"

"I figured Sorren would know something about Winfield, probably even worked with him if Winfield was legitimate."

"I'm still wondering about the timing," I said. "It seems like too much of a coincidence for the pistols to suddenly show up now." I texted Sorren a quick message about the pistols and Winfield, curious to see what he would say.

"I thought the same thing, but the old guy who brought them in never let on if something had spooked him into selling," Teag said. Most people who sell magically-charged objects to us don't say what makes them so anxious to strike a deal. Maybe they're afraid that being haunted will hurt the price. We generally pay well enough for 'unusual' items that the owners make the sale on the spot. I've heard it's whispered that Trifles and Folly is the best place to get rid of 'problem' pieces. Good for business, and good for the Alliance.

Just then my phone let me know I'd gotten a text message. "It's from Sorren," I said. That was odd. It was a few hours before sunset, and Sorren was usually sleeping. He's old enough to be able to stay awake during daylight – so long as he's in a completely dark place – but doing so drains him, so I've heard him say that he avoids it unless absolutely necessary. The fact that he was up now told me he was really worried about everything that was going on.

"And?" Teag asked, watching as I read the message.

"He asked if we could bring the pistols out to his house. He'll look at them later tonight." I paused. "Uh oh. He said to be very careful. 'Make sure you're protected.'" I looked up and met Teag's gaze.

"He sounds worried."

"Yeah. So am I. I think all of the things that are going on are related, I'm just not sure how. But if someone is out to get Sorren, we're bound to be in the crosshairs, too."

Chapter Eleven

I HAD ONLY been out to Sorren's house a few times. It was out in the country, not terribly far from Charleston, but far enough to feel separate from the bustle of the city. The house was just a bit newer than antebellum, small by former plantation standards. The barns held thoroughbred horses, not farm equipment, and the home itself was tastefully decorated. Sorren had told me that the house was one of several he kept around the world, managed through third parties to hide his longevity, and staffed by a handful of loyal and discreet long-time servants.

"Any word from Sorren on the trouble with the other locations?" Teag asked as we headed up the long driveway.

I shook my head. "No, but he may have more to tell us when we see him. Whoever's been targeting Sorren's connections isn't likely to let up until he gets what he wants." Sorren was fairly closed-mouth about the extent of the Alliance's operations. Part of me was curious, but I figured that it was Sorren's way of protecting us. Knowledge was a dangerous thing in our business.

The home at the end of the road was framed by an allée of live oak trees, with white pillars, large windows and a wide front porch. Carefully tended gardens graced both sides of the entrance. "Those flowers are gorgeous," Teag noted. "It's too bad Sorren never gets to see them in sunlight."

I knew from experience that Sorren's home was protected by several types of magical wardings, even more elaborate than the ones Lucinda had placed around Teag and my homes and the store. That was in addition to a modern security system. The wardings were tuned to keep out magical threats and supernatural predators, and while I could feel a shimmer of energy as we crossed the protective barriers, I saw nothing out of the ordinary.

A droning buzz made me look up. Through the canopy of live oak branches, I glimpsed a dark shape in the sky. We were heading for the house not long before sundown. I figured that by the time we got settled in, Sorren would be rising for the night.

"That helicopter looks awfully low," Teag said, squinting.

"And it's coming in at the wrong angle to land," I said, worried as the chopper headed straight for Sorren's house.

"It's not going to land – it's going to crash!" Teag slammed on the brakes. The helicopter slammed into the antebellum house. I threw my arms up over my face to protect myself and huddled in a crash position, eyes squeezed shut.

The explosion rocked our car although we were still half a mile away, and the fireball was so bright it flared red through my closed eyelids. When I dared to raise my head, the whole building was on fire. Its roof was gone, the windows were blown out, and flames leaped into the sky.

"Come on!" I said, unfastening my seatbelt and opening my door. "Sorren's in there – or at least his staff are!"

Teag was right behind me as we jogged closer to the site of the explosion. "There's no way a regular helicopter would cause that big of an explosion," Teag said as we surveyed the damage.

"You think it was a bomb?"

Teag nodded. "Yeah. And flying in got around Sorren's wardings since it wasn't magic."

"A suicide pilot?" The heat kept us from getting anywhere near the remains of the house, but I hoped that if anyone had escaped, we might be able to help get the injured clear of the blast zone.

"Maybe," Teag said. "Or it could have been remote controlled. No way to tell until the fire stops burning."

Fortunately, the wind was taking the smoke away from us as we circled the house. Around back, we found a dazed woman lying in the yard. Teag and I rushed over. Her face was red with the heat and her clothing was scorched in places from the blast, but she was breathing, and her eyes fluttered open as we knelt next to her.

"Can you move?" I asked, eyeing how close we were to the house. It was hot enough that sweat was pouring down my face and my skin felt sunburned. Burning embers floated down all around us, and I flinched as one sizzled against my skin.

The woman nodded, and I got under her shoulder, helping her limp far enough away to be out of the range of the embers and upwind of the smoke. A few moments later, Teag joined us. He was supporting a dazed-looking man with a bloody gash on his forehead.

My heart broke as I stared at Sorren's burning house. There was no way we could possibly go inside without full firefighting gear, and given how hot the flames were and how much of the structure was burning, I wasn't even sure the firefighters would chance it.

"They're inside," the woman rasped.

"Who?" I asked.

"The rest of the staff."

"How many?" Teag asked. He was eyeing the house, but I knew from the look on his face that he, too, had concluded that going in would be suicide. On my few prior visits, I had only met a butler and a housekeeper. I was betting a house this size needed more people than that to maintain it, and I feared for anyone who had been inside when the 'copter hit.

"Two," she croaked. "Ben was in the garden with me," she added with a nod toward the man.

Running footsteps made us turn, expecting an assailant. Instead, a woman with red hair tied back in a thick braid, jeans and a work shirt came from the direction of the horse barn, which was far enough away to be out of danger.

"Patsy! Ben!" she cried out, then drew up short at the sight of us. "Who are you?"

"We work for Sorren, at Trifles and Folly," I explained. "We came by to drop off a package for him."

"Well, it's good you weren't a little bit earlier, or you and your package would be in there," she said with a jerk of her head. "I'm Anna, and I take care of the horses."

I felt sick, staring at the fire as the house was rapidly reduced to a charred shell. *Did Sorren have his day crypt under the house? If he did, will the heat affect him even if the flames can't reach him? And can he get out, if the house collapses on top of the cellar?*

In the distance, I could hear sirens. Teag and I exchanged a glance that told me we were on the same wavelength. *Detective Monroe is going to have a field day finding us here.*

"Get out of here," Anna said. "Go out the back way. It's unpaved and unmarked, so you won't run into the cops and the firefighters on the way out. I'll see to Patsy and Ben."

Teag and I nodded our thanks and ran for the car. The sirens were closer, and I did not want to end up in a holding cell while Detective Monroe tried to figure out what to do about us. Teag's car bumped and jostled as we stayed to the outer edge of the driveway as it circled the burning house, not wanting to leave tell-tale tracks on the grass. We picked up speed as we headed past the horse barn, and followed the two lines of bare dirt that marked the maintenance road. I held my breath as we reached the main thoroughfare, but let out a sigh of relief as I realized it was not the same road we had come in on; this stretch was deserted.

I didn't start breathing evenly again until we were halfway back to the city. "Wow," I said.

Teag had a white-knuckled grip on the steering wheel. "Yeah," he replied. I was still in shock, and I figured he was, too. Things blow up in the movies all the time, but when your friend's house explodes right in front of you, and you know there were people inside you couldn't help, words just aren't sufficient.

"Do you think he –" I started, but couldn't finish.

Teag shrugged, with a pained look on his face. "No way to know," he said. "He's survived this long. It's probably not the first time someone's tried to burn him out."

I would be thrilled if Sorren survived the attack, but that didn't blunt the loss of his staff. They had been in the wrong place at the wrong time – as we nearly were – and whoever had caused the explosion didn't care about civilian casualties. Sorren would be devastated. He chose his household staff very carefully, and many had been with him for years. A few, those trusted with his secret, had served him for decades. Losing them would be like losing family.

"Whoever did this isn't just trying to destroy Sorren," I said, feeling anger rush in to push grief aside. "Whoever's doing these things wants to hurt as many of Sorren's people as possible in the process. He's right – someone's got a vendetta against him."

"After all the years Sorren has been with the Alliance, he's probably made more than a few immortals angry," Teag replied. "But why now? And who?" *Sariel*, I thought. But until we could prove it, we couldn't fight anything, and I was ready to do some fighting.

Teag was careful to keep to the speed limit. We did not need to be pulled over anywhere close to the explosion. He chanced a look at me. "Do you have any contacts at the Alliance? Anyone you could connect with?" He didn't have to finish the thought. *In case Sorren is really gone.*

I shook my head, and forced myself not to tear up, although it felt like I had a rock in my throat. "No. Sorren was my only direct contact. He said it was safer that way."

"Daniel Hunter knows how to contact the Alliance."

I glared at him. "Daniel Hunter might be involved in the explosion. I don't like him and I don't trust him."

"I agree. But he *is* a link. Just something to keep in mind."

I crossed my arms, still badly rattled by what had happened. Someone had tried to kill Sorren. Someone had almost killed us. And whoever it was had almost certainly killed whichever unlucky staff members had been in the house at the time of the blast. I didn't want justice. I wanted revenge.

"Let's go back to your place," Teag suggested. "We can see what's on the news, and I can do some digging online to see what the police and fire investigators found out."

"What about Anthony?"

"He's going to be working late again. Unless you'd rather come to our place. If it would make you feel better, you can even pick up Baxter and spend the night."

Much as I appreciated the offer, I declined the invitation. When we got to my house, I checked to make sure Lucinda's wardings were in place. Since I lived downtown, I was hopeful that whoever had dropped a helicopter on Sorren's house wouldn't do something quite so splashy in a more populated area, but I still resolved to talk to Lucinda about assuring I was protected from overhead threats the next time I saw her.

Teag seemed to be thinking the same thing. "I'll check the wardings on our house when I get home," he said. "Just in case."

Baxter greeted both of us with furry frenzy, and I was particularly glad to cuddle with him as I switched on the TV. Teag poured us each a glass of wine. I had lasagna in the freezer that would make a good emergency dinner, and enough lettuce for a salad, so we were covered for supper. I put the lasagna in the oven and took a quick shower to get the smell of smoke and the light covering of soot off my skin and out of my hair, then I settled in on the couch to channel surf coverage of the explosion, while Teag got a shower and went in my office to work his magic on the web.

"Minute-by-minute coverage of the recent bombing –"

"We'll give you the latest on what could be a terrorist attack right here in Charleston –"

"Reporters are on the scene for updates on a helicopter crash and house fire –"

In each case, a perfectly-coiffed news reporter looked earnestly into the camera against a background of smoke and flames. I stifled a sob as one of the cameras panned to show the scene. Sorren's magnificent old mansion had been reduced to rubble and a few burnt walls.

My phone rang, and I snatched it out of my pocket, hoping it was Sorren. Father Anne's number came up, and her voice was worried. "Cassidy – I'm watching the news and that house fire, is that Sorren's place?"

"Yes it is," I confirmed, but I was leery of going into more detail over the phone. "We haven't heard from him, and we don't know any details. But if we find out something, I'll let you know."

Lucinda called a few moments later, and I told her the same thing. The next time my phone rang, I did not recognize the number, but the voice was familiar, if surprising.

"I told you this wasn't a game." Daniel Hunter's voice was a growl.

"It's about time you returned my calls," I said, sorrow turning quickly to anger. "I've been trying to reach you for days."

"Doesn't matter. Someone got past your boss's defenses. Not too many people could do that. Are you ready to take this seriously yet?"

His arrogance made me angry, and I was already in the mood to hit something. "I've always taken this seriously," I snapped. "Sorren asked me to set up a meeting with you. What can you help us do to fight the problem?"

"Now you're asking the right questions," Hunter replied, with a tone that said he enjoyed being insufferable. "I've been watching the power spikes in the magic around here. I think that something is trying to come through to our world from somewhere else, maybe bring a few of its buddies with it. Whatever it is feeds on the ghosts for energy, and it's munched people on staircases, too. I'm trying to get ahead of it, and you should be doing that, too, unless you want it all to fall apart on your watch." He paused. "Let's wait on a meeting until we see whether Sorren is still around or not." He hung up on me before I could reply.

All Hunter's talking had made me miss the updates about the explosion. I flipped through the channels quickly.

" – helicopter seen right before the explosion…"

" – no flight plan filed, not sure who it belonged to…"
" – house owned by an old family trust, not yet able to find out who lived there…"

I froze as the next channel showed smoldering ruins and EMTs carrying out a stretcher with a body under a white sheet. "No word yet on whose remains were found in the wreckage of the house. Police say three bodies have been recovered, but given the nature of the explosion, it might be some time before we discover who they were."

The reporters seemed so detached, and while I knew that was their job, tonight I wanted everyone else to be stirred by the same rage and need for vengeance I felt, the anger that propped me up and kept me from sinking into despair.

I knew the stories wouldn't update again for a while, so I turned the volume down and leaned back on the couch. Whenever I shut my eyes, I saw the helicopter falling from the sky, saw it hit the house and explode, and watched flames shooting higher than the tallest trees.

I must have fallen asleep, because Teag woke me by calling my name. I shook my head to clear it, and turned up the volume on the news since the background footage had changed again.

"Helicopter was stolen –"

"Pilot believed to have died in the crash, although teams will be sifting through the wreckage –"

"The organization which owned the house has released the names of two of the people killed in the fire –"

Teag motioned for me to turn down the volume. "I found a few leads," he said, sitting down on the couch. "All the law enforcement agencies are fighting over whose turf this is on," he said. "FBI, Homeland Security, FAA, State Police and the Charleston Police – they all want a piece of it."

"And?"

"The Feds know a little more about the helicopter than what's being said on the news," Teag replied. "It was stolen yesterday, which means whoever did this had almost twenty-four hours to upfit the copter as a bomb."

"Do you think someone actually flew it into the house?"

Teag shrugged. "Looks likely, but the Feds aren't saying much – though there was an extra body near the 'copter wreckage."

"What about Patsy and Ben and Anna?" I asked. "Any word on how they are?"

Teag nodded. "I hacked into the EMT report. Patsy and Ben were treated for smoke inhalation and Ben had a concussion. Anna was fine."

"Did they tell anyone they had seen us?"

"Not according to the reports that have been filed so far," Teag replied. "I'd expect Sorren's staff to be trained not to volunteer information. Patsy and Ben weren't really up to doing much talking, and Anna was mostly worried about the other two staff members in the house."

"Can they trace the property back to Sorren?"

Teag chuckled. "As the original owner back in 1670, but since then, the land has passed through a maze of holding companies and trusts. It would take a team of lawyers a lifetime to unsnarl the ownership – which is what I'm sure Sorren intended."

"Anything else?" I was feeling the effects of the day and the wine, and I wanted to know whether Sorren was dead or alive.

"Yeah – and it wasn't what I was looking for," Teag replied. "The NSA measured two big EMF spikes in the last two weeks near Charleston, and the base EMF frequencies jumped up ten percent above normal after the spikes."

"The souped-up ghost activity," I said, meeting his gaze. "And two big spikes could mean magical events that did something to cause that baseline jump."

Teag nodded. "That was my suspicion, although of course the NSA is more worried about terrorists."

I didn't protest as Teag refilled my wine glass. "We've got plenty of pieces, but no idea what the puzzle picture looks like. And I think Mr. Thompson and Mrs. Teller and everyone else who has been warning us about a storm coming are right. Something big is building, but what?" *And how do we fight it if Sorren is really gone?*

Teag was just getting ready to go after supper when I heard a knock at the front door. Most people ring the bell at the door on the side of the piazza, since it's generally considered that the porch is part of the house itself, so it would be rude to walk in uninvited. *Unless you've got a good reason not to want to be seen,* I thought, jumping up to answer the door with my heart pounding. I stopped long enough to grab Alard's walking stick and ready the collar on my left wrist, just in case there was trouble. Teag was right behind me, ready for a fight. No one should have been able to get through the wardings, but with everything that had been going on, I wasn't taking any chances.

Sorren stood on the porch looking as if he had clawed his way out of a grave. His skin was streaked with soot and dirt, and his blond hair was dirty and tangled. Along his arms and on his face I could see newly-healed cuts. His color was normal, suggesting that he had fed, but he looked on the verge of collapse.

"Come in – quickly!" I said, worried about his condition and elated that he had survived. He was limping, which for a vampire could mean anything from broken bones to internal injuries that would kill a mortal. But he was still in one piece, and that was good enough.

"You fed?" Teag asked as Sorren staggered to the couch and sat down. In an emergency, Teag has supplied blood for Sorren to heal.

Sorren nodded. "From the horses," he said, and managed a scratchy chuckle. "Don't worry about them – they're fine. But I needed blood quickly, and they were close by. Healing requires more blood than a normal feeding."

"You were in the basement when the house exploded?" I asked.

Sorren nodded. "My crypt wasn't damaged. Unfortunately, the passageways to the surface collapsed. It made leaving very difficult."

"How did you survive the fire?" Teag asked.

"The crypt was deep enough, and insulated enough, that it kept the flames at bay. The heat, however, nearly got the best of me." Sorren's gaze was haunted. "And although I survived, two of my people were not so lucky." I could hear the sorrow in his voice. "They had been with me for fifty years."

"I'm so sorry," I said.

"Anna said you were there, when the explosion happened," Sorren said, raising his gaze to meet mine. "Tell me what you saw."

Teag and I took turns recounting the helicopter crash and the explosion, as well as the aftermath in the rear yard and our hurried departure. Sorren listened quietly as Teag filled him in on what he had learned online, and I supplied what the news organizations were saying.

"They're wrong and right at the same time," Sorren replied, leaning back against the couch as if his strength was nearly spent. "It is a terrorist attack – but a magical one. But it's not Charleston the bomber is after. It's me. I'm certain of it now. As certain as I am that somehow, Sariel survived."

"More attacks?" I asked.

"There have been attacks on three of my other stores, in addition to the Boston incident and the other attacks I told you about," Sorren replied. "And the bomb at Trifles and Folly. That can't be a coincidence."

"We've had lots of supernatural stuff try to kill us," Teag said. "What makes you think it's different this time?"

Sorren was quiet for a minute, as if he was trying to decide how to answer and how much to tell us. "It started a month ago with threats – emails, letters, packages. Nothing dangerous, but each one a warning that someone was watching me, someone knew how to find me. No hint why or who." He gave a mirthless chuckle. "Over the centuries, I've made my share of enemies. It's not a short list, even among the immortals." Sorren paused. "It's the Nephilim angle that has me puzzled. Nephilmancy isn't a common type of magic. The last time I ran into a nephilmancer, it was more than a hundred years ago. Sariel. I killed his son and until now, I was certain that I had destroyed Sariel, too."

"No other nephilmancers since then?" I asked.

Sorren gave a dispirited shrug. "Not that I've heard of, but I've been asking all my contacts to see what they can find. A nephilmancer is bad enough, but the vendetta angle... that's the real puzzle. The only way I can make sense of it is if Sariel is still alive – and wants revenge." He shook his head. "It would explain the ramped-up ghost activity here in Charleston, if Sariel was calling Reapers to do his bidding."

"Would being dead stop Sariel?" Teag asked. "It's not exactly a deal breaker in our business."

Sorren raised an eyebrow. "His son was completely destroyed. I saw Sariel disappear into a fireball. When the fire was gone, there was no trace of him and no further problems – until now."

"How about someone who might have a grudge on Sariel's behalf?" I asked. "Since it's not just a nephilmancer we're up against, it's one who seems to be stalking you in particular."

"I'll see what I can find on the Darke Web," Teag volunteered.

"And I will tap my resources as well," Sorren said. "Although if Sariel did somehow survive and he's come back for vengeance, he's managed to keep a low profile. The Alliance would have noted his return, if he made it public."

"We might have a thread to start tying things together," Teag said. "What do you know about a man named Josiah Winfield?"

Chapter Twelve

"JOSIAH WINFIELD?" SORREN frowned. "I haven't heard that name in a very long time."

"Back up," Teag said. "Who was Josiah Winfield? Was he with the Alliance?"

Sorren leaned back in his chair and stared off into the distance for a moment. I imagine that after nearly six hundred years, it takes time to remember things. "Josiah Winfield worked with the Alliance on occasion when it suited his purposes, but he wasn't part of it," Sorren said quietly. "He was a supernatural bounty hunter."

Teag raised an eyebrow. "Who pays the bounty?"

"Creatures who have existed for a long time tend to have acquired many enemies," Sorren replied. "There's always someone who wants to even a score."

"I didn't touch the pistols, but just from running my hand above them, I got an image of a fight that didn't look like it went well for Josiah," I said.

Sorren nodded. "He fought a lot of battles, but he died during a duel. That was a loss. Josiah was more principled than many Hunters, the best of a dangerous bunch."

"Hunter? You mean like Daniel Hunter?" I asked. "And what happened to Winfield?"

Sorren was quiet for a moment, and I had the feeling that his thoughts were far away. "Yes, 'Hunter' like Daniel," he said finally. "It's a job description, not a surname. As for Josiah Winfield, he was part of a team that went up against... Sariel. The last time Sariel was here in Charleston, bringing Nephilim across to do his dirty work, it was in 1854. The Yellow Fever epidemic. Except it wasn't just the disease killing people. Sariel summoned Watchers from the other side, and together with the Nephilim, they harvested souls to feed on. Sariel made himself the judge, jury, and executioner."

"Judge," I echoed. Teag and Sorren looked at me. "Mr. Thompson keeps talking about a judge. He told me, 'The Judge comes at midnight'. Daniel also mentioned Watchers and Reapers."

"Now I'm even more convinced that this whole mess has something to do with Sariel," Sorren said. "This can't all be coincidence. But before we do anything else, let me take a look at those pistols."

We went out to the kitchen, where Teag had left the dueling pistols when we came in from the car.

"The man who brought in the pistols said he believed they still worked, but he hasn't fired them," Teag said as Sorren inspected the guns carefully.

"Indeed," Sorren murmured, and as he handled the pistols, I had the feeling he was looking for something specific.

"You said you didn't handle the guns, Cassidy, yet you had a mental image of Josiah Winfield in a magical battle?"

I nodded. "Teag supplied the name. I saw the history."

Sorren set the guns back in their case. "They're

Winfield's pistols," he said. "I saw his mark on the grip. Cassidy couldn't have seen that unless she handled them, and even then, she wouldn't have known what it meant. They're the real thing."

"Since we're all together, how about if I take a look at the pistols myself?" I said, managing to sound braver than I felt. My visions seem to be getting more detailed, but I still can't control my reactions as well as I'd like to. Sometimes, if the vision is strong enough, I don't control it at all.

"Are you up to it?" Teag asked. "It's been a hell of a day."

Just then, the timer rang for the lasagna. "How about we do it after dinner?" I said. "That way I'm less likely to get knocked for a loop by the vision."

Teag and I were both hungry, so dinner did not take long. Afterwards, Teag brought the guns back to the table. "Ready?" he asked.

"Ready as I'll ever be," I said.

I let my hand hover over the box, and got the same ripple of apprehension and danger that I had sensed before. Then I closed my eyes, took a deep breath, and let my hand touch the smooth, burled wood of the gunstock.

The world shifted, and I saw Charleston through the eyes of a stranger.

Josiah Winfield stepped off the train and looked around, sizing up this new place. I ignored the looks fellow passengers gave me, worried glances that took in my leather coat and long gun and considered me suspect.

Let them. I was here to do what needed to be done so they could sleep like babies in their beds at night, none the wiser. And if that meant that my dreams would never be peaceful again, so be it. I didn't particularly like the word 'assassin', and I didn't think it was quite the right term when I wasn't – usually – killing real people, but it would do. Monster hunter. Demon killer. Supernatural vermin exterminator. Those got to the heart of the matter. Then again, it didn't really matter what people called me, so long as at the end of the day, I got paid and I was alive to spend the money.

Even if it meant working with unholy creatures like vampires. I knew who my contact was. Blond man. Dutch accent. Vampire. Funny thing, but if I'd had a different sponsor, I might have been gunning for him. On this job, I take his money to kill something even worse. Nothing personal.

The memories blurred into a jumble. I knew time was passing, but the stream of images gave me only an occasional glimpse of what Josiah had seen. The memories became clear again, and I – or rather Josiah – was fighting for his life.

I had the dueling pistols, one in each hand, and they barked as I pulled the triggers. The Nephilim closed in on me, a tall, misshapen creature that only vaguely resembled a man. Raw-limbed and slack jawed, with rage-filled eyes more fitting to a rabid dog than a human being, the thing came at me relentlessly. I had spent my revolver, and the shotgun pushed the monster back, but didn't kill it, letting it come at me again. I was running out of options, and my comrades were too busy fighting for their lives to bother saving me.

The dueling pistols were a last resort. Normally, a one-shot gun isn't a good pick for a firefight. But these guns were different. Tonight, I had loaded them with bullets I'd made myself. The bullets were a mixture of silver and lead, blessed by a priest, dipped in holy water and rubbed with salt. I figured that had to sting.

The Nephilim came at me, and I fired both guns at close range, closer than I liked, aiming for the eyes. My other shots had opened gaping wounds, and they would have killed a human. But these things weren't human, even if their mothers had been. No, they took after their daddies' side, ugly as sin and mean as a jackal. I'd heard that they could cast an illusion, make themselves handsome enough to bed a woman. Must be true, because no one would let something that ugly near enough to spit on them let alone make a baby.

The bullets hit, tearing into the purpled flesh of the Nephilim, searing skin and muscle as blessed metal met unholy flesh. The thing reared back, roaring in pain, clawing at the holes, and for a moment, I was forgotten. It was the break I needed.

Guns were nice, but I trust in swords. I shoved the pistols back into my belt. They had bought me the time necessary to get in close with my sword while the Nephilim was distracted. The sword was blessed, too, but by powers darker than the padre who had said a prayer over my bullets. I came at the ugly half-demon, a cutlass in one hand and a wicked knife in the other, determined to do justice.

I cast a flicker of illusion to make the monster think I had moved to the left, then I swung hard to the right. In the next breath, I sent a flicker of magic to make the cobblestones slick underfoot, so the creature had to think about staying upright. Then, I struck.

My first hit bit deep into the bone, and the upswing gutted the creature. It got in one good blow with its claws, raking them across my chest. I bit back a scream. But these things don't die easy, so I kept on swinging. Black blood splashed me, but I kept on hacking. First *the forearms, then the neck. Just to be sure, I put the blade deep where the heart should be. Only then did the monster lay still. I stepped back, watching, as the body began to shrivel and fold in on itself until it vanished, pulled clean back to wherever the hell it came from, or maybe to hell itself. Don't matter much to me, so long as it's gone and it don't come back.*

Again the memories shifted and spun. *Time passed. This time, when the images cleared, I was staring down the barrel of a gun. There was a reason a certain street in Charleston got the nickname 'Dueler's Alley'. Straight and nearly windowless, it was like sighting down a sluice. Charleston is funny about honor. Do what you please in the dark with whomever you will, and that's all right. Speak the truth about it to someone's face, and they aim to kill you.*

It would have been a shame if I hadn't engineered the whole damn thing. In the end, it wasn't a Nephilim that got me. No, an upstart demon-spawn got its fangs into me. Poisoned me real good. Even witches couldn't save me, and I'd have blacked my soul to beg a cure from them if they'd been able to fix me.

I could feel the poison in me, burning its way through, taking a little bit of me with each day. I didn't know whether it would kill me or turn me into some new kind of monster, and I didn't want to find out. I guess I could have put my gun in my mouth and pulled the trigger, but that seemed cowardly. So I did the next best thing and challenged the best duelist in Charleston, a man I was quite sure wouldn't miss.

Son of a bitch. I've spent a lifetime dodging bullets just so that, here at the end, I could stand and take one like a man. I'm not a'feared of dyin'. There are worse things. I've seen them. I did not want to be someone else's monster. So here I stood in the early summer heat, pistol in my hand, waiting for my chosen executioner. May God, if he exists, have mercy on my soul...

Abruptly, I was Cassidy again, gasping for breath and holding onto the table for dear life.

Sorren slid the dueling pistols out of reach and Teag moved a cold glass of iced tea close to me. I took the glass in both hands to keep from spilling it and drank it down.

"That must have been some ride," Teag observed.

I finished off the iced tea and set the glass aside, still feeling my heart thud in my chest at the remembered fear of a man who had died in a gunfight more than a hundred and fifty years ago.

"I saw him fight a Nephilim," I said breathlessly, and recounted the fight that I had witnessed.

"How are they different from Reapers?" Teag asked.

"Two different types of evil creatures, both exceptionally nasty," Sorren said. "Reapers are like disembodied ghouls. They feed on the spirits of the dead instead of decaying corpses. But the Reapers themselves can serve as food for bigger, badder spirits – like the Nephilim."

A horrible thought occurred to me. "Could a more powerful spirit consider Reapers like cattle to be fattened up, in order to provide a power boost for some kind of big magical attack?"

Sorren nodded. "It would take a very powerful spirit – or sorcerer – to do that, but it's possible, at least in theory."

"And Daniel Hunter said he thinks someone – or something – is trying to bring other creatures through from somewhere else," I said. "As if Reapers and Nephilim weren't bad enough on their own."

"Those would be the Watchers," Sorren said. "Especially if someone intends to bring a Harrowing, which is what Sariel did back in 1854. The Nephilim are the foot soldiers. Watchers are the generals. They can manipulate people's thoughts, and since – like the Nephilim – the Watchers are fallen angels, they're merciless judges of everyone except themselves."

"And those guilt-fests are the Watchers manipulating our thoughts?" I asked, thinking about the odd moments of crippling guilt I had felt whenever Coffee Guy was around.

Sorren nodded. "Which is further proof that at least one Watcher has come across and is nearby. So Daniel is telling the truth in that, at least. And the fact that you've encountered the 'guilt-fest', as you call it, worries me. It means the Watcher is close enough to stalk you."

"It's the illusion part that worries me," Teag said. "If Nephilim can pass themselves off as human, they're going to be hard to spot." He gave a lopsided grin. "We can't go around shooting everyone who looks like a movie star."

"What do Watchers look like?" I asked.

Sorren shrugged. "They're basically senior Nephilim, so they can make themselves look just as human. They use their good looks to seduce, but there's no reason they couldn't make themselves look average if it suited their purpose – like blending in."

I was beginning to see why the people I'd met in the supernatural protector business seemed paranoid. Handsome Nephilim were bad enough, but the idea that Watchers could look like regular people was downright terrifying.

"What now?" I asked.

"Now, we've got to find out how many Watchers have been brought across, and whether it's Sariel or someone else, we've got to stop him before he can bring down a Harrowing on this city," Sorren replied. "Since Daniel Hunter is being difficult, I'll track him down myself and find out what's he's up to. He's good in a fight, and we're going to need all the help we can get. Not only is the clock ticking – we're way behind."

DETECTIVE MONROE SHOWED up at Trifles and Folly bright and early the next day. She didn't bother with chit-chat. "What were you doing yesterday afternoon?"

I weighed my options. Legally, I didn't have to answer her. I could route all questions through my lawyer, which happened to be Anthony. I could remain silent, make her jump through hoops to get scraps. On the other hand, Monroe was a pit bull, and she wasn't going to go away easily. She might even enjoy the challenge, and we'd be locked in a tug of war. I didn't have time for that.

"Minding the shop and running some errands," I replied.

"A Volvo that looks a lot like your assistant store manager's car was spotted near the big explosion yesterday," Monroe said.

"Big explosion?" Teag had already hacked into the police database, so we knew Monroe had nothing on us. His Volvo looks like thousands of cars in the Charleston area, and Lucinda put a little spell on his license plate that makes it fuzzy for cameras or computers. Monroe was fishing, and I wasn't biting.

"Out at the old Belle Terre plantation," Monroe replied, eyes narrowing as if she guessed I was evading her. "Helicopter crashed into a house."

"Sorry to hear that. Hope no one was hurt."

"Three people were killed," Monroe snapped.

My patience was wearing thin. "I'm sorry to hear that," I repeated. "But I don't know what it has to do with me, or why it brings you here. And I do need to get the store ready to open."

"Have you ever been out to the Belle Terre plantation?"

I met her gaze. "This is Charleston. I've been to a lot of plantations. What's your point?"

"First a bomb goes off in front of your shop. Then a helicopter crashes into a house – one that's got the strangest history of ownership I've ever seen. Funny, isn't it?"

"I'm not sure why you think that everything that happens in Charleston has something to do with me. I'm not that important," I replied, stepping around Monroe and setting out fresh merchandise for the day. "Surely there's something more urgent you need to do."

"There's something off about you and this store," Monroe replied. I wondered if she had a bit of magic herself that fueled her hunches and fed her intuition. "I don't know what it is, but I'm going to find out."

Not if I can help it. "Am I free to go?" I asked, "because I've got a business to run, and you've got an unfortunate accident to deal with, so we both have more important things to be doing."

If Monroe thought she was going to intimidate me into pouring out my soul to her, she was wrong. I've fought demons and vampires and ghouls, stared down Loas and sorcerers, and held my own against hell spawn. She didn't even make my radar of scary things, although having her poking around was likely to be inconvenient.

"Go," she said irritably with a wave of her hand. "But I intend to look into any possible connection between this store and the Belle Terre plantation. And if I find one, I'll be back – you can count on it."

I didn't turn around to watch her leave, although I relaxed a bit when the door slammed shut. It worried me that she might be able to find a connection between the plantation and Trifles and Folly. Sorren was exceptionally careful about things like that. Then again, several centuries ago, no one foresaw databases that stored information indefinitely.

Monroe would figure that any link between the explosion at the plantation and the bomb at the store meant we were hiding something from her, and we were. And, if she could find the connection between the plantation and the store, maybe someone else would, too.

Then again, if the bomber had a connection to Sariel, he – or she – had come here because of Sorren, had already known the connection between Sorren and the store. But despite the attacks on Sorren's other properties, this vendetta seemed especially focused on Charleston. And that meant big trouble for us.

A few moments after Detective Monroe left, Teag stuck his head out of the back room. "Is it safe to come out?"

I sighed. "As safe as it ever is around here." Teag had a glass of iced tea, and I took a swig of my coffee before I went back to arranging the displays.

"You know, I got thinking after I left your place last night," Teag said, moving to the other side of the store to put out the jewelry and valuables we lock up each night. "I wondered whether old Josiah actually left Dueler's Alley, or whether he hung around to keep an eye on things." A gleam came into his eye. "It would be interesting to take Alicia Peters down there and see."

"I was thinking the same thing," I replied. "Josiah wasn't the kind to give up and go home. He instigated the duel so that he wasn't at the mercy of the demon-spawn who poisoned him. And that raises another question. Did he already have an escape plan in place?"

"Sounds to me like Josiah had a love-hate relationship with magic," Teag said, leaning back in his chair. "And from what you've said, he was a little iffy when it came to the afterlife."

"Either that, or he was pretty sure he'd draw the short straw if St. Peter got a look at his resume," I replied. On bad nights, when I couldn't sleep, the same worry had occasionally crossed my mind.

"So there's a better-than-average chance that Josiah didn't move on, if he got the choice," Teag said. "After all, Mama Nadege is still around after all these years, looking after her descendants. What's to say that Josiah didn't pull the same kind of thing? He had an iron will. Purpose and stubbornness – the making of a ghost."

"Monkey fist," I murmured.

"Pardon?"

"It's a phrase Father Anne used," I replied with a thoughtful smile. "Some ghosts stick around because they're hanging onto something. Like a monkey who gets his fist stuck in a bottle trap because he won't let go of the banana inside."

"Odd analogy, but I can see what you mean," Teag said. "And thanks a lot for that image," he added wryly. "Now every time we run into a ghost, I'm going to picture it with its hand stuck in a bottle, holding onto a banana."

I chuckled and finished off my second cup of coffee "I think you might be right."

"What? You're getting the same mental picture too, with bananas?"

I shook my head. "No. You might be right about Josiah. Those dueling pistols are more than just guns," I eyed the matching set warily. "Josiah had them custom-made. He chose the wood and the metal with care, for their magical properties as well as their durability. He built magic into them; runes etched into the metal in places no one can see. Blessings from powerful people. He even made the bullets himself."

"You're wondering whether or not you might be able to use those pistols and draw on that magic, aren't you?" Teag asked.

I nodded. "Those pistols mattered to Josiah in a deep, gut-level sort of way. I might be able to tap into his power."

It wasn't as crazy as it sounded. I had done the same before. On my own without an object I can draw on for power, I don't have combat-level magic. But I do have the ability to see the history of an object and experience an emotionally-resonant few moments of its history. That bond lets me become more of a fighter than I normally am, when I tap into a weapon's resonance. I discovered the ability by accident, using a shaman's walking stick, when I was fighting for my life.

"Dueling pistols only have a single shot each," Teag said. "They weren't meant for sustained combat. So even if you could draw on Josiah's imprint, it's not like he's left you something that will mow down the bad guys."

"Maybe not. But two shots with a little extra magic to go with them might turn the outcome of a fight."

"I'll call Alicia and see if we can get her to go down to Dueler's Alley with us," Teag said.

Before I could respond, we heard a knock at the front door. "That must be Maggie," I said, and went to let her in.

"What a beautiful day!" Maggie said, grinning from ear to ear as she step-hopped her way inside with her crutches. "I bet we're going to get plenty of customers!"

I couldn't resist grinning. "If there are any more of those Canadian tour busses headed our way, you might be right." It was peak season for visitors. Temperatures were cooler than at the height of summer, but compared to up North, Charleston was still comfortably warm. The gardens were in their fall splendor with colorful mums and pansies, along with ornamental kale and flowering cabbages. Fall is a fantastic season to see Charleston, for visitors and for those of us who live here and never get tired of it.

The morning was pretty busy, but I still couldn't get the vision from Josiah Winfield's pistols out of my mind. Maggie went to meet a friend on her lunch hour, and Teag had packed a lunch, so I decided to clear my head and go for a walk.

"Why do I suspect that you're going to end up at the Archive?" Teag said jokingly.

"Maybe because it makes sense to talk to Mrs. Morrissey and see if she knows anything about this Winfield character," I replied, grabbing my purse. "I'll be back before too long," I headed outside, hoping the sunshine would improve my mood.

First, I grabbed a quick lunch at Honeysuckle Café and a couple of lattes to-go. Mrs. Morrissey, the woman who runs the Archive, has a weakness for lattes, and bringing one to her pretty much guaranteed we'd talk a while.

It wasn't far from the café over to the Historical Archive. The Archive is situated in the old Drayton House, a beautiful home built by a family from Charleston's elite. Time passed, things changed, and the Drayton House was bequeathed to the city.

"I'm here to see Mrs. Morrissey," I told the receptionist. No matter how often I visited, I always appreciated how beautiful the place was. The Archive had kept most of the house looking like a grand old home, with period furnishings and paintings. I could almost imagine women in ball gowns and men in formal attire gathering in the parlor for a party.

"Cassidy! How wonderful to see you. And you've brought a latte for me, you darling girl!" Mrs. Benjamin Morrissey emerged from the former sitting room that was now her office with a big smile of welcome. I handed her one of the coffees, and she gave me a quick hug and air kiss, then motioned for me to follow her into her office.

"It's been a little while. I was beginning to think you'd forgotten your way here!" she said, as I sat down in one of the comfortable chairs facing the desk. Mrs. Morrissey went around to take a seat in her own leather chair.

Mrs. Morrissey came from one of the Charleston blue-blood families, and had married well. When her husband died, he had left her well-off both in money and social connections. I guessed that Mrs. Morrissey was in her seventies, still pretty in an elegant way. She was slim enough for St. John suits, and her hair and make-up were always perfect. I loved that Mrs. Morrissey had no patience for Botox or facelifts, meaning that she looked her age in the most graceful way possible. She had been a friend of my Uncle Evan's, and I suspected that she had more than an inkling of what we really did over at Trifles and Folly.

"Oh, I'd never forget," I replied with a chuckle. "And I've got a question I'm hoping you can answer. What do you know about a man named Josiah Winfield?"

Mrs. Morrissey took a sip of her latte and leaned back in her chair, thinking. "Was he from Charleston? I can't place that name."

I shook my head. "I don't think so. He was something of a wandering vigilante who might have passed through the city around the time of the last big Yellow Fever epidemic."

Mrs. Morrissey set her latte aside and stood up. "There's a book upstairs with sketches from that period," she said. "Some are pretty grim, as you can imagine. Photographs were expensive, so a lot of the newspapers still relied on sketches. Come on. Let's see what we can find."

The Archive's big front hallway was a display area for rotating exhibits, and so was the ballroom on the second floor. I'd had some bad experiences with items in a past display, but to my relief, the current special exhibit was on 'Angels in Charleston'.

"Oh wow!" I said, looking at the display. "What's up with all the angels?" The wall display cases had paintings, small sculptures and stained glass panels, Christmas ornaments and jewelry – all of them featuring angels in very Charleston-esque settings.

"Do you like it?" Mrs. Morrissey asked. "It's for the Angel Oak Fundraiser."

The Angel Oak is a huge old live oak out on Johns Island. Scientists say it's at least four hundred years old, and some estimates go all the way up to fourteen hundred years. The tree is a celebrity in its own right, but hurricanes damaged it, and so local preservation societies were raising funds to keep the old tree healthy.

"I never realized there were so many depictions of angels in Charleston," I said, peering into the cases.

"Well you know, they do call us the Holy City," Mrs. Morrissey said with a laugh. That's a nickname Charleston has earned for the large number of churches in the city. No matter where you turn, there's always a spire in sight.

Some of the pieces on display looked very old, while others were modernistic. "There are more in the exhibition room upstairs," Mrs. Morrissey said, warming to the subject. "Some of the pieces date back almost to Charleston's founding. Usually, they were religious paintings of angels watching over the city, or guarding a particular person or family. Down through the years, a lot of artists have been drawn to the angel theme. I didn't realize quite how many until we started to put the display together."

Some of the paintings were 'primitives', done by artists with talent but no training. Others were clearly done by professionals. A few of the paintings even featured the Angel Oak, while others showed angelic creatures holding back threatening shadows and monsters with their glowing swords.

"You know, angels are a theme almost everyone can identify with. Pretty much every belief system has some kind of angels, and we tried to display pieces that show a broad range of viewpoints," Mrs. Morrissey added as I followed her upstairs.

On the way up the broad staircase, I stole a glance at an oil painting of a ball from the late 1800s. It had been painted at the Drayton House during a big party, and tucked into the back, trying not to be noticed, I saw Sorren among the many guests whose faces and outfits had been captured by the painter.

Displaying small collections in the Drayton House is pretty new for the Archive, but the front hallway and the upstairs ballroom are perfect for showing off pieces in a more intimate setting, and donors love it. Upstairs, the old ballroom was decked out in white, silver, and gold. Angels of every size and style graced the room. Some were blown glass and others were punched tin. There were angels of stone and wood, stitched from fabric banners, even woven from sweetgrass. A series of photographs showed the angel monuments from Charleston's fine old cemeteries, and a local baker had created some interesting variations on the idea of 'angel food' cake. Standing in the center was a replica of the Angel Oak itself, a floor-to-ceiling model that still didn't come close to the size of the real thing.

"That's pretty amazing," I said, nodding toward the artist's version of the old live oak. Even though it was a fraction of the size of the actual tree, it was still huge. Although I hadn't touched any of the artwork, the display filled the ballroom with a peaceful vibe, strong and confident. I felt myself relax for the first time in days, enjoying a sense of safety. There in the midst of the angel art, it really did feel like someone was watching over me.

"Isn't the model of the Angel Oak striking?" Mrs. Morrissey said. "The artist received permission from the tree's caretakers to use some of the twigs and acorns from the real Angel Oak. He really captured the essence, don't you think?"

I nodded, looking all around at the artwork. "Whenever there's been a difficult time, we've had a rise in art with angels," Mrs. Morrissey said, leading me around the exhibition. "Yellow Fever, cholera, earthquakes, bombardments, hurricanes, and the like – people turn to making or painting angels. I guess it gives them a sense of comfort."

"So the display is part of the fundraiser?" I asked.

Mrs. Morrissey nodded. "Yes, and I think it will be fabulous. Almost everything here is part of the silent auction to raise money to preserve the Angel Oak. The exhibition premier will be during the donor gala. It's just a few days away – I have a million and one things to do to get ready!"

A grouping of paintings in the far corner of the room caught my eye and I wandered over. I could feel the energy shift as I headed toward the edge of the room, and the feel-good vibe became edgy. The angels in the rest of the display ranged from cute to protective, chubby cherubs to hunky bare-chested guys in white robes with flaming swords. But the images in this painting were much darker and more sinister. The faces of these angels leered or threatened, and their eyes were cold. The artist had painted the background in the colors of storm clouds: black, gray, sickly green, and a shade of purple that was the color of a deep bruise or a wound gone bad. I found myself face-to-face with a painting of three Nephilim.

"Why is this part of a display on angels?" I asked, taking a step back.

Mrs. Morrissey chuckled. "Interesting, isn't it? It's one panel from a series of paintings called 'Nephilim Rising'. I suspect they'll raise a lot of eyebrows. I call them our 'bad boys'. Haven't you ever heard of fallen angels?"

"Of course I have. Those just look like they fell hard."

One of the fallen angels was in its monster-form. A second was robed in black with a cowl that nearly covered his face. The third looked straight ahead with a frightening intensity, strikingly handsome, like a movie star hired to play a psychopath with the flat, dead eyes of a remorseless killer. I shivered, having seen that same look in Coffee Guy's eyes. Whoever had painted these Nephilim had first-hand knowledge.

"I can't imagine anyone getting a sense of comfort from these angels," I said. There was a horrible beauty to them that made it difficult to look away, and a disquieting sense that it might be best to keep an eye on them. Near the painting, the resonance was disquieting and dangerous, as if the room itself was screaming a warning to stay back.

"Unfortunately, you're right," Mrs. Morrissey said. "They were painted by Gerard Astor, an artist from Charleston who gained national – and international – prominence. But Gerard battled some demons of his own, like depression and drugs. This was the last painting he finished before he vanished. Most art historians believe he committed suicide."

I remembered what Father Anne had said, "*Poor, doomed Gerard Astor*"... If he had enough contact with the Nephilim to paint their portraits, it didn't surprise me he killed himself. Especially if the Nephilim came with the same dose of overwhelming guilt that I felt around Coffee *Guy*.

I let Mrs. Morrissey lead me around the rest of the exhibition, although I did not turn my back on the fallen angel painting. The other pieces were light-hearted, inspirational, and gorgeous, and I tried to push the darker images from my mind.

"I think your display is fabulous," I said, surprised at how many different ways there were to fashion angels. I let my hand gently touch one of the carved and painted wooden angels, and felt a warm, protective power resonating from the sculpture. I was willing to bet the same would be true for most, if not all, of the figures. Whether the artists knew it or not, the angels they felt moved to carve carried their own flicker of magic, bound up in the emotional imprint of the artists that made the figures.

Reluctantly, I left the ballroom and followed Mrs. Morrissey to the Archive's library. "Here we go," she said, bringing a large, canvas-bound book down to one of the reading tables. Not everything had been scanned into computers yet, and while doing so was an ongoing project, such things take time and money. Hence the 'stacks', dozens of shelves filled with old volumes organized by the Dewey Decimal System with Mrs. Morrissey's brain as the search engine.

"*The Great Yellow Fever Epidemic of 1854*," I read, looking down at the embossed cover of the large book. Yellow Fever had scourged Charleston from its founding until the creation of modern medicine. A hot, wet climate, mosquitoes and the constant coming and going of strangers in a port city was a recipe for epidemics. But even by those standards, the outbreak in 1854 had been a doozie.

Gingerly, I touched the cover of the book, but no vision appeared to me. Just a persistent sadness, perhaps from others who had looked for clues to the fate of ancestors in these pages.

"I can't imagine wandering around the city with a sketch book in the middle of an epidemic," Mrs.

Morrissey said as I flipped the pages in the oversized book. Black-and-white charcoal sketches caught images of funeral processions, corpses littering the streets, carts filled with dead bodies and mourners of every age and social class. A few old daguerreotype photographs were sprinkled among the sketches, faded with the years.

"They must have realized that the epidemic would go down in history," I mused. The sketches looked like they had been drawn quickly, but with an eye for detail. I turned one more page, and drew in a sharp breath.

"Did you find what you needed?" Mrs. Morrissey asked as she busied herself with another book.

Oh yeah. The next sketch looked like the cover for a fantasy novel. A man in a long duster coat was shooting at five dark, cloaked figures. Bodies lay heaped around the feet of the creatures, and one of the beings gnawed on a human leg bone. Streaks of lightning fell from the sky, and the gunslinger's weapon shot fire.

Most people would have taken the sketch for allegory, mankind versus the plague. I was certain the sketch's artist had witnessed a battle between Winfield and the Nephilim. I took a picture of the page with my phone, and decided to ask Sorren for details later.

"I found the man you asked about, here in the names of the dead," Mrs. Morrissey said, calling me away from the sketchbook and over to where she pointed to a name in a big ledger of the plague dead. And right above Mrs. Morrissey's sculpted fingernail, I saw the name 'Winfield, Josiah. Death by unlawful duel'.

"Looks like he didn't die of the epidemic," she said brightly. "I hope that helped."

"Oh, it did," I replied, still thinking about the battle sketch. I wanted to ask if there had been missing people before the plague broke out, people who started down staircases and never made it to the bottom, but I didn't. I was pretty sure I already knew the answer.

We had to cross the ballroom again on our way out. I was pondering what we had seen in the sketch book. *You're no good at protecting people,* I found myself thinking. *What good were you to the people at Belle Terre? They're dead because you didn't warn them. If you were faster on the uptake, you'd have known they were going to be in danger...*

I caught myself, and shook my head to clear it. Alarm replaced the overwhelming, unnatural tide of guilt. *Sorren said Watchers stood in judgment. That means either a Nephilim or a Watcher is nearby, and we're in danger.*

The room's energy shifted. The lights dimmed and the air was cold. Mrs. Morrissey shivered. "Something's wrong with the air conditioning!" she fussed. "I'll have to have someone take a look at it."

I shook my left wrist, and the old dog collar fell out of my sleeve, but I didn't put the power into it yet to call Bo's ghost to my side. I let my athame slip into my right hand. I could use it in more places than the walking stick, since shooting blasts of flame in a museum is generally frowned upon, except as a last resort. I moved into the ballroom, wary and ready for an attack.

Something moved over on one side of the exhibit, and my gaze traveled toward Gerard Astor's dark, haunting 'Nephilim Rising'. That's when I blinked and caught my breath, because one of those darkly handsome fallen angels was peeling himself off the canvas.

"Who are you?" Mrs. Morrissey spotted the Nephilim as he stepped away from the painting. She had drawn herself up to her full height, chin raised. "No one's supposed to be in here until the event tomorrow night."

The Nephilim did not answer her. He only had eyes for me. I figured that he could sense my magic and wanted to take a bite. Painting Creep sauntered toward us, and there was a lethal, panther-like grace to his movements.

Mrs. Morrissey moved toward the alarm by the door, but Painting Creep was faster, and before I could draw my athame on him, he got between her and the alarm panel. He gave her a shove that sent her off balance, and she fell against a large, solid display table, smacking her head on the way down. She moaned but did not try to get up, and a combination of fear and anger moved through my veins like rocket fuel.

"Get away from her, you bastard." I willed power to my bracelet and my athame at the same time. Bo's ghost went to stand watch over Mrs. Morrissey's fallen form, while the cold force of my magic caught Painting Creep square in the chest. The force sent him tumbling, barely missing some of the large granite angel statues, throwing Creep across the room. I kept myself between him and where Mrs. Morrissey lay, but remembering the fight with Coffee Guy by Magnolia Cemetery, I was afraid this wasn't going to end well.

Painting Creep rose to his feet, then he laughed as if it was all a game to him and headed for me again.

I backed up one step and then another. Painting Creep moved like he had all the time in the world. Bo's ghost lunged at the Nephilim, barking and snapping, and his ghostly teeth managed to rip open the fallen angel's left arm from shoulder to wrist. Dead, undead or other, the bite must have hurt, because Painting Creep gave an angry cry and shook loose from Bo's jaws.

I blasted him with another shot of cold white energy and Painting Creep started to transform. His model-perfect good looks twisted and stretched, and I knew that if he completely transformed, I would never be able to beat him on my own.

I took another step back, and found myself backed up against a marble statue of an angel. It stood two feet taller than I was, with wings partially unfurled. Now, with my back against the smooth, cold marble and my magic wide open, I could feel the vibe that I sensed when I first entered the room. All of these pieces except for 'Nephilim Rising' had a warm glow to them, carved or painted with good intentions, a sense of awe and consecration. The Angel Oak replica had the strongest essence.

I grabbed on to the edge of the angel's wings as I drew my will to me, focusing on that warm glow of power in the art and the tree sculpture, summoning it to envelop me, charging my magic until I could hear it buzz in my mind. I gathered all the power I could hold, and sent it streaming toward Painting Creep in one massive thrust.

The paintings and statues took on an inner glow and beams of light appeared, linking the artwork together like a giant grid, with the Angel Oak at the center. All except for 'Nephilim Rising'. I felt the magic growing stronger, amplified and reflected, taking on more power as it pulled from the strong emotions of the art's creators and beholders.

This time, the magic was a tide, not a single blast, and it rolled toward Painting Creep like an overwhelming, golden wave. It swept over everything in its path without damaging a thing, but when it struck the Nephilim, the surge of magic stopped him mid-transformation, and knocked him off his feet, hurling him back toward the huge, life-sized canvas of 'Nephilim Rising', into the blackness that yawned where his image had once stood.

I expected a crash as his body connected with the large painting, to hear the tearing of canvas and the splintering of the frame, but there was no sound at all. One second, the Nephilim's form was borne on the tide of magic, and the next, he was disappearing into the darkness of the painting. I blinked, and Gerard Astor's masterpiece stood intact as it had been when I first entered the room, except for the fact that it was missing one Nephilim.

Bo's ghost barked, rousing me as I stood there trembling in shock. I turned, trying to pull myself together, and saw Mrs. Morrissey lying on the floor. Bo barked once more, then vanished as I knelt beside my friend.

Mrs. Morrissey moaned and tried to turn over. I helped her onto her back, and her eyes fluttered open. "What happened?" she asked. I could see where she was going to have a goose egg on her head where she had hit the table, and blood matted her hair from a cut on her scalp.

"We were coming back from the stacks and you must have tripped," I replied. I felt awful about lying to her but the truth was much, much worse. "You fell, and I tried to find someone to help, but there's no one else here."

"No, there wouldn't be anyone else right now," she said, her voice sounding thin and reedy. "Everyone else is at lunch."

"Let me call an ambulance," I offered, worried.

Mrs. Morrissey reached up and touched the side of her head, coming away with bloody fingers. "Maybe that would be a good idea. I don't have time to be hurt," she said with a sigh. "There's so much to do for the gala."

I sat with her as I dialed for help on my cell phone. The downstairs door was unlocked, and the EMTs arrived sooner than I expected. Even though I knew it was standard procedure to put her on a backboard and brace her neck, I hated to see Mrs. Morrissey looking so frail. They carried her carefully down the steps, and for a moment I held my breath, terrified that a void might open up out of nowhere and swallow them whole the way it had taken the other missing people, but the stairs remained just steps. I hoped that Mrs. Morrissey would be fine, and out of the hospital soon. At the same time, I was worried about the Archive hosting a big public event with 'Nephilim Rising' on display. That could be a disaster. *Maybe she'll be okay, but they'll postpone the event,* I thought. *At least until we can take care of Sariel and his fallen angels.*

Somehow, I wasn't surprised that Detective Monroe arrived a few minutes after the ambulance crew. "Well, well. You again," she said, eyeing me with a very cold gaze.

"Hello, Detective," I replied.

She looked around the foyer of Drayton House. "Aren't you supposed to be running your shop?"

"Mrs. Morrissey is a friend of mine, and I often consult with her on the history of pieces that come into the store. I brought her a latte, and she wanted to show me the new Angel Oak exhibit. She tripped and hit her head. I called for help."

"You show up in strange places too often. It's a bad habit."

"I didn't think they sent detectives out to follow up on ambulance calls," I replied, thankful that at least this time, my fight with the Nephilim had not left the exhibit hall in ruins. That would have been difficult to explain.

"Normally, I don't," Monroe said. "I happened to hear the call on the scanner, caught your name attached to it, and thought it might be worth dropping by."

I tried to keep a handle on my annoyance, and hoped I didn't look as pale and shaky as I felt. Adrenaline is a wonderful thing in a fight, but once the fighting is over I usually want to throw up. "You don't look so good," Monroe observed.

"It was the blood," I lied. "Blood makes me sick." Actually, since I'd taken up with the Alliance, I'd seen my share of blood, ichor and lots of other really nasty fluids that don't have names and I'd been just fine. I figured it was an answer the detective would accept, and she rolled her eyes as if I had lived up to some unspoken stereotype.

"Go back to your shop. Stay out of trouble. You might just be unlucky," she said, giving me a skeptical glare. "But if you keep showing up in the wrong places, I *will* find out why."

I walked two blocks before I sank down on a park bench and let myself have a good round of the shakes. I wanted to call the hospital to find out how Mrs. Morrissey was, but I knew it would be a couple hours before she was through the emergency room, and no one would release information to me, anyhow.

My head was full of what I had seen, trying to figure out where Josiah Winfield and his pistols fit into the picture. It seemed like too much of a coincidence for his prized guns to show up right when we had monsters and ghost-eating spirits loose in Charleston. I walked back to the store, but we were busy enough with customers that it was over an hour before I had the chance to catch Teag up on what I had seen.

"I've got some news as well," Teag replied when I finally filled him in. "In between customers, I did a little digging on the Darke Web. I looked up good old Josiah Winfield, and also tried to find out more about your mysterious Mr. Thompson."

"And?" I poured the last cup of coffee and rinsed out the pot and filter, then drew up a chair at the break room table.

Teag brought in his half-finished cup of tea and joined me. "Let's start with Josiah. Sorren described him right: Josiah was a combination private investigator/hit man/demon hunter." He grimaced. "He was kind of a splashy guy."

"As in style or blood?"

"Both. Josiah liked to make an impression. He rode a huge, black stallion, and wore all-black clothing and favored a long duster that resembled a priest's cassock."

"That squares with what I saw in the vision, and the drawing Mrs. Morrissey showed me at the Archive."

"He had the pistols, but he also carried a crossbow and a nasty modified shotgun. Oh, and he had a penchant for making things freeze over with magic," he replied, raising an eyebrow.

"Yikes. As in making hell freeze over?'

Teag nodded. "Yep, and that's how he seemed to look at it, too. Not much of a sense of humor. When he rode into town, people got out of his way, especially demons and dark magic types."

"I can imagine that he made an impression."

"He passed himself off as a traveling preacher who did exorcisms. A lot of the magical community doesn't remember him favorably. Apparently, he was known for double-crossing more than one 'colleague' whom he considered to be a little too close to the dark side for his taste."

"Wow. A real fun guy."

"That's just it. Some people questioned whether Josiah was really playing for one side or the other, or both ends against the middle. He shows up doing some sketchy jobs for the Family, and then helps out the Alliance. No one liked or trusted him, but he was good in a fight, so he kept getting asked back to the party."

"What kind of magic did ol' Josiah have?" I asked, sipping my coffee. "That might be important."

"He seemed to have a knack for cheating at cards," Teag replied, "but mostly, he liked freezing things." He raised an eyebrow. "One more thing, Cassidy," Teag said as I rose to check my email. "About Mr. Thompson at the nursing home? He's a direct descendant of Josiah Winfield, right down to the magic."

I raised an eyebrow. "That old guy was a supernatural hit man?"

Teag nodded. "More of a paranormal soldier of fortune. Kinda like Josiah. Jobs done, grudges settled, no questions asked. Depending on who you talk to, Josiah was either a tarnished hero who took care of problems no one else wanted to touch, or an enforcer for powerful society folks who got in a magic-related jam."

"Or a bit of both," I mused.

"Either way, he was a dangerous man in his day. And even though he's dead, we have no idea what he's still capable of doing."

I took my coffee cup to the sink and rinsed it out. "Do you and Anthony have plans tonight for dinner?"

Teag shook his head. "No. Big court appearance tomorrow, so Anthony's holed up preparing."

"Want to hang around and we'll get something to eat? I'm wondering if we can find out more about Josiah."

"Sure," Teag said. "And for the record, I poked around a little – gently – on the Darke Web about Daniel Hunter. Yeesh. One nasty son of a bitch."

"We kinda knew that."

Teag shrugged. "Then consider it validation."

We grabbed a bite to eat and settled back down to see what more we could uncover. It didn't take long for Teag to hit pay dirt. Images of newspaper articles and obituaries came up on screen. I was quiet for a moment, speed reading through an old article that mentioned Mr. Thompson.

"Edwin Thompson did exceptionally well for himself in the stock market," I mused. "That was his profession – stock trading. His clients had above-average returns, too – consistently enough to get noticed. There were allegations of insider trading and cheating, but no one could make the charges stick."

"Numbers magic," Teag replied. "Like the guys who can count cards in Vegas and win every hand, only beyond mortal skill. Josiah was a card cheat, remember? If Thompson's magic helped him see patterns, he could get ahead of the sequence, beat the market."

I nodded. "Which wouldn't be out of the question as a relation to Winfield," I said thoughtfully. "Like with FBI profilers, it's all about finding and predicting patterns."

"Anything else?" he asked.

I was about to say no, then two old newspaper clippings caught my eye. "Hold up," I said, eyes widening. "Now that's interesting."

"What?"

"Didn't you say Thompson was supposed to have some sort of deep freeze magic, like Josiah?"

"That's what I heard on the Darke Web."

"Well according to this, several people around Thompson died in fatal accidents involving ice." I met his gaze. "In and around Charleston." In Alaska, that might not be strange. Charleston didn't get much ice.

"What happened?"

I scrolled down. "One of his business partners, whom Thompson was in the middle of pushing out of the firm, died when his car slid off the road on a patch of black ice."

"We get a few cold days. There can be slippery spots."

"Uh huh. Then two years later, Thompson's ex-wife, who was about to get a big divorce settlement, slipped while walking down a flight of stairs – in front of witnesses – and died."

"Okay," Teag said, drawing out the word skeptically. "That's a big coincidence."

"Yeah," I agreed. "And here's the kicker. The District Attorney back in the Eighties was convinced there was some kind of improper trading going on, and he dogged Thompson. Until he died, of a sudden, massive heart attack."

"I wonder if a guy like Thompson could freeze someone's heart," Teag mused, and I knew he was on my wavelength. "Or maybe cause a clot with ice?"

"Which no one would ever look for before it melted," I replied.

Well what do you know? Old Mr. Thompson wasn't just a curmudgeon and a wizard. From what I'd just seen, it looked like he was also a stone-cold killer.

I turned to Teag. "Anything else?" He nodded.

"I did discover something that Sorren didn't tell us."

I looked up. "Oh?"

"According to the legends, Watchers don't bother destroying ghosts. They take people they believe need to be judged," Teag said soberly. "And they're fond of feeding on wrong-doers who didn't get punished 'enough' by their standards."

"I wonder if that has any connection with the people who have disappeared on the staircases," I said. "Do you think you could find out?"

Teag grinned. "Haven't met a police database I couldn't hack. But don't tell that to my sweetie," he added with a conspiratorial whisper. "You know, don't you, that Sariel hasn't really done his worst yet?"

"I know. And we're going to be at the center of it, when he does. I just want to be as ready as we can," I said. Nice thought. But I had no idea how to make it happen.

Chapter Thirteen

"I CAN'T BELIEVE people pay good money for ghost tours to bring them down here," I said.

"They're getting entertainment," Teag replied. "You've had too much of the real thing."

He was right about that. It was close to midnight, and we were in Philadelphia Alley, a short, straight side street with high, mostly windowless walls that earned its nickname, Dueler's Alley, in blood. Not coincidentally, there's an archway that used to lead directly into St. Philip's cemetery. Convenient, in a macabre way.

"*I* can't believe dueling still happened into the late 1800s," Alicia Peters, our medium, said. She shivered, and rubbed her hands on her arms to warm up although the night was a pleasant temperature.

"It went on longer than that, in secret," Teag said. "Lots of men died. It was a stupid way to settle an argument."

Now that we were here, the whole trip seemed like less of a good idea than it had during daylight. Teag carried Josiah Winfield's dueling pistols in a duffle bag that included his martial arts fighting staff and a variety of protections against supernatural bad guys. I wasn't taking any chances tonight, so I had my athame and Alard's walking stick, plus my agate necklace and the old Norse spindle whorl that helped me focus my magic.

"Let's see if we can make contact with Josiah," Teag said. Alicia found a spot she favored in the alley, and Teag made a protective circle with salt around her, then for good measure, made one for the two of us as well. Salt alone won't hold off the worst supernatural predators, but it keeps most of the general nasties at bay.

Being careful not to smudge either salt circle, I passed one of Josiah's pistols to Alicia as a focal point. I kept the other one. They were both loaded. I had questions for Josiah, but I wasn't entirely certain that if he did show up he would be pleased to see us, so I viewed the loaded pistols as a form of insurance.

Alicia began to sing quietly, swaying back and forth. The alley grew colder, and wind stirred on what had been a still night. I've seen plenty of ghosts who had the power to show themselves or the will to become visible, but my magic can't contact ghosts like Alicia's. Watching her work always made me awestruck and a little frightened.

The air felt thick around us, and I heard a man whistling a jaunty tune. The 'whistling doctor' was one of Dueler's Alley's more famous ghosts, but I was sure that tonight, with Alicia calling to the spirits, we had standing-room-only for haunts. But was one of them Josiah?

"Josiah Winfield," Alicia called quietly. "If you are present, make yourself known."

A handful of pebbles rose into the air and hurled against the alleyway wall. *I'll take that for a 'yes'.*

"We have your pistols, Josiah," Alicia continued. "And we'd like to have a word with you. The enemy you fought has returned. We need to know how you destroyed it."

The air in the alley had grown cold as a winter's night. I could see my breath, a decidedly rare occurrence in Charleston. Gooseflesh rose on my arms and the hairs on the back of my neck were standing up. I didn't need Alicia's gift to know that the narrow alley was chock full of ghosts, and it felt like more were coming by the minute. In the dark corners, I could see wisps of fog, spirits manifesting, waiting to see what would happen next.

Boot steps sounded in the darkness, growing closer. I caught a whiff of bay rum and leather, and knew that Josiah was with us.

"Josiah Winfield. I need to know what you discovered about the Reapers and Watchers you fought," I said, partly addressing Alicia as the conduit to Josiah, and partly addressing thin air. "They've returned, and I think you found out something I need to know."

I give Alicia credit for brass-plated balls, figuratively speaking, because she doesn't just talk to spirits, she lets them get inside her head. I saw the change come over Alicia as Josiah's ghost responded to our call. Her stance became more masculine and arrogant, her expression took on a look that was not her own, and one hand caressed the dueling pistol as if it were a long-lost lover.

"I'm here." Alicia's voice became harsh and throaty as Josiah's ghost spoke through her.

"You fought Nephilim," I replied. "You knew my boss, Sorren. We've got problems, and I think you found out something you never had a chance to tell anyone before you died."

Alicia is a few inches shorter than I am, and you could drop her into any society tea party and she would fit in without missing a beat. So it was jarring to see her give me the once-over like a truck driver, have her gaze linger noticeably at chest level, and then grudgingly rise to meet my gaze with a level prove-yourself glare.

"So that Dutch vampire bastard is still around?" Winfield said. "Figures he'd outlast me." I waited out his stream of profanity and when I didn't pale and didn't flinch, I saw some grudging admiration in his gaze.

"Something is drawing Nephilim to Charleston," I continued. "Reapers and Watchers, too. People go down stairways and disappear. Is it Sariel?"

Instead of answering my question, Winfield looked at the pistols. "You've got my guns." Josiah Winfield's voice had a wistful quality, the kind most sane people reserve for lovers or children.

"You weren't using them anymore," I replied with a shrug.

"True enough," Winfield replied, and Alicia absently petted the gun she held as if it were a lap dog. "Reapers and Nephilim, huh? Bad stuff. What did you say about stairs?"

"People go down stairs and never get to the bottom."

"People with something to hide, or old secrets, maybe a past they'd rather forget?" Josiah's rough cadence was jarringly at odds with Alicia's usual way of speaking.

"Yeah," I said. Josiah chuckled, and the sound sent a shiver down my back. "That's the Watchers. They're like enforcers, hired guns." He gave a hoarse, strained laugh. "Like me, only worse, and they play for the other side."

"What's so bad about Watchers?" Teag pressed. He stood a few feet away, keeping a lookout on the alley entrance and exit so we didn't get surprised.

"Reapers eat regular ghosts. Watchers eat tainted souls," Josiah replied, with a hint of condescension. "Gives them power. But they don't show up by themselves. They're brought across, like the Nephilim, by someone more powerful. Where there are Watchers, there's gonna be a Judge."

"What do I need to know to stop the Watchers and the Judge?" I was desperate to get answers before the connection was broken.

The overwhelming guilt washed over me before Josiah could answer. I saw Teag's face as it hit him, saw him blink back tears and set his jaw to hold his composure. Alicia was silently weeping.

I shook off the guilt, desperate to free the others before we were attacked. "Teag! Alicia! Snap out of it! The guilt is a trick. It's what the Watchers do. It's not real." I couldn't tell if I was getting through to them, but all hell was about to break loose and I couldn't handle it by myself.

Movement warned me that we were about to stop talking and start shooting.

Two unnaturally handsome young men were headed toward us from one end of Dueler's Alley, while two more came from the other entrance. One for every taste: blond, dark, ginger and bald. Teag had pulled himself out of his funk and fell into a defensive stance, his staff in one hand and a magical dagger in the other. Runes blazed at the top of his staff, and the braided cords fastened to the staff juiced up its power with his Weaver magic. I jangled the collar on my left wrist, and Bo's ghost appeared by my side, ninety pounds of spectral, pissed-off golden retriever.

I had the walking stick in my left hand, and one of Josiah's pistols in the other. Alicia still held the second pistol, though I doubted she had any idea how to fire it. I couldn't tell whether she had heard my warning, or whether she was still paralyzed by guilt. That meant Teag and I had to protect Alicia as well as try to get out of this alive, and it was four to two. Lousy odds.

I shot first. Fire surged from the old walking stick. The heat raised sweat on my forehead, and the blast of fire hit Baldy square in the middle of his Italian designer shirt. The beast inside roared as the force of the strike threw him back toward the mouth of the alley, his clothes aflame, flesh burning.

Bo's ghost was already in motion, bounding down the alley at Ginger, who looked like the answer to a Scottish bad girl's wildest dreams. Bo leaped, managing to get three feet of air under him, and tackled Ginger like a lineman. Bo's teeth clamped down on Ginger's shoulder, and his front claws raked down through a black silk shirt that probably cost as much as most people's monthly mortgage payment.

Teag moved in fast while Ginger was down. He's earned every one of his martial arts trophies, without using magic. Now, I heard him chanting under his breath, raising his power. Ginger tore loose from Bo's grip, losing a chunk of flesh in the process, and was halfway on his feet before Teag hammered him with his staff. The crack of wood against bone echoed, followed a split second later by a flash of light. Ginger went down like he'd been Tasered, only Teag's bolt of power carried a magical jolt.

Bo went low; Teag went high. Bo lunged and caught Ginger in the left calf, as Teag used his staff as a fulcrum and leaped, planting a boot with silver-tipped cleats right in the Nephilim's chest. Ginger dropped like a rock, and Teag smashed the butt of his staff down through the pretty-boy's face, following it up with another wallop of magic that made Ginger convulse once and then lie smoking and still.

Blondie was heading my way, while the dark-haired Nephilim hung back as if he was going to let his friends do the heavy lifting. He had coal-black hair and sharp features that made me think of a bird, so I mentally nicknamed him 'Crow'. If he thought he was going to get out of this without rumpling his Armani jacket, he had another think coming.

Half way toward me, Blondie broke into a run. I had spent the afternoon practicing with Josiah's dueling pistol, and I knew its range and expected its kick. I'd used normal bullets for practice, and saved the silver-tipped, holy-water-blessed shot for tonight.

Just a little closer. The damndest thing about dueling pistols is that they were made for short-range fighting, not distance, and they only had one bullet. That meant I had to hold my one shot until Blondie was within forty paces, which was too damn close for comfort.

That's when Crow charged.

I heard a roar behind me, and knew that Baldy had managed to regroup. Teag had his hands full. I had a split second to get off a shot at Blondie before he went for my throat. Alicia was between me and Crow, which meant I couldn't fry him with my walking stick without getting Alicia, too. As fast as Nephilim moved, it looked like both of them were going to hit me at the same time.

A thick fog came out of nowhere, coalescing between me and Crow. *Not fog, spirits.* I caught glimpses of faces and shapes, hazy gray. *Josiah isn't the only dueler who never left the alley.* Though the ghosts of dead duelers looked insubstantial to me, they had enough supernatural heft to slow down the dark-haired

Nephilim, making him fight his way through the fog to get to us. *Bless you, Alicia,* I thought.

Alicia's ghosts bought me the few seconds I needed. I took my shot at Blondie, and got him in the gut. The impact of the shot stopped his momentum, and put a big bloodstain on his abdomen. But I knew what really hurt was the silver and holy water combo, since his veins lit up through his skin from the inside-out and he went down screaming as his whole body started to smoke.

"Alicia – move!" I shouted. The alley ghosts were doing their best to slow the fourth Nephilim, but he was strong enough to fight his way through, tearing free from the spectral hands that snatched at his clothing and pulled at his arms and legs. Crow was almost on her, half transformed. I had seen what those claws could do. I dropped the gun and raised my walking stick, but I still couldn't get a clean shot.

"Get out of the way!" I yelled. And she did, but not the way I expected. Alicia swung to her left, bringing up Josiah Winfield's pistol as if the motion were the most natural thing in the world, and she fired right through the fog, plugging Crow at point blank range without blinking an eye.

"Die, you son of a bitch," she growled as the shot blew the Nephilim's head apart. Just for good measure, she clubbed the creature with the butt of the pistol as he fell, and kicked him square in the throat before his body hit the ground.

Either Alicia had been taking secret bad-ass lessons, or I was witnessing Josiah Winfield in action.

Four dead Nephilim lay on the cobblestones of Dueler's Alley, their bodies already beginning to crumble. Alicia, or maybe I should say Josiah, turned to me and gave me a nod that said I had earned an answer to my question.

"You want to stop the Watchers, you've got to kill the Judge who's bringing them through. Find the entry points, and seal them off," Josiah said. "But you've got to stop them before the Judge brings five of them through. That's all he needs to start the Harrowing, and when that begins, even the Archangels can't shut it down before it runs its course."

"How do we find the Judge?"

Alicia was losing her connection to Winfield. I could see the tension in her features, and her expressions were mostly her own again. For a heartbeat, it looked as if I could see two figures superimposed in the same spot, Alicia and Winfield.

"Find the biggest, baddest sorcerer nearby, and you'll have your Judge," Josiah replied. "Keep the guns. They'll help."

Alicia wobbled then, as Josiah's spirit left her. She looked around at the smoking corpses and at Bo's ghost, which sat next to me, then from me to Teag. "What did I miss?"

In the distance, I heard sirens. No one else might have seen the ghosts or the Nephilim, but the sound of gunshots carries. "I'll tell you later," I said. "Right now, let's get out of here before Detective Monroe shows up."

"OF ALL THE foolhardy, boneheaded moves!" Sorren didn't usually get angry, and when he did, it was very rarely with us. Now, he was annoyed, and that's when I remembered that it's not wise to tick off an ancient vampire.

"I left you a message. You didn't reply." It was the same tactic I had used for years on my mother. Sorren gave me a withering look, which suggested that he wasn't going to be easily dissuaded.

"You know that Nephilim are on the loose. You've been warned that the Reapers like to snack on magic even more than they like to eat ghosts. Watchers are here in Charleston. And you took Alicia with you!" Sorren was pacing the back room at Trifles and Folly. I had received a terse text message telling us to meet him at the store while we were taking Alicia to her house. Sorren had moved into the secret day crypt built into the foundation of the basement beneath Trifles and Folly.

"It was a perfectly logical move," I countered. "We got good information. And we got out okay."

"This time," Sorren snapped. "You are only mortal, Cassidy, and both you and Teag are relatively new in learning to use your magic. Creatures like the Nephilim are ancient." I suspected that Sorren was testier than usual about our safety because he had just lost several people close to him, and that his sense of guilt on this had nothing to do with the Watchers' magic.

"The Nephilim die pretty easily for being that old."

Sorren shook his head, and he may have rolled his eyes. "You haven't actually destroyed them. They can't be 'killed' like that. When you destroy their physical body, it drains them, so they go back to their realm to recover, but they can return – and they remember."

Holy shit. "So Coffee Guy could come back – and he'll remember that Daniel Hunter and I whipped his ass?"

Sorren nodded. "Exactly. Which is why, when I say that I have gained many enemies over the centuries, I mean exactly that. I have been fighting some of these creatures since the beginning of the Alliance."

"Any fight you can walk away from is a good fight," I said, not ready to back down.

I had the feeling that Sorren would have sighed if he had needed to breathe. "Good partners are difficult to come by," he said, and there was a pained note in his voice. "I am painfully aware of how easily humans break."

"Thank you," I said, dropping my argument. "But we've got a job to do. Teag and I went into the alley loaded for bear. We're no use to you if we aren't doing everything we can do to stop the bad guys."

Sorren looked away without saying anything. "There's been another attack, on one of your other stores, hasn't there?" I guessed.

I was willing to bet that he had the same kind of relationship with those stores' owners as he did with my family, working with them generation after generation. We were the only family he had left.

"The store in Quebec was destroyed," Sorren said, his voice gravelly. "Wards breached, everyone dead." I saw grief and anger in his face. "I have worked with that family for more than two hundred years. And I have failed them."

"That's where you were?"

He nodded. "That, and trying to connect with all my locations, strengthen their defenses. Someone is striking at them to get to me, and I'm fucking tired of it."

"Can we at least be certain whether or not Sariel is behind the attacks?" I asked. Teag had stayed quiet through the whole charged conversation, but I knew he was following every word.

Sorren shrugged, and ran both hands through his blond hair. I had never seen him like this, and it rattled me to realize that despite his age, experience and supernatural mojo, he didn't have everything completely under control.

"It sounds like Sariel, but I thought he was well and truly destroyed. I would have bet my life on that." He looked haggard. "I did bet the lives of people who depended on me on that belief. And now they're dead."

Teag laced his fingers together, stretched out his arms, and loudly cracked his knuckles. "Well then, boss, put me to work. Who do you want me to dig up – figuratively speaking?"

I grinned. "We're already in this hip-deep, so it's too late to turn around now. I know you asked Lucinda to bump up the wardings on the store and our houses – thanks for that, by the way. I got the feeling old Josiah might be willing to lend a hand, and we've got Daniel Hunter, plus our usual crew. Whether it's Sariel or someone else behind this, we need to find him and kick his ass all the way back to the Great Beyond."

"Speaking of Daniel Hunter, have you heard from him?" Sorren asked.

I made a face and shook my head. "No. I've left messages. I don't know why he gave me his cell phone number if he had no intention of answering it."

"Daniel has always done as he pleases," Sorren said. "If we're lucky, he'll show up when he's needed, on his own terms. He's a perverse bastard, but he's good at what he does."

"If Watchers cause major guilt trips, then at least one of them is here already," I said. "Josiah told us the Judge would need five."

Sorren nodded. "One Watcher is bad enough. Five would be a catastrophe. Sariel – if that's who's behind this – has us chasing our tails. We've got to get out in front of him if we're going to win. Because he's not just gunning for me. If it's Sariel, he knows how much I love this city, and he'll take down all of Charleston to get to me. I can't let that happen."

"We won't," I promised. But I had no friggin' idea how to make good on that vow.

Chapter Fourteen

ANTHONY WAS WORKING late again, and I didn't have plans, so Teag and I opted for Nicky's Bar, a favorite with Charleston locals, especially the younger King Street and Charleston City Market store-owners. We walked in and half the folks there waved or called out hello. That's one of the things I like about Nicky's. It wouldn't turn away tourists if they showed up, but it doesn't go out of the way to put itself on the map, either. It's a local place, and we love it for that.

"I was able to reach Mrs. Morrissey today," I said. "She's home from the hospital and says she's feeling much better. On the other hand, I was hoping they might postpone the Angel Oak fundraiser. I'd like to figure out how to get that Gerard Astor painting out of there before the Archive is full of people, or we could have a real problem on our hands." I paused, because Teag didn't seem to be listening. "Is everything okay?" He seemed quieter than usual, although with the attacks we both had a lot on our minds.

He sighed. "Anthony figured out that there had to be a link between the bomb at Trifles and Folly and the explosion at Sorren's house. And there's been no hiding the fact that I've come home the last few nights the worse for wear. That scares him, so he gets angry. We had a fight."

Teag made a gesture as if it was no big deal, but he avoided looking at me, and I knew it was weighing on him.

"I'm sorry," I said.

He shook his head. "Nothing for you to be sorry about. I'm proud of what we do. We make a big difference. He's going to have to learn to live with it."

Before I could say anything else, I saw two men heading for our table. "Cassidy! Teag! Mind if we join you?" Kell Winston said. He was with Ryan Alexander, who grinned and slid into a chair on Teag's side of the table while Kell sat down next to me.

Ryan is friend of Teag's and an urban explorer, someone who enjoys going into modern ruins, abandoned buildings, and forgotten places to see what he can see.

"Not at all," Teag said. We wouldn't be able to talk about business, but I think we were both a little relieved. I needed a break.

"What's new?" Kell asked.

"We got mobbed by a busload of Canadians," Teag replied.

"Were they lost?" Ryan is taller than Kell, with chestnut hair and dark brown eyes. They're both close in age to Teag and me, late twenties, and the nature of what we do means we cross paths a lot and work together when we can.

"No, just in need of some vintage jewelry," I replied, taking a sip of my wine. "Has your team recovered from the Blake house?" I asked Kell.

He nodded. "Pretty much. We lost some equipment, but it could have been a lot worse."

We chatted for a while, and Kell and Ryan ordered something to eat. Ryan regaled us with tales of his urban explorer group's most recent adventures, including exploring the old drainage tunnels around the Charleston City Market, and an old cotton warehouse out on the edge of town that was slated for demolition.

"Everyone's in such a big hurry to build new things," Ryan said with a sigh. "But there are so many amazing buildings that could be one-of-a-kind fantastic if someone would just give them a little love."

Considering that preservation and restoration are big business in Charleston and it seems like every other house has a historic plaque, I was amazed anything had been overlooked. But that's what UrbEx'ers do – they go looking for the beauty in ruins, finding the hidden gems in places others never notice.

"If I spend enough time with Ryan, I feel like I'm in one of those commercials to adopt a shelter dog – only he wants everyone to adopt an old building," Kell quipped. "Seriously, though, since we teamed up, it's been amazing. Our group can document hauntings and paranormal activity in places no one else has been – except for graffiti artists – in years. And Ryan's team helps us navigate safely in places that aren't exactly, shall we say, up to code?"

"Found anything really interesting recently?" I asked.

Ryan leaned forward. "Actually, yes. Which is one of the reasons I'm glad we ran into you two tonight. We've been out at your favorite place – the old Navy Yard."

I shivered. Ryan and Kell both know I've had bad experiences out there. "I'm telling you, there's a lot of bad mojo there."

"Believe me, we know," Kell said. "But even after what happened at the Blake house, these buildings are too good to pass up. Ryan wants to get in and explore before all the good old places get rehabbed and sold to businesses." The old Navy Yard had been getting a slow make-over for years, with the hope to convert the land someday into a profitable business park. Unfortunately, the area's bloody past and bad luck – pirates, epidemic victims, military casualties – wasn't easily erased.

"Have you ever seen the old power generation plant?" Ryan asked. "It's a prime spot for exploring. The first two times we went out to the plant, it was pretty clear that no one had been there for a long time. But when we went back last week, we found a large burned circle on the concrete at the bottom of a flight of steps." Ryan looked to Teag and me for a response. "I mean, that sort of thing doesn't happen spontaneously. No blood. No suggestion of foul play, but there was a perfect circle there in a room where it hadn't been before – and a bunch of salt all over the place."

Ryan pulled out a photo and showed it to us. The basement room was mildewed and badly lit. Paint peeled from the walls in sheets and from the ceiling, wires and old pipe insulation dangled like industrial Spanish moss. A large, scorched circle was clear in the middle of the floor. Just like something someone with a lot of magic power might use to summon a creature from beyond.

"You're sure what you found was salt?" I asked.

Ryan nodded. "Yeah. Why?"

"People who believe in magic think that salt is protective," Teag replied.

"You think someone did some kind of ritual in there?" Ryan asked, raising an eyebrow.

Teag shrugged. "Who knows?"

I glanced at Kell. "Kinda reminds you of what we saw at the Blake house, doesn't it?"

Kell leaned forward and studied the photo. "That's weird. You think there's some Satanist cult in town?" I didn't have the heart to tell him that the real answer was worse.

"Did you find anything else unusual at the old power plant?" I asked.

"We aren't the only ones to have been there recently," Ryan said. "There were at least two different sets of footprints in the mud near the back door. We saw the same footprints in some of the dust inside. But here's the weird part – it looked like there was a third set of prints near that circle in the basement – and whoever made them was barefoot."

"Trust me," Kell broke in, "that is not the place any sane person would take off his shoes."

Teag and I exchanged a glance. *A supernatural creature like a Watcher wouldn't care.*

I looked over at Kell. "What did your folks find out?" I asked.

"People have said the place was haunted ever since a technician got electrocuted back in the nineties." I'd heard the rumors. The power plant sat outside the city limits, a hulking concrete box of a building, but so far, no one had bothered to tear it down, even though a new generation plant had taken over its job a long time ago.

"Yeah, that's what I've heard," I replied. Teag nodded and started typing on his phone, so I figured he was either looking up intel on the power plant, or hacking into a satellite that could give us a visual if Google didn't do the trick.

"What happened?"

"Since other sites have been pegging lately, we figured we'd go back and see if the power plant was juiced up – supernaturally speaking," Kell said.

I sighed. Of course he did. Charleston might be on the verge of a supernatural smackdown, but for Kell and his people, it would be like a neon sign offering free ice cream. Unfortunately, I couldn't warn them off without having to explain what I knew, and their eagerness to explore could put the ghost hunters right in the middle of the danger. If we couldn't keep them away, they might be safest if we went with them.

"Harry clued us in to things being weirder than usual out there," Kell continued. "You know him? The homeless guy who's usually caging coins in the median by the traffic light out that way?" I could picture Harry, a short, grizzled-looking guy who held a cardboard sign claiming to be a disabled vet.

"Yeah, he's a decent sort."

"He helps us keep an eye out for the cops, and we try to help him out with whatever he needs," Kell said. "So anyhow, Harry told me spooky stuff was going down, so I got the crew together and we went out to have a look."

He paused to take a bite of his food. "Our meters started going bonkers as soon as we went inside," Kell said. "EMF, audio, orbs – you name it. Melissa, the psychic who comes along sometimes, was freaking out because she said she could hear ghosts screaming." He had our full attention. "Harry said he wanted to show us something really weird down in the basement. We let him lead us, since he knows the place better than anyone. He started down to the basement with a flashlight. I was right behind him, a few steps back. All of a sudden, his flashlight goes dark, and I hear Harry yell. I thought maybe he was playing a trick, or the flashlight failed, you know?" Kell paused. "So after a moment, we went on down. We looked all around. No Harry. We called his name, but he didn't answer. Not only that, but there weren't any fresh footprints in the dust at the bottom of the stairs. He just vanished."

"What happened then?" I was afraid I knew what happened to Harry, and I bet that if Teag ran a search on him, we'd find that somewhere in Harry's past, he had been charged and acquitted of a crime, just like the other men who disappeared.

"We got out of there fast," Kell replied, sounding embarrassed. "Weird, huh?"

I exchanged a glance with Teag. I was sure he was thinking what I was thinking. We needed to make our own trip out to the old power plant and see for ourselves what was going on. *Two big circles for major magic – two Watchers brought over from Beyond. Three more, and it all goes 'boom'.*

Kell sipped his beer. "The poltergeist activity is getting worse. We kept getting hit with pebbles and little chunks of plaster that were definitely thrown – they didn't just fall off the ceiling. Doors slammed and opened on their own. We heard engines humming, but nothing was turned on."

"What about the room with the burned circle?" I asked.

Kell met my gaze. "That was pretty strange. All through the building, there was so much EMF activity I actually thought someone was playing with us, faking it. The ghosts were more aggressive than ever. But the closer we got to the room with the circle, the quieter it got, until the last length of hallway and the room itself – nothing. Total null."

That didn't surprise me, if Reapers liked taking a bite out of ghosts to stoke up their energy, heck, maybe they liked a snack or two between plagues and disasters. I imagine hell spawn get peckish, too.

"You guys really know how to get around," Teag remarked, finishing off his ale. "What about that old motel you said was out near the Navy Yard?"

Kell nodded. "We've been there. There was plenty of graffiti, doors ripped off, lots of damage, so we're certainly not the first to go there. But we had heard a story about a young man who killed himself there in one of the rooms. Another guy hanged himself in one of the bathrooms when he found out his girl married someone else." In other words, good ghost-hunting.

"This was our second time at the motel," Kell went on. "The first time, we didn't get anything except a couple of blurry orbs." Orbs were balls of light caught on camera, and many ghost hunters believe they are spectral images.

"This time, orbs were popping up all over the place. Cold spots. Poltergeist stuff – doors and windows slamming, flying pebbles, objects falling. And the same feeling that we had at the power plant, that the ghosts really wanted us to leave."

I looked to Ryan. "Any evidence that people had been in the building lately?"

He frowned. "Yeah. And if we hadn't been trespassing ourselves, I might have called the cops. The only thing is, I'm still not sure whether what we saw was human, or just some big animals. The prints were strange."

"Oh?" I asked.

Ryan nodded. "We saw several hoof prints. Gouges in the walls and rips in the carpet that looked like a bear had gotten loose in there." He had photos, too. I was grateful, because it saved Teag and me a trip that was not likely to be in our best interests.

He paused. "The other difference was the smell. Some of the rooms at the old motel stank like nothing I've ever smelled before."

There's a reason people say something 'stinks like the pit of Hell'. Supernatural creatures, especially those from the less enlightened realms, tend not to adhere to mortal notions of hygiene.

"What I really want to know," Kell said, "is what's causing this big surge in supernatural activity? From what I'm seeing on the ghost hunter forums online, lots of other people are asking the same question."

I was pretty sure I knew, but it wasn't an answer I could share. You can't un-know something, just like you can't un-see it. And for all that ghost hunters and paranormal investigators believe the truth is 'out there', very few people really want to have their nice, normal mental framework of how the world functions totally turned on end.

"Would you two mind sending me copies of those photos?" I asked. "I promise not to reveal my sources," I said with a smile. "But I have some friends who might be able to figure out what caused the things you saw."

"I was hoping you'd ask," Ryan replied, grinning. He pulled a flash drive from his pocket. "Here. Kell and I put the best photos on this. Don't worry – we know how to scrub the digital images so that they can't be traced. But if you give it to someone in law enforcement, do me a favor and wipe it for prints, okay?"

He wasn't joking. Ryan's group of explorers is very careful not to damage property or steal left-behind items, but they still trespass, break, and enter. Teag and I did a lot of the same in service to the Alliance. The police were likely to take a dim view of such things. That made it awkward to do your civic duty when, in the process of committing a misdemeanor, you happen upon someone committing a felony.

"It's probably something new with college students," Kell said. "You know, some kind of hazing or role playing game. I certainly don't want to kick off another one of those 'Satanic panic' mass hysteria things. But I do think it bears looking into." He shrugged. "Something about the whole thing felt... wrong."

"Since we don't know if the people behind this are dangerous, you might not want to go back, at least until things calm down a little," I suggested, hoping they would take the hint. I liked both Kell and Ryan, and the people I had met from their groups seemed like nice folks. I didn't want anyone to get hurt, and I sure didn't want anyone in the way when the time came for us to take down the ghost-chompers.

"That's okay," Ryan said. "There are plenty more abandoned buildings near Charleston, and more haunts than Kell can shake a stick at. But if you do find anything out about what we saw, I'd love to know."

The conversation turned to more mundane topics like the weather, travel plans and mutual friends. When we reached the street, Kell and Ryan headed to their cars, and Teag and I walked a couple of blocks back to where we had parked by the store.

"I don't want our friends getting involved in this," I said. "Someone's likely to get hurt."

"If we warn them off too much, they'll realize we know more than we're telling, and they'll try harder to be involved," Teag cautioned.

"You know we're going to need to go out to that power plant and get a look at what's going on," I said.

"Yeah, I figured. Out of the frying pan, into the fire."

"Let's hope that Sorren gets back quickly, with reinforcements," I said. "We've got to shut Sariel down before more Watchers can get through."

Chapter Fifteen

UTILITY PLANTS ARE meant to be brightly lit. No one designs them to be prowled around in the dark. Everything echoes and huge pieces of equipment make for strange shadows and lots of hiding places. But here we were, making our way through the dust and darkness. Faint moonlight struggled through the old plant's high, dirty windows, but it barely made a difference in the gloom.

"Not too hard to follow the trail," Teag muttered. Once again, we were outfitted for a small supernatural war. Teag and I each had one of Josiah Winfield's pistols, cleaned and reloaded and ready for action. I had my athame and my walking stick, Bo's collar, and a satchel full of everything from witch mirrors to jack balls to some *gris-gris* powder, and I was wearing every protective amulet I owned. Teag had his fighting staff, his *espada y daga* fighting blades, some other nasty-looking knives, and an assortment of magically-charged knots and amulets. Teag was wearing a vest he had made with magical protections woven into its warp and woof, and he had gifted me with one right before we set out. I was happy for any extra protection I could get.

I was pretty sure that he also had a few highly-illegal ghost-scrambling weapons courtesy of Chuck Pettis.

Tonight, Caliel came with us, and as a Voudon houngan, he had his own powerful protections. With luck, that included being under the watchful, protective eye of the Loas. Caliel, like Lucinda, was a descendant of Mama Nadege. He could throw down with the big boys. Sorren led the way. We were ready for trouble.

Huge generators the size of trucks loomed like sleeping giants, casting long, dark shadows. Darkened light fixtures hung from the high ceiling, and it did not take much for my imagination to turn them into hovering predators. I've seen pictures of old power plants built around 1900. They had soaring ceilings and big windows, resembling huge railroad terminals like Grand Central Station in New York City. This plant was far too new to have any architectural character. It was a big, concrete box, as ugly as it was functional.

Habitation changes the energy of a place, and so does abandonment. It's like the difference between sleeping, and dead. The power plant had stood empty for decades, and all the energy imparted by the bustle of living beings going about their business had faded away long ago. What remained was a dead husk, energy-wise, but dead things have a way of coming back to life in the most disturbing and dangerous ways.

"Someone's called up some bad magic, very strong," Caliel said as we ventured deeper into the deserted power plant. "Can you feel it?"

We all nodded. To me, the taint of dark magic felt like something sticky and foul on my skin. The feeling grew stronger as we moved farther into the bowels of the abandoned plant.

"Kell said that the big generators and the offices are on this floor," I said, "and the lower floors are mostly wiring and conduits."

"Unfortunately, that's where we're headed." Sorren led the way. Dressed all in black, he was ready for a fight. He wore two swords, his favorite weapons.

"There are the stairs." Teag's voice was flat. He was probably just as frightened as I was at the prospect of going down those steps where Harry had disappeared. Hell, going down into the underground, lightless subfloor was frightening under the best of circumstances, even when black magic and supernatural monsters weren't involved. We were going in where fallen angels had not feared to tread.

Somewhere in the distance, water dripped and rats squeaked. I tried not to think about the roaches and other vermin skittering around our boots and I wondered if this was the way the guys who explored those old Egyptian tombs felt as they descended into the unknown.

We stopped at the top of the stairs. Sorren turned to Caliel. "What do you sense?"

Caliel closed his eyes and I felt a ripple of power brush against me as he gathered his magic. "On the stairs, nothing. Lower down, remnants of dirty magic, very dark. And..." his voice drifted off. "I don't want to say until I know for sure." He shook his head and muttered something in the island language I had heard him use to invoke the Loas. "Some bad shit happened here."

"But the stairs are safe?"

Caliel gave me a lopsided grin. "Nothing here is safe, but whatever took Harry is gone from the steps. And if you're right about the Reapers and the Watchers, then the rest of us are safe, unless you've got some past sins you'd like to confess?" He chuckled as he said it, but there was truth beneath the humor.

I couldn't help glancing toward Sorren. He had been a thief before he had been turned, and what he had done in the centuries since then likely went beyond breaking and entering. Sorren gave me a wan half-smile. "Don't worry, Cassidy. The Reapers aren't looking for vampires. We're not on their menu. They want mortal prey."

Still, I held my breath as we carefully made our way down the steps. Our heavy-duty flashlights barely made a dent in the pitch black darkness. Sorren didn't need light to navigate, but Teag, Caliel, and I did. While the power plant was 'abandoned', I wasn't sure that meant the shadows that waited for us were empty.

Sorren was in front. I went next, followed by Teag. Caliel took up the rear, chanting and singing to the Loas to ask for their protection.

Nothing happened. I let out a long breath when we reached the dirty concrete floor of the second level. The ceiling was a lot lower than in the generator room. This level held wiring, pipes, and conduits – a maintenance sub-floor to keep the main generator room from being too cluttered.

Harry had vanished into thin air on those narrow concrete steps.

"Someone came this way," Sorren said, pointing to smudged footprints in the dust. Cobwebs hung from the exposed rafters and the tangle of wires and pipes overhead was close enough that I could have put up a hand and touched them.

We made a careful search of the room. In places, Teag, Caliel, and Sorren had to duck to avoid hitting the low-hanging wires and the pipes that ran just inches over my head. I shivered each time something brushed my hair.

I was afraid we might find Harry's body in a corner, overlooked by Kell's ghost hunters. I was hoping that we'd find him holed up, stoned or drunk but alive, but I feared something much worse had befallen him. Unfortunately, Harry was nowhere to be found.

"I feel power, called and dispelled," Caliel said. He moved up to the front with Sorren. Teag fell back to guard the rear, and I played my heavy-duty flashlight around the room. Sorren would sense any humans nearby, and some types of supernatural creatures, but I didn't know if that included Nephilim, and I did not want to find out the hard way. Any angel fallen far enough to end up here had a rough descent.

"Someone's done dark magic, close by," Sorren agreed.

A strange odor lingered in the air, something I associated with an old, unpleasant memory. Then I knew what I smelled: burned meat and hair. That wasn't a good omen.

"Look there." Sorren pointed to a place where the dust had been swept clear. A large area, probably six feet by six feet, had been cleaned off down to the concrete, and charcoal and salt circle of power had been drawn on the stained old floor. The circle had been smudged open in one place, so whatever it was made to contain had either been freed or dispelled. I was pretty sure that anything called up in that circle was something I did not want to meet.

A black chicken feather wafted down through the air. *What's a chicken doing down here?*

"Oh, oh, oh." Caliel was standing over a blackened lump, and as we drew closer, I wrinkled my nose at the smell of rotting meat.

"What is that?" Teag asked, as our flashlights showed bits of yellow bone amid the blackened, charred surface. I saw a smaller lump nearby.

"Someone's offered a burnt sacrifice," Caliel said, "and whatever they used the circle to conjure, they called a Loa to help them." He pointed to a smudged marking on the concrete. It was a *veve*, the elaborate drawings that were the signature of the Voudon Loa, powerful immortal beings that sometimes meddled in the affairs of humans.

"I don't recognize that *veve*," I said.

"Best you don't," Caliel replied. "No good reason to call that Loa. Marinette Bois Sech is cruel and powerful, and if she's involved, we've got big trouble, you can be sure of that."

"Then the things over there –" Teag asked, pointing at the blackened lumps.

"They're the price Marinette charges for her help. A black pig and a black rooster. Burned alive." Caliel was already drawing the *veves* for Papa Legba and Damballah Wedo, protective and very powerful Loas. Sorren examined the large circle while Caliel sprinkled salt and chanted, dispelling any remaining dark energy from whoever had called down Marinette's spirit. "There's a reason she's feared. She does terrible things and she's the patron of monsters. Some say she's the protector of werewolves," Caliel replied.

Werewolves have a patron Loa? I resolved to discuss that further with Sorren, once were well gone from this creepy place.

"What about that circle?" Teag asked. He stood with his back toward us, watching the rest of the floor to avoid being ambushed. "Did someone bring a Watcher through?"

Sorren straightened from where he knelt next to the circle. "That's exactly what I think happened. We need to be gone from here. The sooner the better."

"There's another floor," Teag said. "Kell's people were freaked out enough after Harry disappeared and they found the circle that they didn't try to go farther. But I found the blueprints online. There's another subfloor, probably used mostly for storage, underneath this one."

"All right," Sorren said. "Let's have a look. But we'll make it quick."

The upper floors had smelled of mold and dust, decay and disuse. The smell that rose from the lower floor made me think of fetid swamps in the dead of summer. Not a scent I expected to encounter indoors.

"Stop." Sorren's voice made us freeze in out tracks. "There's a lot of stagnant water down here," he said. "No idea how deep or what's in it. But there's something out there, and I don't think we want to meet it. Back up slowly. Now."

We were halfway back up the stairs before things started jumping out of the water like catfish on a summer's day. I remembered the tentacles of the pool monster at Tarleton. Our flashlights barely cut the gloom, but I got enough of a look to know I did not want a close-up. Black, wriggling things leapt into the air, trying to reach the stairway and us. Slimy and bulbous, they reminded me of individual octopus tentacles or impossibly large slugs, except for their gaping mouths.

One of the things landed on the open metal stairway ahead of me and I blasted it with a shot from the walking stick. It writhed as it shriveled and bits of it flew off, landing in the water with a muted plop. In the next instant, the dark water roiled as the creature's companions fought over who got to eat the leftovers. My stomach lurched.

More of the things heaved themselves up onto the steps. They looked like snakes without heads. Open, lamprey-like maws were all I could see, no eyes or ears, no skull. Eating machines, hungry for fresh meat.

"What are they?" I asked, sickened and horrified.

"Leeches," Sorren replied. "Only they've been exposed to very powerful magic."

"Leeches?" My voice rose a note. I'd had an unpleasant, unforgettable encounter with leeches when I was a kid, swimming at my grandma's pond. These were super-sized. We were going to have to fight our way back up the steps.

Teag hit one of the thrashing monsters with his staff, knocking it back into the water. I had to be careful with the walking stick, because I didn't want to hit anyone with fire, and I wasn't sure whether or not any of the equipment around us might be flammable.

One of the monster leeches hurled itself into the air and lay wriggling at my feet, its open maw flexing as it sought flesh. I leveled my athame and a brilliant, white light flared as my power sent it flailing through the air. Leeches don't fly well, thank all the gods and spirits.

The leeches must have smelled blood, because the water boiled with them. They crawled over one another in their frenzy to reach us, and more than once, we saw one of the uber-leeches reach escape velocity only to be grabbed and pulled back into the stagnant depths by a hungry fellow bloodsucker.

I would have loved to have just torched the lot of them, but I had no way of knowing what else lurked in the shadowed recesses. If there were left-over cans of gasoline or other flammables somewhere above water level, I could set up a fatal fireball that would wipe us out along with the leeches.

Sorren slashed at the leeches with his swords, sending bloody geysers into the air as he cut them in half. The leeches writhed and wriggled, blood spurting everywhere, until they rolled into the depths of the filthy, stinking water to be consumed by their fellow monsters.

I promised myself time to throw up if we survived the encounter.

Caliel let out a yelp, and scrambled back as a leech thrashed toward him, intent on the fresh, hot blood it sensed. Sorren grappled with one of the leeches that had managed to get a grip on his leg, and I watched, sickened, as he yanked it free, its maw red with blood.

"Get up the stairs!" I yelled. "I'll blast them once we're clear."

No one needed to be told twice. We all scrambled up the metal stairs, and I turned and loosed a blast of cold magical force from my athame. The brilliant white light hit the writhing leeches, hurling them free of the steps, throwing them back into the fetid water and tearing some of them into little bits for good measure. Their bloody remnants served to distract the rest of the monsters from following us, as they fought over the spoils.

I was shaking as we reached the relative safety of the second floor. "Keep moving," Sorren urged. "I think we've gotten the wrong kind of attention."

We had awakened the spirits tied to this place. Whatever bound their restless shades to this godforsaken ruin had shaken them from their restless sleep, and now they were looking to take their annoyance out on those who had interrupted their eternal slumber.

The night outside was still and hot. Yet here in the power plant, it had grown so cold I expected to see my breath. Shadows and half-seen images darted around the edges of my sight, and the sense of being watched was oppressive and overwhelming. I glimpsed faces in the shadows, human forms and glowing orbs.

"Run!" Caliel shouted. I smelled a whiff of pipe smoke and heard a dog bark angrily at the pursuing spirits, suggesting that Caliel had persuaded Papa Legba's spirit to buy us time to escape.

We took the steps two at a time back to the main floor, and Sorren dropped back, swords in both hands, ready to fight. Teag and I were in front as we sprinted for the doorway with Caliel close behind. We were running flat out, anxious to be out of that cursed place. Sorren came last, though with his vampire speed he could have easily lapped us all.

We cleared the doorway to the outside and slammed the heavy metal door into place. Caliel used a flicker of magic to turn the deadbolt, although whether or not the things that pursued us would be slowed by something as mundane as steel was debatable.

Three out of five of the Watchers were already here. Two more, and all hell would break loose, "On the bright side," Sorren said, "I've finally gotten through to the Briggs Society. Archie's been around a time or two. He'll have some ideas on this. Be ready to go at seven tomorrow night. The Briggs doesn't wait for anyone."

Chapter Sixteen

WE STOOD OUTSIDE a two-story brick building on the edge of the old part of town at seven o'clock the next night. An engraved bronze plaque by the door read, 'Briggs Society. Explorers welcome. Ring bell'.

A day had passed since our adventure at the power plant, and I had barely regained my wits and nerve. But with Charleston on the brink of a supernatural apocalypse, none of us had time for a mental health day. So here Teag and I were with Sorren, on the front steps of a building I had often passed but never noticed, as an obnoxiously loud doorbell summoned attention from within.

"You really think this friend of yours can help?" I asked.

Sorren shrugged. "It won't hurt to ask. Archie's one of the few people who's likely to realize something bad is going on." The brick Georgian building looked staid for such things, but Sorren had taught me how much could hide behind a well-heeled facade.

Before I could ask any more questions, a man in an honest-to-goodness butler's uniform came to the door. He looked like something out of Hollywood central casting, tall and lean, complete with a hang-dog expression.

"Password, please?" he asked in a cultured baritone.

"Hurly-burly," Sorren replied without batting an eye. The butler nodded and stood aside.

"Welcome, Mister Sorren." He looked Teag and me over. "Guests? I wasn't told."

"Cairo Protocol, Higgins," Sorren replied without a pause. "Colonel Donnelly will understand."

"Very well, sir. Right this way, sir."

I felt as if I had stepped into the Victorian era. Everywhere I looked, the rooms were filled with treasures and mementos from around the world and from every culture and time period. African and Pacific Islander masks vied with Ming vases, Chinese statues, Japanese kimonos, and Samurai armor. In the center of the foyer, where most establishments would have put a nice table with a huge floral arrangement sat a taxidermied Percheron horse wearing full steel barding.

The foyer was a rotunda with an overhead dome ringed with windows that, while dark now, probably set the room in a bright glow during the day. Portraits hung on the walls dating back hundreds of years. I wondered if Sorren was a founding member, and if so, how he kept his true nature a secret. Then I took a second look at the paintings. I recognized some of the names. John Cabot, the explorer. Henry Hudson and George Bass, also explorers, along with Gaspar Corte-Real, and Sir John Franklin. Every one of them known for being daring explorers – and for disappearing without a trace.

Teag looked fascinated as we followed Higgins down a hallway. More portraits lined the walls; bronze castings, marble busts, and ornate Indian statues were showcased in nooks every few feet. I was certain that the Killim carpet beneath our feet was original and priceless. Although many of the doors we passed were closed, those that were not exposed equally well-appointed rooms filled with furnishings I recognized as antique and expensive. I was sure that I had glimpsed a couple of paintings thought to have been lost or destroyed in wars long past, and I longed to find out what the numerous glass display cases contained. The one case I was close enough to peer inside held a very old, leather-bound book with the title *My Story* written by Virginia Dare. My eyes widened, but there was no time to ask questions to investigate. Even at a distance, curiosity warred with prudence, since my Gift warned me that many, if not most, of the objects carried supernatural power.

That's when the name 'Briggs' connected for me. Benjamin Briggs had been the captain of the *Mary Celeste*, which was found floating and deserted in 1872, and no trace of Briggs, his family or the rest of the crew has ever been found. *If there's anyone who knows anything about people who vanish into thin air, it seems like we've come to the right place.*

"This whole place is filled with Spookies and Sparklers," Teag whispered. I wondered now how many of the items Sorren had 'disposed' of for us had found a permanent home here, and what made this fine old building a suitable containment area.

"In here, sir." Higgins opened a door and stepped to one side. Sorren murmured his thanks and strode into the room, and with a glance and a shrug, Teag and I followed.

"Sorren, my good fellow. What brings you out tonight – with guests, no less?" The speaker was a florid-faced man who looked to be in his late sixties. Tall and raw-boned, everything from his elocution to his bespoke suit was utterly upper-crust. He stood in a well-appointed parlor. Dark wainscoting and hunter green paint gave the room a decidedly masculine feel, while the sculpted plaster ceiling, crystal chandelier, and antique Aubusson carpets softened the overall impression of the room. I was not surprised to find more exquisite paintings adorning the walls, along with a tapestry I judged to be several centuries old and likely Belgian in origin.

"May I present Colonel Archibald Donnelly," Sorren said, and our host inclined his head in acknowledgement. "Colonel, this is Cassidy Kincaide and Teag Logan, my assistants."

The Colonel nodded, and gestured toward a small seating area near the fireplace fitted with antique Delft tiles. "I don't have anything on hand for you, Sorren, sorry to say, but can I offer either of you two a bourbon?"

Teag and I declined. Colonel Donnelly poured a drink for himself and sat down in a brocade wing chair. "Haven't seen you around the Club in quite a while, Sorren. A few of the members have asked about you. Heard about the fire. Damned shame. Into a bit of trouble, I presume?" The Colonel lifted a shaggy eyebrow, and his blue eyes were clear and bright, with more than a hint of mischief. I was willing to bet he had been a hell-raiser in his younger days.

"You've felt the disturbances?" Sorren asked.

Colonel Donnelly snorted. "Hell's bells, man. Of course I felt them! Wouldn't be worth my salt as a necromancer if I hadn't. Question is: what are you going to do about it?"

"Josiah Winfield's ghost is back. So is Daniel Hunter. Someone is bringing Nephilim across, and several

Watchers have already crossed over," Sorren said. "At least a half a dozen people have vanished. Trouble's brewing, and whoever is behind this is either nursing an old grudge or trying to get me out of the way. Maybe Sariel, back from the grave. We're going to need high-powered help, Archie. That's why I came to you."

So many of the objects in the room carried such strong magic that it was difficult to keep my mind on the conversation. The parlor was filled with Victorian clutter: a terrarium full of mandrake, botanical drawings of flora and fauna I was pretty sure didn't exist in the natural world, and a suit of armor that looked more like a space suit for a creature with decidedly non-human appendages.

If I concentrated, I could hear many of the items whispering to me, making me all kinds of promises if I would free them, trying to seduce me with flattery and visions. I folded my hands in my lap, determined not to touch anything. Teag's attention seemed to be riveted on the tapestry, and when I looked at the large, intricately woven picture, I realized that it was chock full of magical sigils and symbols. It fairly glowed with power, and I couldn't begin to imagine how it might look to Teag's Weaver magic.

"Talk to me about Reapers and Watchers, Archie," Sorren said. "Half a dozen or so men started down stairways and never reached the bottom. All had questionable backgrounds, but no convictions. No blood, no bodies. Just vanished."

Archibald Donnelly nodded. "Sounds like Watchers, all right. They feed on the people they judge, and a powerful sorcerer like Sariel could use them to reflect power back to him. As for Reapers, they're minor demons, harder to catch than they are to destroy. Slippery devils. But someone has to call them from the Lower Realms, and frighten them into following the rules." He sighed. "Otherwise, they'd just be snatching folks left and right. That alone tells you we're going against someone with real power."

Donnelly shook his head. "'Course, the Reapers don't realize that they're just the cows being fattened for slaughter. Kind of like supernatural batteries. They store blood power for the sorcerer to use for his big event." He paused. "The Watchers are senior Nephilim, and they help the sorcerer do whatever he means to do."

"So the sorcerer needs the Watchers to call down a Harrowing," Sorren said. "Familiar territory, Archie. Remember?"

Donnelly nodded. "Aye. And I thought we eliminated the most likely suspect a long time ago."

Sorren leaned back in his chair and closed his eyes, rubbing his forehead with his hand in a very mortal gesture. "So did I. I'm certain that Sariel's son Samuel was completely destroyed. And until now, I would have bet my life that Sariel was permanently gone, too." He shook his head. "But everything points to Sariel. I just don't know how he managed to survive."

"We've seen supernatural spikes all over North America increase in the last month," Donnelly said. "You know the kind of chaos that's been going on. It's not like the Family to be so blatant. More like some kind of supernatural terrorism."

I glanced toward Sorren. "You said that some of your properties and stores were attacked. Were there attacks on any of the Alliance's operations that aren't primarily connected to you?" I wracked my memory for strange things in the news lately. Sad to say, since TV and internet news collect stories from all around the world and feature the worst in the headlines, every week is full of horrors.

"There's always violence in the world somewhere, and it's not always due to the supernatural," Sorren replied. "But lately, the Alliance and its allies have seen a sharp uptick in weird attacks that seem to have a common magical thread."

"That serial killer in New England," Donnelly said. "Witnesses describe a 'movie star handsome' stranger who was last seen with the victim and then vanishes without a trace."

"The shooter in that big workplace killing," Sorren added. "Was a woman – odd in itself, since men are more likely to commit that type of crime. But what's really worrisome is that the shooter's co-workers described her as being in a new romantic relationship with a tall, dark and handsome stranger and how dramatically she changed after she started dating him." He paused. "And of course, there's no trace of the boyfriend or that he ever existed."

"There have been a dozen smaller killing sprees that fit the pattern," Donnelly added. "The killers have all been women or gay men, all the model of good citizens, caring friends, well-behaved neighbors, hard-working employees and diligent family members. Then out of the blue one day, the killer wakes up and slaughters their nearest and dearest – family, neighbors, co-workers, pets, friends – and commits suicide. In every case, the killer had a notably good looking new lover for a few weeks before the murders, and that lover disappears without a trace after the deaths."

"Nephilim," I murmured. *As if the dating scene wasn't scary enough.*

"Clearly," Donnelly replied. "The question is: why?"

"To keep us distracted," Sorren replied. "I've been running around trying to keep my people safe, and I can't be everywhere at once. The Alliance is stretched thin responding to all these recent dark magic incidents, thinking they're unrelated."

"Which they appear to be," Donnelly added, "if you're looking for a relationship among the victims or the mortal killers. But the real connection –"

"Is the vanishing boyfriends," Teag said. "The Nephilim. And I bet the police figure the killers just murdered them and the bodies haven't turned up yet."

Sorren nodded. "Add to that the stairway disappearances, and both the police and the Alliance are so busy with the distraction, the real predator slips in unnoticed."

"When you looked into the stairway disappearances, did you look beyond Charleston?" I asked Teag. That's when I realized why he had been staring at the tapestry on the wall. It was the full panel of the 'Mystic Capture of the Unicorn', the seventh of the famous Unicorn Tapestries. No museum in the world had had more than tatters of the Mystic Capture since the 1700s, but here it was in its full glory. Not only was the panel priceless, it was one of the lost treasures of the art world. And it was staring me in the face. Apparently the Briggs Society specialized in vanished artwork as well as missing explorers.

Teag brought his attention back to the discussion. "I saw that there had been some in other cities, but don't forget – the stairway people might have just been reported as missing persons, without a mention about the steps. That would make it almost impossible to see the pattern, and I wasn't really looking outside of Charleston."

"People vanish every day," Donnelly replied. "Most do so on purpose, to escape bad debts and awful love affairs. Some fall prey to criminals or bad fortune. But others disappear because of magic – either their own or someone else's."

"Sariel brought down his 'judgment' on Charleston the last time because he thought it was a 'wicked' city," Sorren said. "He called it a 'Harrowing'—a rather Old Testament-sounding phrase for mass murder. What if Sariel meant to come back and cause a Harrowing here in Charleston because he knows it's particularly meaningful to me?" Sorren said. "And what if he brought his Nephilim through early to cause just the kind of distraction we've seen, so that neither I nor the Alliance would be prepared to fight him here?"

Donnelly sipped his bourbon. "You've got some big 'ifs' to that theory, but given what we've got to work with, it makes more sense than anything else we've come up with."

"It would explain how three Watchers got through without us realizing it," Sorren said. "Even Daniel Hunter is coming in late to the game. There was just too much magical 'noise' going on to notice."

Donnelly nodded. "Makes sense. Distracts everyone, plenty of blood for the Reapers and Nephilim to feed on, causes you heartache, and sets you – and Charleston – up for a big fall."

A question had been nagging me. "None of these missing staircase people ended up here by chance, did they?" I asked. "Since disappearing without a trace seems to be a common theme among the members I've seen pictured."

Donnelly chuckled. "No, I can assure you, none of those stairway people ended up here. As for vanishing, it's something we know more than a little about here at the Briggs. Since explorers by definition go into the unknown, they sometimes find themselves beset by dark or unstable magic." He shrugged. "Some of our members blundered into old ruins or tombs that were set with powerful curses. Others tinkered with objects or knowledge they didn't fully understand. Some just managed to be in the wrong place at the wrong time when a powerful magic user was doing a major working."

"So your society commemorates those explorers who've gone missing?" I asked.

Donnelly chuckled and glanced at Sorren, whose lips quirked upward, just a bit. "Not completely, Miss Kincaide. It's true we remember them. We also use magic to find them – or to discover what happened to them if they're beyond finding. And if they've been transported somewhere – or 'somewhen' – outside normal time and space, we give them a place to come home to, where people will actually believe their mad tales."

"And the artwork?"

Donnelly gestured to the walls and shelves crowded with artifacts and artwork. "Some works of art are just that – pieces from the artist's imagination. But others, especially pieces by some of the great masters, are imbued with magic of their own." He raised an eyebrow. "You know something of how strong emotion colors an object?"

I nodded. "Yes. First-hand."

"Now imagine a piece of artwork that contains bits of the creative spark of the genius who made it, or perhaps still retains some of the magic used by its creator." His gaze told me he was utterly serious. "A famous painter or sculptor facing a deadline for a powerful patron might be tempted to call on supernatural powers for help, or bargain away part of his soul for fame."

He gestured again toward the masterworks on the walls. "Down through the ages, some of those masterpieces were taken from display by their rightful owners, the supernatural creatures who made and kept those bargains with the artists. Others were taken by the artists themselves, long after their mortal lives ended, when claiming ownership would have been controversial or dangerous. The rest are here because they pose a danger to the mortal world. Quite a few of the pieces are portals to places you don't want to go, or doors that could admit things you don't want to meet. We keep them – and you – safe."

Sorren cleared his throat. "Back to Reapers. You're a necromancer, Archie. Can you conjure the spirits of some of the men who vanished and find out what took them, and why?"

Now I understood why Sorren had told me to ask the shop owner next door for something of Jonathan's that he had left behind when he disappeared, and why Teag had been sent to find something that belonged to Harry.

Donnelly looked resigned, as if the request had not caught him by surprise. "I rather figured this wasn't a social call," he remarked, although his half-smile softened his words. "You want to confirm whether Sariel is the real power behind this, and shut him down – like last time."

Something I did not understand flickered in Sorren's eyes. "Whether or not it's Sariel, there's a nephilmancer using Reapers and Nephilim in Charleston, and bringing Watchers across. As far as I'm concerned, that's a declaration of war. If we can confirm that it's Sariel, all the better. But whether or not we know his name, it's time to bring the battle to him."

Donnelly's eyes took on a hard glint. "That's a reasonable request in an unreasonable business." He nodded curtly. "All right. I just need a little time to set this up. There's no such thing as a 'simple' working when it comes to necromancy."

He poured bourbon for Teag and me although we hadn't requested it, as if he assumed the evening's work would require it. I could tell from Sorren's slight flush that he had fed recently. After Donnelly left the parlor, I took a sip of the bourbon and began to move around the room, peering at the treasures though I was careful not to touch anything. Teag had begun at the same spot but was working in the opposite direction.

"Is that one of the missing Faberge eggs from the Russian Revolution?" I gasped, marveling at a jewel-encrusted egg on a golden stand.

"Yes – and the other six are here somewhere, too," Sorren chuckled. "As are the most potent of the famous works that were 'destroyed' over the years in fires or disasters. The society took them because they were dangerous – you of all people should understand the possible consequences when objects carry a supernatural threat."

I did indeed, but at the moment, I was overwhelmed by what I was seeing. It occurred to me that I had no difficulty believing in fallen angels, demons, and ghosts, but was mind-blown by artwork that had mysteriously survived fires, war, and cataclysm. I also noted a few objects with engraved plates that made my eyes bulge.

'Medallion from the Lost City of Z, courtesy Percy Fawcett 1927', read one tag next to a golden pendant. 'Stone from the North Pole, courtesy of Roald Amundsen, 1932' said another tag. I remembered reading about both men, and realized the gift dates were after their so-called disappearances.

"How does this place keep it quiet when they've got all these missing art treasures?" Teag asked. "What's to keep authorities from barging in and finding the art – and the missing people?"

Sorren smiled. "The Briggs has its own defenses, built up over the centuries, as well as formidable guardians. That's not something you need to worry about."

Against one wall was a large glass curio cabinet. It was filled with small sculptures from several vanished civilizations, wax carvings and poppets I wouldn't have touched on a bet, strange coins and amulets and a variety of other items that looked like a time-traveler's souvenir collection.

"That's a cabinet of oddities, or *wunderkammeren*," Sorren said, noting my interest. "Members bring back things from their travels as mementos, or in some cases, to make sure they don't fall into the wrong hands." I made sure to keep my hands clasped behind my back, since I was certain I didn't want any accidental visions from the pieces in the display case.

Half an hour later, Higgins returned. "The Colonel requests your attendance," he said, and ushered us out of the parlor. We followed Higgins down a long corridor filled with more portraits and impossible pieces of artwork. I noticed that the butler stayed just far enough ahead of us to discourage conversation. Sorren seemed to know his way around, but Teag looked as nervous as I felt.

Higgins stopped at a pair of double doors at the end of the hallway. He opened the doors ceremoniously, and stood aside. "This way, please."

The huge space might have been a ballroom a century ago. Now, it was empty of furniture except for a few *wunderkammeren* around the walls, giving it a cavernous appearance. The parquet floor was exquisite, as were the heavy velvet draperies that covered the floor-to-ceiling windows. I glanced upward at the high ceiling with its molded plaster decorations, and realized that the patterns there were composed of magical symbols.

Thirteen huge windows. Thirteen astrological signs incorporated in the plaster designs overhead, one for each of the conventional zodiac signs as well as Ouroboros, the tail-devouring serpent. Power was built into this room, and the single figure in its center who beckoned us forward fairly shimmered with magical energy.

"Wait!" I said, coming to a dead halt. "That's one of Gerard Astor's paintings!" I pointed to a dark, moody canvas that hung on one of the paneled walls. It was taller than I was, and the images it depicted were life-sized. Set against a background of shadows and flames, Nephilim stalked toward the beholder. Some were incredibly handsome men with a predatory gleam in their eyes, while others had begun to transform into their true, monstrous state, black-winged and sharp-toothed. I recognized Baldy, the dark-haired one I'd nicknamed Crow, and Blondie from the Nephilim who had attacked us in the alley. One of the fallen angels was Asian, while the fifth's skin was dark as ebony. A fine net of silver chain hung over the canvas, fastened into the wall on all sides, and it looked to me as if it were designed less to protect the painting from onlookers than to protect the viewers from the painting.

I shuddered, remembering what Coffee Guy had looked like for real, and how the Nephilim at the Archive had peeled himself out of a similar painting. I thought that the silver mesh net was a wonderful addition. That made me worry about Mrs. Morrissey, and I resolved to find a way to protect her, as well as any attendees who viewed the exhibit. "His work is in another display at the Archive."

Sorren frowned. "Astor made a deal with Darkness to achieve his fame, and it drove him mad. He either didn't realize, or didn't care, that his paintings could be used as portals for Nephilim to enter our world. Though he became very famous, his paintings cost a lot of lives."

"I thought he disappeared," I said, remembering what Mrs. Morrissey had told me. After the fight with the Nephilim I encountered at the Archive, I had no trouble believing that Astor's paintings were cursed.

"He did," Sorren replied. "The Alliance saved his life and removed him to a safe location, where he was cared for until he passed away."

"So some of these people who've vanished, the artists and explorers, didn't always disappear on their own, by accident?" I had known that the Alliance operated in the shadows and out of mortal channels. Now, I was glimpsing a side of it I had never considered, and it made me uncomfortable.

"Regrettably not," Sorren replied. "Remember – I know a thing or two about 'vanishing' myself." That was true. Immortals needed to be able to fake their own deaths and then reinvent themselves as someone else. "Some of our members realized the danger of what they had created or discovered, and agreed to disappear in order to keep themselves or their creations from being misused. Others, like Astor, had their minds destroyed by dark magic. We took them for their protection and everyone else's safety, gave them the best care possible, and provided a secure home. It's a bad business, but there's no way around it. And before you judge, try to imagine the alternatives."

The thought of someone with Gerard Astor's dark power painting Nephilim portals at the whim of drug cartels, Third-World despots, or organized crime bosses chilled me to the bone.

Archibald Donnelly stood in the centre of the ballroom floor. Like the building itself, Colonel Donnelly was far more than he appeared. Donnelly had been wearing a button-down shirt, sport jacket, and khakis when we first met him, standard casual attire for upper class men at leisure in Charleston. Now, he was dressed all in gray from head to toe. He wore a silver pentacle the size of a half-dollar coin on a chain around his neck and rings of silver, jet and obsidian on his fingers. I looked down at the smooth wooden floor, and realized that a large circle had been worked into the design of the wood itself. That circle was overlaid with salt and charcoal. Large pillar candles burned at the four quarters of the circle, and the smell of freshly-smudged sage filled the room.

Inside the circle, I saw the items Teag and I had supplied to Sorren. Harry's dirty, worn backpack looked forlorn, and Jonathan's carabiner held the keys to the beat-up motorcycle that was his pride and joy.

Higgins closed the doors after us, remaining on the

inside of the room. He threw a heavy bolt, and then ran his hand down the opening between the two doors, murmuring under his breath as a golden glow sealed the doors shut. When he turned back to us, he no longer looked the part of a butler. Higgins stood taller, straighter, chin raised, and he met my gaze with a smirk as if he had anticipated my surprise.

"Let's join the circle, shall we?" he said. He led Teag and me over to where Sorren already stood on the outskirts of the warded circle. As we followed him, I noticed that Higgins wore an Indian *talwar* sword on his belt, and a *kila*, a three-sided dagger, as well, an excellent weapon for fighting demons.

Someone – maybe Higgins – had brought in the duffel bag from Teag's car that contained our weapons. That meant Donnelly expected trouble, and we were expected to be more than bystanders. Teag and I were already wearing the protective vests Teag had made with magic woven into them. Now, we grabbed the rest of our gear and went to stand in between the candles at the cross-quarters.

"Take hands and make a circle," Donnelly said. I looked to Teag on one side and Sorren on the other. We couldn't reach each other and remain outside the circle.

That's when I noticed the ghosts. Some of them slipped out of the shadows and the corners of the room, while others stepped down from their portraits. A few just appeared out of the air, gone one moment, present the next. I recognized many of the faces from the paintings in the other rooms, explorers whose luck had run out, or who chose not to leave the society when their time was up.

Donnelly's magic made them nearly solid, and the ghosts stepped up to the outside of the wardings to take our hands. The man on my right was dressed like a Spanish conquistador, while the man on my left had the look of a French fur trader. The ghosts came from every century, including a few I recognized from TV specials when I was a kid. Women explorers too, the unsung heroines of history, pioneers and traders, seafarers, aviators, and astronauts. Just a few of the Briggs Society's members, coming at the Colonel's call to venture once more into the unknown.

To my surprise, the ghosts' hands felt cold and solid to the touch. I did not squeeze because I did not want to know what would happen. When the circle of our bodies was complete, Donnelly murmured words of power, and a cold incandescent barrier leaped up where the circle was marked on the floor, separating Donnelly from us.

Donnelly took out a dagger from his belt and put three slashes cross-wise on his left wrist. He shook his bleeding wrist, casting a spatter of blood within the warded circle.

"Jonathan, by your connection to this object, I call your spirit to this place and bind it to my will."

Another shake. "Harry, by your connection to your possession, I call your spirit to this place and bind it to my will."

A third shake. "So I have willed it. So mote it be!"

The curtain of power flared and I looked away, since I dared not break the connection of the circle to raise an arm that would shield my face. The power rippled and gleamed with an iridescent light. Donnelly's figure glowed and as he spoke the words of summoning, he became a larger, more commanding presence, someone to be reckoned with.

When the glare faded and I looked again, two new figures stood within the circle. The ghosts around the perimeter had grown solid enough that if I had not known they were specters, I would not have guessed it. I strained for a better look through the shimmering warding, and recognized Jonathan, the clerk from the store next to Trifles and Folly, along with a bearded young man who looked familiar. I guessed that he was Harry.

I gasped when I got a good look at their ghosts. They were gaunt, sunken in on themselves as if they had been hollowed out. Deep, bloody scratches marked their arms, thighs, and faces, and the raw wounds on their arms and lower legs looked as if something had been gnawing on them. Deep shadows obscured their feet and warred with Donnelly's magic to draw the ghosts back into the darkness.

"You are bound to speak only the truth," Donnelly commanded the spirits. "Who took you from the staircases?"

"Black spirits," Jonathan replied, his voice strained by fear and pain.

"Shadow things," Harry replied, and screamed from a torment we could not see.

"Desist!" Donnelly commanded in a thunderous voice, and the darkness around the ghosts rolled back. He turned his attention back to the ghosts. "You were alive when you were taken?"

Both Jonathan and Harry nodded. "When did you die?" Donnelly asked.

"In between," Jonathan replied.

"In the black place," Harry said.

"What happened to your bodies?" Donnelly pressed. Harry and Jonathan looked at the shadows held at bay by the necromancer's power, and then back to the Colonel.

"Taken," Jonathan said, and even speaking in fragments seemed to take all of his energy.

"Eaten," Harry added.

"What then?" Donnelly asked. The two shadows faded in and out, as if even the Colonel's magic could not hold the remnants of their souls for long.

"Black ghosts... witch... circle... man appeared." Jonathan's voice dropped in places, but it was enough to piece together what he had witnessed.

"I don't know," Harry wailed, looking panicked. He was the most recently dead, still new to his fate.

"Help me!" Harry pleaded. "Dark place. Bad ghosts. Chains on the ceiling." As I watched, Harry's ghost grew brighter and dimmer by turns, then began to pull apart like a piece of wet tissue, separating strand by strand until only his scream remained.

Jonathan's spirit jerked back and forth as if pulled by opposing forces, until with a lurch one side, the ghost dissipated. A loud bang made us all jump. Donnelly said the words of power that revoked his circle, and the shimmering lights fell. At that moment, the Gerard Astor painting tore itself apart and five Nephilim wrested their way through the silver chain that covered the canvas. I could see their skin blacken and smoke where the silver burned them, but they tore the chain asunder anyway, never taking their predatory gaze off us.

A brilliant light flared, and a golden wall of power enveloped the room, like a dome descending from the center of the ceiling. It covered the walls and windows, the doorways, floor and ceiling. We were sealed in – with the Nephilim.

"What the hell is going on?" Teag shouted.

"The Briggs Society is defended," Donnelly replied. "Nothing has ever been able to get through our protections. Since we have so many volatile items, we've got some internal protections too. This room is now on lock-down. Nothing gets in or out until the battle is over."

"And if we don't win?" I asked.

Donnelly's expression was unreadable. "We have half an hour to contain the threat. At that time, the defenses purge this room and reset."

"What does that mean?" Teag asked, as we circled to keep the Nephilim in view.

"Nothing good," Sorren muttered. "You don't want to know."

"Can't you override it?" I yelped.

Donnelly shook his head. "Regrettably not. Seemed like too much of a risk. I'll bring it up at the next board meeting—assuming there is one."

The five fallen angels came at us at a full run.

Higgins and Sorren moved faster than mortal speed, clashing with the two closest Nephilim, the ones I had nicknamed Baldy and Blondie. Sorren had a sword in one hand and a dagger in the other, and he ran toward the fallen angels with a shout, wielding his blades with deadly force. The Nephilim were unarmed, but that did not make them less dangerous. Sorren's sword bit deep into Baldy's right arm, down to the bone. The Nephilim snarled and flung the blade clear, showering the room with black blood. He swung a fist at Sorren, catching him on the shoulder and throwing him several feet across the room.

Sorren rose with a roar and barreled toward Baldy, catching the fallen angel in the gut with one of his blades. Baldy screeched and raked Sorren's face with its nails, leaving bloody tracks down his skin. Three of the ghosts from our circle rushed in to help, solid enough to grab at the Nephilim's arms and legs to help Sorren.

Close by, Higgins fought with his *talwar* in one hand and the three-sided *phurba* knife in the other, as more of our ghostly comrades threw themselves at Blondie to hold him back. Higgins moved with deadly speed, blocking the Nephilim's blows. He kept his *talwar* wheeling at head height, while he struck with the *phurba* any time Blondie tried to get close. It was a fearsome defense, and his opponent shrieked in anger, denied an easy kill.

I wondered why the Nephilim didn't just transform and fight in their monstrous shapes, when I realized that Donnelly was chanting. Still within the circle, the necromancer's magic might not have the same control of the fallen angels as he did over the spirits of the dead, but he could dampen the Nephilim's magic enough to keep them in their human form. And while human Nephilim were hard to kill, they were a damned sight worse when they turned into monsters.

Unfortunately, that left us shy one fighter, since while Donnelly was busy squelching the Nephilim's magic, he couldn't join in the battle. From my perspective, an equal number of Nephilim to humans is already an unfair fight. The ghosts were definitely on our side, but their best efforts couldn't do any real damage, so they focused on slowing down the fallen angels.

Three Nephilim came running toward Teag and me—Crow, Ebony, and Asian Dude. I went left, Teag went right, and the ghosts that Donnelly had summoned for the circle went right up the middle. Nephilim weren't

Reapers, so the ghosts had no fear of them, and empowered by Donnelly's magic, the ghosts were solid enough to run interference between us and the Nephilim.

I didn't have time to watch, because I had problems of my own. Crow, the Nephilim coming for me, had the good looks of a rich boy gone wrong: high cheekbones, a cleft chin and thin, sensual lips with a lock of dark hair that he flicked out of his eyes with a casual toss of his head. Maybe I was supposed to be impressed, but I had seen what these guys looked like for real, and that destroyed their appeal.

Bo's ghost was already beside me, and he lunged for Crow, managing to score a deep bite on the fallen angel's left wrist until the creature flung him loose. While he was preoccupied with Bo, I raised my athame with one hand and clutched my spindle whorl with the other, drawing on the memory the whorl held of its previous owner, a Norse witch named Secona. That boosted my power, and I channeled my magic through my athame.

A cold-white torrent of power erupted from the athame and caught Crow full in the face. He staggered, blinded and battered, as Bo sprang for the throat. Two ghosts, one in the uniform of the British Indian Army and another in the parka of an Arctic explorer, rushed at the Nephilim and grappled with him, keeping him from coming closer to me. I saw the ghost of a Conquistador and another in an aviator jacket struggle to hold back Ebony while Teag battled Asian Dude. I dared not use Alard's walking stick for fear of catching the house or my allies on fire. But I had one of Josiah Winfield's pistols, loaded and ready, and Teag had the other one.

I dropped the spindle whorl back in my pocket, drew

Josiah's gun and fired, knowing that I might not get another shot. As I did so, I hooked my magic into Josiah's weapon, letting the memories of its previous owner run through me, gaining a temporary advantage as his knowledge became mine.

Silver is unpleasant to vampires in the real world because it gives them a rash, not because it destroys them. Same with holy water. Nephilim, on the other hand, are highly allergic, on top of not much liking getting a bullet to the heart. I'd used one of Josiah's special rounds, packed with silver, iron, and obsidian and both blessed and baptized in holy water. Before I could lower my pistol, Crow lurched forward, shoving me hard enough to hurl me across the room and into one of the Society's *wunderkammeren*. The closet of oddities smashed open, showering me with its strange and singular wonders, momentarily stunning me as glimpses of the pieces' power and history flashed past me.

Crow screamed and tore at the raw wound on its chest. Its skin began to blacken, first near the wound and then radiating outward from the point of impact along the veins. If that's what a supernatural allergy looks like, there isn't a big enough EpiPen in the universe to contain it. The blackened veins began to glow red, and the Nephilim's once-handsome face contorted, bone structure halted mid-morph, so that it was a grotesque combination of man and monster. His eyes were bloodshot and bulging, lips swelling and blue. The red glow became fire burning through thousands of arteries, veins and capillaries. The fallen angel let out one more ear-splitting scream and then blew apart into hundreds of blood-soaked gobbets.

Teag let loose on Asian Dude with Josiah's other gun

a second later, splattering his remains over the other half of the ballroom. That left three more of the fallen angels to battle, and I could see that Donnelly was tiring fast. If his magic failed and the Nephilim got their full powers back, it was going to be ugly. Then again, we had less than half an hour to worry about it, before the Briggs Society's protections destroyed us and the Nephilim. Around us, the golden containment dome had begun to pulse slowly.

"Why is the gold light blinking?" I yelled.

"It's warning us," Higgins shouted back. "It will blink faster and faster the closer we get to the half-hour mark." *And if we weren't done by then, ka-boom.*

Sorren and Higgins were battling Blondie and Baldy old school, with swords and hand-to-hand combat, and the fact that it wasn't a quick rout for either of them provided dim prospects for success for Teag and me, if the Nephilim could put up that kind of fight against a vampire and whatever-the-hell Higgins was. There was one more Nephilim on the loose, and he was closing on us fast. Getting up close and personal with these guys was a recipe for disaster, and with Josiah's one-shot pistols done for, I needed some distance weapons, pronto.

Teag got between me and Ebony, circling his staff warily. He loosed two of the knots from the rope that hung from his belt, releasing stored magic to replenish himself. In the next moment, the staff was in full motion, runes blazing, moving swifter than I could track in a complicated series of circles and figure-eights, designed to keep an attacker at bay and make it impossible to grab the staff. Ebony tried to come past Teag, probably figuring that he could survive a thump or two from the staff, and drew back, shrieking, as the staff connected with a charge of magic like a high voltage shock.

I hit the Nephilim with a blast from my athame, and the cold power drove him back a pace. I'd learned from the first encounter, and aimed for the face. Bo's ghost followed up with a deep-throated growl and a lunge nearly throat-high, sinking his teeth into Ebony's arm. The Nephilim shook free, howling in rage and pain.

Where the staff had connected with Ebony's arm, the skin was blackened, and his eyes glowed red with malice. I had managed to get to my feet, and I looked at the scattered contents of the oddities cabinet, desperately searching for a weapon. The golden containment dome was blinking more quickly.

"Teag, catch!" I yelled. I hurled two objects his way. One, an old net of knotted rope, landed near Teag's feet. The other was a thin, sharp piece of coiled steel with a handle. Teag was the martial arts expert; I figured he'd know what to do with it.

I needed more mojo if I was going to do any more blasting with my athame, and even the spindle whorl could only replenish me so much. Then I saw a flat metal disk with a sharpened edge. It was a *chakram*, an Indian weapon, and I'd seen someone on television use something like it. I figured it was worth a shot, assuming I could handle the damn thing without losing a finger. There were a lot of weapons I might not be able to pick up and easily use, but I knew how to throw a Frisbee.

No time for second-guesses. I picked up the *chakram* as carefully as I could. As soon as my skin touched the elaborately etched brass I had a vision of old India, and I knew I was seeing the memories of the weapon's former owner. I sank my waning magic down into those memories and pulled with my remaining strength,

channeling the skill and knowledge of that long-ago
warrior and taking them into myself. Without hesitation,
I flung that sucker at Ebony, who was circling Teag. I
aimed for his throat, but he was quick enough to side-
step just enough that the razor edge sank into his left
shoulder instead, severing his arm.

I glimpsed a silvery sliver of steel lightning, and then
another. Bone-deep cuts opened up on the Nephilim
from shoulder to hip from Teag's metal whip. Each time
the whip hit, a flash of green fire burst from its hooked
tip, and then the coiled steel retracted, peeling a strip of
skin with it.

"Cassidy – the net!" Teag shouted.

I scrambled for the net at his feet and threw it
over the bleeding Nephilim. The net was weighted,
so it spread and fell evenly. The Nephilim screamed
again as the rope net glowed with silver fire. The
fallen angel collapsed to his knees, shrieking threats
and trying to tear the net apart, while its magically-
strengthened fibers burned his hands. Teag brought
his boot down on the nearest edge of the net, and
as soon as he made contact with the rope, I felt his
magic channel through the fibers, until the net was
a brilliant silver. With a final screech Ebony writhed
beneath it and then fell still.

I looked up just as Higgins got inside his opponent's
guard. His curved blade slashed Blondie through
the neck, while his triangle-bladed knife stabbed the
monster right in the heart. The Nephilim gave a last,
ear-piercing wail and exploded.

The magical golden energy was flashing like a strobe.
We were nearly out of time. I really did not want to be
stuck for eternity with a bunch of Nephilim. But we

had minutes left to fight before the Briggs Society would handle the problem for us.

Sorren was getting the best of his attacker, though from the way both of them were bloodied, the fight was between equals. Sorren thrust his sword deep into Baldy's belly, sacrificing his shoulder to take a wicked slash in return. While the Nephilim was impaled on the blade, Higgins drove his *phurba* two-handed into the fallen angel's back, between the ribs, and into the heart. The creature burst apart, covering Sorren and Higgins with its blood.

The golden dome strobed. "We won!" I shouted, looking at Higgins and Donnelly. "How do we tell the house that we won?"

In the next heartbeat, the flashing golden light winked out. "Don't worry, madam. The house always knows," Higgins said in a cool voice as if I had merely inquired about when dinner would be served.

We looked around at the ruined ballroom. The Nephilim had been destroyed. Donnelly lowered his arms, brought his chant to a close, and walked the circle clockwise to release his wardings, then extinguished each of the candles. The ghosts acknowledged us with nods and gestures of approval, and vanished.

"How many times do we have to kill these guys?" I asked.

Sorren shrugged. "They'll keep coming back as long as the nephilmancer is around to call them."

Though Donnelly had not been involved in the physical fight, the toll that the magic took was clear in his face. He looked as exhausted as I felt, only he wasn't soaked with Nephilim blood.

"Sorry about the cabinet," I said, looking back with

chagrin at the broken piece of furniture and its spilled contents.

"Seems to me that the cabinet provided exactly what you needed, when you needed it," Donnelly replied, raising an eyebrow as his gaze traveled from the metal whip in Teag's hand to the old net, to the brass *chakram*.

"What is that thing, anyhow?" I asked, nodding toward Teag's new weapon.

"It's an *urumi*," Higgins replied. "A favorite of the gent whose ghost you might have seen in the British Indian Army uniform – Nain Singh Rawat, one of the greatest *pundits* of all time." He pointed to a portrait that had managed to escape being spattered with gore. In it, a dignified Indian man with angular features and a stern expression stood proudly as he was presented with a gold medal by a scholarly-looking man in a top hat. Glancing around at the other paintings, I recognized some of the other ghosts who had tried with all their spectral might to protect us, and I offered up my silent thanks.

"Did we get anything useful from all this?" Teag's tone was sharp, and I knew that meant he was dead tired.

"Confirmation that the Reapers are behind the stairway disappearances," Sorren replied. "And a clue to the whereabouts of another Watcher portal."

I thought back to the fragments Harry's ghost had been able to share. "Bad ghosts. Dark place. Chains on the ceiling." One place came to mind, to anyone familiar with Charleston's bloody past.

"The Old Jail," Teag and I said in unison.

Sorren nodded. "My thoughts, exactly."

"But we don't know whether the Watcher is already

here, or about to come," I protested. "And come to think of it, I didn't feel the overwhelming guilt that I've always felt before a Nephilim attack."

"That's because the Nephilim who attacked us were already inside the Briggs Society, and our protections would keep a Watcher well away," Donnelly said.

"Cassidy's right about the danger from a new Watcher, but we're in no condition to do anything about it tonight," Sorren said firmly. Worried as I was, I knew I was not up to another fight, and by the look of it, neither were Teag or Sorren.

"What now?" Teag asked.

"I'll see both of you safely home, and we regroup tomorrow night," Sorren said.

I looked at the mess the battle had made. "What about all this?" I asked. "We trashed the place."

Donnelly chuckled. "There's more magic in the Briggs Society than dreamt of in your imagination," he said. "Higgins and I will make sure it's taken care of." He glanced at the net, *chakram* and the *urumi*. "In the meantime, at least for the duration of the present emergency, keep the weapons. They suit you. I believe their former owner would be proud to see them used for a noble fight."

"We can't have you leaving looking like that," Higgins said, shaking his head. "Come with me. You can clean up before heading out." Just like that, he was back in butler mode, and I vowed to ask Sorren for the real story some time when we weren't up to our necks in Nephilim.

It turned out that the Briggs Society had guest rooms, and Higgins led us each to comfortable sleeping quarters with private bathrooms. When I emerged from a hot shower, I found that my blood-soaked clothing had been removed and a fresh outfit, exactly the right size, awaited me. Next to the clothes, the *chakram* lay on a black leather pouch, spotless and shining. I resolved not to question the magically miraculous concierge service and happily got dressed, tucking my wet hair back in a tail.

When I came downstairs, Teag and Sorren were dressed in clean outfits as well, and except for a few fresh cuts and bruises, we looked none the worse for the wear. "Keep me updated, Sorren," Donnelly said as he waved good-bye and Higgins walked us to the door. "If I can help, I will. Hell of a task, this."

Sorren's lips quirked. "Oh I will, Archie. Believe me, I will." With that, we stepped outside to find Teag's Volvo right where we left it several hours before. I turned back for one last look at the Briggs Society, but the Georgian brick building was nowhere to be seen. In its place were three white clapboard Charleston single houses that looked as if they had been there for the better part of a century.

"Where –" I stammered. Teag turned around and stood, dumbfounded, as well.

"'When' is a better question," Sorren said with a chuckle. "That's what I meant about the Society being able to protect itself. It appears and disappears on no particular schedule, not always in the same place, and it never stays long."

Which could mean that those explorers from other times might still stop in for a hot toddy now and again, in the past or future. Thinking about it too hard made my head hurt. I got into the car, leaned back in the seat, and was asleep before we reached my house.

Chapter Seventeen

I WAS RESTLESS, so I decided to take a walk the next morning, after we opened the shop. "I'm going over to the Lowcountry Museum," I said. "Lucinda's exhibition should be ready to open, and I wanted to ask her about what Caliel said when we were at the power plant."

"Take the rental car," Teag said. "We don't need another Nephilim incident. If Sariel is behind this, then you and I are a way he could get at Sorren. Please – drive."

I sighed. It was sunny and mild and the idea of a walk to clear my head was attractive. Still, I couldn't argue with Teag; there had been too many attacks to be careless, and I didn't relish another run-in. "All right," I conceded. "I won't be long."

My car wouldn't be out of the body shop for a while, so I appreciated having a rental, which saved me from needing to borrow Teag's car. I took the long way to the museum since I wanted to enjoy the sunshine and get some perspective on all the weird stuff that had been going on. Teag and Sorren and I had fought some scary supernatural plots before, but this series of attacks was personal, and that made it worse – as if someone planning to kill tens of thousands of people wasn't bad enough.

As I drove past one of the Ghost Bikes I slowed down. The front wheel was turning slowly, but a few seconds later it spun wildly, and the bike began to shake and shudder, as if it were trying to tear free of the chain that held it to the telephone pole. *Hurry,* it seemed to say. *Time's running out.*

The Ghost Bike incident rattled me, and I took a few deep breaths when I parked in the Lowcountry Museum's lot. Big banners proclaimed 'Voodoo and You: Loas and the Lowcountry', and other banners included pictures of items on display. It looked like everything was ready to go, and I knew it would be a real accomplishment for Lucinda to bring off a successful exhibition.

I navigated the receptionist and ignored the velvet ropes that prevented museum-goers from entering the exhibition before it opened. Lucinda and her team had gotten a lot done since my last visit. I kept my hands behind my back, resolutely not touching anything. I could hear Lucinda talking with her assistants, and did not want to interrupt, so I killed time by taking a stroll around the display cases.

One set of banners traced the history of Voodoo from its African and Caribbean roots. All around the space were large paintings of Loas like Papa Legba, Baron Samedi, and Erzulie Dantor along with their *veves* and the Catholic saint associated with that Loa. The glass cases held candles, dolls, shrines, and charms, showing how the practice of Voodoo – or Voudon as many preferred – differed depending on the time period and the location. The exhibit was fascinating and before I knew it, I had made my way around the room.

I found myself staring at a life-sized effigy of a woman sitting in a chair. Her eyes blazed red, and all around the chair were paper flames. A taxidermied black goat lay at her feet along with dried salvia, sprigs of lavender, and a bowl of candy. Behind her was a picture of Erzulie Dantor and a painting of a black pig. 'Brule Marinette' the small sign said, and explained that Marinette had been a mambo who helped to start Haiti's slave revolt when she sacrificed a black pig and called on the spirit of Erzulie Dantor to free her people. Marinette, the sign added, was caught by the slaveholders and burned alive, and each year, an effigy of her was burned to honor her martyrdom. I stared at the papier-mâché face with its red eyes and shivered.

I heard the hoot of an owl, and a ghostly gray creature flew past me, brushing my face with its wing feathers before vanishing. When I looked back at the figure in the display case, real flames burned all around the chair and effigy, yet there was no smoke, and nothing inside the case was catching on fire.

I watched, terrified, and realized that the woman seated on the chair was no longer made out of papier-mâché. She was real, and I could see the rise and fall of her chest. Marinette's blood-red eyes fixed on me, and she rose to her feet amid the flames. I backed away, certain that a glass case could not contain the power of an angry Loa.

The figure took a step toward the glass, and the fire licked at her bare feet and the hem of her dress, but did not burn. Marinette raised one hand and pointed directly at me. Her mouth began to move, but I could not hear what she was saying, although from her expression, I figured it couldn't be good.

"*Arretez!*"

Lucinda's voice came from behind me, strident and commanding. She continued speaking in a Caribbean patois, and then her voice began to rise and fall and she closed her eyes, raising her hands. Her whole body shook, and when she opened her eyes, her expression changed and I had the distinct feeling that someone else was looking out at me. I caught a whiff of citrus and basil, and knew I was in the presence of a second Loa who had possessed Lucinda.

The flames in the glass case surged higher. The paper figure and wooden chair should have been burning, but they weren't. Marinette's lips pulled back to bare her sharp, discolored teeth, and her gnarled hands scratched at the inside of the glass with yellowed nails. There was a reason 'Marinette Bois Sech' meant 'Marinette of the dry arms'. As I watched, her body withered in the flames, skin stretching across her bones tight as a mummy, showing every rib and bone. Her fire-red gaze was fixed on me, and she reached toward me, closing her fist in a grasping gesture.

I could not breathe, and my stomach clenched. It was a struggle to stay standing, and I felt as if I were being squeezed by strong arms so tightly I feared my ribs might break.

That's when I realized two more people were chanting, and saw that Lucinda's assistants had come out of the meeting room. They stood against the wall, letting the mambo work, but their eyes were closed, faces uplifted and hands open, quietly reciting the Lord's Prayer and the Hail Mary, a reminder of Voudon's long, interconnected relationship with Catholicism. I couldn't speak aloud as I struggled for breath, but I silently started to chant along with them, hoping that it would help Lucinda gain the power she needed to repel the entity in that case before it broke free.

Flames filled the glass case, though I felt no heat. I thought that surely the sprinkler system would turn on, and I feared that the museum would catch fire. Marinette's hold on me tightened, and I dropped to my knees, gasping, as the world spun around me. A new scent, pipe smoke, told me that Papa Legba was nearby, and I hoped it was not so that he could see my soul across to the afterlife. I gasped once more and fell face-down onto the museum floor. Everything went red as my air-starved body fought to stay conscious, and then black as I lost my fight.

"CASSIDY." LUCINDA'S VOICE seemed far away, but I followed it, hoping to find my way out of the darkness. "Come to me." I couldn't see where I was going, but I held tight to Lucinda's voice and the sound of chanting. Gradually, the darkness grew lighter, and with a gasp and a shiver, I came back to myself to find that I lay face-up on the cold tile of the exhibition room.

"I'm glad you found your way back," Lucinda said. She was kneeling next to me, and from the worry in her eyes, I knew that what I had seen and felt had been real.

"Is she –" I turned toward the glass case, but the figure and the flames were once more just made of paper.

"Shh. Don't say the name. She's gone," Lucinda said. Her white pantsuit and pink silk blouse were the perfect background for the large silver necklace she wore, a powerful protective amulet.

"I need to talk to you," I managed.

Lucinda nodded. "I didn't figure this was really a social call. But let's get you off the floor and settled first, shall we?"

Lucinda helped me to my feet and one of her assistants brought a chair from the meeting room and another gave me a glass of cold sweet tea, then her staff went back to work without a word, sparing me more embarrassment. Lucinda waited until I had finished the tea and gotten my breath back before she spoke.

"Did you touch anything before the Loa manifested?" she asked. Lucinda knew my talent, so it was a reasonable place to start.

I shook my head. "No. I knew better. I walked around and looked at the displays and read the signs, but that's it."

She glanced toward the glass case again, but nothing had changed. I drew another deep breath and realized that I did not feel bruised or damaged, although in the middle of the attack, I could have sworn that Marinette was going to break a rib or two. Lucinda seemed to guess my thoughts.

"It was a psychic projection," she answered my unspoken question. "Nasty stuff, and something that takes a lot of power to pull off. But not real. A warning – or a threat."

I nodded. "And the spirits you called, where they really here?"

Lucinda laughed, a deep, smoky chuckle. "Oh yes child, they were here! If you want to thank them, send over a bottle of pink champagne for Erzulie Freda and some rum for Papa Legba."

I resolved to stop and pick up both on my way back to the store that afternoon. "Did Caliel talk to you, about what happened at the power plant?" I asked.

Lucinda shook her head. "I've been mostly ignoring my phone for the last couple of days trying to get the exhibition ready. Fill me in."

I told her what happened at the power plant, and she listened with a worried expression. "If someone's conjured... that Loa..." she said with a nod toward the case, "they're playing a dangerous game. You do not want to mess with her."

"Why would someone involved with Nephilim and Watchers call for... her?"

Lucinda frowned and thought for a moment. "You know that Voudon – like all religions – has picked up bits and pieces from a lot of influences over the centuries, right?" I nodded. "That's especially true with the Catholic saints, since African slaves weren't allowed to pray to their own gods, so they represented their gods with saints to be able to worship without being punished."

That much I knew. "Over the years, people have said a lot of things about Voudon, much of it mistaken," she continued. "But there is a belief that comes up, time and again, that says that at least some of the Loa were once fallen angels." She shrugged. "It's a very gray area for practitioners and scholars, tied up with strange texts like the *Book of Enoch* and its Watchers –"

"What did you say?" I looked up sharply. "Watchers?"

Lucinda nodded. "Why?"

I didn't think I could possibly explain the Briggs Society and figured that I shouldn't try, so I left out details and told Lucinda about the summoning circles found at the power plant and the Tarleton House and what Henry and Jonathan's ghosts had told us – and the possibility that a Watcher was about to enter through the Old Jail.

"You really have stepped in it this time, haven't you?" Lucinda said, shaking her head. "My, my, my."

"Do you think there's a real connection between... her... and the Watchers?"

Lucinda shrugged. "It doesn't matter what I think. What matters is that whoever is summoning the Nephilim and bringing through the Watchers either believes there's a connection or just wants help waging war. And... she is always pleased with blood and fire."

Great. Just great. Bad enough that we've got killer evil angels and a scary-powerful sorcerer with a grudge running around, now there's a bad-ass Loa to worry about.

Lucinda laid a hand on my shoulder. "Sorren's been fighting these kinds of things for a long time," she said. "Trust him. And remember – you've got friends with some pretty cool talents." She gave me an encouraging smile. "Charge up that agate necklace of yours in the moonlight. It'll help protect you. And you know that Caliel and I will be glad to help whenever you need us."

"Thanks," I replied. "And I really did enjoy the exhibition – well, at least until it attacked me."

"Take it as a compliment," Lucinda replied. "You and Teag are both important to Sorren, and so is Trifles and Folly. If one of his enemies is behind this, you're going to be on his hit list. So walk softly, and carry a big wand."

WE HAD A store full of customers when I got back, so Teag couldn't grill me on what happened at the museum, although he seemed to pick up on my jitters as soon as I walked in. We sold some estate jewelry to vacationers from New Hampshire, a beautiful old mirror to an interior decorator, and a fancy French clock to a guy from Seattle, although I have no idea how he planned to get it home on the plane. We had a lot of browsers as well, so it took Teag, Maggie, and me to keep everyone happy and answer all the questions. When five o'clock came and I flipped the sign in the window, we all let out sighs of relief and leaned against the cases.

"Wow! What a great day!" Maggie said after we had locked up the valuables and closed down the register. "But I'm beat. I'll see you on Monday – I'm going to go home, put my feet up and order pizza!" With that, she hobbled out of the shop, still on crutches but doing a lot better. Teag and I looked at each other.

"Your trip to the museum lasted quite a while," Teag said, arching an eyebrow. "And I'm betting you and Lucinda weren't just chit-chatting. So, spill. What happened?"

"I promise to fill you in over dinner, but I'm starving. And if we're going to kick Nephilim butt tonight, I need to fuel up."

I caught Teag up on everything that happened as we ate, and then he dropped me off at my house so I could take care of Baxter and get a quick nap before it was time to go to the Old Jail. I slept on the couch, but my dreams were dark and I woke up to find Bax licking my nose, looking at me worriedly.

"Just bad dreams," I reassured him – and me. I held him for a few minutes, stroking his silky white fur. Since the trouble with the Nephilim, we had stopped taking our nightly walks around the block, which meant Baxter only had our small backyard garden to explore. We played a lot of Frisbee. I figured that counted a bit for weapons practice, since I now had the *chakram*, but I missed the freedom of a good walk and the conversations with neighbors, and I'm pretty sure Baxter did, too.

"Not too much longer, I hope," I told him as we came back in from the garden. "Once we save the world, you and I can go back to taking nice, long walks." I hoped it would be that simple.

Midnight came faster than I would have liked, and Teag pulled up in front of my house with Sorren riding shotgun. I slid into the back seat, with a sack that held all my gear. I guessed that Teag had his weapons in the trunk. We didn't have too many more 'special' bullets for Josiah's guns, but both pistols were reloaded, and I had a few spare rounds in my pocket. Along with the new weapons Teag and I had gained at the Briggs Society, I should have felt more confident, but I'd had my fill of Nephilim, and I knew the war hadn't even really begun yet.

We parked several blocks away from the Old Jail and walked. Charleston is a pretty safe city, if you don't count the ghosts. Our path took us past one of the old cemeteries, and a shower of pebbles reminded us that the ghosts remained terrified of the Reaper threat. *The living would be afraid and angry too, if they knew how much danger they were in.*

The Old Jail is a big, imposing structure in daytime, and more so at night. It's been a cursed site for a long time, since the land beneath the Jail was used as a hospital and a pauper's cemetery before the Jail was built back in 1802. The front section is a boxy stone castle, with an octagonal tower in the back. Until it was finally closed in 1939, the Jail held about three times as many prisoners as it was designed to house. Evil, grief, and misery are steeped into the stone. It's no wonder the

Old Jail is considered one of the most haunted sites in a very haunted city.

I had toured the Jail in daylight, and even though I'm not a medium like Alicia, I was sure we were being watched by unseen eyes. The pictures I took were full of orbs, even though it was a clear afternoon without rain or fog. The Jail once housed Charleston's most notorious prisoner, serial killer Lavinia Fisher, who was hanged in the back courtyard. Many people thought Lavinia's spirit never left, and her ghost is one of the most frequently seen. Confederate and Federal prisoners of war were held at the Old Jail, along with pirates, leaders of slave uprisings, and common criminals. Conditions were brutal, and some inmates didn't survive long enough to meet their date with the hangman.

Dark place. Bad ghosts. Chains from the ceiling. No one could argue about the Old Jail being a dark place. Even now, a lingering sense of doom pervaded its shadowed passageways. Plenty of the people whose spirits might have remained here certainly qualified as 'bad'. But I knew right away where Harry's ghost meant when he talked about chains.

There's a room near the entrance that was once an interrogation chamber. Historians debate exactly how things were done, but many folks believe prisoners were suspended from chains and either left to hang painfully in their bonds or beaten to coerce confessions. It's one of the most haunted rooms in a spookapalooza building. And that's where we were heading.

I was surprised when Caliel and Chuck Pettis – Clockman – met us just inside the Old Jail walls. "We're the cavalry," Chuck said. I could hear him ticking from a few paces away, which meant he wore hundreds of watches sewn into his military-issue Kevlar vest. He once had a premonition that if his clocks ever wind down, he'll die. From the sound of it, he was pretty safe tonight.

"Lucinda told me what happened at the exhibit," Caliel said with a nod in my direction. "Bad stuff."

"This place is hotter than usual," Chuck grumbled, and I knew he meant supernaturally, not temperature-wise. Although the grounds around the Old Jail were empty except for us, I felt as if I were suffocating in the press of a large crowd.

"Yeah," I agreed. "Let's get this over with."

Caliel opened the lock with a flicker of magic, and the door swung wide. We used the tour entrance, and it led us straight into one of the Jail's narrow stone corridors. The temperature inside was noticeably colder than the warm evening air, and the hairs on my arms and neck rose with the sense that we were not alone.

Down the hallway, a door slammed shut. A flash of light zipped through the darkness just at the corner of my vision, and I glimpsed a greenish yellow orb in the distance down the long corridor, bobbing up and down in midair as if daring us to chase it.

It sounded like the spirits of the Old Jail were waking up. I could hear the sound of chains dragging across the floor above us, while in the distance, a metal cell door rattled violently as if shaken by a prisoner desperate to get out. Sorren led the way. Teag and I were right behind him, while Chuck and Caliel brought up the rear.

I felt something brush against my arm, but no one had passed by. The Old Jail's shadows crowded around us, and our flashlights did not seem up to the task of pushing away the unnatural darkness. Off to one side,

I thought I glimpsed a woman standing next to one of the narrow windows, but when I turned my head she was gone.

More thumps sounded above us, sending my heartbeat racing. Since we had no idea of what – or who – we might encounter, we came well-armed. I had my athame in hand, and Bo's ghost already walked beside me, head down and hackles up as if he expected trouble. Teag and I both wore our protective woven vests along with our amulets, and he had both his staff and his *urumi*. The *chakram* Colonel Donnelly had given me hung in a scabbard at my belt. I didn't want to set the place on fire, so I had left my walking stick at home tonight, but both Teag and I carried Josiah's dueling pistols. I noticed that Teag had his jack ball out and was twirling it to fend off unfriendly spirits. I pulled my jack ball from my pocket and did the same.

Chuck depended on technology for protection. He had an EMF grenade in one hand and an odd homemade weapon in his right hand that looked like a ray gun out of an old-time science fiction movie. Sorren had a sword in each hand. He had healed already from the wounds he had taken at the Briggs Society. Teag and I still sported bruises.

Caliel was dressed in a black shirt and dark jeans, but when he removed a charcoal scarf from around his neck, I could see that he wore a large necklace made of pieces of mirror set into metal that made a wide collar. I knew it protected him against spirits and witches, who could become trapped within the mirror and lose their power. Around Caliel's left arm was a black band with the *veve* of Baron Samedi, the keeper of cemeteries. I picked up the scent of rum and cigar smoke, and I bet Caliel had made an offering to the Baron for our protection before he set out this night.

The closer we got to the room with the chains, the more active the Old Jail's spirits became. For an empty building, the darkened corridors were full of footsteps, the sound of chairs sliding across bare boards, clanging metal and rattling chains. Some startled us, but most were muffled, as if just making themselves heard taxed the strength of these ghosts. Disembodied voices whispered, wailed and screamed, then fell to an indistinct buzz. I was as keyed up as a hummingbird on caffeine, and I wanted to be done and out of there.

Sorren pushed open the heavy door to the chain room and we all braced for battle. Our flashlights shone into the darkness, illuminating several old, rusted chains with manacles that hung from the ceiling, props for the ghost tours. On the worn wooden floor beneath the chains was a freshly-marked circle drawn in salt and charcoal. Four burned-out candles sat melted and sooty at the quarters. Black chicken feathers littered the floor.

"We're too late," Sorren said. "The Watcher has made it through."

"Uh oh." I pointed to the chains and manacles overhead. They had begun to swing, slowly at first, and then more violently, though there was no draft in the room.

"Ouch!" Teag said as the door tried to slam shut and rammed his shoulder. Those distant voices were closer now, and their tone had changed from frightened and mournful to angry.

Shadows loomed on the walls, and dark shapes took form, stepping away from the plaster and into the room. Bits of stone from the ceiling pelted us. The temperature dropped until it was cold enough that I could see my breath. Orbs danced around the room like a cloud of fireflies, zipping toward us and emitting a nasty shock when they got too close. I ducked as one came right at my face.

Teag cried out as one of the shadows raked his arm, solid enough to tear through his sleeve. Bo's ghost was barking loudly, running at the wraiths, snarling and snapping his teeth to keep them at bay. Heavy footfalls on the stairs and commotion in the hallway told me the Old Jail's ghosts were massing. I blasted the wraiths with my athame, sending a cone of cold silver force against them. They parted and drew back, then rushed forward again, as if they knew my strength was limited.

The runes on Teag's staff glowed brightly as he circled it slowly overhead, jabbing it toward any ghost that ventured too close. Each time he stabbed it into the dark figures, the staff's runes flared and the ghosts receded as if stung. The room was far too small for him to use his *urumi* or for me to hurl my *chakram* without seriously injuring one of our companions or ourselves, though I thought the silver fire of Teag's razor whip might give even ghosts pause.

"Let's get out of here," I yelped.

"You've got that right," Chuck said. "Everyone get out. I'll cover you." We hurried out the door as Teag kept it open.

Chuck pushed to the fore. "Fire in the hole!" he shouted, tossing his EMF grenade and ducking, throwing an arm up to cover his eyes. We all did the same. There was a flash of bright light, a high-pitched squeal, and a burst of electro-magnetic energy that ghosts hated.

"Go!" Chuck shouted, pausing only to retrieve the spent shell of his grenade. We thundered down the stairs, while behind us, the ghosts swarmed in a swirling, green-gray cloud. Faces came to the fore, only to be clawed back into the mass. Skeletal arms reached out of the cloud with clawed fingers and sharp nails, ripping at our clothing and scratching our skin.

"Run!" Sorren fell back so the rest of us could escape, slashing through the ghosts with his swords, which had taken on a faint glow. Chuck took up a firing stance behind and to the right of where Sorren stood, so that nothing could get past them. He aimed his ray gun-lookalike and squeezed the trigger. Thin lightning bolts crackled from the gun's snub nose, branching again and again until they were as wide as the corridor. The threads of lightning buzzed and snapped with electricity, and the cloud of spirits drew back abruptly.

Once the rest of us were out, Sorren and Chuck ran for the door, and Chuck paused to fire one last lightning net at the cloud of spirits as it massed to come after them again. In a few more steps they were clear, slamming the door behind them. That's when we realized that we weren't out of danger yet.

The broad gravel lot around the Old Jail was filled with ghosts. They crowded along the inside of the high wall, shadows and wraiths dark as storm clouds, while others were orbs, bobbing and weaving. One thing was clear: they were between us and the exit.

"I've got this." Caliel stepped forward. "Buy me a couple of moments and shine your lights into my mirrors."

We did as he told us, and the mirrors lit up, reflecting the light back toward the spirits, which kept their distance from the silvered glass that could trap them in a new and smaller prison. Caliel reached into his backpack and drew out a flask and a cigar. He opened the flask and the heady scent of spiced rum wafted on the air. A second later, he lit the cigar in his other hand.

"Stay behind me, and work your way toward the back gate," Caliel said in a low voice. Then he began to sing and chant, dancing a slow, swaying salsa toward the ghosts. His chant matched the rhythm of his steps, and he kept his eyes on the darkness as he held up the rum and the cigar toward the night sky.

We edged our way toward the break in the high stone wall as he drew the ghosts off, step by step. *This isn't going to work. They're wicked fast. We can't get out of the gate before they catch us.*

Orbs sparkled in the night air like snow, translucent and twinkling. In the deep shadows I could hear heavy breathing and shuffling steps. A woman's voice rang out in a peal of high-pitched, hysterical laughter, and I guessed Lavinia Fisher was enjoying the outing.

The back lot was where the gallows once stood, and before that, nameless dead were committed to unmarked graves in the potter's field beneath our feet. Outcast and condemned, scorned and misbegotten, the angry dead's terror of the Reapers increased their thirst for vengeance.

We had gone as far as we could go. The ghosts did not leave the Old Jail yard exit unguarded, even while most of their number bunched around Caliel, who was still singing and swaying, waving the cigar in the air. I could trace the glow of its embers in the darkness. The ghosts dampened the normal night sounds of the city, the honk of car horns and the hum of engines, conversations and barking dogs, strains of music playing through distant open windows. The jail yard was unnaturally silent, and where the darkness blotted out the stars, orbs danced.

Caliel's voice rose, and he took several quick steps backward toward us and the exit. Still chanting, he bent and poured out the rum in a half circle, then dropped the lit cigar to set the alcohol on fire, a fleeting buttress between us and the darkness. Caliel ripped off the black armband with the *veve* and cast it into the fire.

"Lord of the Cemetery and Lord of the Grave, Lord of the Dead and the Watchman of Graves, come forth!" Caliel shouted.

Smoke rose from the flames, far out of proportion to the fire. I blinked the tears out of my eyes as the wind shifted, and when my vision cleared, I saw four men standing in the fire between Caliel and the ghosts.

Caliel had called on the Ghedes, the Voudon Loas of the dead, to save us.

Baron Samedi I recognized. Tall and gaunt, dressed in a top hat and Armani tuxedo, he had the hanged man card from a tarot deck tucked in the wide purple ribbon around his hat and a pair of sunglasses missing one lens. In one gloved hand he held a black cane with a knob that looked like a human hip. The empty sockets of his skull face stared into the darkness. He was the gatekeeper to the afterlife, and a fearsome adversary.

The other three Ghedes were just as fearsome. Baron La Croix, reclaimer of souls, was a short, fat man in a tuxedo who looked as if he enjoyed the finer things in life. Baron Cimetiere was huge; in his tux he looked more like a bouncer at a nightclub, but I knew he was the protector of graveyards. The fourth man wore his fine clothing with the ease of a con man and the lethal grace of a hit man. Baron Kriminel, the hired muscle of the Ghedes.

Baron Samedi raised one hand, palm out toward the ghosts and I heard a voice that echoed like it had been spoken in a crypt. I could not make out the words, but the ghosts drew back like a wave from the shore, parting behind us to clear our way. Like my companions, I ran.

We did not stop running until we reached the car, a few blocks away from the Old Jail. Sorren, who could move faster than any of us, matched our pace to avoid leaving us behind. Caliel came last, casting frequent glances over his shoulder, but the powerful Loa he had invoked had kept their bargain. I shivered, wondering about the cost. The Ghedes did not work for free, and those who called on them for deliverance needed to be ready to pay their price.

"That was not what we expected and more than we bargained for," Sorren observed as the rest of us stopped to catch our breath. We stayed in the shadows beneath the branches of the old live oaks, unwilling to risk adding a chase from the Charleston police to our troubles.

"There's a third Watcher, and we missed our chance to stop him," Teag said, bending over to catch his breath, his hands on his thighs.

"How long ago was the magic worked?" I asked Caliel. "And thanks for saving us."

Caliel gave a wide grin. "My pleasure. As for the magic, it wasn't done in the last few days – the energy was too dispersed for that. I think Harry's ghost told us what it could, but the dead lose their sense of time, since it means nothing on the Other Side. He told us what had happened, not what was about to occur."

Sorren swore in Dutch. That was a sign he was tired and worried. "If Sariel is really the cause of all this, then he's three steps ahead of us, and we can't afford to lose," he said. "We've got to figure this out – and fast – or a lot of people are going to die, and it will all be because of me." He paused. "Let's go talk to Mama Nadege, and see what she makes of it."

Chapter Eighteen

IT'S ONE THING to have studied Charleston's history or read about it in books. It's something entirely different to walk the cobblestone streets and old alleyways with someone who saw those events first-hand.

Charleston is a beautiful city. It overlooks the harbor, and its streets are filled with marvelous antebellum houses, elaborate wrought iron gates and secret walled gardens. But Charleston also has a dark side. For decades, before the Civil War, it was the biggest slave market in the United States. The beautiful homes, wealthy plantations and genteel life enjoyed by wealthy Charlestonians were made possible by blood and suffering. Duels and pirates took more lives. That darkness taints a city's energy. Much as I love Charleston, its shadowy undercurrent draws the wrong sort of supernatural crowd.

We headed into the historic district, down streets that had remained largely unchanged for hundreds of years. Tourists love the glimpse these narrow passageways provide to the city's long-ago past. On the surface, the alleyways and side streets are picturesque. But roiling beneath the picture-perfect facade are the stone tape memories of horrors even the walls can't forget, as well as ghosts that can't move on, and supernatural creatures you don't want to meet in the dark.

Sorren led us to a narrow alley that still looked much as it did in the 1700s. Chuck stayed behind to watch the entrance, giving us a nod to go ahead. Long ago, there had been ramshackle shanties for the enslaved craftsmen and house servants who had belonged to a powerful family in a big house at the end of the street. Some of those slaves brought Voudon with them from New Orleans or the Caribbean. That power still lingered, after all these years.

"Good evening." A deep, rumbling voice with a Caribbean lilt greeted us from the shadows, and a dark-skinned man dressed in a white, loose-fitting linen outfit stepped out to greet us.

Sorren smiled. "I think that's supposed to be my line," he replied.

The man laughed, a rolling basso sound, and grinned widely. "Mama told me to come here tonight," he said. "She knew you were coming. I'm Solomon, one of her helpers." He seemed so lifelike, I could almost overlook being able to see through him when he turned away from the light.

"There's trouble coming," Sorren said as we followed Solomon into the shadows of the alley. The slave quarters were long gone, but as we walked the cobblestones, it didn't take much imagination to see those shanties on either side of us, or to believe that the ghosts who once lived in them were watching us with suspicious, dark-eyed stares.

"Trouble's already here, that's the truth," Solomon said. There were street lights at the entrance to the alley, and a few gas-fired coach lanterns on the walls as we ventured farther inside, but the light did not seem to be able to hold back the darkness. I shivered.

At the end of the street, a gas light cast a glowing circle, and in it stood an old African-American woman in a long, white dress. Her hair was bound up in a many-colored wrap, and on a chain around her neck, I saw a metal disk with the *veve* of Papa Legba.

"Welcome back, children." The old woman's voice was strong. Her hands had seen hard work, but her back was unbowed and fire danced in the depths of her dark eyes.

Sorren and Caliel made a little bow. Teag and I did the same. "Mama Nadege," Sorren said, respect clear in his voice. "We are honored by your presence."

"I told Solomon to expect you," Mama Nadege replied. "Bad things are happening, Sorren, and they're about to get worse. We've been here before, yes we have."

"Have we?" Sorren asked intently. "That's why I came. The Watchers are returning, and I'm almost certain Sariel is behind it, but I thought he'd been destroyed."

Mama Nadege closed her eyes and lifted her hands to the sky, murmuring in a sing-song voice for a moment. She seemed to get the answer that she was seeking, and turned to Sorren.

"They are gathering," she said, and the *veve* on the chain at her throat had a silvery glow. In the distance, I heard a dog howl, and caught a faint whiff of pipe smoke. That meant that Papa Legba was nearby, too.

"How many?" Sorren asked. "And how did they get through without our knowing?"

"Sariel has his ways," Mama replied. "You know of three Watchers, but a fourth has arrived. Only one more, and the Harrowing will begin."

"I thought Sariel had been destroyed. It's been a long, long time," Sorren replied. "Obviously, I was wrong. And if it's really him, how can I make sure that this time, he can't come back?"

"Sariel knows that Charleston is dear to you. Of all your places, Charleston is closest to your heart," Mama said. "You destroyed his son. Had you forgotten? He has not."

"I haven't forgotten," Sorren replied gravely.

Mama nodded. "Sariel survived, and since then, he's regained much strength. But whether he is as strong as he was before, without his son, we won't know until we face him in battle." She paused. "Why now? Because he has been biding his time and he has reached a point where he believes he can win."

"I'll need your help," Sorren said.

Mama Nadege chuckled, a throaty, vibrant sound. "Oh, you can count on me son, and Caliel and Lucinda will help you. Sariel's not quite ready to strike yet, but it won't be long. Gather your team. Find his weakness. Then we must take the fight to him before he brings the last Watcher through."

"Like last time," Sorren said, and I saw sorrow and determination in his features.

"Aye," Mama Nadege agreed. "There will be a cost. But there is no choice. Now go, with the blessing of the spirits," she said, holding her outstretched hand toward us in blessing. And then, as I watched, Mama Nadege's image faded to nothing.

"How does she do that?" Teag murmured. We both knew that Mama Nadege had been dead for more than two hundred years, but even from the afterlife, she had the power to appear real and solid, and to make an impact in the mortal world.

"So what do you think?" I asked. "Do we have a chance of beating Sariel?"

"The mortal world isn't the true home for Sariel or his creatures, so coming across weakens them. That's our opportunity," Sorren added. "Striking before they have their power at full strength."

"Or what?" I asked, meeting Sorren's eyes. Because of his long bond with my family, I'm one of the few, like Mama Nadege, who can look him straight in the eye with impunity.

"The last time Sariel appeared, when Josiah Winfield helped fight him, we came very close to losing," Sorren said quietly.

I shuddered. "Then we'll have to stop him," I said, swallowing back my fear. "Whatever it takes."

THE NEXT NIGHT, Teag and I met Anthony at the Historical Archive for the Angel Oak Fundraiser. I had promised Mrs. Morrissey that I would attend, and I was anxious to get another look at the exhibit, now that I had more experience with angels than I ever thought I'd get this side of the afterlife.

The old Drayton House was lit up with twinkle lights in the crepe myrtle trees on either side of the walkway and in its walled garden. There wasn't a parking place for blocks, so I was glad we had walked from Teag and Anthony's house. Before we even reached the door, I could hear the strains of a string quartet playing in the garden, the hum of conversation and the clinking of champagne glasses.

"I'm so glad they brought the Drayton House back to life by making it the Archive headquarters," Anthony said. He's on a couple of historical preservation boards, and his appreciation of old houses remains unspoiled by memories of nearly being killed by murderous ghosts. "I like what they've done with it."

On one hand, I felt bad that we weren't out hunting for Sariel. But Sorren had felt we needed a day to regroup. He had given Teag a list of items to research on the Darke Web, and said he needed to check with some of his supernatural sources before we took the next step. Sorren seemed concerned about a showdown with Sariel, and that made me downright worried. So going to a swanky event and rubbing shoulders with Charleston society was as good a distraction as any.

Every downstairs room was comfortably full of upper-crust Charlestonians dressed to impress. "Anthony! Good to see you," a man said as we entered, and Anthony grinned, shaking his hand and chatting. Anthony's law practice serves a well-heeled clientele, so he worked his way around the room for a few moments, shaking hands and trading small talk.

"Cassidy and Teag! It's been a while – nice of you to make it," someone else said from the crowded foyer. Most people knew us from Trifles and Folly. My family had been in Charleston since the city's founding, so I recognized a number of the older guests as people my parents knew before they moved to Charlotte.

Most of the city's Who's Who milled about in the foyer or out in the garden. I scored a flute of champagne from a passing waiter, along with a bacon-wrapped scallop from a tray of passed *hors d'oeuvres*, and Teag did the same. Finally, the crowd shifted and I spotted Mrs. Morrissey at about the same instant she saw us.

"Cassidy! Teag! I'm so glad you're here." Mrs. Morrissey waved to us where she was ensconced in a wing chair in the middle of the old house's parlor, surrounded by some of the city's blue-bloods and the Archive's most enthusiastic donors. We made our way over, and I was glad to see that other than a barely-noticeable bruise on her forehead, Mrs. Morrissey looked fully recovered. She noticed the antique walking stick I wielded with a bit of over-the-top glam. "Love that cane," she said. "Quite an antique – I can't believe you're actually using it!"

"What's the use of having something if you never take it out of the case?" I said with a smile. She had no idea just how much 'use' Alard's walking stick got, or how lethal an 'accessory' it actually was. While I didn't intend to use the walking stick indoors, I figured I should have it with me for the walk there and back.

"You won't believe the news!" Mrs. Morrissey bubbled. "We received a phone call yesterday from a man in Belgium of all places, who wanted to purchase 'Nephilim Rising' for his collection! And he didn't hesitate when I named the price – isn't that marvelous?"

I managed to keep a straight face, although I was certain that Sorren was her mysterious Belgian. "That's fantastic," I said. Although the painting was downright dangerous, the money raised would go to support the Historical Archive, which was a worthy cause. "Do you have to ship it to Belgium?"

Mrs. Morrissey shook her head. "No. But he was most insistent that he be able to have the painting picked up this morning. Said he had one of his people in Charleston who would be leaving soon, and he gave instructions to bring around a cashier's check and have the painting sent with his agent. So we started this year's fundraiser off with a bang!"

Bless Sorren, he managed to get the painting out of the Archive before it could cause havoc with the gala and more people got hurt. I owed my patron a great big 'thank-you' for that.

By the time Mrs. Morrissey was ready to lead the guests up to the ballroom, Anthony had rejoined us, standing just behind Teag. Anthony's suit was an updated Michael Kors take on classic Southern seersucker, complete with the pastel bow tie and suspenders combo that decorously announced 'old money'. Teag wore a European-cut jacket and slacks without a tie and looked smashing. I noticed that he brought his leather messenger bag and bet it was full of weapons, just in case. I had thought about wearing a pretty dress, but decided that a pant suit and flats might be the better choice. The jacket hid my athame and Bo's collar beneath my sleeves, and I'd managed to work in Alard's walking stick as an accessory. Sad when you pick what to wear to a party based on how well you could fight monsters while wearing it.

The party moved upstairs, where more waiters with champagne and *hors d'oeuvres* awaited, plus a cellist who was seated in the back corner where 'Nephilim Rising' had been.

"Uh oh," Teag murmured, nudging me. "Look who's here."

I barely had time to glance around before I heard an unwelcome voice behind me. "Why am I somehow not surprised to see you here?" Detective Monroe said.

I almost didn't recognize her, since she wasn't wearing the boring dark suits I'd seen her in before. She cleaned up better than I would have thought, when she wasn't scowling. Her hair was simple but flattering, and a touch of tasteful make-up softened her features. She had also opted for a well-tailored pant suit and flats, and I bet she had made the choice for the same reasons I did. I was also pretty certain there was a gun holstered beneath her jacket and a badge in her purse.

"Detective," I said. "I didn't realize you had a fondness for the arts."

Monroe gave me a look. "I have a fondness for making sure gatherings like this go smoothly, especially given the odd things that have been going on lately." She nodded toward a man who stood with his back to us, talking to two men I recognized as members of the City Council. "Besides, my boss thought it would be a good idea to be seen here, so here I am."

She eyed the walking stick and made a face. "Bit of an affectation, isn't it? What's next, one of those long cigarette holders?"

"I felt like adding a little cinema chic for the cause tonight," I lied. Given that my pantsuit had satin tuxedo-jacket lapels, I could be forgiven for going Hepburn.

Monroe rolled her eyes. "Whatever. If it's a trend, I don't think it's going to catch on."

Just then, Anthony returned with fresh champagne for the three of us. His expression changed when he recognized Monroe. "What a surprise, Detective," Anthony said in a cool voice as he handed us our drinks. Anthony casually laid a hand on Teag's shoulder and moved to stand slightly between me and Monroe, a protective gesture the detective couldn't miss.

"No reason for concern, Counselor," she said, confirming that she recognized Anthony as well. "Just making small talk." And with that, she headed off, though I noticed she wasn't indulging in the champagne.

"Trouble?" Anthony asked *sotto voce*.

Teag shook his head. "Not yet, anyhow. Probably not a bad idea to have some plainclothes officers here, considering the crowd."

I wasn't convinced, but I said nothing. Instead, I looked around at the art and the magnificent sculpture of the Angel Oak that dominated the ballroom. Closing my eyes for a moment, I could sense the shift in the room's energy without the Astor painting. The vibe was cleaner, untroubled. To my surprise, the energy also felt healing, as if it were reacting to how stressed, tired and generally beat up I felt and it sent me a rush of much-needed replenishment. I opened my eyes and blinked, feeling much better, and caught a glance from Teag that indicated he had experienced the same boost.

"Care for a petite quiche?" I turned as the waiter spoke and startled. The server who smiled above a silver tray of expensive noshes was cover model handsome.

"Sure," I said, managing to brush his hand as I took the canapé. He moved away and Teag managed to snag a quiche before he was out of reach. I glanced around at the rest of the serving staff. They were all good-looking enough to make me very nervous.

"Sometimes a pretty face is just a struggling actor," Teag murmured, guessing my thoughts.

He was right, but I was too worried about the possibility of Nephilim waiters to let it go. "I'm awfully peckish tonight," I said with a smile. "I'm going to check out what's being served." With that, I moseyed and mingled through the crowd, making sure I checked out what each waiter had on his tray, brushing close enough to make contact with bare skin. To my relief, absolutely nothing supernatural happened.

Since I had dispelled the threat of an impending Nephilim attack and Detective Monroe was off paying attention to something other than Teag and me, I indulged in a few rare moments of relaxation. I savored the bellini I'd gotten from one of the waiters along with a nibble of asparagus and prosciutto, and let myself enjoy the cellist's solo. Teag had gone off with Anthony, so I dawdled, making a slow circle of the ballroom to look at all of the angel-themed art. I placed bids for the silent auction on several local-artisan pieces that I liked, items for the store and a pottery piece with especially nice vibrations that I thought I would keep for myself. Since I'm a big fan of the Archive and Mrs. Morrissey is a huge help with research, I figured I could spare an extra donation on top of my annual pledge.

As I made my way around the room, the giant model of the Angel Oak in the center drew my attention. Once I had seen all of the pieces of art for auction, I found myself standing beneath the gnarled, spreading limbs of the tree, staring up at its canopy. Even at one-fifth scale, the artist's massive installation brushed the ballroom's high ceiling and sent out limbs that nearly reached all four walls.

"Impressive, isn't it?" Mrs. Morrissey said, coming up beside me. "It's not really for sale, although I've had a couple of inquiries, if you can believe it!"

"What will happen to it once the fundraiser is over?" I asked. I hated to think that the beautiful piece might be dismantled permanently, although it would surely need to be taken apart to get it out of the ballroom.

"One of the big bank buildings downtown wants to put it in the atrium for several months," she replied.

"Then both the Lowcountry Museum and the University have expressed interest." Mrs. Morrissey smiled. "I'm just impressed with how life-like it is, and how well the artist incorporated pieces of the real Angel Oak."

I hadn't been out to Johns Island to see the Angel Oak in a long time. If the replica here in the ballroom was any indicator, I decided that the real tree's resonance must be exceptionally powerful. My magic registered calming vibrations, and a sense of serenity and patience that was often in short supply. "I wish I had room to take it home with me," I said. "It makes me feel calmer just standing next to it."

Mrs. Morrissey chuckled. "You're not the first person to say that," she replied. "I think that's part of the reason so many locations want the installation. Everything today makes us all jittery and keyed-up. When you find something that calms you down, you want to hang onto it."

Someone called her away just then, and just as I was about to move on, Teag and Anthony caught up with me. "Let's get out of here before Anthony spends any more money," Teag said, but his tone held affection and humor. "He's already placed a couple of generous bids, and if we win, I don't know where we'll put the stuff!"

Anthony shook his head with a smile. "There's always room for a good piece of art. We'll just move things around." He gave me a conspiratorial look. "Don't forget – a high bid challenges the competition to bid more, which benefits the Archive."

"Have you seen everything?" Teag asked. "Are you ready to move on?"

I nodded. Although the ballroom was spacious, the art display took up a lot of room. It felt crowded, and there were probably people downstairs who hadn't had a chance to come up and mingle. "We'd probably better clear out so that more donors can look at the art," I replied.

We said our goodbyes to Mrs. Morrissey and headed out. I glanced around, looking for Detective Monroe, but didn't see her. That was fine with me.

Despite the air conditioning, the fundraiser seemed crowded and stuffy, so the cooler air outside was a relief, and I looked forward to the prospect of a nighttime stroll. Yet by the time we were half-way to Teag and Anthony's house, I felt antsy, and I noticed that Teag was paying more attention to the shadows around us than to Anthony's attempts at conversation.

I should have bid more on that piece of art. Pretty ungrateful, considering that it was my fault Mrs. Morrissey got hurt. I wasn't fast enough or smart enough to protect her. The least I could have done was bid more. She helps us out a lot with research. Selfish, selfish, selfish –

I caught myself and turned toward Teag just as he reached for his messenger bag. "Watcher-guilt!" I warned. "That means trouble!"

"Maybe we can get home –" Teag started to say, but then something dark, fast and solid leaped out from the shadows behind us, taking Anthony down with it.

"Anthony!" Teag shouted. He ran for the Nephilim, which was still in human form, and got in a solid kick to the monster's head that would have dropped a normal opponent. The Nephilim barely registered the blow. Teag pulled a three-sectioned bo staff out of his bag, and with a snap and a twist, the sections came together to make a six-foot fighting rod. In his other hand was his dagger. Josiah Winfield's pistols were back at his house, too bulky to easily carry in public.

I didn't dare fire either my athame or my walking stick for fear of hurting Anthony. Three more Nephilim were heading our way from the other direction. The waiters at the party might not have been fallen angels, but these pretty boys sure were.

I shook my left wrist, and Bo's ghost appeared by my side, already growling. He'd had a taste of Nephilim lately, and he sounded ready to get some more. I had the walking stick already up and leveled, and let loose a torrent of fire that caught the Nephilim on my right full in the face while Bo snarled and leaped at the Nephilim in the center.

Teag was giving the Nephilim that had attacked Anthony a first-class beat-down, striking with his staff, dodging in and out to drive his dagger down again and again through the Nephilim's back. He couldn't use his *urumi* with Anthony pinned under the fallen angel, but the dagger and staff together should have been a lethal combination.

Anthony was fighting, trying to wrest free from the Nephilim's grip. I heard what sounded like six muffled shots, and the Nephilim's body jerked with each one.

"Drop your weapons! Charleston Police!" The voice came out of the darkness, but I knew it had to be Monroe. Now she'd gone beyond annoying. She was likely to get us killed.

The three Nephilim coming toward me never slowed down. Bo went for the man in the center, sinking his teeth deep into the flesh of his shoulder. A shot fired, and went straight through Bo's ghostly form, while his snarling spirit never loosened his grip.

Teag landed a hit to the skull of the Nephilim that had Anthony pinned, hard enough to score a home run. Instead, the bloodied fallen angel stood slowly, revealing the mere shell of a body, its chest blown away. Anthony scrambled to his feet, covered in blood, a gun still clutched in his right hand. Teag gave one flick of the *urumi* and the razor whip blade took the Nephilim's head clean off its shoulders. It lurched toward Teag, arms outstretched and hands clutching, before it finally toppled to the ground and the body disintegrated.

"What the fuck is going on?" Monroe grated, and it was clear she was pissed off. Some choice – get shot by a cop or slashed to ribbons by a fallen angel.

The Nephilim I fire-blasted barely broke stride, although his clothing burned away and his skin charred to blisters. I sent a column of fire toward the center Nephilim, which wouldn't hurt Bo but caught the fallen angel right in the face.

"I said drop your weapons!" Monroe snapped.

"Can't," I shouted. "Not unless you want to see these guys cut us up where we stand. I could use some help here!"

"Ask yourself why they're still charging us after they've caught on fire," Teag yelled as he cycled his staff overhead, keeping a wary eye on the Nephilim on the left. Although the collapsible staff was metal instead of wood, I saw that he had engraved runes into the surface that were glowing like embers.

He stepped forward and gave a shake of his wrist. The *urumi* snaked out with a *zing* and struck the Nephilim around the waist, tearing through his shirt and peeling off a strip of flesh with it.

With a roar, the Nephilim on the right began to shift. Blood-red leathery skin replaced the charred flesh, ripping through what was left of the burned clothing. Its claws scrabbled against the cobblestones as it began to run toward me, reaching for me with the sharp talons on its long, muscular arms.

This time, I blasted the fallen angel with my athame, which threw him into the air and sent him tumbling down the street. A dark figure stepped from the shadows, and I saw Monroe draw down on the Nephilim.

"Get the hell out of there!" Teag warned. "That thing isn't human."

Before Monroe could get more than a word of the Miranda warning out of her mouth, the Nephilim crawled to his feet and turned toward her beneath the streetlight, giving her a good look at just what we were fighting. The Nephilim backhanded Monroe and came after me at a run.

I'll give Monroe credit. She rolled, came up in a crouch and got in four shots, all of which took the monster in the torso. He never slowed down, although the shots made a bloody mess of his back and would have killed a human. Her aim was good, but her bullets weren't as effective as what Chuck Pettis and Daniel Hunter had used on the other Nephilim. Apparently, Chuck and Daniel favored larger caliber guns than standard police issue, and silver-holy water rounds that didn't come with regulation gear.

Now that Monroe was shooting at the fallen angels instead of at us, I could focus on the real threat.

Anthony had figured out that his bullets weren't going to stop the Nephilim, but getting shot distracted them just fine. So he took aim at the monsters one by one, setting them back on their heels long enough for Teag and me to strike. I was still in shock over Anthony even owning a gun let alone shooting one, but I wasn't going to turn down help no matter how unexpected. The same went for Monroe, so long as she kept shooting *them* and wasn't shooting *us*.

"Out of bullets," Anthony said grimly.

"Get behind me – and stay there!" Teag ordered. We still had three Nephilim to go. Teag lashed the Nephilim closest to him with his *urumi*, and the steel blade was crimson with blood, flaying the fallen angel with every stroke of the razor-sharp lash. I wished I had my *chakram* or Josiah Winfield's pistols – preferably both – and wondered whether or not what we had with us was going to be good enough.

Monroe followed Anthony's lead, once she figured out she couldn't drop the Nephilim, and her shots slowed our attackers. I alternated blasting fire with the walking stick and the white-cold force I could project from the athame, but I couldn't keep it up forever. The bullets kept the Nephilim from transforming, but I doubted Monroe had a neverending supply. Bo's ghost kept at the fallen angels, dodging after them with bared, bloodied teeth. He chomped down hard on the hamstring of Teag's target. When the Nephilim went down onto one knee, Teag caved in the side of its skull with his staff and followed up with a full-power kick just for good measure. The fallen angel collapsed, and Teag jammed the end of his staff down on the base of the Nephilim's neck, severing its spine. The corpse vanished.

Two down, two to go. Anthony was wounded and Nephilim claws carried taint, so he'd be in bad shape if we didn't end this fight quickly. Teag and I were tiring fast. I was afraid that the gunshots would summon more police. That was likely to get Teag and me shot and civilians wounded when the Nephilim turned on the cops.

The Nephilim I battled was half-changed. I hit him in the chest with a column of fire and he roared with anger, but he kept on coming. His right hand slashed across my shoulder deep enough to destroy my jacket and draw blood from four parallel gashes. On sheer reflex, I sank my power down into the cobblestones and the earth beneath my feet, and to my surprise, something answered.

We were South of Broad Street. Much of this area was reclaimed from the water by dumping the rocky ballast of ships into the busy harbor. Unnatural ground and old ocean bed was a natural magnet for spirits. I felt my power fan out to the old homes along the street with their long-suffering ghostly residents, and I called out for help to the duelists and drunkards and vagabonds who had breathed their last along these gutters. I'm not a medium and I'm not a necromancer, but when I touch haunted objects, the ghosts respond. And tonight, I needed their help.

Bo's spirit grew more solid, and hurled himself at the Nephilim closest to me. Monroe still looked bushwacked by what was going on, but the half-turned fallen angels were close enough to anyone's definition of monster that she decided to strike first and ask questions later. She had emptied her clip into the Nephilim, and the fact that they kept on coming must have convinced her that they were the bad guys. We could hash it out later, if we were all alive to argue about it. Now, Monroe went after the Nephilim's backs, pistol-whipping one and pulling a truncheon from somewhere to hammer away at their skulls.

Teag's *urumi* had both of the Nephilim stripped nearly bare of skin. Deep cuts to the muscle and tendons should have stopped them, but they kept on coming. Anthony hurled rocks from the gutter, and he pitched like a major leaguer, but we just didn't have the firepower to bring these suckers down.

I saw a blur, and one of the Nephilim flew through the air. He landed on the *chevaux de frise* atop the wrought iron fence behind us and stuck like a gigged frog. Another blur, and the last Nephilim stopped in his tracks, with a steel sword protruding from his chest through his heart. A second later, his head was torn from his body. The corpse shuddered and convulsed, then crumbled to ash. Sorren stood behind him, a bloodied sword in his hands.

"I have never been so glad to see anyone in my life," I said shakily, lowering my walking stick. Bo's ghost rubbed against Sorren, gave me a tired doggy smile, and vanished.

"What... the hell... happened here?" Bloodied and bruised, Detective Monroe staggered toward us. I'll give her props – she had to make a split-second judgment on whom to back, and she picked the right team.

"What do you think happened?" Sorren asked. I recognized the honeyed tone of compulsion.

"I have no idea," Monroe replied, less forcefully than before. "Those men looked normal, but no one human can take that kind of damage –"

I wasn't Detective Monroe's biggest fan. We'd never be BFFs, or do a girls' night out. But right now, I felt for her. She was used to a world where there wasn't such a thing as monsters, where everything made sense, and where the simplest explanation was the best. And she had just tumbled into the Twilight Zone.

"You fought bravely," Sorren said in a voice that was almost impossible to resist. "Why did you follow Cassidy?"

"I know there's more going on than what she's saying," Monroe said as if she were in a trance. "I figured I'd follow them, see where they went. Wondered what the lawyer has to do with it. Where there's smoke there's fire."

I could tell that Monroe was fighting the compulsion, but her voice had taken on a dream-like quality. Anthony moved forward, and his expression was equally intrigued and repelled, but Teag vigorously motioned for him to be quiet.

"What did you see?" Sorren asked.

Monroe's answer was halting. I'm sure for a by-the-book cop, fighting monsters strained every rational synapse in her brain. "I saw... monsters. Or people dressed up like monsters. Or terrorists that looked like... monsters."

There's a moment when people encounter the supernatural and it turns their world upside-down. Some people can deal with it. Most can't. Monroe might be obnoxious, but she was a good cop. She just wasn't cut out for this kind of thing. Neither were ninety-nine percent of the people on this planet.

"You saw an attempted drive-by shooting. The shooters were after Cassidy, Teag, and Anthony," Sorren said quietly. "You ordered the attackers to disperse, and they did not heed your orders. Then as they drove away, you fired your weapon into the air as a warning and finally into their vehicle. There were no monsters. Nothing unusual happened. Just three people fighting off an attack. Do you understand?"

Numbly, Monroe nodded. She'd had the courage to stick around and help, even though she had no idea what was going on and didn't actually like us. And now she could go back to her everyday existence, disbelieving in magic and monsters, secure in her very normal world. I envied her – just a little.

"You're going to walk back to your car," Sorren instructed. When you get there, you'll remember helping to scare off the drive-by. That is the report you'll make. And in the future, you'll realize that you have more important things to do than to pay attention to what Cassidy, Teag, and Anthony are doing." Sorren looked toward us and cocked an eyebrow with a sardonic smile.

"I understand."

"Go now, and remember nothing else."

We remained silent as Detective Monroe turned and walked away. When she was out of sight and out of earshot, we all gave a sigh of relief.

"How did you know we needed help?" I asked.

Sorren shrugged. "I was afraid there might be problems at the gala. That's why I made sure the painting was gone early. Once it was dark, I thought I should check in. I'm glad I did. Circumstances delayed me, for which I apologize."

"I think we might have broken about a dozen or so laws, at least." Anthony sounded a little woozy. Teag turned toward him with concern just as Anthony's knees gave way and he collapsed to the sidewalk. He was bleeding where the Nephilim had struck him, and he looked pale.

"Oh God," Teag said. "We've got to get him inside and get help."

"I've seen you fight in tournaments," Anthony said, looking up at Teag unsteadily. "But not like this. You went Batman on their asses."

"Guess that makes you Robin," Teag said, worry pinching his features tight. "Where the hell did you get a gun? You hate guns."

"But I love you," Anthony mumbled. "And what you do is dangerous. I figured... it would come in handy." His eyes rolled into the back of his head and he fell silent.

"Sorren, please," Teag begged.

Sorren laid a hand on Teag's shoulder. "We're not far from your house. Let's get him inside. It's likely not as bad as it looks." Sorren scooped Anthony into his arms as if he were lifting a small child, and we walked the last block to their house. I was holding my breath and when we crossed over Lucinda's protective wards, I exhaled.

Sorren laid Anthony down on the couch. "Let's take a look at those gashes." Teag fetched the special first-aid kit, and Sorren cleaned and dressed Anthony's wounds with practiced skill. "He's had quite a shock, and he's lost some blood, but he'll be fine with rest," he said after he finished. "I'll send Dr. Zeigler over right away to have a look at him, in case those cuts are tainted."

"Will he remember?" Teag asked.

Sorren nodded. "Yes. He bought that gun and learned to use it of his own free will. While he struggles with belief in the supernatural, he believes you. So, yes. He will remember. All of it." That was going to make for an uncomfortable conversation later, but we were in too deep to worry about it now.

Sorren glanced from Teag to me and his eyes narrowed. "As for the two of you," he said, "let me take care of those cuts." Sorren's injuries were already healing on their own.

Teag swore that he was all right with Anthony on his own, and Anthony was sleeping soundly, thanks to a root tea from Mrs. Teller and some help from Sorren. Sorren made a call, and promised that Dr. Zeigler would stop by in the morning. An hour later, Sorren and I left to walk to my house.

"You bought the painting at the auction," I said as we walked.

Sorren chuckled. "I figured you'd hear about that."

"Where are you going to hang it?"

"I've got somewhere in mind where it will fit right in with the décor."

I turned to look at Sorren as we walked up to my piazza door. "Thank you for showing up tonight. I really thought we were toast."

Sorren's expression was a mix of regret and hesitation. "I may have gotten us all into something over our heads this time," he admitted. "But tonight, I could make a difference. So I did. Good night, Cassidy."

I stepped across the wards, into safety. "Good night, Sorren."

Chapter Nineteen

THE NEXT NIGHT, Teag and Sorren and I sat at my kitchen table, combing through the information we had collected, searching for a way to get an advantage against Sariel. Anthony was doing well enough that he demanded Teag come over and reconnoiter with Sorren and me – that was his word, 'reconnoiter' – so that we could carry on. I decided that when all of this was over, I was buying Anthony dinner and a bottle of the best scotch I could afford.

"Sariel's powerful, and he's ruthless," Sorren replied. "So were the others I've fought over the centuries. But with most of them, it was strictly business. With Sariel, it's personal. That need for vengeance makes him especially dangerous – and he was bad news to begin with."

Sorren looked tired. I wondered if a combination of worry and blaming himself for Sariel's re-appearance was wearing on him. If so, it was a perfectly normal, perfectly human response for someone who was neither normal nor human. I walked over to the counter to pour myself a glass of wine.

"What was Sariel, before he became a nephilmancer?" I asked.

"More than one hundred years ago, Sariel was a judge who didn't feel that he received justice, so he appealed to a Power that would enable him to set things right – at least, according to his views. He made a bargain with the Darkness."

Sorren stared off for a moment, remembering. "The thing is, long ago, the man who became Sariel was a pretty decent person. Back then, he was Judge Asa Larson. Had a reputation for being stern but fair, and he was a family man, pillar of the community."

He shook his head. "Then things went wrong. His daughter married a homesteader and went West. Many people did, after the war. The daughter and her husband settled out in the Oklahoma territory, set up farming, and did well for a time. Then word came that the daughter and the other settlers had been killed by a bandit gang."

"And the bandits got away," I supplied.

Sorren shrugged. "No matter how many crimes the bandits were linked to, they never seemed to get caught."

"Corrupt officials?"

"Maybe. Or perhaps just incompetent ones." Sorren gave a sad smile. "There was no DNA analysis, no forensics. It was much easier to get away with murder." Something in Sorren's voice gave me the sense that he knew the truth of his statement first-hand.

"So the Judge went out West, decided to take things into his own hands," Sorren continued. "He hired some vigilantes, and tried to bring the bandits to justice."

"Sounds like a dedicated father to me. Extreme, but dedicated."

"The bandits were cruel, brutal men." Anger smoldered in Sorren's eyes. "No one would have missed them if Larson had been successful. Even the local sheriffs helped. But your West has a lot of barren, open land. And Larson didn't count on the bandits having a *bruja*."

"A witch."

"Yes. Larson set out with his gunslingers toward a place in the desert the bandits had made their bolt-hole. Thirty men went in. Two came out: Larson, and one other survivor."

"Was it the witch, or the bandits that defeated him?" I asked.

"According to the stories, it was the witch," Sorren replied. "It was not a fair fight. Larson survived, but the battle changed him, and he was even more fixated on revenge than before."

"So Larson decided to try another route?"

Sorren nodded. "Larson's grief and frustration drove him mad. When the Almighty allowed his daughter to die and didn't use Larson and his vigilantes to bring judgment, Larson cursed God and sought the power he needed elsewhere."

"As in, becoming a nephilmancer," I said.

"Yes," Sorren replied. "Larson went looking for a deal with whoever could bring the bandits down. He went to several mortal crime lords, but because of his reputation as a judge, none of them would trust him. Finally, mad and destitute, he made the proverbial deal with the Devil – or near enough."

"So how did his son factor into this?"

Sorren reached down and lifted Baxter onto his lap. Baxter did one turn around and settled in, content to allow Sorren to scratch his ears.

"One of Larson's sons disavowed him," he replied after a pause. "But his younger son, Samuel, went along, whether to protect his father or avenge his sister, no one knows." He paused. "The son that cut him off made Larson dead to him and made it his business to go to war against Larson and people like him."

Holy shit! "So Daniel Hunter –"

Sorren nodded. "Yeah. He's Asa Larson's other son. One big dysfunctional supernatural family."

"And did Larson eventually get his vengeance against the bandits?" Listening to Sorren talk about history as if it happened yesterday was more gripping than any reality show. I had to restrain myself from making popcorn.

"He did. But everything has its price. Larson's vow gave him over, body and soul, to an entity known as Sariel who wanted access to this mortal realm," he said. "Sariel promised Larson that the bandits would pay for their crimes, and they did." He was quiet for a moment.

"Whatever atrocities the bandits had committed, what Sariel did – through Larson and his son, along with Nephilim he now controlled – avenged the murdered settlers tenfold. The bandits were tortured, mutilated, burned, vivisected, and their souls were cursed to eternal torment. Larson got his revenge. But the price was his own soul, and quite possibly, his son's as well. Maybe he and Samuel went to their judgment willingly," Sorren said with a shrug. "Maybe not."

"How did you get involved?"

Sorren grimaced. "Larson – now Sariel – drew the attention of the Family." He didn't have to explain. The Family is often behind problems the Alliance steps in to fix. They're the supernatural equivalent of organized crime.

"The Family made sure he got the resources he wanted, until he emerged as an exceptionally powerful nephilmancer and a possible threat to them," Sorren replied. "Up to this point, I had been only marginally aware of the situation. But when Sariel returned from the West, it became clear that he was a problem the Alliance needed to handle."

"Because of the Watchers?"

Sorren nodded. "The power of being judge, jury, and executioner corrupted him."

Teag had brought a bag of Krispy Kreme donuts with him, and the 'hot now' smell of sticky, warm glazed goodness wafted up from the open box in the middle of the table. I had already eaten two, and I doubted a third would go well with my wine, so I pushed the box aside.

"Anything else you can tell us about Sariel?" I asked.

Sorren reached into his pocket. "Actually, I was going to let you see for yourself," he said. And with that, he produced a battered ring from his pocket and placed it on the coffee table.

"I wore this ring in the battle that claimed the life of Sariel's son," Sorren said. "I suspect that if you touch it, you'll see – and you'll have all the answers you might want about exactly who – and what – we're up against."

"Hold on," Teag said. He produced a strip of cloth about as wide as his hand and about a foot long. Woven into the fabric were runes and markings, and even without touching the cloth, I knew that Teag's Weaver magic was imbued in the warp and the woof.

"I made this to see if I can piggyback with Cassidy's visions," he said. "Let's try." He lifted the ring and placed it onto the strip of fabric, then held the end of the strip between his thumb and fingers. "Okay, Cassidy," he said with a grin. "Do your stuff."

I took a deep breath and reached out toward Sorren's ring. As I touched the metal, I closed my eyes, and I felt the jolt of power as my magic showed me a vastly different time and place.

Thanks to the ring, I viewed the scene through Sorren's eyes. I stood on a sprawling lawn bounded by large live oak trees. Wisps of fog hung in the air, and Spanish moss drooped from the trees' gnarled branches. Beneath my feet lay the unmarked graves of generations of dead slaves, restless spirits far from home. Such gravesites were common in the Lowcountry, and Sariel and his Reapers had been feasting, bringing across more Nephilim, increasing their strength to win bigger spoils.

We were here to stop them. This night, fast and strong wouldn't be enough. We were going to need every advantage we could get – and no small amount of luck.

Sariel came over the hill first, followed by the scarred, half-human thing that was once Samuel. Where Judge Larson's alliance with Sariel had preserved his outward appearance, Samuel's years of following his father into battle on their quest for vengeance had left him battered and broken. Half of Samuel's face had been badly scarred by fire, costing him an eye. He moved with a hitch in his gait from old wounds, and his left arm was crippled. Still, he followed, his eyes alight with the same cold malice that animated his father.

We waited in the shadows, cloaked by amulets and wardings. Sariel strode down into the old graveyard and spread his arms, raising them to the sky as he began to chant. Samuel kept watch behind him, with a sword in one hand and a pistol in the other.

Wind rustled through the live oaks' branches, stirring the moss at first, then tearing at it with force as the breeze became a howling maelstrom. Behind Sariel, it looked as if the night sky itself were ripping open, a jagged tear inky black against the starry heavens.

Sariel's chant grew louder, and through the rip, I could see shadows descending. Twisting, bat-like shapes emerged from the tear in the sky: Nephilim, tainted spirits born of blood and debauchery that hungered for souls. Sariel had brought five Watchers through already, and the Yellow Fever that now claimed tens of thousands of lives would not end until we destroyed the ones who brought the Harrowing down on Charleston.

Columns of light flared, one from each corner of the burying ground where my allies had concealed themselves. Inside each warded column was a powerful magic user: witch or warlock, mambo or houngan, even a Cherokee shaman. The shimmering light lit the open field more brightly than moonlight, and as I watched, the light began to stretch out between the pillars and over our heads, until we were enclosed in an iridescent dome.

Magical barriers prevented whatever came through that rift from harming those outside the dome or from retreating back from whence they came. If our magic was strong enough, Sariel would not be able to bring more of his minions through the rift, and his Harrowing would end with his destruction.

Until then, we were trapped inside, along with Sariel and his Nephilim.

"Now!" I shouted, and my allies cast off the charms and spells that had hidden them from Sariel's view. They rose from the shadows, and power surged in arcs through the air, hitting the Nephilim and Watchers. The monsters shrieked and screamed, twisting as our magic consumed them. The air smelled of sulfur and decay.

A dozen Nephilim had come through the rift along with the five Watchers. We had our hands full. I ran for Sariel, sword raised. Gunfire would not harm him; that, we had learned the hard way. But the steel blade in my grip had been spelled by a master witch, and it gleamed a cold, blue light as if it were eager to taste blood. Samuel stepped between us and leveled his gun at me.

I felt the bullet from Samuel's gun tear through my chest but I kept on going. Another shot, another sharp, agonizing pain, as a second bullet ripped into my left shoulder. Still, I ran. That was why we had left Sariel and his son for me to battle. I was hardest to kill. I dodged the next two bullets, and the fifth grazed my temple. I was close now, and before he could shoot me point-blank, I dove and rolled, fast enough to move out of the way in the instant between the pull of the trigger and the flash of the muzzle.

Samuel screamed a curse and turned on me with his sword, tossing his gun to the side and drawing a knife from his belt. He was no longer fully human and it showed in his quick reactions and in strength nearly equal to my own. Sariel saw us close on each other, but the magic onslaught from my allies kept Sariel out of our fight. My allies kept the strikes coming, positions always changing, moving targets Sariel could not find to hit.

"You have been judged and found guilty." Samuel announced as our swords met each other. "I will be your executioner."

"Not today."

Unlike his father, Samuel was mortal. His enhanced abilities came from an amulet on a leather strap around his neck. I could see the strap now, and as my blade *screeched down the steel of his sword, Samuel buried his knife hilt-deep in my belly. I gasped, but took the pain, stepping toward him to slash my knife across his neck, severing the leather strap and then, reversing course to slit his throat.*

Samuel's body toppled to the side and I nearly fell with him. Dark blood spilled out from the gash his knife had torn in my abdomen. My bullet wounds were already healing, but they hurt like hell. And as Samuel's body hit the ground, Sariel finally realized what I had done.

"My son!" he screamed, mad with rage. Sariel turned on me, the other attackers forgotten, and gathered his power for a fatal blast.

I raised my sword and prepared to fight, resigned to my own destruction.

A blinding flare of light struck Sariel squarely in the forehead, and he froze. Blasts of fire burned at Sariel's back, followed by cold so sudden and intense that it raised a heavy skin of ice over his entire form, immobilizing him. Wave upon wave of magic struck him, and only then did he realize that I was just the bait.

His mouth was already forming a killing curse when a column of iridescent light fell around him, imprisoning Sariel. I could see the rage in his face, and knew that he wanted my blood. My allies sent their power coursing towards Sariel, enveloping him in a ball of fire and magic. I heard a scream, smelled burning flesh, and then he and the flames were gone.

I opened my eyes and saw Sorren watching me intently. The ring tumbled from my hand onto the table. Teag stirred in his chair, and looked at me with an expression of awe. "Is that how it always is for you when you touch something? Damn, girl!"

I gave a rueful chuckle. "Yeah, pretty much. Sometimes it's worse."

It took me a moment or two to process what I had seen. Sorren doesn't share many items to give me visions, and I'm pretty sure I know why. I always come away with more clues to who Sorren is – and was. I think that makes him uncomfortable. Memories and emotions hit me that weren't part of the intended message. Mostly, what I pick up is loneliness.

"So Sariel's son was sucked into the family madness," I said. "And in the last battle, you went after Samuel knowing it would distract Sariel so the others could attack and bind him."

Sorren nodded. "Yes."

"The people who helped you, the ones with magic," Teag asked, "are any of them still around?"

Sorren chuckled. "No. They were either mortals who died a long time ago, or they were destroyed in one battle or another over the years. I'm the only one left. Except for Sariel."

"That battle we saw was fought somewhere near Charleston?" I asked. "Did he pick the city for his Harrowing because of you the last time, too?"

"The battle was about fifty miles from here, out on a large plantation," Sorren replied. "And no, the location was one of convenience – for Sariel. Charleston was a prize ripe for the picking, its climate suited to pestilence, which has always been a feeding ground for the demonic."

"Now, he's bringing the fight back to Charleston again," I mused. "You cost him a son; he's going to make you pay by destroying a city."

"I don't have any mortal descendants," Sorren replied. "Hadn't gotten around to that when Alard turned me. Over the centuries, I made very few fledges, and most of those whom I made disappeared or have been destroyed."

I thought of Mrs. Butler, out at Palmetto Meadows. Someone had raised wards around the nursing home, and I was willing to bet Sorren had something to do with it. Had he taken other precautions to protect her as well?

"How do you plan on fighting Sariel this time around?" Teag asked.

"That's a good question," Sorren said. "There's even more at stake now. Charleston is a bigger city. An epidemic now could kill ten times as many as back in 1854."

"Can we assemble a team like you had the last time?" I asked. "Can the Alliance send anyone?"

Sorren shrugged. "On the first question – yes, we can assemble a team, but the skills and magic will be different from what I had to work with before. As for the Alliance, they're the ones who sent Daniel Hunter, and they're providing help in other ways." He gave me a wan smile. "No matter how much of an ass Hunter might be, he's good at what he does."

I don't like trophy hunters in the normal world, but I thought of the demonic creature Coffee Guy had begun to turn into, and decided that I wouldn't mind if Daniel Hunter bagged and stuffed it and hung it on his wall.

"The attacks you've been battling all over North America, they weren't just to harm people you cared about," Teag said. "It's also stretched the Alliance thin, keeping them from massing against the real strike."

Sorren nodded. "I fear you're right. The Alliance doesn't dare risk leaving those other locations undefended. But it means that we've got to fight Sariel with the resources we've got. And hope that they'll be enough."

Chapter Twenty

THE NEXT DAY at noon, Baxter and I were scheduled to go to Palmetto Meadows. I was ready for something to take my mind off Nephilim, Watchers, and sorcerers. Still, instead of my purse I took a backpack with some of my weapons, and I wore Bo's collar and had my athame up my sleeve. Just in case.

Seeing the smiles from the nurses when Bax and I walked into the lobby lifted my spirits, and I knew that to the residents, 'dog day' was the highlight of their week, or what they remembered of it.

All the more reason why I was surprised when sour-faced Becky stopped me before I got to the reception desk. "What is that dog doing in here?" she demanded, eying Baxter disdainfully.

"We went through this last week," I said. "Baxter is a therapy dog. This is our usual day to visit," I replied.

"I didn't hear anything about that," Becky snapped. "You'll have to go outside until I can confirm."

I walked back through the door with Baxter, perplexed at Nurse Becky's rudeness. That's when I realized that I hadn't felt the shimmer of the wards that protected the nursing home. *That's odd – and disturbing.*

There wasn't time to ponder it, because Judy came hurrying out to meet me, looking embarrassed. "I am so sorry," she said, glancing over her shoulder to make sure Becky hadn't followed. "She's new… doesn't excuse –"

I shrugged. "Forget about it," I said. "Baxter doesn't care, and neither do I." I paused. "It is okay for us to come in?"

Judy nodded. "Yes. Hell, yes. And I made sure Becky won't bother you. Come on in." I followed her, and Baxter trotted in like a celebrity. All he needed was sunglasses.

"What's new today?" I asked.

"Absolutely nothing, which is how I like it," Judy said. Being around Judy always made me feel good. I wondered if she had that effect on the residents, too, and whether it was part of her magic. If so, I hoped the nursing home paid her double.

"You want something before we start? Coffee? Water for Baxter?"

"No thanks. We're ready to get going," I said as we entered the activity room. I noticed a large framed canvas of an ancient live oak tree with engraved brass name plates on different limbs and branches. A side table beneath the canvas held a bouquet of fresh flowers and a silver candelabrum with unlit white taper candles.

"What's that?" I asked. I couldn't help noticing how much the live oak looked like the Angel Oak.

"Do you like it?" Judy asked. "It's been in the works for a while, but they just hung it up over the weekend, so don't feel like your memory's slipping. We added the flowers and candles to make it look festive."

I got up close and looked at the plaques.

"They're in memory of residents who have passed on," Judy said. "It's our way of honoring them. I think you realize that the staff here gets pretty attached to them."

Like the real Angel Oak, the tree in the mural had thick limbs and lots of twisting branches, heavy with leaves. There were already a lot of small plaques commemorating former residents.

A few heads turned when Judy had buzzed Baxter and me into the activities room. Several older ladies began to clap, and Baxter – the little show-off – pranced a few steps on his hind feet. Mrs. Peterson and Miss Henderson were playing cards. The TV on the wall was showing 1960s sitcoms, and four residents sat on the couch, some watching, and some dozing. Over to one side, I saw Chuck Pettis and Mr. Thompson playing checkers. Chuck saw me and waved, so we went over there first.

"Nice morning," Chuck said. He had a different vest on today and I couldn't hear his protective watches ticking, so I wondered if he switched to digital when he wasn't demon hunting. I noticed he had an umbrella next to his chair, although it was a sunny day. Next to the umbrella lay a worn backpack. I was willing to bet he had even more 'surprises' in his backpack than I had in mine. I guess we both felt jumpy.

"Looks like it's going to be a nice day," I replied.

"Humph." Mr. Thompson did not look up, but he did look down at Baxter, who presented himself to be petted. I lifted Bax and looked for a nod to say it was okay to put Baxter in his lap. Baxter cuddled in and looked up with his black-button eyes, confident he could melt even Mr. Thompson's heart. Old Man Thompson finally relented and managed half of a smile.

"Cute little fellow. Reminds me a lot of a dog I used to have. Tilly. Did I ever tell you about Tilly?" he asked as his gnarled, calloused hand stroked Baxter's head.

I smiled and shook my head, ready to hear Tilly's story again. Meanwhile, I noticed that Mr. Thompson, Josiah Winfield's descendant, had his cane tucked beside him on his wheelchair seat. *Interesting. He might need a cane to get out of his wheelchair. Or it might be handy as an athame.*

I watched Mr. Thompson as we chatted about the weather. His topics were random, and he repeated himself a lot. But his eyes were clear and sharp, and I wondered how much of his 'dementia' was a game.

Chuck seemed to guess my thoughts. "You've got me," he conceded, and he looked up to meet my gaze. "Happens most of the time we play. He beats me fair and square."

Huh. I know dementia patients have moments of clarity, but if Mr. Thompson won most of his matches, I was willing to bet that he was faking at least some of his decline.

I took Baxter back from Mr. Thompson, careful not to touch his skin. "I'll let you two get back to your game," I said, and led Baxter away, though I felt Mr. Thompson's gaze on us as we left. I still wasn't sure whether he was friend or foe.

Bax and I made the rounds. I felt like the handler for a rock star, while Baxter strutted his stuff. Don't ask me how, but that little show-stopper knows when he's got the spotlight. The nursing home is mostly older ladies and a few long-lived men. Even the old guys who were as crusty and hard-bitten as Mr. Thompson melted for Baxter. I looked the other way as they slipped him broccoli and Brussels sprouts, cauliflower, and green beans. He ate like a pig, and it was clear from the furtive looks that the residents all felt like they had put one over on Judy and me.

Baxter fairly bounced from one resident to another. Yet all the while as I smiled and made pleasant conversation, my mind kept straying to the present situation, aka the impending doom of Charleston. Sariel was out to get Sorren, and he didn't care how many thousands of people he killed to do it. I remembered a t-shirt I had seen about not annoying T-rex because we're crunchy and yummy with BBQ sauce, or something like that. That's how I felt: utterly not up to the task of saving the world in a pissing match between two immortals.

Baxter, however, lives in the moment, and at the moment, he was a superstar. After we had chatted with about a dozen ladies, I spotted Helen Butler out in the garden. Baxter and I made a beeline to see her.

Mrs. Butler looked up as we opened the door to the garden. Her lined face lit up for a few seconds with expectation, then fell when she realized we weren't who she was waiting for. Still, she brightened when she saw Baxter. "Now aren't you a cute little fellow. What's your name?"

We had this conversation every time, but I'd learned to take it in stride. "He's Baxter," I replied.

"Baxter," she repeated, stroking his fur. "I wish my gentleman caller was here to see him. He'd like Baxter." I didn't have the heart to tell her that Sorren, in his own way, was extremely fond of the little dog.

"I'm sure he would," I replied. "Will he be stopping by sometime today?"

Mrs. Butler frowned, thinking. Maybe it was a trick of the light, but I thought I could glimpse how pretty she had been, years ago. "I don't know," she said, looking unsure. "Maybe. He... comes and goes." She waved a shaky, spotted hand toward an album on the table. "Have you seen my pictures?"

We had time for this. Even if the world tottered on the brink of extinction. I sat for a moment, and Mrs. Butler held Baxter on her lap, and together we flipped through the faded pages of her scrapbook that lay next to knitting needles and a skein of yarn on the garden table.

"Look at that!" she said, pointing to a photo that was yellowed with time. From the styles, I guessed that it was from the 1940s. The young woman who would become Mrs. Butler was a knock-out in a bathing suit, having fun at a picnic near a swimming hole. "My, we were daring, weren't we! Jumping off the rocks like that. What were we thinking?" It seemed hard for me to imagine the frail nonagenarian jumping at all, let alone diving into what looked like an old quarry. I gained a better appreciation for what Sorren had seen in her.

"Well," she said as we finished looking at the pictures. "You've got to get going. If you see my young man, let him know I'll save him a place at dinner." She picked up the knitting needles and shook out the half-finished scarf she was working on. "I'm making this for his birthday," she confided.

I gave her arthritic hand a gentle pat. "I will be sure to let him know you're expecting him for dinner," I said. She rustled Baxter's ears one more time, and then waved good-bye as he and I made our way back inside.

Becky kept her distance, but she never let me out of her sight, even though Judy was officially accompanying me. "She must really not like dogs," I said under my breath.

Judy shrugged. "I don't know what's up with her. Boyfriend trouble, maybe. Becky's only been here a month, but she's the type that lets everyone know her business. She started seeing this guy – good looking, but kinda stuck on himself." Judy rolled her eyes. "My bet is that he's a player, and she's just caught him at it."

I glanced at Becky, and saw her glowering at us from the far side of the room. "Maybe they'll kiss and make up," I replied. "I hope she's not that grumpy with the patients."

"She used to be fantastic with them. Now she's moody as all get out, snaps at the other nurses, and there's no pleasing her." Judy sighed. "Well, never mind. You didn't come here for the gossip!" We kept moving around the room, and I resolved to ignore Becky, focusing on all of Baxter's fans.

"We try hard to keep the patients happy," Judy said, "but we just can't do everything. I feel so bad about letting them down. I mean, we try, we really do, but it's never good enough. I wish we could do more."

Judy's uncharacteristic guilt-trip made me realize my own thoughts had begun to spiral. And that meant trouble. Once I shook off the guilt attack, I could tell that something was wrong. Baxter growled, and the hair on the back of my neck stood up.

"Can you hold Baxter for a moment?" I asked Judy. I briefly touched her skin in the process, and felt the static shock of magic meeting magic. A guilty look in her eyes told me she knew exactly what the shock meant.

"Judy – I know this is a strange question, but Becky's new boyfriend, you said he was good looking?"

She nodded. "Like he walked off the cover of a romance novel."

Uh oh. "I want to check something out. I'll be right back." I headed for the big windows that looked out on the walled garden.

"He's rather handsome, isn't he?" Miss Peterson said. It was the kind of comment that, coming from a prim lady in her nineties, might have made me smile. But I wheeled around, and looked out the plate glass windows, following where she pointed out a newcomer to her friends. A *GQ*-worthy Nephilim stared back at me with a dead, soulless gaze from the walled garden.

"Oh my God," I murmured under my breath. I hurried back to the activities room. The smell of smoke made my heart beat faster. I rounded the corner, and saw orderlies helping residents toward the exits.

Chuck Pettis was standing near the television, taking charge of the situation. "Don't worry! Everything will be all right. We'll clear the air," Chuck said in a voice both comforting and authoritative. The nurses looked grateful for his help as they pushed wheelchairs and assisted residents with walkers and quad canes.

"Chuck, we've got problems!" I said.

Coffee Guy stared back at me through the glass from the garden, as if he were not only looking right at me, but for me.

"Wards are breached," Chuck hissed under his breath. "We're under attack." I noticed that he was holding his umbrella and had grabbed his backpack.

"Mr. Thompson, it would be a good idea to go outside until the smoke clears," Nurse Judy suggested. I took Baxter back from her, and held him close against me.

"I'm staying right here," Mr. Thompson said, raising his chin. There wasn't a hint of confusion in his blue eyes now, and the set of his jaw said he had no intention of hiding from a fight.

I turned in a slow circle. Two of the walls had nice, big windows that looked out on the garden surrounding the building. Lush grass, trees, and flowers filled the space between the activity room's windows and the high brick wall that surrounded the Alzheimer's wing. Outside of the windows, standing on the grassy 'moat', were four model-gorgeous Nephilim already in the courtyard. My heart sank as I recognized them as fallen angels we had already fought—and thought we had destroyed. One of them was definitely Coffee Guy, back to cause more trouble. With him were Baldy, Blondie, and Ginger, the ones who jumped us in Dueler's Alley.

"We've got to get everyone out now," I said to Judy, going to help push Miss Henderson's wheelchair to the door. I looked toward where I had last seen Helen Butler. She and another patient were still in the garden off to one side. They were talking with a nurse and didn't seem to notice the intruders. But I knew that the Nephilim were bound to notice them soon.

Shit. I had my athame up my sleeve, Bo's collar on my left wrist and my *chakram* was in the small backpack I used instead of a purse, along with Josiah's pistol. I had hoped to speak privately to Mr. Thompson about the gun, since he was a descendent of Winfield's. I'd taken a hell of a chance bringing a weapon into the nursing home, but now I was glad. Sorren had gone to ground, and he'd be no help in the bright sunlight. I could speed dial Teag or Father Anne, but it might all be over by the time they got here.

Something big exploded nearby. I wheeled, and realized that the kitchen was on fire. Another explosion rocked the building, and the alarms shrilled. Sprinklers clicked, but no water sprayed from them.

Trapped. In the distance, I could hear the nurses cajoling the patients to stay calm as they moved them into the hallway and away from the kitchen and common room. I felt sick. Everything in me wanted to get the elderly residents out to the parking lot and away from the fire, but I knew that with Nephilim around, it was more dangerous out there than it was in here.

The smoke was getting thicker. Two of the orderlies were trying to put out the kitchen fire with extinguishers, but it was too much for them. The alarms were ringing loud enough to be heard even for residents who had turned off their hearing aids, and strobe lights flashed to warn the deaf.

"Three of us, four of them," Chuck said tightly, coming up to stand next to me. He released a hidden clasp, and his umbrella became a short sword. Mr. Thompson sat in his chair facing one of the windows. He held his cane like a lance, steadied on the arm of his walker. I tucked Baxter into my backpack and I took out Josiah's pistol and the *chakram*, fastening the pack closed. The pistol went into my waistband at the small of my back, and the *chakram* snapped into a leather strap on my belt I had worn, just in case.

"Four of us." I looked behind me and saw Nurse Judy. I had not noticed the silver pentacle she wore on a chain around her neck. Maybe she had kept it hidden before, but now it lay outside the neckline of her scrubs. I remembered the jolt I had felt when our skin touched.

"What are they, and what do they want?" she asked.

"They're fallen angels, and they want to kill us to settle an old score," I said.

"Then screw them," Judy said, as if it was the kind of thing she heard every day. "Nobody messes with my patients."

We stood facing the broken windows. I searched the garden for Helen Butler and her companions, unsure whether they had managed to come inside or whether they were still outside. Either way, they were in danger. Commotion filled the hallways as orderlies and nurses tried to move confused residents along the escape route.

"I've got to find Mrs. Butler and the people who were in the garden," I said. "We can't leave them out there."

The alarms blared and I heard voices raised in confusion. "Is it the Germans again?" I heard a frail voice ask. "Do we have to go to the bomb shelter? I've forgotten where it is."

"Quit burning the roast!" a man shouted. "How many times do I have to tell you to turn down the oven!"

"Everyone stay next to the wall and move toward the door!" one of the nurses ordered, a calm, confident voice in the midst of chaos. The smoke was getting worse, and without the sprinklers, the fire would spread fast.

"Chuck – distract the Nephilim!" I yelled. "I've got to get people out of the garden."

"What's wrong with the doors?" I heard the question repeated over and over. Outside the windows, the Nephilim smiled. My heart thudded. Coffee Guy wasn't with the other three anymore.

No sprinklers, and the doors to the outside don't work. Nephilim in the garden, and probably more at each exit. They aren't here to fight us. They're here to make sure we burn.

Chuck headed toward the windows, drawing the three Nephilim toward him. I slipped out the side door, heading toward where I had last seen Mrs. Butler. We were locked in, on fire and under attack, so I had no idea how I was going to protect her, but I knew for Sorren's sake – and for my own conscience – I had to try.

I went around the corner toward the small seating area where Mrs. Butler had shown me her photo album. Two dead orderlies lay like broken dolls next to the garden bench, and pages ripped from the album fluttered on the wind.

Coffee Guy held Mrs. Butler against his chest like a shield. Her eyes were wide and she still held her knitting in one hand. Mrs. Butler struggled harder than I would have expected for a woman her age, kicking at her attacker's shins, but I knew she would be no match for the fallen angel's strength.

"Is this what you're looking for?" Coffee Guy asked.

"Let her go!" I said, as Bo's ghost materialized next to me. I had my athame in my right hand, but I couldn't get a clear shot at Coffee Guy with Mrs. Butler in front of him.

"Did you come to rescue Sorren's pretty girl?" Coffee Guy taunted, tightening his grip on Mrs. Butler. "I'm glad you're here. You can tell him how she died – before we kill him, too."

"Leave Sorren alone!" Mrs. Butler yelled, and drove her knitting needles into Coffee Guy's shoulder with desperate strength. The Nephilim howled in pain and threw her to one side with brutal force. I winced as she hit a concrete planter and lay still, her neck bent at an unnatural angle.

I had a clear shot and I took it, blasting Coffee Guy with the white-cold force from my athame, sending him slamming against the brick wall. Too angry to think about my own safety, I struck him again and again, pounding him against the bricks until his head was a bloody mess. Bo lunged at the Nephilim and his sharp teeth snapped shut on the fallen angel's throat, bringing my attacker to his knees.

Eyes blurred with tears of loss and rage, I grabbed the nearest weapon, a heavy cast-iron lawn chair, and slammed it down onto Coffee Guy's head, putting one of the legs down through his skull. The fallen angel's corpse crumbled and vanished.

I ran to where Mrs. Butler lay, hoping against all odds. The truth was clear as soon as I knelt next to her. Her eyes were open and staring. I felt a surge of guilt and failure that had nothing to do with the Watchers, wondering how I would ever face Sorren when I had let him down so completely.

"Cassidy! Get out of there!" Chuck shouted. I ran back inside, and an instant later, the windows shattered, sending shards of glass everywhere; they lodged in the tables and the upholstered chairs, sliced through my skin and embedded themselves in the walls.

Chuck emptied the clip of magically-enhanced bullets from his gun into Blondie's head and chest. From the recoil and the effect, I figured he was packing something larger than Detective Monroe had used. Silver-obsidian-iron-blessed bullets made a big difference, too. The fallen angel crumpled to the ground and vanished, but Baldy stepped from the shadows to take his place.

"Oh, that is so unfair," I muttered.

"Bastards," Mr. Thompson growled. His cane was made of gnarled ash, a yard-long athame. Blue light burst from its tip, enveloping Baldy in a cocoon of ice. Maybe Nephilim didn't have hearts to freeze, or maybe they were just tougher than Old Man Thompson's mortal victims. The ice held for a moment, but before either Chuck or I could attack, Baldy broke free with a savage growl. And Ginger was right behind him, and they'd added Painting Creep, plus Crow, the dark-haired fallen angel from Dueler's Alley and Asian Dude, one of the bad boys we had fought at the Briggs Society. *Damn.*

"Take this!' Nurse Judy muttered. She had no wand. Instead, she extended her right arm palm out, turning the gem in her ring toward the window. Green fire arced from her ring and hit Baldy full in the chest, holding him in place. Mr. Thompson's eyes narrowed and this time when he sent a blast of magic from his cane, a dagger of solid ice lodged deep in Baldy's chest like a frozen lance. Blood bubbled from the wound and the fallen angel collapsed as his body gave a final shudder, then disappeared.

Four Nephilim sauntered toward us, seemingly undeterred by the fact that we'd already dispatched three of their buddies. It didn't help that Nephilim could fly, and landing in the walled garden was a lot easier than scaling the walls to get out. They didn't need to hurry. We were the ones inside a burning building.

The ghosts of Palmetto Meadows had begun to gather. Maybe they wanted to watch us fight the monsters, or perhaps they sensed that some of the residents might soon be among them, if we couldn't tame the fire and smoke soon. But I glimpsed their presence near the memorial tree, silent witnesses to our skirmish with the forces of Hell.

The smoke was getting thicker despite the broken windows. In the hallway, I heard screams and sobbing, shouts and prayers. I wanted to help the staff get the patients to safety. But nowhere was safe until we dealt with the Nephilim. Then the fire doors triggered, and we were cut off from the hallway, locked in the activity room with three fallen angels, and fenced in all around with a brick wall too high to climb.

I pushed my athame back up my sleeve and snapped the *chakram* free, leaving Josiah's pistol jammed into my belt. Ginger stepped through the shattered glass coming straight at me, while two others advanced on Chuck and Mr. Thompson. I sent the *chakram* flying.

Ginger flinched an instant too late. The *chakram* hit him in the chest, slicing bone-deep, right through to the ribs. A large flap of flesh hung from the bones, splattering blood across the broken glass that still clung to the window frame. The Nephilim staggered forward, howling in anger and pain. Bo's ghost lunged, chest high, and sank his teeth into Ginger's right shoulder. As the Nephilim struggled, Chuck flicked his wrist and sent a silver dagger into the fallen angel's left eye. Bo released his jaws, and Ginger fell to the ground, convulsing, before disappearing in the next instant.

"Got another one of them," Chuck muttered.

"Watch out!" Judy shouted, and shot her green fire over my shoulder so close it singed my hair. She caught Painting Creep full in the face, and while he was trapped by her magic, I grabbed Josiah's pistol, took aim and shot that son of a bitch right through the heart with Winfield's special bullet. He dropped like a rock.

Baxter whined quietly from the backpack, and much as I hated to admit it, I was as scared as he was.

Two Nephilim left. I prayed that they didn't get more reinforcements. Crow ran toward Mr. Thompson, who brought his ash wood cane up like a rifle. He shouted a command, and ice formed on the Nephilim's skin and clothing, frosting his hair white. The fallen angel slowed, and I wondered whether Old Man Thompson was trying to freeze his blood or stop his heart.

But in the next breath, Crow shook off the ice and came at Thompson with a roar, lifting him out of his wheelchair and throwing him across the room. Thompson twisted as he flew through the air, and managed to hang onto his cane. He fell hard, but he was tough enough to roll into a ball, a move that told me he had long practice and plenty of experience with fights.

Judy ran over to him, and I put myself between Crow and them, hoping to buy time. I got in a shot with my athame that sent the Nephilim halfway across the room, but I knew it wasn't putting him down for good. Then I realized I had made a big mistake.

I had forgotten about Becky.

Becky charged out of the activity room's side parlor armed with a kitchen knife in each hand. I don't know what hold her fallen angel boyfriend had on her, but her eyes were glazed and her lips pulled back over her teeth in a snarl. Meanwhile, the Nephilim I'd just hit with my magic got to his feet and looked ready to rumble.

I couldn't fight off both Becky and Crow at the same time. As Becky ran at me, the last fallen angel, Asian Dude, started to transform into his nightmare beast form. This just kept going from bad to worse.

Becky was closer than the Nephilim, and if I didn't stop those knives, I'd be mincemeat before the fallen angel got to me. Baxter barked angrily from my backpack.

Bo's ghost snapped and harried Crow while I went after Becky. Josiah's gun only held one shot, so I grabbed it by the barrel and swung it like a club. I slammed the butt against her right hand, and she lost her grip on one of the knives, which I kicked to the far corner of the room. She got me good with the other knife, opening a deep cut on my left forearm that hurt like hell. I brought the dueling pistol back for a second blow and this time, I nailed Becky right in the temple. She sagged like a sack of potatoes, and while she was on her way down, I kicked the bloody knife from her left hand, just in case. I hoped she was down for the count, because Crow was closing fast.

Out of the corner of my eye, I could see that Chuck was losing ground against Asian Dude. It was in its monster form, a purplish-black, fanged and clawed creature from a nightmare, and it stood at least eight feet tall with muscles all the steroids in the world couldn't give a mortal.

Chuck hit the monster with his sword and two of his silver throwing knives, but the creature just bellowed in rage and kept coming. He zapped it with the ray gun look-alike he had used at the Old Jail, but that only slowed the Nephilim down. I hoped Chuck had more surprises in his pack, because I couldn't help him and still protect Judy and Mr. Thompson.

The room was growing smokier by the minute. We would probably have been dead already if the Nephilim hadn't broken all the floor-to-ceiling windows on their way in. I heard sirens in the distance, but I wasn't counting on them getting here in time for a rescue.

More ghosts lurked around the edge of the room. I would have expected them all to appear as frail old people, but maybe they got to choose, because many of them looked as they had in their prime. Most of the men wore military uniforms from the World Wars. Some of the women wore ball gowns while others sported cocktail dresses or shirtwaists with matching hats and white gloves. They watched the fight with interest, staying well back out of the way.

"Hey soldier boys!" I yelled. "We could use a little help here!"

Bo got his ghostly teeth into Crow's thigh, and refused to let go. The ghostly old soldiers swept forward, some toward Crow and others toward the monster Chuck battled. Like Bo, they were solid enough to grab arms and legs, dragging the fallen angels back and slowing them down. I was willing to take all the help I could get.

While Crow and Asian Dude struggled to get loose, my gaze fell on the silver candelabrum under the memorial tree canvas. I dove for it and came up swinging. Damn, it was heavy. Holding it by its base, I swung with both hands, slamming it into Crow's head so hard I crushed the side of his skull. Blood streamed down his ruined face and fluid poured from his eye, but he kept on coming.

He smacked his fist into me and sent me reeling. I lost Josiah's pistol out of my belt, and it went spinning away. Even though I was seeing double from the impact, I swung the candelabrum again, aiming this time for the front of his face. The silver burned his skin as it made contact, breaking his nose and caving in his cheekbones. His remaining eye fixed on me with a bone-chilling hatred.

Crow raised his fist to hit me again. Bo snarled and chomped down on the fallen angel's wrist, while the old soldiers tackled him, throwing him off balance. It was the break I needed. Running with all my might, I angled the candle-holder side of the candelabrum toward the Nephilim and charged at him with my full strength, ramming the six separate prongs into his chest with enough force to break ribs. Then I let go of the candelabrum with my right hand and shoved my palm right against his chest. I let my athame fall down my sleeve into my hand, called on my power, and blasted that cold force right through his body at point-blank range.

It tore a hole right through his body, as if I'd shot him with a cannon. Crow sank to his knees and fell face-first onto the blood-covered floor, then disappeared.

That left the Asian Dude in full monster mode. It swung a clawed hand at Chuck, but he ducked and got in a good, deep slash with his sword. The bloody blade's silver gleam betrayed its magic.

I didn't want to get close enough to Asian Dude to try my candelabrum trick again, but I whacked it good on the wrist when it tried to take a swing at me, and got backhanded out through one of the ruined windows for my trouble. Lucky for Baxter, who was still in my backpack, I fell on my side. The walled garden had been great for keeping befuddled residents in, but now that we needed a way to escape, it made it damn near impossible to easily get out. The air was filled with smoke, and part of the roof was burning. We were running out of time.

I picked myself up, aching all over. My lip was swollen and bloody, and the gash I'd taken on my arm was bleeding pretty badly. The scratches from the Nephilim's claws burned, and if I survived the fight, I'd have to deal with their poison.

My *chakram* glinted in the sun, and I grabbed it, running back in to the fight. The last Nephilim was heading for Judy and Mr. Thompson. Chuck was on the floor, crawling to his knees for another round.

"Hey ugly!" I yelled, trying to distract Asian Dude. I hurled my *chakram*, and caught it in the neck, but it wasn't straight on, so the razor disk just loosed a fountain of black blood instead of taking the monster's head off. Now it was really pissed.

Mr. Thompson croaked a word of power, and a white blast shot from his cane, rooting the Nephilim to the floor with a thick layer of ice from the waist down. Some of that ice made the tile slick, and I slid, and slammed into the memorial tree canvas on my left side, knocking the wind out of me.

Judy fired off another green blast from her ring, hitting Asian Dude square on. Bo sank his ghostly teeth into the Nephilim's right leg, while the old soldiers rushed the monster from the front. Chuck came up on one knee and aimed the biggest damn handgun I'd ever seen in my life at the fallen angel's back.

As soon as my skin touched the memorial tree artwork, I felt a surge of powerful emotion: sadness, hope, acceptance, and even joy. I was drained and fading, so I latched onto the vivid memories and feelings that permeated every inch of the canvas. The artist's passion. The grief of family members. The dedication of nurses like Judy. The bittersweet memories of people like Mrs. Butler.

I thrust my power into the canvas, pulling the surge of those emotions into me, recharging my magic. And then I sent it all blasting toward Asian Dude with a full-throated battle cry of defiance, feeling as if I had opened a fire hose of magic that poured through me and out through my raised palms.

My blast of magic hit just as Chuck pulled the trigger, and my head rang like a bell at the sound of the shot. The bullet and my force magic tore through Asian Dude, taking off its right arm and half of its back and showering the room with gore and blood. The bullet slammed into the door to the reception area, splintering it from top to bottom.

The last Nephilim collapsed to the floor in a bloody heap. Small ash heaps marked where the other fallen angels' bodies had disintegrated. The old soldiers saluted and winked out, along with the rest of the ghostly onlookers. Bo barked at me urgently, as if to remind me that the building was on fire. Like I could forget. Chuck was crawling around, gathering up our weapons and stuffing them in his bag.

Even with the broken windows, the smoke was getting thick. My lungs ached, and my eyes stung. Baxter had gone quiet in my backpack and I was worried. Overhead, the ceiling creaked ominously. In a few more minutes, it wouldn't matter that we had defeated the Nephilim. We were all going to be dead from the fire.

"Get everyone into the garden!" I yelled to Chuck. It might be walled, but it was outside, and there had to be a door somewhere for lawn maintenance that we could use to escape. Then again, it was probably locked to keep the residents from wandering off.

"You get the nurse. I'll get Thompson," Chuck ordered. We sucked in deep breaths of air, then charged back into the activity room. The smoke was thick enough that it was like fighting my way through heavy fog and it hurt to breathe. I found Judy slumped over Mr. Thompson, grabbed her by her wrists, and yanked her toward the garden with all my might. It wasn't gentle, but it beat burning to death.

Chuck was right behind me, carrying Old Man Thompson in his arms. We reached the far wall of the garden and looked back toward the nursing home. Most of the roof was on fire, and it looked like it could collapse at any moment.

"There's a door!" I said, pointing farther down the wall. Chuck pointed his gun at the lock and fired. The door swung open into the parking lot, which was starting to fill with emergency vehicles. Just as Chuck fired, the roof's main beams snapped with a crack as loud as gunfire, and the whole thing collapsed inward with a rush of flames and embers.

Chuck shouldered Old Man Thompson's limp form, and I had my shoulder under Judy's arm, dragging her with all my might.

Chuck and I made our way halfway across the parking lot before we collapsed. Firefighters rushed past with their hoses, but it was too late. Palmetto Meadows was gone. I dropped to the ground, sobbing beside Judy who was scratched and cut from having been dragged halfway across an asphalt parking lot. But she was alive, dammit. And so was I.

I looked for Chuck. He was doing CPR on Mr. Thompson, but I had the sinking feeling that it was too late. Paramedics ran toward us, shouting, but I was too hazy to understand what they were saying. One of them pressed an oxygen mask over my face and tried to make me lie down, but I fought him off, then pulled Baxter from my bag. He was struggling to breathe, and before the EMT could stop me, I tore off my mask and put it over the dog's face. The paramedic didn't argue, he just got another mask for me, while another member of his team took care of Judy. A paramedic eased Chuck away from Thompson and got him a mask, while two more took over caring for Thompson, giving it their best shot.

Baxter coughed and snuffled, but he was breathing more easily, and I hugged him close. The paramedics loaded Judy onto a cart and put her in an ambulance.

Another piece of the roof collapsed, and in the chaos, Chuck managed to get to his feet and throw his backpack with all of our weapons into his car before anyone noticed. Thank God: if someone official had glimpsed even half of what was in there, we'd be headed to prison before dinnertime.

Chuck refused treatment, but the cut on my arm was bad enough that I knew I was going to need stitches. Antibiotics, too, although whether they would be good against Nephilim taint, I wasn't sure. If they weren't, Mrs. Teller and Dr. Zeigler could fix me up. I was groggy and sore, bruised from head to toe, and my lungs felt like they were on fire, but all I could do was hug Baxter and marvel that we were still alive.

After I could talk, I tugged on the sleeve of the EMT who was giving me oxygen. "What about the others?" I rasped. "The patients?"

He looked away. "I'm sorry. You four are the only ones who made it out."

Chapter Twenty-One

THE DRUGS THEY gave me in the hospital knocked me out while they stitched up my arm and sent me into a deep, dreamless sleep. When I woke up the late afternoon sun streamed through the window, and Teag sat next to my bed.

"How –" I started to ask, but my throat was too raw to finish. Teag helped me sit up enough to drink from the glass of water by the bedside.

"I hear things," he shrugged. *Then again, it would be like Teag to have his computer to pop up an alert if I ever get admitted to the ER.*

"Baxter?"

Teag smiled. "He charmed the firefighters and the EMTs and was eating someone's sandwich when I arrived. Pretty tough for such a little guy. Maggie's watching him at your house. We closed the shop early."

I closed my eyes and let out a deep breath. "Chuck and Judy?"

"Chuck's the one who called me," Teag said. "He's banged up, but says he's been worse. I can't get anything official on Judy, but I think she's going to be okay." He gave me a look that told me that he knew more than he was saying and not to ask questions while other people might be listening. *Which meant he had hacked the hospital computer.* "Mr. Thompson?"

Teag shook his head. "He didn't make it."

"All those people –"

"Yeah. I've been watching the headlines on my phone. No complete death count yet." I could hear the sorrow and anger in his voice.

"Sorren." I didn't have to elaborate.

"Yeah." Teag's one word spoke volumes.

How do we tell a vampire that his last mortal lover is dead – murdered by an old enemy to strike a blow at him? I didn't relish having that conversation, but I also didn't want Sorren to find out on television. "He's not up yet."

Teag shook his head. "Soon."

We sat in silence for several minutes, and then I heard footsteps coming our way. Teag tensed, and while he had not brought any weapons into the hospital, as a martial arts champion he could do pretty good damage without them. The curtain pulled back, and Detective Monroe stood in front of an angry nurse.

"I am going on record as having advised against this," the nurse said. "She's only just woken up."

Detective Monroe didn't look worried. "I'll be brief." She looked at me, took in my injuries, and shook her head. "You, again. Just unlucky, or is there more to the story?" Her voice was brusque, but she didn't seem quite as harsh as before the attack after the fundraiser. I was hoping that Sorren's compulsion had stuck. She was the last person I felt like dealing with right now.

Teag bristled, but I signaled him to cool down. "Hello," I rasped. "I feel like hell."

"What do you know about the fire?" she demanded. I reminded myself that despite Sorren's glamouring, I was one of the surviving witnesses to the fire at the nursing home, and since Monroe knew me, it was only natural for her to come looking for information. The rudeness was nothing personal.

I shook my head and winced. Every muscle in my body ached. "Nothing. We were in the activity room. All of a sudden, there was smoke."

"Therapy dog day?" she asked. I nodded. "Anything unusual?"

Where would I even start? "There was a new nurse named Becky. She was acting really strange right before the fire started." That much was true. It hurt to talk, but I figured Monroe wasn't going to leave until she got something useful.

"What about the other nurse, the one who survived? Judy."

"We were trying to get patients to safety. It all happened so fast." I had a coughing fit that felt like someone was tearing my esophagus with fish hooks. Monroe winced.

"How about Chuck Pettis? You know him?"

"Seen him around." I used the minimum number of words possible. Full sentences hurt more. "Usually at the nursing home." True again. I generally only saw Chuck if we were working on a situation, or during his visits to see Mr. Thompson.

"Know anything about the old guy who died in the parking lot? Thompson?" Monroe's voice was brusque, but I saw a glimmer of emotion in her eyes. The deaths made her angry, too.

"Played checkers. Liked Baxter. Grouchy."

The nurse came back to the doorway. "Time's up, officer. Doctor's orders." I could see by the glint in the nurse's eyes that she didn't mind pulling rank to get this interloper out of her domain.

Monroe gave me the once-over again as if to assure herself I hadn't faked my injuries. "All right," she said. "We were done anyhow." She met my gaze. "I may have more questions. Try to stay out of trouble."

With that, Monroe departed. After the nurse had seen her out, she came back to check on me. "I'm so sorry," she said, refilling my glass of water. "I tried to get her to come back later, but she insisted, and we can't do much when it's the police –"

I fluttered my fingers. "It's okay." But I was thinking about the nurses at Palmetto Meadows who had fussed over Baxter and who died trying to protect their patients. The lump in my throat made it hurt worse, and tears started.

The nurse shook her head. "See? I knew she shouldn't have bothered you so soon after everything. Why don't you try to rest?" She glanced at Teag as if to shoo him out, but I managed a whimper and a small headshake, and she relented.

"All right, if she says so," the nurse said to Teag. "But let her get some rest before we sign her out." They had promised me I could leave around seven, and I was going to hold them to it.

When she left, Teag leaned forward and gave my hand a comforting squeeze. "We're not going to leave you alone," he promised. "I'm staying to take you home, even if they make me sit in the waiting room until then. Maggie's at your house for a while – she absolutely insisted – and then Father Anne will be over to sit with you until midnight. Chuck said he'd stand guard overnight, unless Sorren wants to."

He slipped my cell phone into my left hand. "Keep this where you can reach it." Then he brought me Bo's collar and my wooden spoon from the bag in my dresser, fastening the collar on my left wrist and giving me my athame in my right. "Better have these handy, too." He managed a slight smile, but I knew he was worried about me.

I fell back asleep, and the next thing I knew, it was time to leave. I didn't relax until we were in Teag's car, pulling out of the parking lot without any Nephilim in sight. I sighed and leaned back in my seat.

"What's the plan?"

"That depends on you," Teag said, sliding his gaze my way for a moment. "How are you – really?"

"Exhausted, but otherwise not as bad as I expected," I answered truthfully. My throat didn't hurt quite so much now. "The cut on my arm was deep. They stitched me up, but I'd like to get Mrs. Teller or Sorren's doctor to take a look at it, just in case there was any taint on that thing's claws." I'd rather not do battle with the forces of Hell for a couple of days, but I knew we might not have the luxury of choosing the time and place.

"I already thought about that," Teag said. "And Mrs. Teller is expecting us. Plus I did some digging on the Darke Web, to see what I could find on Watchers and Judges," Teag said. "Most of it we knew. But I found something interesting. Bringing a Watcher through seems to unbalance the supernatural status quo. Meaning that whenever a Watcher comes through, there's usually also some kind of big supernatural brouhaha."

My mind raced. "So –"

He nodded. "Yeah. I tracked the weird stuff and attacks against when the Watcher circles showed up. And I'd say the theory holds true."

I groaned. "Great, but does it tell us how to predict another Watcher? Or what happens right before the shit hits the fan? Because if we've got to be busy fighting off Nephilim and giant leeches and crazy ghosts, it doesn't leave much time to fend off Sariel and his Watchers."

Teag grinned. "I've got a theory, but not a good way to test it. From everything I've pulled together, it looks like the stairway disappearances happened a day or two before the big supernatural disturbances. And the most violent disturbances happened near where the Watcher was being brought through."

I thought about it for a moment. The Old Jail. The power plant. Tarleton House. Stairway disappearances happened before all of them, and they had all been places where we fought off monsters.

"But there are only three rings that we've found," I protested, thinking aloud. "Sorren said there had to be five Watchers for Sariel to turn into the Judge from Hell."

"About that," Teag said, his voice tight. "Ryan called not long after you left the store. He and his team had gone out exploring again. They went out to that abandoned motor lodge – used to be the Debonair Motel back in the Sixties, and it's been abandoned for decades."

I knew the place. It was one of those one-story drive-up places where all the rooms opened toward the driveway, like something that belonged on Route 66. When the big highway opened, the Debonair Motel was a casualty. It closed a long time ago, but the building still stood, looking more decrepit every year.

"And he found a Watcher circle?"

Gail Z. Martin

Teag nodded. "Yeah. Said it looked like it had been there for a while – which might mean that it was earlier than all the others. That would match when the first stairway disappearances happened, and when Valerie started to complain about the ghosts."

"What about the other attacks?" I asked. "Like at the Briggs Society? Or today?"

Teag grimaced with frustration. "I'm not sure. Today I'd classify as a personal attack, not a 'disturbance'. I'd say that the Nephilim targeted Palmetto Meadows either because of Mr. Thompson or to get to Sorren by hurting Mrs. Butler. Same with the attacks at the Archive and the museum and the cemetery. In each case, the Nephilim had the chance to hurt Sorren by killing people close to him – you, Lucinda, and Father Anne."

I realized that we weren't driving Teag's normal route to my house. "Where are we going?"

"First, to see Mrs. Teller and have her take a look at your arm. And then, I figured you'd want to be at Trifles and Folly at sunset, when Sorren wakes up," Teag said. He jerked his head toward the sun that was low in the sky. I sighed. This wasn't a conversation I was looking forward to having.

Mrs. Teller clucked her tongue and shook her head when she saw my arm, but her powders and potions took some of the pain away, and when she was finished, she assured me that the wound had been cleansed. Teag and I made the trip to Trifles and Folly in silence. We had only been in the store for a few minutes when the sun dipped below the horizon. Right on cue, the cellar door opened. Sorren isn't usually that prompt leaving his day crypt, and by the look on his face, I knew he sensed that something had gone terribly wrong.

407

He looked from Teag to me, and relaxed a bit, as if his first fear was for our safety. "What's happened?" he asked. I've seen Sorren angry, pensive, and worried, but never panicked. And it was real panic that I glimpsed in his eyes, although he strained for outward calm.

"Sorren, I'm so sorry," I started. That was when he took in my bruises and the fresh stitches. I'm sure I still smelled of hospital antiseptic, and blood.

"Nephilim attacked Palmetto Meadows," I said as gently as I could. "They set it on fire." I swallowed hard. "The doors wouldn't open. We fought them, but we couldn't stop the fire. None of the residents made it out."

Vampires can stand absolutely still. They don't breathe, and their hearts don't beat. Sorren looked like a pale marble statue, his expression one of despair and loss. He closed his eyes, and bowed his head, struggling for control. "You're sure?"

"I hacked the fire department computers," Teag said quietly. "And the hospital. The only ones who got out were Cassidy, Chuck Pettis, and one nurse. Edwin Thompson died, too."

"Tell me what happened." Sorren's voice was low and soft, but it fairly vibrated with tension. He was like a steel cable stretched taut enough to snap, fists clenched, jaw locked.

We went into the break room. Teag made hot tea, and added plenty of honey to mine. I was going to need it in order to talk. Sorren sat, head down, staring at his clasped hands, unmoving.

I went through the whole thing, while Teag and Sorren listened in silence. Now that I was moving around, my arm hurt even with the pain medication I'd taken at the hospital. I felt like I had been run over by a truck, and my head had started to pound. But right now, I was pretty sure that Sorren was hurting worse.

"You saw her today?" Sorren asked finally, in a voice barely above a whisper, tight with emotion.

"I sat in the garden with her and looked at pictures from a long time ago," I replied. "She fussed over Baxter. And she told me her 'young man' was coming to visit her." I choked up and had to pause. "She fought the Nephilim, Sorren. She stabbed him with her knitting needles and kicked him in the shins. She gave him hell, up to the last."

Sorren choked back a sob. "That's my girl," he said brokenly. "I went to visit a few days ago. I just never thought –"

I didn't know what to do, so Teag and I just sat in silence with him. Outside, twilight became full dark.

"Helen was so beautiful," Sorren said finally, and I remembered how stunning she had been in the old photos, probably more so in person. "Smart. Perceptive. She knew what I was, and she cared for me – and kept my secret." In his ragged voice, I heard centuries of loss and loneliness. Someday, inevitably, Teag and I would be gone, too. Sorren would remain. I did not think that I could go on, were our roles reversed. Yet Sorren did. We sat together in silence for a while.

"We have work to do." Sorren said finally, channeling his grief into anger. "And this time, I will make sure that Sariel *stays* dead."

Just then, Teag's phone rang. He stepped away for a moment, and when he returned, his expression was worried. "That was Father Anne. She wanted to let us know that there were two more stairway disappearances today. And if my calculations are right, then that means we've only got a day, maybe two, to figure out where Sariel is going to bring through his last Watcher, and when – if we want to save Charleston."

WE GATHERED AT my house. I wouldn't listen to the objections Sorren and Teag raised. I knew that I needed sleep and medication better than anyone, but there was a job to do, and a city to save. After the horror of Palmetto Meadows, I did not want to see the same kind of destruction play out a thousand-fold with an entire city.

While Maggie dog-sat, she had made a pot of home-made chicken soup, so the house smelled wonderful. Baxter's bark was a little hoarse, but he was certain all the visitors were there to see him, and if Teag and I hugged him tight and held him a little longer than usual, he wasn't going to complain.

I tried to hurry Maggie out as tactfully as possible. She stood her ground, hands on hips. "Cassidy Kincaide. You think I don't know what goes on at that shop. I may be old, but I'm not clueless! Y'all go out at night and get rid of bad haints and dark magic. Well," she said, standing up straight and looking me in the eye. "I can't fight and I don't have magic. But I do cook. And an army moves on its stomach. So while you plan your battle, I'll make sure no one goes hungry." She relented a bit. "Please, Cassidy, let me help. After all, I was there when Jonathan disappeared, and I'd taken a shine to the boy."

Dumbfounded, I nodded. "Sure. And Maggie," I said. She turned back to look questioningly at me. "Thank you."

Usually, my dining room table holds catalogues and packages. We cleared that away, and created a war room. Tonight, we'd called out the troops. Father Anne was there, and so was Chuck Pettis. Lucinda and Caliel came, plus Mrs. Teller and Niella. I was surprised when Archibald Donnelly walked in, but Sorren was expecting him. Even Daniel Hunter showed up, though I noticed that the rest of the crew greeted him with reserve.

Teag mapped out the locations of the ghostly upsets on a big whiteboard, along with the stairway disappearances and the four Watcher circles. He added the places Sorren or the rest of us had been attacked, along with the dates.

"You can see the pattern," Teag said, sounding like a professor. "Each time there's a stairway disappearance – feeding the Reapers to juice them up for the big strike – a few days later, that's when the Watcher comes through while we're sidelined fighting the big supernatural threat."

"While *you're* sidelined," Daniel Hunter said. "I've been stalking the Watchers, and trying to break through their protections to stop one from coming through." We all turned to look at him.

"Don't get me wrong," he protested, raising a hand to forestall comments. "The threats you were fighting had to be dealt with. I'm just saying that going up against these guys when they're bringing their last major player across from wherever-the-hell he comes from isn't going to be a walk in the park."

"Where were the newest stairway disappearances?" I asked.

Teag pointed to a spot just outside of the City of Charleston. "Out here. On Johns Island."

Father Anne frowned. "Johns Island? That's an odd location." Johns Island is separated from the mainland by the Stono River. It's only slightly smaller than Long Island or Martha's Vineyard, although those islands are much better known. Part of it is a nature preserve, and most of the rest is high-end condos.

"Two men and a woman disappeared. That's more people at one time than any of the other disappearances," Teag noted. "In each case, the people had sketchy backgrounds with prior acquittals or inconclusive investigations. Witnesses saw the person start down a stairway inside a house or business. The person was clearly visible at the top of the stairs, but disappeared before he or she reached the bottom. No one found anything – no footprints, no hair or clothing: nothing."

"So if the disappearances happen a few days before the Watcher comes through and the supernatural disturbance occurs, we'd better be prepared for trouble in two places," Mrs. Teller said. "Because the kind of 'disturbances' you're talking about need someone to put them down. But somebody's got to go stop those Watchers."

"The thing is, we don't know where the disturbances are going to happen," Teag said. "Or where the Watcher is going to come through."

That's when it hit me. "We know part of it – I think," I said. Everyone turned to look at me. "When I fought the Nephilim at the Archive, I drew on the power of a model of the Angel Oak that incorporated some pieces of the original tree. And at Palmetto Meadows, it was the Donor Tree artwork resembling the Angel Oak that helped me channel my magic to fight another Nephilim. If that tree is as old as they say with deep, wide roots –"

Magic has always regarded trees with respect, and included them in the most powerful rituals. Mighty oaks, flexible birch, handsome ash – from the Druids on down to today's Wiccans, we sense the power in these old, towering, majestic creatures. Like Yggdrasil in the

Norse myths, huge old trees draw in the essence of the Earth itself through their roots, and stretch toward the stars. The Angel Oak was said to be at least five hundred years old—maybe over a thousand. Beings that live that long are powerful – and Sariel would want to take advantage of all that stored magical mojo.

"I think Cassidy's on to something." To my surprise, it was Daniel Hunter who took up for me. "Each of the places where a Watcher has come through was located near a natural well of power. Tarleton House was over the old Charleston earthquake fault line. The power plant displaced a huge old cemetery. That abandoned motel was in a flood basin. The Old Jail created its own power-well with its history." It didn't take much to follow his train of thought. "And the Angel Oak has more than a thousand years of history, with roots that practically go all the way down to China," Lucinda said. She nodded. "I think you're right."

"Predicting where the supernatural disturbance is going to hit will be harder," Caliel noted.

Teag pointed to his map. "Every time, the disturbance happened within a ten mile radius of the place where the Watcher came through. For the Angel Oak, that means somewhere on Johns Island. And since the supernatural seeks its own, it's likely to be somewhere with a restless past."

"Bloody Bridge," Sorren said. We all turned to look at him. "The battle, back during the Civil War."

A battleground was a natural well of power for the supernatural. It had all the elements to keep spirits mired: violence, strong emotion and conflict. Just the kind of place to create a supernatural uproar, turbocharge the ghosts and get them riled up and dangerous.

"So," I said. "Who gets assigned to which team?"

I was pretty sure I knew part of the answer, but it needed to be said aloud. "I'm going to the Angel Oak," Sorren said, and I saw a killing glint in his eyes.

"Me too," I chimed in.

"And me," Teag replied.

"Count me in," said Lucinda. "I haven't forgotten the damage to my exhibit. I've got a bone to pick with this Sariel."

"You're gonna need back-up," Daniel Hunter said. "So I'd better be there."

Chuck Pettis gave a harrumph. "If you're going, then I'd better go – to watch you," he said.

"I'll head up the strike team for the battleground," Colonel Donnelly said. "Right up my ally, as a necromancer, war ghosts and all." He gave a curt nod of his head. "We'll handle it."

Father Anne gave him an amused, sidelong glance. "Me, too. I do know something about setting the dead to rest," she added wryly.

"We'll help with the ghosts," Niella and Mrs. Teller said. I could see that Caliel was torn, but in the end, he nodded.

"If Lucinda's with you, I'll go to the battleground," he said finally. "Just don't go having all the fun without us," he added.

"Then it's agreed," Sorren said, and I could see in every line of his body that he was ready for a fight. "And if you finish early at the battleground, come help us out. We'd better be in position early, because it's all going to hit the fan tomorrow."

Chapter Twenty-Two

"THIS CAN'T BE good." The approach road to the Angel Oak was closed off. A scribbled sign on a piece of cardboard said that the gift shop had been closed due to a gas leak.

"Convenient," Teag muttered.

"Very." We parked the car in a maintenance driveway, and hefted the bags with our weapons. My arm hurt, but painkillers were out if we were going to fight. By the time we were back at the entrance to the road, the others had joined us, grim-faced and determined.

We walked beside the rough gravel road toward the tree. The land around the Angel Oak has been kept undeveloped to preserve the tree, so it was really dark. The only light came from the security bulbs on the small gift shop. That glow was barely enough to show the silhouette of the tree, but even so, the huge size was breathtaking.

The Angel Oak is gigantic. People who have been to plantations or gardens in the South have seen plenty of live oaks, but nothing like the Angel Oak. At more than sixty-five feet tall and over twenty-five feet in circumference, the tree is epic. No one is quite sure how old the tree is. I had heard people say five hundred years, while others argued more than a millennium. The Angel Oak has limbs that are almost ninety feet long and more than eleven feet thick. Being in its presence is awe-inspiring, like going to the redwood forest or seeing the ocean for the first time. Even people without magic know subconsciously that the tree is a place of power.

Sariel knew it, too.

We got to the tree first. Sorren signaled us to stop and wait in the shadows while he scouted. He returned in a few moments.

"Sariel's not here now, but he's been here. Most likely to cause the gas leak problem and guarantee no one would interrupt his ritual," Sorren reported.

Score one for Teag's analysis, I thought.

We all knew the plan, so we had our roles and our places. Teag and I paired up and moved to the right. Lucinda and Sorren went toward the back of the tree. Chuck and Daniel went left. There was no telling how long we had before Sariel showed up, and we had a lot to do.

Lucinda began to walk a circle widdershins around the Angel Oak, carrying a walking stick that belonged to a powerful houngan ancestor. She used charcoal mixed with sage and salt to form a sacred circle, and carried a burning sage smudge as she walked and chanted. At one point, she stopped to drape a small rag doll over one of the Angel Oak's low branches and hung a single old shoe by its laces, to send a message to the spirits on the Other Side. Then she set several cobalt-blue bottles upside-down over some of the tree's smaller shoots so that they stood upright. Those were 'witch bottles', meant to trap less powerful evil spirits. Lucinda laid an offering to the Loas at the base of the great tree: eggs and white flowers, a bottle of rum, several cigars, and a wreath made of leaves.

Chuck and Daniel walked across the open area around the tree, bending down every so often to nestle something into the grass and dirt. Both men were even more heavily armed than usual. The big handgun Chuck had used at the nursing home was in a holster on his belt, and a bandolier across his chest held silver-modified bullets, EMF grenades, a couple of dangerous-looking cylinders with wires and dim red lights, and that odd ray gun he had used at the Old Jail. He also had something that looked like a sawed-off shotgun but with more wires and a power pack. I was in favor of anything short of C4.

Daniel wore a similar bandolier with bullets and shotgun shells that were likely as magically modified as Chuck's. He was packing the handgun he had used at the cemetery, and in the moonlight, I thought I saw silver runes running down its barrel and around its grip. Daniel also had something else that looked like a cross between a shotgun and a harpoon, with a sharp silver blade. I also saw some wicked-looking knives on his bandolier that I bet were custom-made and customized for hunting supernatural prey.

Teag and I wore thin bullet-proof vests under our clothing, with protective woven vests beneath them. With luck, that would protect us from direct hits both mundane and magical, although no one sells 'anti-Nephilim' rated body armor, even on the Darke Web. We looked. The stitches in my arm were wrapped up with gauze and padding. Sorren had shown up with shirts for both of us that were supposed to be made out of a 'cut-proof' fabric. That might reduce the damage from a knife, but I was willing to bet it hadn't been tried against fallen angel claws.

I had one of Josiah Winfield's dueling pistols, and Teag had the other, and we both had enough ammunition to get in a couple of shots. Bo's collar was on my left hand, and Bo had been beside me since we reached the Angel Oak, waiting until he was needed to bite one of the Nephilim on its ass. I had Alard's walking stick hanging from a strap on the left side of my utility belt, and my athame up my sleeve in a wrist holster. The *chakram* hung on my right side. In my pockets, I'd stashed my Norse spindle whorl to amplify my magic, packets of salt and a couple of other protective charms, and I was wearing my agate necklace.

Teag had his battle staff, a couple of knotted ropes to replenish his magic, and his *espada y daga*, a dagger and sword set. He had extra daggers in a bandolier, and the silver-edged *urumi* whip sword coiled in and hanging from a strap at his belt. He wore his *agimat* and hamsa charms, and in a pouch on his back, he had two new weapons, the battle net from the Briggs Society and a second net he had woven himself. Teag's version was knotted with magic and soaked in colloidal silver.

We each had one more, new weapon. The day after I had gotten out of the hospital, Teag and I found a package from the Briggs Society that contained two unusual-looking weapons that were a cross between a knife and a pair of brass knuckles. The note with them just said, 'Best, Archibald'.

Sorren made an initial walk around the perimeter, and then stood to one side, watching and ready. He wore two swords, and a couple of knives. And as a vampire, he *was* a weapon.

We hunkered down, waiting.

I worried that Sariel and his Nephilim might have spotted our cars, despite the efforts to hide them. I'd forgotten something important: fallen angels can fly.

One by one the Nephilim landed, each of them with darkly handsome faces and ruthless eyes. Coffee Guy was back for a replay, and so was Painting Creep from the Archive, along with the other five Nephilim Chuck and I had fought at the nursing home. Seeing them again was lousy enough, but Ebony was there from the Briggs Society artwork and a new one I hadn't seen before with long, sandy-colored hair. When they moved away from each other, Sariel stood among them, although I'm damned if I knew how he got there.

Scarred and twisted, Sariel had not weathered the centuries well. Sorren's immortality came from being a vampire. The Nephilim were otherworldly creatures, and had never been men. Sariel's long existence came from magic, and magic has a cost.

Sheer hatred glowed in Sariel's eyes. His skin was marred by white scars that looked like branching lightning bolts, and mottled by diseased, discolored masses. He looked centuries old, but that didn't make him less dangerous. I'd watched a lot of kung fu movies where the old guy whips everyone's asses.

I felt the Watchers' presence even before they touched down. A wave of crippling guilt washed over me, reminding me of every broken promise, every mistake, every time I let someone down.

It's your fault all those people at the nursing home are dead, the dark magic whispered in my brain. *You weren't good enough. You're going to fail now, like you've failed everyone who ever depended on you.*

"Watchers," Teag muttered. I was pretty sure he was right. Four newcomers were equally handsome to the Nephilim but they looked a little older, more distinguished, and moved with a grace that comes with wealth, power, and consummate self-assurance. If the Nephilim looked like underwear models, the Watchers looked like A-list movie stars. Homicidal, psychopathic movie stars.

Sariel, on the other hand, was butt ugly.

Bo's ghost growled, and then I felt him nudge my hand. I looked down and met his gaze. My right hand went to the agate necklace, while my left felt for the spindle whorl in my pocket. *It's a lie.* I struggled to cast off the Watchers' magic. *I never failed Baxter, or Bo, or Teag, or Sorren, or Maggie –*

With a deep breath, I drew on the powerful emotions and memories of my grandmother's spoon, the wood I had taken for my athame. *Not true!* I concentrated on the resonance my touch magic read from the athame, the love and warmth and acceptance, the bond of family, and I gathered power from those images and thrust out with it as if I were hitting a plate glass window with my fists.

The Watchers' illusion shattered. I saw Teag and Chuck shake themselves out of the trance. Daniel didn't look fazed, and it occurred to me that he might not give a damn whether or not he let anyone down. Lucinda was still chanting. If the Watchers' poisonous suggestions had any power over her, it did not show.

Sorren raised his head like a viper about to strike, and I saw malice in his gaze. I could only guess what guilt the Watchers had tried to lay on him, for the people he had killed and those he could not rescue. The expression on Sorren's face said he had reckoned with regret and made his peace.

Game on. Everyone seemed to move at once. A blast of white light came from one side of the clearing and then the next, and gray shadows flew through the air. Three of the Nephilim screamed as Chuck's explosives fired flexible metal nets that wrapped Baldy, Crow, and Coffee Guy in silver-coated mesh.

Teag and I attacked. Teag's sword blade passed easily through holes in the net, running Crow through the chest. I loosed a blast of fire from the walking stick at Baldy, setting him aflame as he struggled to free himself from the net that burned with silver and hot metal. Chuck leveled his ray gun and sent lightning bolts blazing toward Coffee Guy, electrifying the metal net and sending blue sparks into the air.

The fourth Nephilim, Asian Dude, ran at Daniel, who had his high-caliber magiked-up handgun out, and he started blasting away. Being corporeal is a bitch; bullets hurt. Chunks of the fallen angel's flesh flew off in a bloody spray, bones shattered, but the infernal thing didn't stop coming until Daniel put a silver-tipped bullet through its head and shattered its skull. The corpse vanished.

One down. Eight to go—plus the Watchers.

I felt the tendrils of the Watchers' power trying to creep back into my brain, hoping to slow me down with remorse. I tuned in my power to my agate necklace and my onyx bracelet, and the tendrils receded.

The Nephilim were tearing their way through the nets. Boy, were they pissed. Red, seeping welts criss-crossed their skin, and their fingers were bloodied and slashed to the bone where they had pulled the chains apart. Coffee Guy's pretty face was ruined, as if the murderous look in his eyes didn't already spoil the effect. He was already starting to shift to his true, purple-skin, winged bat-out-of-hell form with savage claws and powerful muscles. The other Nephilim were shifting as well, while the Watchers stood back, letting the foot soldiers take the first assault.

I recognized the Nephilim heading for Teag. He was Ginger, one of the fallen angels at the nursing home, and so was Blondie, the monster running toward Chuck. All I had to do was think about Helen Butler and all of the other nurses and patients who had died, and my blood ran hot. I sent my *chakram* flying and sliced through both of Coffee Guy's wings, sending him thudding to the ground with a screech as the *chakram* embedded itself in the ground.

He was back on his feet quickly, stalking toward me and I knew from his expression he intended to finish what he started.

I grabbed the walking stick and blasted him with fire. I couldn't hold it long, so I made it as hot as my anger, fueled by the memories of power in Alard's cane and the images of those old ladies who didn't deserve their fate. Coffee Guy let out an ear-splitting howl as his skin crisped and peeled away. I had to lower the walking stick and regroup or the magic would drain me dry, and when I did, Coffee Guy just kept coming. He was a charred mess, with blackened strips of skin hanging from his body and burned bone showing through the gashes, but he never slowed down.

Stay out of reach. I had learned that lesson the hard, painful way. Coffee Guy dove for me, but I slipped past him. Without his wings, his advantage lay in strength and those long, sharp, tainted claws. I was fast and small, and my Kevlar and knife-proof shirt were more protection than I'd had before, but I wasn't going to bet them against a supernatural boogeyman.

Coffee Guy swiped at me again, and this time, his claws raked against my shirt. I felt the pressure of their sharp points, but not the pain. The shirt worked. I'd figure out how to word that in a five-star online review later. *Repels hell spawn claws.* Yeah, that would go over well.

I wheeled, and this time I had Archie's brass knuckle talons on my right hand. Nephilim hide is tough, but the blades were sharp as scalpels with a micron-thin coating of silver. I hit him with my full strength, clawing down through the muscles on his forearm to the bone.

I was covered in Nephilim blood, but the strike let me dance back out of his range long enough to drop my athame into my right hand. I dodged this way and that, making him follow me, until I had him where I wanted him, and then I channeled all my rage into my athame's blast of cold, raw power.

It struck Coffee Guy square in the chest and threw him backwards – right onto the razor-sharp edge of my *chakram*, which was still lodged in the ground. He landed with his full weight and then some, driving the curve of the blade through his spine. Coffee Guy writhed for a moment and gave one last, hellish scream, before his body vanished. Two down, seven to go.

Sorren and Daniel battled Baldy and Crow. Ebony and Blondie stalked Lucinda. That left Painting Creep and Ginger for Teag and me. Chuck went to help Lucinda, freeing her to concentrate on her magic and leave the fighting to him. The last Nephilim, a guy with sandy-colored, shoulder-length hair who looked like he'd walked off the cover of a romance novel, remained on the edge of the fight, taking time to choose his prey. I hadn't seen him before, and that worried me. How many more Nephilim could Sariel muster up if he needed reinforcements? I was pretty sure I didn't want to find out.

Through it all, Sariel and his Watchers hung back, and I had the feeling that Sariel was enjoying the show, letting the Nephilim wear us down so that we were easy pickings. He was building a bonfire, and although I figured that couldn't be a good thing, I had more immediate dangers to worry about.

Teag loosened one of the rope knots that hung from his belt, using the stored magic to refresh his energy. I hadn't found a way to replenish my magic, and I was sweaty and winded. Holding onto the spindle whorl helped some, and I tried to catch my breath. Fire shimmered in the runes carved into Teag's fighting staff as he wheeled it overhead. Ginger watched Teag warily, while Painting Creep eyed me. It was the look of a predator deciding which prey was easiest to kill.

I won the bet.

With a growl, Painting Creep sprang at me, and this time, the claws punctured the knife-proof shirt, and raked my left shoulder. I returned the favor, plunging the silver-coated obsidian blades deep into his neck. For an instant, we were locked together, with his claws caught in the tough fabric of my protective shirt and my knives snagged in his leathery skin. Teag seized the opportunity and hit the monster's head like it was opening day at Wrigley Field.

Painting Creep howled and threw me clear. I tumbled across the ground, and came up just as Ginger grabbed for Teag's fighting staff. It shrieked as its hand burned on the runes, but all it needed was the chance to pull Teag close enough to grab. The fallen angel yanked Teag's arm hard enough to nearly dislocate it, then lifted him overhead like one of those movie monsters.

I had Josiah Winfield's dueling pistol locked and loaded. One shot: I had to make it good. I steadied myself and squeezed the trigger, firing at Teag's assailant. Fire spewed from the muzzle along with the bullet, which took off the back of Ginger's skull, raining blood and brains onto the dirt. The monster tottered for a second and then as Teag struggled free, the body crashed to the ground and disappeared.

No time to celebrate. Painting Creep came back at me with a snarl, grabbing my right arm to pull me in for the kill. I raked my brass knuckle blades down his face, sinking one of the blades into an eye as Bo's ghost leaped at the Nephilim's back and chomped down hard on the arm that had a hold of me. Painting Creep let go, howling, ichor spilling from his ruined eye, and Teag finished him with his short sword through the neck.

Sorren and Daniel made quick work of their two Nephilim. Crow had changed into his monster form, and Sorren went after it with both swords, landing a deep gash across its chest and taking off one arm. Sorren had taken his share of damage, with a cut down one cheek and four slashes across his chest. He got in another strike with his sword, then dodged out of the way as Daniel plugged Crow full of lead and silver with several rapid, accurate shots that left very little meat on the shattered bones. The carcass dropped to the ground and vanished.

Sorren kept Baldy busy with his swords while Daniel edged into position and fired his harpoon gun. The silver-steel blade went right through Baldy's back, its point protruding out the front, before Daniel gave a mighty jerk to the rope and hauled the barbed tip backward, raking its blades through the Nephilim's guts as Sorren landed a clean sword stroke that sent the fallen angel's head rolling.

Three Nephilim left. Blondie was fighting Chuck, Sandy went after Teag and me. Daniel Hunter circled Ebony, waiting for a chance to strike, and Sorren turned his attention to the Watchers, in case those bad boys decided to get into the fight. I covered Teag while he reloaded one of Josiah's pistols with the special bullets, sending a blast of flames from my walking stick. Teag had pulled out one of his silver-soaked fighting nets, and was jostling it in his left hand like a bullfighter with a cape.

"Here kitty, kitty, kitty," Teag mocked as I reloaded my pistol.

Nephilim don't have much sense of humor. Sandy howled and came at Teag in a dead run. Bo's ghost leaped into the air and sank its teeth deep into the Nephilim's shoulder, ripping open a wide, ragged gash.

Teag had been practicing with the net. He flicked his wrist and the net snagged over the fallen angel's clawed hand. Teag dove to the ground in front of me, dragging Sandy with him, and presenting me with a point-blank headshot. I squeezed the trigger of Josiah's gun and the Nephilim's skull exploded. His body was gone before it could hit the ground. Chuck fried Blondie with his ray gun and then took off his head with a sword for good measure while Daniel caught Ebony in a fusillade of gunfire and his silver-bullet-ridden body crumbled to dust.

That left the Watchers, Sariel, and however many Reapers Sariel could conjure up. The odds weren't in our favor.

Archibald Donnelly and the rest of our team had gone to Bloody Bridge to battle Reapers. I wondered how they fared, and if they would make it here in time to lend a hand. That depended on whether Sariel had an unlimited number of shadowy hench-spirits. But they weren't here yet, so if we were going to be rescued, we'd have to do the rescuing ourselves.

A breeze stirred the cobalt blue spirit bottles, with the clink of glass on glass. The lone shoe twirled as another gust stirred the heavy, warm air. A moment's stillness, a pause in the carnage.

Enraged at the defeat of the Nephilim, Sariel shrieked a command, and dark shapes swarmed from the bonfire. They danced in the flames, and for a moment I saw the twisted faces and gaping maws of nightmare and legend. Reapers, come at the command of their master.

"Go!" Sariel commanded.

The Reapers rushed toward us like a dark tide. I knew what they could do to ghosts. I didn't want to find out first-hand what they could do to people, and I had no intention of letting them near Bo. I used one of the bags of salt in my pocket to make a quick protective circle for me and Bo's ghost, but it wouldn't hold against anything too strong or determined. Inside the circle, Bo snarled and snapped as the Reapers surrounded me, and the night air grew cold.

"You have *got* to be kidding," Teag groaned. Sariel was not going to let us interfere with his final act of vengeance. As we fought on, Sariel continued the ritual that would bring the fifth Watcher through and rain chaos down on Charleston.

That was not going to happen on my watch.

I held out my athame, sending a cold white burst of force. The light and force went right through the Reapers. Chuck lobbed EMF grenades left and right, setting off brilliant flashes. Each time, the Reapers screeched and drew back, but the grenades weren't destroying them, just making them back off. Sooner or later, Chuck was going to run out.

Teag wrapped his silver-infused net around himself, covering his head and torso. A Reaper came at him fast, shadowy hands outstretched to grab and rend. Instead, the Reaper let out an earsplitting cry of pain as it touched the silver. Teag snapped his metal whip, and the silver-coated blade snaked through the Reaper shadow. The Reaper twisted and screeched, pulling back fast. Teag had won a round, but there were so many Reapers and his whip, like my athame and Chuck's grenades, only drove them back. We weren't destroying them.

Sariel was already making a circle for his last, grand working. All he had to do was bring across his fifth Watcher, and then he could unleash the Harrowing on Charleston, killing tens of thousands of people and getting his vengeance on Sorren. Unless we lived long enough to stop him.

Sariel and his Watchers had juiced up their mojo consuming Reapers and drawing power from deaths of the stairway disappearances. We'd had nothing more than a good night's sleep. No wonder Sariel had stayed out of the fight himself. He was saving his magic for the big finale.

"You've lost, Sorren," Sariel shouted. "You and your pathetic soldiers will be the final sacrifices. When the fifth Watcher comes through, this city and everyone you have loved in it will pay for their transgressions in flames."

Sariel stood before a blazing bonfire. "Marinette! Come to us! Aid us and you will have death a-plenty to feed on!" In the dancing shadows of the firelight, I spotted a skeletal image of a woman. Dry skin was pulled tight as a mummy across bone, and tangled dirty hair fell shoulder-length on a flowing red dress. Crabbed hands clutched black feathers, while her red eyes pierced the darkness, and her bony feet shuffled on the dry ground.

This was Marinette Bois Sech, the Voudon Loa, the one to whom Sariel had made the sacrifices at the power plant. I thought I was already as terrified of the Watchers as I could get, but the fearsome sense of old magic that rolled off Marinette was nearly heart-stopping in its intensity.

Sariel wasn't the kind of bad guy who wastes time monologueing. While the Nephilim kept us busy, he was drawing on Marinette's power to open a gateway and bring through the last Watcher. It didn't take much to guess what was in it for Marinette. Death and fire were enough for her. Sariel would start by killing us, and then slaughter thousands of people – but he would wait to destroy Sorren until he had made sure everyone and everything Sorren cared about was gone.

The air rippled and shimmered over Sariel's bonfire, then tore in two, revealing a black void. The Watchers were chanting with Sariel, and any second now, the fifth Watcher would come through, and the killing would begin. We had to stop it. I just didn't know how.

Wind gusted through the Angel Oak's branches. The cobalt blue bottles rattled. The wind grew stronger. The bottles clinked and grated against each other. The whole Angel Oak glowed with an eerie internal light. It lit up the bottles so that their deep blue shone in the night.

Spirit bottles.

Lucinda shouted a word of power and raised her walking stick. The bottles rattled again, more forcefully, deep sapphire blue against the night.

Reapers drifted closer, drawn by the power of the spirit bottles. Lucinda sang, the Angel Oak's leaves rustled, and the wind hissed like a giant snake. Too late, Sariel saw what was happening, but by then, he had lost control. The spirit bottles called to the Reapers, drawing them into the beautiful gem-colored prisons that clouded and darkened as the devourers were trapped inside. The big tree shuddered as the last of the Reapers vanished into the spirit bottles.

That just left Sariel, Marinette Bois Sech and the Watchers. A sorcerer with a vendetta, a bat-shit crazy Loa and four high-ranking fallen angels with another Watcher fighting his way between worlds.

Marinette's spirit grew more solid as the flames of the bonfire rose. Sariel was working his magic, opening the gateway to Hell. We were fighting as hard as we could, and losing. The fifth Watcher struggled through the ether to get to the opening between our world and his. We had seconds left if we were going to stop a cataclysm.

Without any kind of signal, we charged at Sariel and his Watchers, determined to go down fighting rather than letting him destroy Charleston.

Sariel's magic was tied up in his working to open that portal and bring the fifth Watcher through. He didn't dare break away to fight us. He needed his Watchers to wreak vengeance, but until the fifth one joined them, they didn't have a starting line-up. And we gave them no choice except to fight or let us cut them down where they stood.

The Watchers chose to fight.

"Leave Sariel to me!" Sorren snarled.

"Now where would the fun be in that?" a voice questioned from the darkness behind the fire. Archibald Donnelly, necromancer extraordinaire, emerged from the shadows wearing a safari outfit complete with pith helmet. Behind him were Caliel and Father Anne, as well as Mrs. Teller and Niella. They all looked worse for wear, skin streaked with dirt and blood, but they had made it in time, and they looked mad as hell.

Donnelly raised a churchwarden pipe, holding the pipe bowl in his palm and pointing the stem directly at the portal. The Watcher was fully framed in the ragged opening of the rift between worlds, about to step through the doorway. "Encumber!" Donnelly thundered, and the Watcher receded from the opening, as if he had been pushed far back a long corridor.

"Don't you know better than to muck around in the Netherworld when there's a necromancer around?" he chided Sariel. He turned to Sorren. "I'll hold the gate. You deal with that sorry son of a bitch."

Chuck was already firing at the Watchers. He let out a string of curses, lobbed an EMF grenade, then took careful aim. At the instant the grenade exploded in a burst of electromagnetic energy and cold light, Chuck squeezed the trigger again. Watcher One screamed in rage and pain as the modified bullet tore into his shoulder.

Lucinda and Caliel joined forces and took on Marinette Bois Sech. The dangerous Loa's figure had grown nearly solid enough to step out of the fire like a god made flesh. Lucinda never stopped chanting and singing, even when she loosed a torrent of green fire from the tip of her walking stick, which held the remembered power of all the mambos and houngans who had owned it across the generations. Lucinda's fire hit the apparition square in the neck and face. The green fire met with Marinette's own flames, red as hell. Fire vied with fire, a test of wills, but for the moment, it halted Marinette's advance.

The night smelled of blood and otherworldly ichor, salt marsh and sweat. I caught a whiff of tobacco and the smell of rum. Over to one side, Daniel's harpoon gun sank its silver-tipped spear right through Watcher Two's chest. Enraged, the Watcher reached down and yanked the spear back out, hurling it back at Daniel so fast that Daniel barely saw it coming. The harpoon sliced deep into Daniel's thigh and he cried out.

Father Anne came at Watcher Two from behind, with a pearl-handled, thin-bladed knife that had its own brand of nasty magic. She stabbed the blade through the Watcher's neck so that the point came out the other side, and then pulled fast and strong, slitting his throat from the inside out. Father Anne doesn't mess around. Watcher Two sank to the ground but instead of disappearing, his whole body trembled and then he rose, ready to fight. It was going to take more than a slit throat to put a Watcher down. That was a very bad sign.

I was busy with Watcher Three, but out of the corner of my eye, I saw that Mrs. Teller and Niella had retreated to the doorway of the nearby gift shop, where they crouched over the dim flame of a candle. I figured they were casting some kind of Hoodoo protection spell, and I just hoped they'd be quick about it. A brilliant light flared, and Watcher Three staggered. Over his shoulder, I spotted Chuck with his juiced-up ray gun, and he gave me a grim smile. I followed up with a blast from my athame. I charred Watcher Three's face and Chuck went for the kill, sending the Watcher's head rolling, but I was tiring quickly, and I knew one more blast was probably my limit.

Sorren was fighting Sariel, while Donnelly's magic focused on the portal and Watcher Five, who still hadn't come through yet to our world. Sariel's power enabled him to nearly match Sorren's speed and strength, and it was quickly evident that he knew how to wield the sword he had drawn. Sorren went on the offense with both swords, but his strike missed while Sariel's sword cut a deep gash in Sorren's thigh.

Sorren snarled, and I could see his fangs. "One of your Watchers is down. The rest will die soon. Give it up. The game's over."

"I can still destroy you and yours," Sariel returned. "Marinette! Goddess! Lend me your strength!" The strain of holding open the portal and fighting off Sorren's attack was starting to take its toll. In response, Marinette turned from where she withstood the assault from Lucinda and Caliel. I heard a horrible laugh, and then Marinette vanished and Sariel's whole stance changed. For a split second, I thought I saw Marinette's image overlaid on his, and then Sariel's lips twisted in a vengeful, triumphant smile as the Loa possessed him. The transformation was terrifying.

Sorren had his swords, but juiced up with Marinette's power, Sariel pulled one of the metal parking signs out of the ground, swinging it one way and the other, first jabbing with the sharp metal sign and then using the concrete that still clung to the other end as a cudgel. It was far beyond his natural strength, and I wondered if he would find his body badly damaged when the Loa finally departed. That would be cold comfort if he beat us into the ground before then.

The concrete end caught Sorren in the chest, sending him flying with enough impact to break ribs. Sorren was back in the fight in the blink of an eye, dodging in and around the deadly metal and concrete to sink both his blades deep into Sariel's belly and side, ripping the blades sideways as he pulled them free so that blood gushed and entrails bulged.

Teag sparred with Watcher Four, managing to keep him at bay, but the Watcher tired of the game and with a howl, shifted to his beast form. I was pretty spent after taking out Watcher Three, but I gathered enough of my strength to channel more magic through the walking stick, and a blast like a torch burst from the end of the cane, hitting Watcher Four square in the torso. He shrieked and swung at Teag and me with his claws, but I managed to dodge the worst of the strikes, though the sharp nails opened new cuts on my shoulder. I staggered, weakened by the outlay of energy needed to use my magic.

The instant the flames subsided, Teag leaped on the Watcher's back, slashing with his knife and his dagger, flaying the skin from the fallen angel's frame. The beast swept Teag aside with one powerful arm, sending him flying across the lot to land hard on his back.

We were losing, fast. A storm was rolling in, and dark clouds now filled the sky. The air felt thick with power, tingling with electrical charge, like right before lightning strikes.

Sorren was holding his own against Sariel, but he was bloodied in a dozen places. His shirt hung in tatters, and three deep gouges across his face barely missed his eye. He looked like he was getting the worst of the deal. Caliel and Lucinda had gone to help. Caliel had drawn blades, and teamed up with Sorren to box Sariel in, forcing the nephilmancer to watch two opponents at once. Lucinda channeled her magic through her staff, hitting Sariel with a burst of power to drain his strength, giving Sorren and Caliel opportunity to regroup between strikes.

Chuck held something that looked like a cross between a cattle prod and a flame thrower. Chuck's high tech weapons worked like a charm on disembodied creatures like wraiths and malicious ghosts, but it was always a toss-up how they'd affect corporeal creatures. His weapon was holding Watcher One at bay, but it didn't look likely to destroy the creature, and no battery lasts forever.

Daniel had either run out of ammo or decided it wasn't doing the trick. He had regained his silver-tipped harpoon and had a long knife in the other hand. He had fought Watcher Two to a stand-off, but Daniel would eventually tire, and the Watcher would make his move. Father Anne dodged in and out of all the fights whenever opportunity presented to land a blow with a knife spelled and consecrated to be doubly damaging to supernatural creatures. The only problem was, Watchers could take more damage than Nephilim, and we were running out of ways to blow them to smithereens.

Teag had regained his feet, uncoiling his razor-sharp *urumi* steel-and-silver whip-blade, lashing out at Watcher Four. Our 'knife-proof' shirts and Kevlar vests had deflected the worst of the damage, but now they were torn and we were bloody and bruised, achingly tired. Sooner or later, we were going to lose the focus necessary to do magic. That's what Sariel was counting on.

Watcher Four rushed me, and I slashed at him with my brass knuckles knife in one hand as I brought my athame up at point blank range and reached for all the magic I could muster to blast him backward. The fallen angel swung one of its heavy fists and I went sprawling at the base of the Angel Oak, its hard roots scraping across my skin. Bo's ghost lunged and snapped, positioning himself between me and my attacker, and the Watcher backed off, but it was clear he was waiting for me to tire.

I wasn't going down without a fight.

I dug my fingers into the ground to push myself up, and felt a shiver of power run through my body. Roots. Tree roots. Not just any tree. The ancient Angel Oak. And in my mind's eye I could see all those roots, tangled and interwoven over the centuries, drawing life from the depths of the ground and stretching leaves toward the stars.

"Teag!" I shouted. "Pull on the fabric of the roots!" I ran for the trunk and threw my arms out wide, pressing my back and palms against its rough bark, expecting any moment to feel the Watcher's claws. Bo's ghost was right in front of me, growling a warning for the Watcher to keep his distance.

Thousands will die and it's going to be your fault. You failed. You weren't good enough. The Watchers knew I was tired, and the insidious tendrils of guilt and doubt snaked toward my mind now that I was almost too weary to fight them away. *You might as well die. All that blood on your hands...*

Overwhelming remorse and guilt swept over me, tearing a sob from my throat. My hands splayed against the bark of the broad trunk, holding me up. That's when I realized something important.

Remorse can cripple you and make you give up. Or it can be the hard lesson that puts steel in your spine and gives you the strength to fight the headwind.

In that moment, I used my touch magic to draw on the strong emotions the Angel Oak had witnessed in all its long life. Humans had sought it out for shelter or as a canopy for their happiest times. Animals and birds made their homes in its branches. Storms battered it. Rain nurtured the tree and sun warmed it. I glimpsed images that swept past me, too numerous to see clearly, spanning centuries. And something more. After all those years, the Angel Oak wasn't just alive.

It was *aware*.

I thrust my magic deep into the heartwood of that ancient tree as my feet stood among its roots. Teag was sending his weaving magic down into the mat and fiber of those roots, into the sprawling, complex tangle that supported and fed the tree. The root mass for a big oak could be many times bigger than the spread of its branches, and the Angel Oak's branches were enormous, which meant its roots probably sprawled halfway to Atlanta.

Magic charged the air all around me. The breeze picked up again, swinging that lone shoe and clinking the spirit bottles together. That's when I realized that more than the tree was feeding my magic.

Someone had entered into the tree itself.

"Father Gran Bwa, Father Damballah Wedo, hear us in our time of need!" Lucinda cried. "Lend us your aid!"

The smell of cigars and rum was strong now, and I could feel another spirit alongside the Angel Oak's own awareness, a powerful being far more ancient even than the oak, beyond immortal to timeless. Gran Bwa, Loa of the trees and Earth, one of Voudon's most powerful mage spirits had answered Lucinda's call. He wasn't alone. I blinked my eyes, trying to make sure I was seeing right, but I glimpsed a huge, white snake above me, its massive body coiled round and round the thick trunk of the Angel Oak. It was Damballah Wedo, one of the oldest Loa, a source of life itself.

I felt the Loas' power tingle down the bark of the huge old tree, and sensed the awareness that was the Angel Oak connected with the ancient and powerful beings that had taken rest in its branches. My touch magic saw it all in images, not words, but I knew the tree and its guests had come to an agreement.

The Angel Oak began to glow, as if millions of fireflies alighted on every inch of its huge, twisting branches and its thousands of leaves. Standing beneath its gigantic canopy, hands on its rough trunk, I could feel the thrum of old power, as sure and steady as a river's course. I willed myself into that flow, committing my magic to it, drawing it up through me heedless of the cost, knowing that such power was not made for mortals to wield.

I thought of all the blood that soaked the ground beneath the Angel Oak. Our blood. Nephilim and Watcher blood. Legends say blood does strange things to trees. Now, that ancient tree was waking up.

Teag felt it too, and so did Lucinda. I could see them rally, see the surge of magic fill them with new energy. The Watchers weren't of this world. They couldn't draw on that power. But we could.

Teag snapped his whip blade, and the silver-edged razor sang through the air, slicing through Watcher Four's back and laying open his ribs. He got the fallen angel on the blade's recoil as well, slicing through the muscles and tendons that would have held the wings if the Watcher transformed. His opponent gave a feral cry and turned on Teag, just in time for the long razor-sharp blade to snake across the attacker's perfect face, cutting into the cheek, blinding him in one eye and taking off half his nose.

I heard a crunching, crackling noise and yelped as the ground beneath my feet trembled. The Angel Oak's roots rippled beneath the dirt, then tough tendrils burst from the hard-packed ground, and wrapped themselves around Watcher Four's feet.

Teag had his fighting net, and he used it to snare the Watcher's grasping hands as his *urumi* went for the legs. The flexible blade snapped around the fallen angel's ankles, and hamstrung him in a spray of blood. In the next heartbeat, Teag's sword took Watcher Four's head right off his shoulders. *Another one bites the dust...*

I raised my walking stick and pointed it at Watcher Two, who was still standing despite everything Daniel and Father Anne threw at him. I thought about Helen Butler and Edwin Thompson, about the nurses at Palmetto Meadows and the old ladies who took such joy from Baxter's visits. I thought about how horribly they died, trapped in flames and smoke, because of Sariel. I took all my regret and remorse over not being able to save them, and turned it into molten hot vengeance. Then I willed the power of the Angel Oak and its unearthly visitors to channel through me, through my walking stick. Maybe it would kill me. Maybe not. But I would be avenged.

A torrent of flames burst from the tip of the old walking stick. I felt the power sweep up from the roots and down through the trunk, heard the hiss of

Damballah Wedo and the soft lilt of Gran Bwa, felt the presence that was the Angel Oak and let it all flow through me, growing hot in my rage and sorrow, and felt it explode through the walking stick.

The fire didn't just hit Watcher Two. It incinerated him.

Chuck was covered with blood. Some of it was his own. Most of it, I hoped, was from the fallen angels he had blown to bits. Now, he leveled his shotgun with the odd wires at Watcher One on the other side of the Angel Oak, the one who had eluded the roots that grasped for his feet and ankles and was streaking toward Lucinda faster than Daniel Hunter could intercept.

The shotgun barked and something streaked out of it. Instead of a bullet, what hit Watcher One made him light up like a Christmas tree, waves of blue electricity running up and down his body. It only lasted a few seconds. That's all it needed. He collapsed to his knees from a dose of high voltage electricity that would have fried a mere mortal.

"I am so done with this shit." Daniel Hunter was holding something that looked like a cricket bat studded with obsidian blades. A *maquahuitl*, the weapon ancient Aztecs used when they were severely pissed at someone. He swung the *maquahuitl* with all his might, and it took the Watcher One's head right off his neck, smashing in one side of it for good measure. The severed head stuck to the blades, as if Daniel were batting a gory home run. The fallen angel's body collapsed to the blood-soaked ground.

Sorren, Lucinda, and Caliel still battled Sariel, while Donnelly made sure the fifth Watcher didn't come through the portal. Sorren had a sword in each hand, bloodied to the elbows and spattered with gore. His shirt and jeans were soaked with his own blood from deep gashes. Sariel had Marinette's strength to bolster him, and I wondered if the Loa was the only reason the nephilmancer was still on his feet. The Angel Oak's roots twined around his ankles, as if the old tree knew it was Sariel who had lit the bonfire. Sariel was bleeding heavily from deep gashes on his arms and thighs, and the belly wound alone would have put a regular fighter on the ground. Mad resistance glittered in Sariel's eyes, and I knew neither he nor Sorren would yield short of destruction.

We didn't have that kind of time.

I grabbed the *chakram* from the ground and made a Hail Mary throw, aiming at Sariel. The razor disk missed his neck but lodged in his shoulder. It was the distraction Sorren needed. One sword split the nephilmancer from shoulder to hip, while the other severed his head, just for good measure. Sariel wasn't getting back up from that, even with a Loa possessing him.

Marinette's spirit shrieked in rage as Sariel's body failed. She tore loose from the corpse, rising like a destroying angel above the blood-soaked ground. Lucinda blasted her with the green-lit power of her staff, and Caliel struck with his blessed swords, but the malicious Loa wheeled on them, a frenzy of teeth and claws.

The Angel Oak was still against my back, and my hands gripped its rough bark. I listened to the images that my touch magic unlocked, and I knew that the Angel Oak was not happy at having its long slumber disturbed. It despised the death and blood; it feared the fire.

The reading I got from the Loas was different. Lucinda's power had called them, and they came, observing before they decided whether or not to intervene. Marinette's involvement troubled them, but

I feared they would see the struggle as mortal business, and thus beneath their interest to intervene.

If I could sense the tree's perceptions because I was touching the Angel Oak, maybe the tree and the Loas could hear me, too. I tightened my grip on the tree and opened my mind to the Oak, feeding it images more than words. The stairway disappearances. Reapers. So many deaths. Sariel's desire for vengeance – and what he intended for Charleston. The information passed out of me at a breathtaking speed, and I felt drained when it ended, but I had the definite feeling that I had been heard.

We can't defeat Marinette by ourselves. Please, please help, I begged.

I felt the ancient power of Gran Bwa and Damballah Wedo rouse. Marinette Bois Sech was one of their own, and she had overstepped.

Gran Bwa's spirit sank into the Angel Oak, and the branches shook as the tree's limbs began to move. One huge limb lay on the ground. Now, animated by the Loa, it swept the bonfire aside, scattering the brands and obliterating Sariel's warded circle. Abruptly, the portal winked shut, trapping the fifth Watcher in the Netherworld where he belonged.

The spirit of Damballah Wedo, the great white snake, slipped down the Angel Oak's many branches, spreading out over the limbs and twigs, out into the leaves. The breeze stirred and the Angel Oak bent as if from a hurricane's force. As its limbs came close to where Marinette's spirit raged, I saw the snake's thick coils reach out from among the leaves and wrap themselves around Marinette like an anaconda. Marinette bucked and fought, but Damballah Wedo was stronger. When the snake engulfed Marinette, the vision blinked out, and so did the presence of the Loas.

The Angel Oak looked as it always did. The glow had faded, the limbs and branches were in the positions they had held for centuries, roots beneath the soil once more. Beautiful and ancient, nothing suggested that it had been a participant in a battle for the soul of the Holy City.

Caliel and Lucinda stood at the base of the Angel Oak where the offerings lay, thanking Gran Bwa and Damballah Wedo for their help. Father Anne, Chuck, and Daniel limped around stomping out embers and kicking dirt over the burning remains of the bonfire. Donnelly remained staring warily at the empty space where the portal had been. Only now did he lower his churchwarden's pipe athame, sure that the threat was over.

The bodies of the Watchers vanished, returning to the Netherworld. That left Sariel's remains. When Marinette's spirit left him, the true extent of the damage was apparent. Sariel looked as if he had aged decades, and his body was nearly as dried-out and bony as Marinette's. Sorren retrieved Sariel's severed head, then picked up the body. He looked at Father Anne and Lucinda. "This time, I need to be sure he doesn't come back," he said. They nodded, and left with him toward the dark trees at the back of the park.

Daniel and Chuck scoured the grounds to gather up weapons, spent shells and any other evidence of our work. Except for the scorch mark where the bonfire had been, and the torn-out metal parking sign, our battle left few physical traces. The offerings beneath the tree stayed. There was no harm in leaving them as tribute.

Mrs. Teller and Niella joined us once they were certain the fighting was over. I didn't blame them. Mrs. Teller was up in years, and Niella wasn't a trained fighter. Still, that hardly meant they were defenseless, and I had seen Mrs. Teller hold her own in more than one tough situation.

"Wow," Niella said, surveying the scene. "That was really something."

"We knew we couldn't help with the fighting, so we did what we do," Mrs. Teller chimed in. "We found a doorway and set a protection spell over all of you, against the forces of darkness."

"I'd say it worked," I replied. I had been in enough battles to know that the smallest things can affect the outcome, one way or another. We had squeaked out a victory, and it had taken all of us to do it.

Niella gave me an appraising look. "Girl, we need to get all of you back home where we can doctor you up before those cuts go sour. You look like a hundred miles of bad road."

Her comment reminded me of how many places on my body hurt like hell. Bo's ghost lingered next to me, making sure I was all right. Out of old habit, my left hand reached for his head to ruffle his golden fur and tousle those soft ears. Though my hand slipped right through his apparition, Bo gave me that goofy grin I loved and desperately missed and then, vanished.

We had saved the city, prevented tens of thousands of deaths, and no one would ever know.

"I don't know about you, but I could use a beer, a shower and a pint of blood, not necessarily in that order," I quipped tiredly. Then I sobered quickly as I got a look at Teag.

Teag limped toward me. He had been gashed across the chest and left shoulder, and his shirt was soaked with blood. A deep cut slashed one thigh as well. He was dangerously pale, and swayed on his feet. I ran to him just as his eyes rolled back in his head as he dropped to the ground like a rock.

"Archie! Over here!" Sorren appeared next to Teag in a blur. He dropped to his knees next to Teag and pressed his bloody arm against Teag's lips, forcing some of the fluid into Teag's mouth though it looked like Sorren had little blood to spare. "He's fading." Donnelly hurried over and knelt on the other side.

"Hold onto him," Sorren commanded, withdrawing his arm. "I can't give him enough blood to heal him. I'll have a doctor waiting for us."

"I don't have any supplies –" I started.

"Leave that to me," Donnelly said. He laid his hand over Teag's forehead and spoke a few words of power. That's when it hit me. Teag was dying. Sorren wanted Donnelly to bind soul to body long enough for us to try to save him.

Chapter Twenty-Three

SORREN'S PRIVATE DOCTOR, Dr. Zeigler, met us at my house.

"There are enough supplies in the dining room for a hospital," Maggie said when we arrived. "A man named Higgins brought them by not long ago." I glanced into the dining room and saw sufficient medical supplies for a mobile surgical unit. "I've got hot tea ready, chicken soup and my grandmother's homemade poultice," she added, bustling around the kitchen despite her crutches. Mrs. Teller and Niella went to help, since they had managed to escape the battle unscathed.

"Let mama add some of her powders to that poultice," Niella suggested. "It'll cure that demon claw taint." All of us had deep cuts from the Nephilim and Watchers. Those wounds would turn bad quickly if they weren't tended, and it seemed a waste to survive the battle only to die of blood poisoning. Dr. Zeigler conferred with Mrs. Teller, debating what ingredients to add to the poultice. After a few minutes of discussion, they came to an agreement, and Mrs. Teller adjusted the mixture, working it into a green paste with an odd botanical smell.

Donnelly carried Teag into the living room, and the rest of us limped behind him. Maggie must have had an inkling of what we were going to be in for, because she had thrown plastic tarps and bed sheets over the couches, to keep the blood off the upholstery.

"He's lost a lot of blood," I said, as Dr. Zeigler went to work on Teag. I didn't like how pale he looked or how shallowly he was breathing. Donnelly remained at one end of the couch, his hand never leaving Teag's forehead.

Maggie took one look at Teag, blanched, and then regained her presence of mind, guiding me to a chair before I fell over. "Sit," she commanded. "Before you do more damage to yourself."

Sorren's injuries would have killed a mortal. I could see from his face that he was in pain. He was already healing, but that meant he needed to feed. Sometimes, in an emergency, he fed from Teag, but tonight Teag was not in any shape to spare the blood. Caliel had taken only light damage, so he offered his arm to Sorren, whose pallor improved after a few swallows.

Our 'knife-proof' shirts had deflected some injuries, but they were never meant to stand up to the kind of fighting we had done. Taint from the claws wouldn't hurt Sorren because his ability to heal was supernatural, but the rest of us mortals needed serious patching up. Mrs. Teller fell in naturally beside Dr. Zeigler, adding her magic to his medical skills as they cleaned and treated Teag's wounds, some of which needed stitches and butterfly bandages in addition to magic. Higgins's supplies included IV packs, fluids, and pints of blood. Dr. Zeigler checked for a compatible blood type and got Teag hooked up.

A bad bruise purpled Teag's cheek, and one eye was swollen almost shut. He had a split lip, and enough cuts on his arms and shoulders that it looked like he had gone through the windshield of a car. I wondered how I would ever explain his condition to Anthony, and knew that if Dr. Zeigler and Donnelly couldn't save him, I would never be able to face Anthony again.

We all sat in silence, watching them work, fingering charms or murmuring prayers under our breath. Blood and tears mingled on my cheeks, and Baxter laid a tentative paw on my leg, offering comfort. I swept him into my lap, tears wetting his silky fur.

Finally, Dr. Zeigler stood. "He'll live," he said, with a nod toward Donnelly. Donnelly looked haggard and bleary-eyed, as though the strain of sustaining Teag's life had taxed his already hard-used reserves.

"He's not going to be a happy camper for a few days," Dr. Zeigler observed, peeling away what remained of Teag's blood-soaked shirt. "But the poultice should reduce the fever, and the cuts should heal cleanly, especially with the blood Sorren was able to give him. The injuries would be bad enough if the damage wasn't supernatural, but the dark magic makes it worse." He rose. "He needs to rest for a few days, and that means in bed with no activity. I don't want anything putting a strain on his system or pulling at those stitches."

Teag's color had already improved, and his breathing was steady. Now that he was out of danger, I realized just how awful I felt. "So," Dr. Zeigler said, "let me take a look at your shoulder."

I didn't argue. It felt as if the work of the evening had come crashing down on me all at once, and now that the adrenaline of the fight had faded, I was bone-weary and ached all over. I glanced around at my comrades in arms. Daniel Hunter stood by himself watching out the window, and although he was bloodied like the rest of us, he refused Dr. Zeigler's treatment. I had already figured out that Hunter was something more than mortal. Chuck put up with being stitched and bandaged with the reserve of an old soldier. Lucinda's injuries were minimal, since she had been largely out of the hand-to-hand combat. She looked utterly spent from the magic she had channeled, and dug ravenously into the food Maggie set out. We were too tired to eat, and too spent not to replenish ourselves. Everyone hailed Maggie's cooking, and she beamed. Donnelly found a chair on the other side of the room and sat down, then leaned back and fell asleep almost immediately.

"Father Anne," Sorren said in a voice that was strained but resolute. "Fill us in on what happened at Bloody Bridge."

Father Anne's short dark hair was bloody on one side from a scalp wound and she had stitches from deep cuts on both arms. "We got to the battle site before dark," she said, "and stayed low until the park closed. Caliel set wardings while Mrs. Teller and Niella had powders and charms to drive the Reapers toward where Archie would be waiting for them," she nodded toward Donnelly.

As Father Anne talked, Mrs. Teller and Niella made their way around the room with Dr. Zeigler, helping to cleanse and bind up our injuries, adding a touch of magic to the medicine. Neither of the root workers looked injured, though they, too appeared spent from the energy invested in their magic.

"Archie warned the ghosts not to rise at sunset. Most of the ghosts heard him, but some either didn't hear or didn't understand." Father Anne shook her head. "As soon as they rose, the Reapers were on them. And then we were on the Reapers. I think there's something in the Reapers' magic that forces the ghosts from cover, because the ones we saw were trying to get clear or struggling to stay out of the way. The Reapers shredded any ghosts they got close enough to touch."

"My charms and wardings worked with the ones Mrs. Teller and Niella set, to steer the Reapers right to Colonel Donnelly," Caliel added. "And just to be sure, I set out an offering to Ghede Nibo. He's the patron Loa of war dead and watcher of cemeteries, and he's got no patience for anything that harms the souls in his territory."

"We herded the Reapers toward Archie, and let him use his necromancy to send the Reapers back where they came from," Father Anne picked up the tale. "Meanwhile, Caliel and I did our best to get the ghosts of the battle dead to cross over. Most of them were ready to go. That meant there was nothing for the Reapers to draw energy from, so Archie made quick work of them."

"I wouldn't exactly call it 'quick work'," Donnelly protested from where he sat, not even opening his eyes. "Though I have to say that I appreciated the help from Ghede Nibo. I think it's fair to say that the Reapers didn't expect a necromancer or a Ghede." He smiled tiredly. "Then we closed down that party and came over to bail you out."

I knew his comment was a friendly jab at Sorren, but tonight that had been exactly what happened. Without the help Donnelly and the others had provided in the last part of the fight at the Angel Oak, I was pretty sure we would have lost several lives, even if we had been able to defeat Sariel.

Pounding on my door made us all jump. Chuck and Daniel both moved toward the entrance, ready for a fight. Maggie shooed them back and peered out the window. "It's Anthony," she said worriedly, and I nodded for her to open the door.

"Where's Teag?" Anthony said, bursting into my front hall. "Something's happened. I know it. Where is he?"

Before I could get to my feet to escort him in, Anthony glimpsed Teag lying on the couch. Teag's eyes were closed, and Dr. Zeigler had hooked up an IV for fluids and a blood transfusion. Anthony's eyes widened, and he stormed into the living room.

"My God! What the hell? He needs to be in the hospital!" Anthony looked ready to plow his way through us if need be to make that happen. Dr. Zeigler stepped in front of him, and Anthony stopped dead in his tracks.

"Let me through," Anthony said levelly.

"He can't go to the hospital."

"Because you don't want to answer questions from the police?" Anthony challenged.

"Because those wounds are supernatural," Dr. Zeigler countered. "If he's not within strong wardings, they'll attract supernatural predators, and Teag's too weak to fight them off."

"Then ward the hospital."

"Not possible," Lucinda snapped. "Too big, too many people, too much going on. Lots worse things in a hospital besides germs. Things that feed on blood and death. Supernatural parasites, scavengers. He's protected here."

"Protected?" Anthony echoed. "Look at him! You call that protected?"

"That's enough." Sorren stepped forward. He did not raise his voice, and he did not use glamouring or compulsion. He didn't need to. When a nearly six-hundred year old vampire wants your attention, he has the presence to make people listen.

"Teag is out of danger," Sorren said. "And within these wards, he is safe. I will not allow you to put him at risk, and I think you want what is best for Teag..."

Sorren took the wind out of Anthony's sails. Just like that, his bluster crumbled, and he looked worried and frightened enough to throw up. "I got home early and found a notarized power of attorney and Teag's will on the kitchen table," Anthony said unsteadily. "With a note that said things might go badly tonight. I went to the store but no one was there. I called the hospitals. Nothing. So I came here. And... oh my God," he said again, as if seeing the rest of us for the first time.

We were all covered in blood, clothing shredded, some of us with stitches and others with the faint pink scars of magically-healed lacerations. Sorren looked much better than he had when we left the Angel Oak, but his wounds hadn't fully healed yet, and he looked more like a casualty than a victor. "You look like you've been to war," Anthony said quietly.

I met his gaze. "We have been. The creatures we pushed back tonight intended to destroy us and the whole city – and they probably wouldn't have stopped there."

"The whole city?" Anthony echoed, looking as if his world had come unmoored.

"Probably most of the South, like they did the last time, back in 1854," Sorren replied. He was tired enough that he made no attempt to hide his fangs, and

I saw awareness dawn on Anthony as he glimpsed the points of Sorren's eye teeth.

"Supernatural vigilantes," Anthony murmured. He glanced toward Chuck and Daniel, who definitely looked the part. His gaze hesitated on Mrs. Teller and Niella, and I guessed he recognized them from the market. Lucinda regarded him coolly, and Caliel had gone into the kitchen to make a small offering of rum and cigars to the Loas for their help.

"That's as good a term as any," Father Anne replied. Blood splattered her white clerical collar and the iron cross that hung from a chain around her neck. "We face down the demons in the dark, so the rest of you don't have to."

"The police –" Anthony started.

"The police don't have the means to fight what we fight," I replied. "They'd die. We do what we do because we're specialists."

"You mean, you have magic." Anthony said. I nodded. He ran a hand back through his hair. "Shit," he said, and I could practically watch the gears turn as he put it all together.

"Decide," Sorren said. "I can make you forget everything you've seen here tonight and you can go about your business, but that forgetting will include Teag."

Anthony pulled himself together and looked at Sorren levelly. "No! Hell, no! I may not really understand this, but even if it got me disbarred, if Teag's here, I'm staying."

Sorren stepped aside and let Anthony move past him to kneel next to the couch. He reached up and took Teag's hand. "I guess if worst comes to worst, I can always be your *consigliere*," Anthony said with a rueful half-smile as the tears rolled down his cheek.

"Nah… we're the good guys, but thanks. If you can keep our secrets, we'll keep yours," Father Anne said. Donnelly pushed a glass of bourbon into Anthony's hand.

"Buck up, old boy," he said. "Any battle all your people live through is a mighty fine fight."

Dr. Zeigler made a slow circle around the room once more, checking on all of us to assure himself we were patched up. He lingered over Teag, checking the IV lines and Teag's vital signs, then looked to Anthony and Sorren. "I'll be back in the morning to check on him. He'll be fine for tonight." He gave the rest of us a nod and let himself out. Zeigler's a good guy. Not only does he make house calls, but he knows his way around supernatural injuries, and manages to keep everything off the authorities' radar. I assume Sorren pays him a hefty retainer.

Archibald Donnelly picked up his pith helmet from the table. "He doesn't need my help anymore," Donnelly said with a nod toward Teag. "Bloody fine show we put on tonight," he said, clapping Sorren on the shoulder. "Always happy to lend a hand." He gave Sorren a broad wink. "And thanks for that painting. I'll make sure it gets exactly the spot it deserves."

Chuck and Daniel insisted on keeping watch on the porch, and I wasn't going to stop them. The others made their goodbyes and straggled out, until only Sorren, Maggie, Teag, Anthony, and I were left.

"Is my room ready?" Sorren asked with a hint of dry humor. There's an old, windowless root cellar in the basement where I keep a futon for him in case of emergencies.

I nodded. "Get some sleep. We'll keep an eye on Teag."

Maggie was managing without her crutches, but she had pushed herself enough that her limp was obvious. "You were a trooper," I said. "Thank you."

Maggie shrugged. "What are friends for? I'm glad everyone's all right." She leaned down to scratch Baxter's ears. "But I'm dog tired."

I jerked my head toward the guest bedroom. "Go ahead. I'm going to turn in soon." Once Maggie headed down the hallway, I went to the linen closet and brought out a pillow and sleeping bag for Anthony.

"Figured you might as well be comfortable, since I didn't think you'd leave the room," I said.

Anthony took the bedding appreciatively. "Thanks, Cassidy. Sorry I was such an ass."

"We threw a lot at you all at once," I said. "And you were worried." I shrugged, then winced as the movement hurt. More than anything, I just wanted to get cleaned up and fall into bed. Dr. Zeigler had given me some painkillers, and with Chuck and Daniel on guard duty, I thought I'd break down and take the pills to get a good night's sleep.

Anthony glanced over at Teag, who was still sedated and sleeping. "Panicked is more like it. Thanks for taking care of him. You really think he'll be okay?"

"You heard the doctor. He needs to rest, but he should be fine after all the stitches heal up," I replied. "Now, I've got to get some sleep." And with that, I tucked Baxter under my arm and headed for bed.

Two weeks later, Teag, Father Anne, and I stood in Magnolia Cemetery. The sun was just setting over the marshland behind the graveyard. Technically, the memorial park was closed, but Father Anne and Sorren had pull with the administrator, so for once we didn't have to worry about being caught and thrown out after hours.

Sorren joined us just as the sun dipped below the horizon. "They did a nice job with the headstone," I said as he walked up.

The dark granite stone was unpretentious, but I knew a memorial of that size had cost plenty, as had the lot beneath the spreading branches of an old live oak. Mrs. Butler's remains had never been recovered from the wreckage of Palmetto Meadows, so there was no body, and since she had no living relatives, no funeral was held. That's why Sorren had asked us here, for a private memorial.

The stone read 'Helen Wadsworth Butler' with her birth and death dates, along with a carved heart, a dove, and the words 'Forever remembered.' Most of the time, that kind of epitaph is an overstatement, but for Sorren, it would be very true.

"Am I late?" Archibald Donnelly strode across the well-trimmed lawn, managing to avoid the gravestones though the cemetery was not lit for night visitors.

"Right on time, Archie," Sorren said. Donnelly was wearing a well-tailored suit, though the cut looked about a century out of date. He came up to stand with us, and read the inscription.

"Can't tell you how sorry I am about this, Sorren," Donnelly said. "Do you have what I asked for?"

Sorren nodded and reached into a pocket, withdrawing a World War Two-vintage man's watch. He handed it over to Donnelly, who took it carefully between both hands. Donnelly closed his eyes and began to murmur. A faint mist gathered near the headstone, glimmering with flecks of light. The mist thickened and in another moment, a figure stepped out of the fog.

This was Helen Butler as she had been seventy years ago, the beautiful, sassy girl from the old photograph. Sorren stepped toward her, and at least from where I stood, when he held out his hand to her, it looked as if she clasped his in return.

"I'm sorry I couldn't protect you," Sorren murmured. "I failed you."

Her laughter carried on the night air. "Never. You were always there. You didn't think I knew, but deep inside, I did. And at the end, you made me remember the old days. You gave those back to me – to us."

"My friends will make sure your crossing is smooth," Sorren said, his voice tight with emotion. The grief in his eyes was at odds with how young he appeared. *Even though he knew this day would come, I guess it never gets easier.*

"I had a very good life, a long life," Helen said, and reached out to touch Sorren's cheek. "Not as long as yours, but long enough. I'm glad I had a chance to say good-bye before I left."

Sorren wasn't crying, but I was. Teag looked a little misty, too. In Father Anne's business, it's necessary to have a game face for doing funerals, but I could see in her eyes that she was touched.

Sorren leaned toward Helen's apparition, and they shared one final kiss. Then she stepped back and waved good-bye. Donnelly murmured again, and the mist dissipated. Next to me, Father Anne began to read quietly from the *Book of Common Prayer*.

"Oh God of grace and glory, we remember to you this day…"

Teag walked me to my car when the service was over. The insurance company had finally processed the paperwork, and I had a new blue Mini Cooper. He slung his arm over my shoulder and I put mine around his waist, partially out of camaraderie, and partly to keep from tripping over gravestones in the dim light.

"All's well that ends well?" he asked.

I glanced behind us. Father Anne and Archibald Donnelly were walking toward the parking lot. Sorren remained behind, head bowed, standing in front of the headstone.

"Yeah," I said, "as well as it can be, I guess. And better than it could have been."

Just then, my phone buzzed, and I pulled it out of my pocket. It was a text message from Kell. *I meant what I said about taking you to dinner. Pick a nice place and we'll make it a night on the town.*

Teag read the message over my shoulder. "So? You gonna go?" I must have hesitated, because he gave me a stern look. "Life's too short to miss out on the good stuff," he said. "Anthony and I are clear on that now." He shot me a grin. "Besides, if you start going out with Kell, we can double date."

Despite everything, I chuckled. "Go ahead, twist my arm," I said, though I had already intended to take Kell up on the offer. *Sounds good to me,* I texted. *Is there a restaurant in Charleston that isn't haunted?*